THE CHAMPAGNE CONSPIRACY

Center Point
Large Print

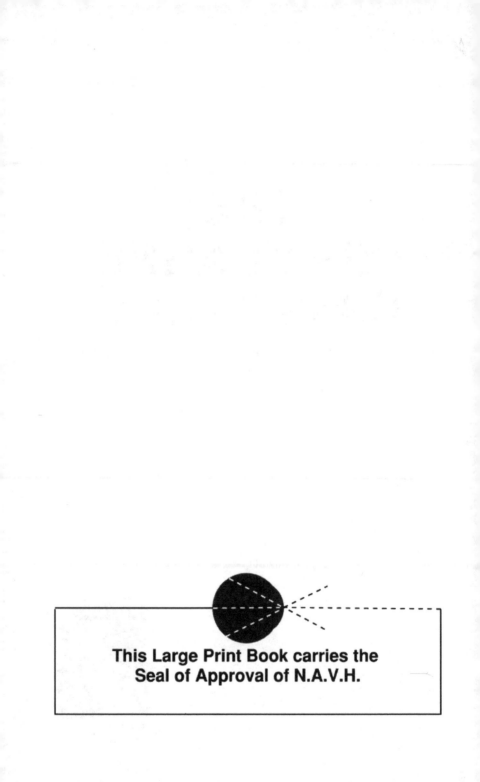

**This Large Print Book carries the
Seal of Approval of N.A.V.H.**

THE CHAMPAGNE CONSPIRACY

A Wine Country Mystery

ELLEN CROSBY

CENTER POINT LARGE PRINT
THORNDIKE, MAINE

This Center Point Large Print edition
is published in the year 2017 by arrangement with
St. Martin's Press.

The text of this Large Print edition is unabridged.
In other aspects, this book may vary
from the original edition.
Printed in the United States of America
on permanent paper.
Set in 16-point Times New Roman type.

ISBN: 978-1-68324-348-9

Library of Congress Cataloging-in-Publication Data

Names: Crosby, Ellen, 1953– author.
Title: The champagne conspiracy : a wine country mystery / Ellen
Crosby.
Description: Center Point Large Print edition. | Thorndike, Maine :
Center Point Large Print, 2017.
Identifiers: LCCN 2016059555 | ISBN 9781683243489
    (hardcover : alk. paper)
Subjects: LCSH: Montgomery, Lucie (Fictitious character)—Fiction. |
Vintners—Fiction. | Vineyards—Virginia—Fiction. | Large type books. |
GSAFD: Mystery fiction.
Classification: LCC PS3603.R668 C45 2017 | DDC 813/.6—dc23
LC record available at https://lccn.loc.gov/2016059555

For Martina Norelli,
bookseller extraordinaire,
with thanks and love

In victory you deserve champagne
and in defeat you need it.

—NAPOLÉON

The rich are different from you and me.

—"THE RICH BOY," F. SCOTT FITZGERALD

ONE

It all started with the dress. I lifted it out of the old steamer trunk and it took my breath away. A gossamer concoction of sea green chiffon, hundreds of copper, silver, and pale green glass beads in patterns like a stained-glass creation from Tiffany, with a sexy zigzag hem of silver fringe that glittered, even by the light of the yellowed bulb that barely lit this dim corner of the attic. I had never seen it—you don't forget a dazzling couture number like this—but it had been beautifully and lovingly preserved, as though one of my long-dead relatives expected to pluck it out of its hiding place and shimmy off to a madcap night of too much dancing and drinking and making out with some guy in the backseat of his roadster.

When I found it, I had been in one of my periodic bouts of overzealous cleaning, which usually happened when the stress piled up and I needed to do something to feel I could restore order and control to some part of my life. Somehow, sorting through boxes and trunks of the discarded detritus that had belonged to generations of ancestors usually did the trick.

Plus—and here is the more mundane reason—there was the coat drive in the middle of January.

Francesca Merchant, who ran the day-to-day operations of my vineyard's tasting room and managed all our events, had shown up at work a few days earlier and announced that Veronica House, the local homeless shelter and food pantry, was collecting winter coats. Any jacket or coat donated in good condition would be given to the guests who came to the center, especially the ones who insisted on sleeping outside in spite of the dangerous temperatures in this record-shattering arctic cold winter.

Donations of men's coats were the most urgently needed, since the majority of people who used Veronica House's services were homeless men. So I scoured the attic, searching for whatever had been stored there and forgotten by family members. I also wrote Frankie a big check.

When I gave it to her, I told her about the dress I'd found during my attic foraging. That afternoon the two of us were sitting on one of the big leather sofas by the fireplace in the main room in the villa, the rambling ivy-covered building where we poured and sold wine and hosted our indoor events. Frankie had just placed another log on the fire and we both had our hands cupped around steaming mugs of coffee to keep warm on a day when the highest temperature would still be only a single-digit number.

"You've got to show it to me," she'd said, her eyes lighting up like a child at Christmas. "It sounds amazing. A real flapper dress. I bet it's drop-dead gorgeous.

"It is. I've never seen anything like it. It must have cost someone an absolute fortune."

"Let's go see it," she said. "I can't wait another minute. Does it fit you?"

"I have no idea." I set my cup on the heavy wooden coffee table.

"You mean you didn't try it on?" She grabbed my hand and pulled me up. "Come on, you have to. And you're giving me a great idea."

We took my Jeep over to the house. By then I'd brought the dress downstairs and hung it on the back of the door to my closet like a guilty secret, along with a shimmery silver satin slip that was obviously meant to be worn underneath, since the dress was completely sheer. Whoever the owner had been had also owned the matching beaded headband. All that was missing was a long roped strand of pearls and a little silver flask filled with illegal hooch, since the dress had to be straight out of the Prohibition era.

"It's perfect for you," Frankie said the moment she laid eyes on it. "With your dark hair and fair coloring, you'll look stunning in it."

I was sitting on the old wedding ring quilt in the middle of my bed, watching her run a hand over the elaborate beading like a professional appraiser assessing its value, her head cocked as if trying to discern its provenance.

9

"I don't think so, Frankie," I said. "Look at that slip. It's satin and it's as fitted as a glove. No room to wiggle around in. It's for someone who is really slim."

Frankie spun around, hands on her hips, and gave me an admonishing I-dare-you look. "Like you."

I shook my head. "It's not a dress to wear anymore; it's something to look at, like a work of art—"

But she had already taken the dress off its hanger and was holding the short silver slip with its spaghetti straps up against me. "Size looks just about perfect, if you ask me."

"I don't think—"

"I'll leave the room, so you can try it on."

I glared at her. "My bra is going to show under those itty-bitty slip straps. I'm wearing a red racer-back bra. It'll look terrible with the green chiffon."

"Enough with the lame excuses. So take off your bra. Come on, it was the Roaring Twenties. Women parked their corsets in someone's bedroom when they went to parties, so they could be . . . available." She gave me a roguish look. "Who needs underwear?"

"I . . . uh . . ."

"Come on," she said again. "What are you scared of?"

"Nothing." Just unnerved at how the dress

10

seemed to have bewitched us both. "All right, give me a minute."

She left and I got undressed. A few minutes later I said, "Okay. Just don't come too near me. She must have smoked like a chimney. Now that I'm wearing it, the fabric reeks of stale cigarettes."

The door opened and Frankie walked in, her hands flying to her mouth, which was open in a big round O.

Finally she said, "You perfect little jazz baby, you. Lucie, you look fabulous. I swear, that dress was made for you. Wait until Quinn—"

I held up my hand. "Hold it right there. What did you have in mind? Wear it the next time we're bottling wine? Or maybe out in the vineyard spraying for powdery mildew?"

She wagged a finger at me. "No, no, no . . . I'll tell you when you're going to wear it. At our Valentine's Day party next month. We'll make it a Roaring Twenties dinner dance. Girls come dressed like flappers with rouged knees and beaded headbands and guys with pomaded hair and gangster suits with wide ties or knicker-bockers and two-toned shoes."

"What Valentine's Day—"

She wasn't listening. "And because I know you won't turn me down, because you have a heart of gold that's as big as all outdoors, we'll make it a fund-raiser for Veronica House. We'll do the villa up like a party out of *The Great Gatsby*, call it

11

our 'Anything Goes' evening." Her eyes had a dreamy, faraway look and I knew she had already mentally planned the entire evening, right down to the gin rickeys we'd drink and the Charleston we'd dance to. "It'll be such fun, something to break up the winter doldrums. Everyone's going to want to come."

"It's a good idea, Frankie," I said, "but I'm not wearing this dress. It's probably been in that trunk in the attic for nearly a century and, like I said, it smells like it."

She came out of her reverie and snapped her fingers, a quick syncopated beat like jazz. "Not a problem. My tailor knows someone who specializes in cleaning vintage clothing. Leave it with me."

"It's too low-cut."

"It is not. You always wear jeans and T-shirts or those long, flowing dresses that cover up everything. About time you showed off what a great figure you've got."

"It's so short."

"Lucie—"

"You can see my foot."

As well as she knew me, it was the one subject I couldn't talk about without betraying how self-conscious I still felt about my twisted, deformed left foot, the one remaining injury I still dealt with after a car accident eight years ago.

Frankie was silent for a long moment, and when

she spoke, her voice was gentle. "And what of it, Lucie? It's part of who you are. Let me tell you, in that dress the last thing anyone's going to be looking at is your foot. You need to stop being so self-conscious. No one else gives it a second thought."

"I don't know—"

"Wear it," she said. "I mean it. We'll keep it a secret from everyone, and when you walk into the room, you'll wow 'em all." She pressed her hands together as if she were praying and threw me a pleading look. "You need to move on. Do it in this dress. And, for the record, you've got great legs."

Once upon a time, I'd been a runner. Cross-country in high school and college. I'd been good.

I gave her a lopsided smile. "Well, at least one great leg."

She burst out laughing, and just like that I knew I was going to wear the dress at our Valentine's Day Roaring Twenties *Great Gatsby* "Anything Goes" Veronica House dinner dance, like Cinderella going to the ball.

But I did draw the line at glass slippers.

That evening, I asked my brother, Eli, who was older by two years, if he knew whom the dress had belonged to. We had just put Hope, my sweet niece and his three-and-a-half-year-old daughter, to bed and I had asked him to come into my bedroom because I wanted to show him something.

I took it out of the closet and held it up. "Any ideas?"

Eli gave me one of those looks men give women when they think you're asking a trick question and they need to get the answer right. Then he stared at the dress, studying the sheer sea green fabric with its intricate beading, as if the answer might be spelled out in code in the beads. Finally he looked up and said, "Probably some woman who was related to us, if you found it in the attic."

"Why, thank you, Sherlock. Aren't you helpful? *Which* relative?"

"A skinny one." He grinned and ducked as I threw a balled pair of socks at him. "Jeez, Luce, how should I know? Me and clothes? Come on. Ever since Brandi walked out on me, I have two requirements for what Hopie and I wear. No visible stains and it doesn't look like someone slept in it."

But the dress had worked its magic on my brother as well, because a short while later I heard him in the sunroom sliding effortlessly from one jazz number into the next on the Bösendorfer concert grand piano that had been our great-grandfather's wedding present to our great-grandmother. The music of Cole Porter, Rodgers and Hammerstein, Gershwin—swingy, upbeat tunes that the wearer of that dress would have

14

danced to, doing the Charleston, or the Black Bottom, or the Lindy hop. I held up the dress against me one more time and, in the privacy of my bedroom, I hummed along to Eli's songs and pretended to dance, imagining myself wearing that sexy, beguiling dress as I wondered what life had been like in the hedonistic, let-the-good-times-roll decade that had roared.

TWO

When you run a vineyard, you never know who is going to walk through your front door and ask to try your wine, maybe stick around for a couple of drinks. We get all denominations: friends, lovers, families, the rare single guest who sits alone. They arrive in varied states of sobriety or inebriation, especially if they've been touring the local vineyards all day, to drown sorrows, celebrate victories, find a new love, get over an old one, or maybe just to kick back and relax. Thankfully, what we don't usually get are trouble-makers looking to pick a fight.

Until today.

To begin with, we were closed. Then there was this guy's attitude, the way he barged into the barrel room—the place where we perform the alchemy of turning grapes into wine—like a gun-slinger bursting into the saloon through a pair of

15

swinging doors. I looked up from helping Quinn Santori, my winemaker, who was filtering wine into bottles with a glass thief, as the man's eyes connected with mine across the room. I knew then that even a KEEP OUT: EXPLOSIVES sign on the door wouldn't have been a deterrent.

But what surprised me more was that I knew him. Not personally, but I would have recognized Gino Tomassi anywhere. He was California winemaking royalty, the grandson of Johnny Tomassi, one of the pioneering winemakers who had emigrated from Italy to California in the early 1900s and planted some of the first grapevines in the Napa Valley. Later, after Prohibition ended, Johnny, along with Louis M. Martini, Cesare Mondavi, and a few other iconic names transformed the region into a winemaking empire some called "the American Eden."

What I didn't know was what Gino Tomassi was doing in my winery at ten-thirty on an early-February morning. But before either he or I could say anything, Quinn cleared his throat and set the thief down on top of a wine barrel.

"Well, well, well," he said in a deadpan voice, "look what the cat dragged in. What are you doing here, Cousin Gino?"

Cousin Gino.

I was used to Quinn's secretiveness about his past life in California—he seemed not to have one—so the idea that he was related to the

Tomassi wine dynasty was about as likely as, say, discovering he was also a long-lost member of the British royal family and potential heir to the throne. Quinn almost never spoke about his family, except for his mother, who had passed away nine months ago, and once, with bitterness, about a father who had abandoned him and his mother shortly after he was born.

All I knew about his mother was that she was Spanish and that when she died last spring, Quinn had returned to the Bay Area for several months to take care of her estate, pack up her things, and sell her house in San Jose. If he was related to Gino, it was on his father's side.

Gino gave Quinn a grim smile, like the two of them shared a secret they wished they didn't know. "What else would I be doing here? Come to see you, Quinn. Introduce me to the pretty lady, why don't you?" His eyes roved over me.

Gino's nickname in the wine business was "the Silver Fox," as much because of his luxuriant silver hair as his shrewd—some would even say predatory—business acumen building the Tomassi Family Vineyard from a prominent California winery into a nationally known brand. I'd also heard a darker story about ties to the Mafia, thanks to an old childhood friend who was now the biggest mob boss on the West Coast. So far, it was all just rumor and unsubstantiated claims; Gino claimed it was a personal relationship and nothing more. But as the saying goes, when you lie down with dogs, you get up with fleas.

He was standing there watching us, like a stage director casting a critical eye over actors who have just fumbled their lines. In person, he was shorter than I'd expected and stockier, but maybe that was because his flamboyant personality projected an image of someone tall and commanding. He wore an expensive-looking cashmere camel overcoat over a double-breasted navy pinstriped suit and had a white silk scarf draped around his neck. Quinn and I had on faded jeans, old wine-stained sweatshirts, fingerless mittens, and down vests to ward off the damp chill of the room. I wondered how long it had been since Gino had gotten his hands dirty in the barrel room like we did. Just now he seemed miles out of our league.

But he had baited Quinn, using me as the pawn, and I resented it. "I'm Lucie Montgomery, Mr. Tomassi. I own this winery." I glanced at Quinn. "You didn't tell me you had family." I paused and gave him my sweetest smile. "In town."

Quinn's mouth twitched, but he turned to Gino and said with contempt, "That's because the last time we spoke was—what, Gino, twenty years ago?" Before Gino could reply, he added, "How'd you find me?"

Though I think what he really wanted to know was *why.*

Gino looked around the room. By California

standards, certainly compared to the vast empire he owned, which sprawled across Napa and Sonoma on either side of the Mayacamas Mountains, my entire operation in the charming, bucolic village of Atoka, Virginia—population sixty—must have seemed like very small potatoes to him. Thirty acres of vines planted on a five-hundred-acre farm given to one of my ancestors in appreciation for service during the French and Indian War, Highland Farm sat at the foot of the Blue Ridge Mountains in a region better known for raising thoroughbreds, hunting foxes, and playing polo than for making wine.

"I've always known where you were," he said to Quinn. "You didn't think I wouldn't keep track of you, did you? I offered you your first job, remember? Tried to give you a hand up. Bring you back into the family business."

Quinn snorted. "You've got a hell of a nerve, Gino. It stopped being my family's business after your father screwed my grandmother out of her share of it. You couldn't have paid me enough to work for you. Not then, not ever."

Gino's face looked like thunder, but he kept his voice level. "Your grandmother came to my father for help because she was desperate after your grandfather lost his shirt on a bunch of lousy business deals. My old man was struggling, but he took out a loan to bail her out and she *gave* him her share of the vineyard in return. My father helped your grandmother, Quinn. The same way I tried to help you." He shook his head and tapped his forehead with his finger. "*Testa dura*," he said to me. "Bull-headed. Always thinks he's right. Always has to do everything the hard way. His way."

I didn't disagree with him about Quinn's stubbornness, but I wasn't about to say so—at least not to Gino Tomassi. "What does bring you here, Mr. Tomassi? Surely it's more than a family reunion, or that you just happened to be in the neighborhood. Atoka's not even on most maps."

This time his smile showed a lot of teeth. "Call me Gino."

"Gino," I said, "to what do we owe the pleasure?"

"You're clever, Lucie Montgomery. Smart. I've been keeping an eye on you, too. You run a good vineyard."

So he already knew who I was. The compliment about my vineyard shouldn't have pleased me as much as it did, especially since Quinn was obviously upset by Gino's out-of-the-blue appearance. Even I knew by now that Gino hadn't dropped by to say "How's every little thing?"

He had an agenda and he was doling out information in small bits.

"I have an excellent winemaker," I said.

"I know you do." His eyes held mine, a penetrating stare, but then he swiveled his gaze to

20

Quinn. "Okay, Quinn, you're right. I didn't just happen to stop by. I wanted to see you about something, ask you some questions."

Quinn's expression hardened. "You must be in a lot of trouble if you came all the way from California to find me."

"A bit of trouble." Gino inclined his head like he was conceding the point. "I was wondering if you knew anything about it."

"About what?"

"About why I'm being blackmailed."

Quinn had been about to pick up the wine thief and begin filling another bottle. He set it down and said, "I have no clue. The Tomassi family has enough skeletons in the closet to fill a cemetery. Which one did someone decide to rattle?" He paused and added, "This time."

"No," Gino said, "this is something different."

"Explain 'different.'"

Gino walked over until he was standing in front of Quinn and me. He dropped his voice to a conspiratorial whisper, although there was no one but the three of us in the barrel room. "I got an e-mail a few days ago. Whoever sent it called himself—or herself—'an anonymous friend.' Said they knew something about Johnny. My grandfather . . . your great-grandfather." He watched Quinn carefully, and I realized he was waiting for some reaction, for Quinn to give away that he knew what this was about.

Quinn glanced at me, his face as expressionless as a poker cardsharp. "His real name was Gianluca Tomassi, but everyone called him Johnny."

"I know who Johnny Tomassi was," I said. "But I didn't know that he was your great-grandfather."

Gino looked dumbfounded. "Are you kidding me? You never told her who you are? Never told her about the family?"

"No. I did not tell her about the family." Quinn banged his fist on the wine barrel and the thief jumped. I grabbed it before it could hit the floor and break.

"Why not?" He still seemed stunned.

"Because I didn't. Get to the point, Gino."

For a moment I thought Gino was about to reach over and grab Quinn by his shirt and tell him to show some respect for his elders. Then he shrugged. "It's a long story. And it's . . . how shall I say? Complicated."

Quinn folded his arms across his chest. "I don't know anything about any blackmail. And I'm damn sure I don't want to get involved with family problems." He gave Gino a hostile look. "*Your* family problems. Especially complicated ones."

"Let me make something clear." Gino stabbed a finger in the air, punctuating his words. "I'm not asking if you want to get involved. I'm telling you that you are. Better you hear this from me, Quinn. I'm doing you a favor by coming here myself."

"Before this goes any further," I said, shooting a

warning glance at Quinn, "maybe we should find a warmer place to finish this conversation."

The two of us had been there filling bottles for a staff meeting at the end of the day, where we would decide the blend for a new wine—a sparkling white like champagne. By definition, anyplace you make wine needs to be cool and dark because heat and light destroy it. But this was early February and the bitter cold of the outdoor temperatures, in the teens, even more frigid if you factored in the windchill, had seeped into my bones in spite of several layers of clothing, heavy boots, and the fingerless gloves.

"Fine," Gino said, "but this is between Quinn and me, Lucie. No outsiders. You understand."

Quinn shook his head. "Forget it. You're the outsider, Gino. Lucie owns this vineyard. Either she stays or we don't talk. You brought her into this the minute you walked through the door. Besides, whatever gets said, I want an impartial witness. You know how I feel about the Tomassi side of the family keeping their word."

Gino's face became a mottled shade of red. "This better not get out. I mean it."

Quinn shrugged. "Apparently, it already did get out and someone does know, or they wouldn't be blackmailing you. Whatever *it* is."

Gino turned to me. "I want your word you won't discuss anything about what I'm going to say. You understand?"

"I know how to keep my mouth shut," I said. "As long as you're not asking me to do anything illegal."

He shot me another penetrating look and I had a feeling this was probably going to come down to splitting hairs and semantics. *Define illegal.*

"Let's go upstairs to the office," Quinn said. "And get this over with."

I reached for my cane, which was propped behind a wine barrel, and caught the flicker of surprise in Gino's eyes. But he said nothing, just followed Quinn and me to a staircase that led to a mezzanine where our offices and the winery laboratory were located. At the bottom of the stairs, my bad foot buckled and I grabbed the railing. Instantly, I felt Gino's hand under my elbow, the chivalrous gesture of a gentleman helping a lady.

I froze. "Thank you, but I can manage. You don't need to do that."

"Sorry." He withdrew his hand. "What happened?"

Most people don't ask. An old person using a cane is someone who needs a little extra help and you don't give it a second thought. Someone young like me is a different story—maybe a debilitating disease or a birth defect, possibly an accident. Either they don't want to talk about your disability because it makes them uncomfortable or they figure you don't want to talk about it because you live with it.

Gino Tomassi wasn't most people. "Eight years ago I was a passenger in a car that took a corner too fast in the rain and hit one of the pillars at the entrance to the vineyard," I said.

"I'm sorry. Tough break."

"My doctors told me I wouldn't walk again, but I did. So it could have been a lot worse."

Gino glanced sideways at me and I could feel him studying me and taking my measure. There aren't many women in my profession, so we have more to prove. A woman with a disability in my profession has a hell of a lot more to prove. "You're tough, Lucie Montgomery. I've heard that about you."

"Thank you."

We climbed the stairs together in silence, Gino slowing his pace to match mine. I guessed him to be in his mid- to late sixties, with the Santa Claus potbelly of someone who relished his food and drink. Up close, I could see old acne scars and a lived-in, deeply lined face, his hooked beak of a nose, strong mouth, and a ship's prow forehead that set off that combed-back mane of silver hair. More than any physical characteristic, though, what came through was his force majeure personality, a combination of ego, charm, cunning, and—so I'd heard—ruthlessness. A man who enjoyed the limelight, high-stakes games, and the adrenaline rush of anything. Whoever was blackmailing Gino had rattled his fortresslike sense of security, intruded into his inner sanctum. I wondered what he was hiding.

Quinn reached the office first and opened the door. After the raw chill of the barrel room, the warm air blasting at us as we walked inside felt good.

A few years ago, Quinn and I had nearly doubled the acreage we'd planted in vines, which required remodeling the winery to accommodate our increased production. One of the biggest changes involved moving our offices from the villa to the winery so they'd be adjacent to the lab, which saved a lot of running back and forth. The new, larger space was L-shaped, with the lab on the long side and our desks on the short side, along with a sofa bed, coffee table, and two club chairs. A full-size refrigerator took up the far corner of the room; two long counters contained a sink, a microwave, racks of test tubes and beakers, and enough opened bottles of wine to make you think we'd had a hell of a party the night before. Picture windows on opposite sides of the room looked out on the interior of the barrel room and the outdoor crush pad, so we could always see what was going on, inside and out.

It was obvious whose desk was whose. Mine was immaculate; Quinn's looked like something had exploded on it. I had made a stab at domesticating the place by hanging a poster of one of our summer festivals on the wall next to our desks and one of my mother's oil paintings—the vineyard in spring, when it was lush and green—above the navy blue sofa.

Gino pulled a pair of reading glasses out of his inside breast pocket and peered at the signature at the bottom of the painting. "Chantal Montgomery. A relative, I presume?"

"My mother," I said. "My sister designed the poster."

"Do they work here, too?"

"My mother was killed twelve years ago when her horse threw her jumping over a stone wall on our property," I said. "Mia works in an art gallery in Manhattan."

"I'm sorry about your mother," he said in a surprisingly gentle voice. "How old were you when she died?"

"Twenty."

He slipped his glasses back into his pocket, and I noticed his hand trembled a little. "I lost my beloved mother when I was sixteen. It was devastating."

Quinn pulled the club chairs up to the coffee table so that they faced the sofa. "Have a seat, Gino," he said. "Take the couch."

Gino shrugged out of his beautiful coat and carefully laid it across the arm of the sofa. He

27

sat and said, "I could use something to wet my whistle."

"White or red?" Quinn asked.

"Red. One of yours, of course." Gino indicated the collection of bottles on the counter. "How about that open bottle of Cab?"

Quinn walked over and picked up the bottle of our Cabernet Sauvignon Reserve. "We brought it up from the barrel room yesterday to see how it's developing." He cleared his throat. "I wouldn't mind knowing what you think."

I knew it cost him something to say that. Pouring wine for customers in the tasting room is one thing. They don't want to know what strain of yeast you used or the type of fermentation or how long you let the fruit hang on the vines. Pouring wine for a winemaker means you're going to get a critique of everything, from obvious flaws to acidity, the characteristics of the fruit, any off aromas, tannins, overall balance—technical stuff.

Gino stretched out an arm along the back of the sofa and regarded Quinn. "I speak my mind; you know that. How long has it been in your cellar?"

"Three years."

Gino raised an eyebrow. "I know left-bank Bordeaux producers who would jail you for infanticide if you opened a Cab after only three years."

Quinn turned red. "Yeah, well this is Virginia, not the left bank of Bordeaux. Three years is nothing when you've been producing wine for centuries. Virginia resurrected what was left of its wine industry in the eighties, after the Civil War and Prohibition. The 1980s. Do you want to try it, or give me a lecture?"

"You don't need to be defensive. Pour already."

Quinn filled a wineglass and gave it to him. "I don't like to drink alone," Gino said.

It was 11:00 A.M.

Show me a winemaker who drinks at all hours—I'm talking about drinking, not tasting and spitting—and I'll show you someone on the road to alcoholism. It's something we've got to guard against constantly in our profession. But this seemed different, more like liquid courage before he explained why someone was blackmailing him, so Quinn filled two more glasses and handed one to me. We sat in the chairs across from Gino.

He lifted his glass. "*Cent' anni.* May you have a hundred good years."

If you've ever witnessed a winemaker sampling a wine, it's like watching someone swish mouthwash in his mouth once he's finished examining the color, swirling the liquid furiously in the glass to release the aromas, and burying his nose in the bowl. We waited while Gino performed the familiar ritual and finally swallowed the wine.

When he was done, he nodded as though he approved, and I felt Quinn start breathing again next to me. "It's got a good balance and I can see where it could be in a few years, once the tannins settle down," Gino said. "Good fruit, but the acid is still there, as I'm sure you know. More Bordeaux-style than California. When did a *paesan* like you start making French wine?"

I answered him. "My mother was French. She came from a family of French winemakers."

Gino set his glass down on a file cabinet next to the sofa. "Family," he said. "It always comes down to family."

"What does?" Quinn asked. "Why is someone blackmailing you about Johnny?"

Gino leaned back against the sofa again and crossed one leg over the other. "I don't know how much you know about your great-grandfather," he said. "*Really* know about him. Other than the story of the poor young immigrant arriving in America with nothing but the shirt on his back and managing to save enough money to buy land in Napa and plant some of the first vines. He kept the place going during Prohibition by making sacramental wine for the Church, instead of ripping out his vines and planting orchards like so many others did. That's what saved his bacon. Sacramental wine. After that, he and Louis M. Martini and Cesare Mondavi and a couple of others from the old country waited it out until repeal. It took a while—Americans had developed a taste for the hard stuff, not wine, during

Prohibition—but eventually things started picking up."

Quinn waved a hand, dismissing him. "I don't need a history lesson about how hard Johnny worked to make California wines respected. Practically carried the industry on his back, according to family legend. Him and Nonna Angelica." He winked at Gino. "I heard other stories, too, how Angelica could be a *testa dura* herself. Run the vineyard as good as Johnny could. In fact, some people thought she did once they got married."

Gino gave a so-what shrug. "Maybe so, but she loved Johnny more than anything in the world. Did everything she could to burnish his legacy and sideline anyone who got in his way. She was tough, your great-grandmother was."

By now it was obvious why Gino was being blackmailed. "Someone found out something about Johnny that you don't want to get out," I said. "Or Angelica. They've been dead for what, sixty years? Seventy? It must be pretty bad for you to want to cover it up after all this time."

"Lucie's right. What could matter so much now? What happened?" Quinn asked. "Don't tell me they robbed a bank and now the money has finally turned up somewhere?"

Gino punched his fist into the palm of his other hand. "Dammit, don't joke about this. Johnny was a good man, a good father, a good businessman, a

31

good friend." He kept emphasizing *good* with more fist smacking. "Plus, he was devout, did so much for the Church, gave thousands of dollars to Catholic charities, but never wanted anyone to know. And Angelica . . . she was always all about the family. Everything was for the family. She was a good woman, too. Went to Mass every day of her life."

He hadn't answered the question, just danced around it. It seemed to me Quinn had struck a nerve, or come close to it. And like they say, going to church every day doesn't make you a saint, any more than standing in a garage turns you into a mechanic.

"Why don't you tell us what it is?" I said to Gino.

He picked up his wineglass and drained it. Without asking, Quinn found an open bottle of Valpolicella on the counter and showed it to Gino, who held out his glass for a refill.

In just about every language or culture, there is a maxim about the relationship between wine and what it does to inhibitions. In the Talmud, it's written that when wine enters, secrets exit. In Russia, the proverb goes that what a sober man has on his mind, the drunken man has on his tongue. And of course there is the Latin platitude everyone knows: *In vino veritas.* In wine, there is truth.

Gino drank the Valpolicella, a moody, troubled

32

expression on his face. Finally he looked up. "Did you know Johnny was married to someone else before he married Angelica?"

Quinn's stunned look answered his question. "It must not have been for long. I never heard about it."

"It wasn't," Gino said. "Barely two years, less as an actual marriage, if you know what I mean. Her name was Zara, and as soon as she came to Bel Paradiso, she was nothing but trouble. Angelica forbade anyone to speak about her after she died."

Bel Paradiso, I knew, was where the Tomassi estate was located at the foothills of the Mayacamas Mountains outside Calistoga. It looked like an Italian castle, complete with turrets and towers and crenellated walls, even a picturesque draw-bridge that pulled up over a small man-made moat. The label of every bottle of Tomassi Family Vineyard wine was emblazoned with a watercolor painting of Bel Paradiso that made it look as though it were floating above the clouds like a distant fairy-tale kingdom.

I figured Zara must have passed away, since divorce was such a taboo in the Catholic Church in those days, especially among the devout Italian and Irish immigrant communities.

"Why didn't Angelica let anyone mention Zara?" I asked. "Was she jealous?"

Gino played with the stem of his wineglass.

"Jealous wasn't the half of it. Angelica was Johnny's sweetheart since they were kids. Their parents grew up in the same village in Italy. When Zara came along—she was a knockout, a real stunner—Johnny fell hard for her, and it broke Angelica's heart. It didn't take long before he realized what a mistake he'd made. Zara, who was a city girl from the East Coast, hated being on a farm in the Napa Valley. After Zara died, Angelica was still waiting," he said. "But this time she had conditions. When she married Johnny, she banished Zara and any memory of her from the Tomassi family history. No photographs, no nothing."

"So this blackmail has something to do with Zara?" Quinn asked.

Gino nodded. "She went and got herself pregnant."

"And Johnny wasn't the father?" I asked.

He looked uncomfortable. "No one really knows. You see, Zara died in an accident at the farm. She went out for a walk by herself one afternoon and didn't come back. By the time they found her at the bottom of a ravine, she was dead. She must have fallen and hit her head on a rock. The baby didn't make it, either."

"How awful," I said.

"Downstairs in the barrel room, you said it was complicated," Quinn said to Gino.

"The e-mail I got from the blackmailer claims

34

that the baby lived. And that there's a birth certificate to prove it."

"I don't understand," I said.

Gino drank more wine, and this time, Quinn refilled his own glass and topped off mine. "Zara was cremated and Johnny scattered her ashes somewhere on our land in Sonoma," Gino said. "There's no marker, since Angelica wouldn't have it. If the baby was still alive, then—"

"Johnny covered it up." Quinn finished his sentence.

Gino nodded.

"Why would he do that?" I asked.

Another coded look passed between Gino and Quinn. "Two reasons," Gino said. "Either the baby wasn't his, or it was and Angelica wouldn't allow Zara and Johnny's child in her home."

"Angelica sounds like a very tough lady," I said in an even voice. "That's heartless."

"How'd you find out all this?" Quinn asked. "If no one ever talked about it."

Gino gave him an ironic smile. "One day when I was about ten, I was out in the woods by the family chapel at Bel Paradiso. I tripped over a tree root and ended up in a little clearing I'd never seen before. It looked like someone had tried to conceal the remains of a bonfire, maybe even a funeral pyre. Some of the trees were singed, too. When I got back to the house, I asked Angelica about it. She told me some cockamamy tale about burning old vines, which I knew wasn't true, and later I overheard her arguing with Johnny, telling him to make it go away, talking about Zara. The next time I went back, all the burned trees had been cut down and you'd never know there'd been a fire."

He looked out the window to the crush pad, and I followed his gaze. In the distance, the hazy purple silhouette of the Blue Ridge Mountains faded into the bleak winter white sky. "Eventually, I got the rest of the story from my father, one of those deathbed confessions," he said. "Angelica had taken all of Zara's things out to the woods and burned them. He told me to look closely at the exterior of the chapel and I'd find the places where the wood was still charred from the heat."

His gaze returned to Quinn, whose mouth was set in a pinched, grim line.

"What?" Gino said.

"You actually thought I knew about all this, didn't you? Is that why you came straight to me after all these years?"

Gino didn't answer right away, and then the penny dropped.

"Why, you—" Quinn's hands balled into fists and he started to get up.

"Quinn, calm down." I tugged on one of his arms and pulled him back into his seat. "Don't."

He shook me off and leaned in toward Gino.

"You think I'm the one who's blackmailing you, you son of a bitch, don't you?"

Gino didn't flinch. "Your grandmother was my father's sister, my aunt. If he knew, it stands to reason she knew, too. And maybe she passed that information on to your father. We both know there's no love lost between our families."

"You have a lousy memory, Gino. My old man walked out on my mother and me right after I was born. We didn't share any father-son confidences." There was a lifetime of bitterness in his words, which broke my heart. "It's not me. I'm not blackmailing you, though I'm almost sorry I'm not. And now that you've found out what you've come for, I think you should go."

Gino held up a hand. "Not so fast. You know I had to ask. In my place, you would have done the same thing. Besides, you're not the only person around here I've come to talk to. Zara's father was a big-shot congressman from San Francisco, Ingrasso his name was, who kept getting reelected—thirty-eight years I think it was—so Zara never really lived in California. She grew up here. Plus, her family had money, a lot of money, so Johnny had married himself an heiress. That's how he kept the Tomassi Family Vineyard going. Anyway, Zara's grandnephew—her brother's grandson—still lives in D.C. I'm meeting him, too, after I leave here."

"I don't understand," I said. "If Zara's baby

survived, so what? Maybe you have a long-lost relative you never knew about. Big deal. Why the blackmail?"

"Johnny left the vineyard in equal shares to his heirs," Quinn said. "Meaning my grandmother and Gino's father. Angelica's children. If there's another heir, someone potentially can claim part ownership of the Tomassi Family Vineyard."

"After all this time?" I asked. "That's two—or three—generations ago, depending."

Gino put a hand to his forehead as if massaging a migraine. "California isn't like other states when it comes to inheritance laws and estate settlement. Our heritage is Spanish, not English, and our legal system reflects that. In California, there's no statute of limitations on probate."

"Are you saying the will was never probated?" I asked.

The look in his eyes answered my question, but he responded anyway. "The only asset in Johnny's estate was the vineyard, so my father and Quinn's grandmother decided not to bother with probate just to clarify the title on the deed. Save themselves a bit of money."

"Oh," I said in a faint voice.

"What if the kid wasn't Johnny's?" Quinn said. "Problem solved, right? There is no third heir."

Gino leaned forward, resting his elbows on his knees, and clasped his hands together. "Yeah. If it wasn't his, problem solved."

He didn't sound convinced.

"You believe Johnny was the baby's father," I said.

"I don't want all this ancient history stirred up. It's family business. It's private." There was an edge in his voice. Once again he hadn't answered the question, just danced around it.

It seemed to me there was something else Gino didn't want to talk about. Something worse than the scandal of an illegitimate child that still haunted him after all these years.

I chose my words carefully. "Whatever happens, the blackmailer is indirectly bringing up the circumstances of Zara's death. Is that what's really bothering you? That maybe it wasn't an accident?" Gino's eyes met mine and I knew I'd guessed right. "You said Zara and Johnny's marriage wasn't a happy one and Angelica wanted her out of the picture."

"I will not discuss that subject," he said with icy finality. "Don't even bring it up."

"Wait a minute." Quinn sat up, frowning, and looked at the two of us. "Hang on. What are we talking about here?"

"Murder," I said.

THREE

Maybe I was right about the reason Gino didn't want the Tomassi family history resurrected: Zara didn't fall and accidentally hit her head out walking alone on the farm. Someone had killed her and covered it up.

And the most logical suspects were Quinn's great-grandparents, Johnny and Angelica Tomassi. One or both of them had murdered Johnny's first wife and gotten away with it for nearly a century.

Or maybe they had until now.

For a long moment the room was silent except for the whir of the blower forcing heat through the vents and the quiet hum of the refrigerator.

Then Quinn said in a tense voice, "What if Lucie's right?"

"It was an accident," Gino said. "So drop it, both of you."

"Only because Johnny and Angelica said it was an accident," Quinn said.

"I said, drop it." Gino's voice cracked like a whip.

"You at least ought to go to the police about someone blackmailing you," I said to him. "Or the FBI. Extortion is a federal crime."

Gino shot me an incredulous look. "I will do nothing of the kind. There's no need for the police or anyone else to be involved."

Quinn got up and raked his hands through his salt-and-pepper hair. "Oh, for God's sake, cue *The Godfather.* You're talking about *omertà.*" He walked over to the counter with its assortment of open bottles of wine. I thought he was going to pick up yet another bottle to polish off, but instead he seemed to collect himself before he came back and stood behind his chair, gripping the back of it with both hands. "Welcome to how the Tomassi family does business, Lucie. Justice the same way they took care of things in the old country. No need to bother with cops or any of that legal crap. It's much more efficient when you handle things yourself, right, Gino?"

"You watch your smart mouth, Quinn. You're damn right I'll handle it myself." Gino looked like he was a heartbeat away from coming off the couch at Quinn. "I hired an ex-cop, runs his own PI agency now. He'll take care of this. My guy thinks we're dealing with an amateur, maybe even someone just fishing. He's asking for a quarter of a million dollars by Friday. He'll let me know where and when."

Quinn threw himself into his chair again and we exchanged looks. Gino could probably find that much cash behind the sofa cushions at home. We'd have to take out a loan, with the vineyard as collateral.

"You ought to be thanking me," Gino said to Quinn. "I'm protecting you, too. Your reputation, your family's honor."

"You're doing this for yourself. For the Tomassi Family Vineyard. You'd take a chain saw to my family's branch of the family tree if you could."

I didn't like where this was going.

Whatever Gino's private investigator had found out would be swept under the carpet—or more likely, buried forever. And what about the black-mailer? Would Gino teach him a lesson? Or her? Would he get his old friend the mob boss to take care of it? Was that what he meant by handling it?

"There's something else," Gino said to Quinn.

Quinn gave him a look full of contempt. "With you, Gino, there always is."

Gino ignored him. "Your mother ended up with Angelica's old steamer trunk, since your grand-mother—Angelica's daughter—got all of her mother's jewelry and most of Angelica's personal effects after she died."

"What of it? Mom kept that trunk in our attic and used it to store her own things. For years she kept her wedding dress in it, until she finally gave it to Goodwill."

"I know you sold your mother's house a few months ago," Gino said. "I told you I've been keeping an eye on you. So I was wondering, what happened to the trunk?"

I knew exactly what he was talking about. Quinn had shipped it to Virginia when he was still in California, a beautiful old steamer trunk of burnished wood, with leather straps, an elaborate brass lock, and a high-domed top. The intertwined initials *APT* were barely visible in faded gold. The shipping company had brought it to my house instead of Quinn's, since there had been no one home at his cottage, and I'd phoned him to ask about it.

"Can't you just accept the delivery?" he'd asked. "I'll move it over to my place once I get back."

But when he returned from California, we both thought he was going to move in with me, and so the trunk had stayed in the basement of Highland House, my home. Quinn, however, slowly but surely began finding reasons why he needed to sleep on the sofa in the office or at his cottage. The idea that we were going to live together went up in smoke, and neither of us had brought it up since then.

Quinn stared at Gino without batting an eye and said, "I shipped it here. Why? There's nothing in it now except stuff that meant something to my mother, stuff she saved of mine, like my old report cards, school photographs. I think my high school yearbook is there, too." He shrugged. "Unless you want the Tomassi christening gown."

"That was handmade in Italy. Sure I want it," he said. "What about Angelica's photo album? The one with the pictures of Johnny and her after they first got married, the early days of the vineyard, and my father and your grandmother when they were kids."

A muscle moved in Quinn's jaw. "What about it?"

"So you do have it." Gino sounded pleased. "I'd like it. It should be at the vineyard, since it's part of our history. I'll pay you for it if you want."

"Don't insult me. What else, Gino? I know you. You want something else besides that album."

Gino moved his wineglass around on the coffee table as if he were considering a move in a chess game. "You're like your father. He had a good bullshit-detection meter, too."

"I wouldn't know. And leave him out of this."

Gino stopped playing with his glass. "The blackmailer claims to have proof the baby lived. Maybe Angelica kept something. Maybe it's still in the trunk."

Quinn shook his head. "No one's had access to it, so whatever it is, the blackmailer didn't get it from me."

"It's in my basement," I said. "Where it's been ever since the movers delivered it from California last fall."

"I'd like to look at the album, and I'm going to be here all week. I could send a courier to pick it up and bring it to my hotel in D.C. At least let me have the pictures duplicated. I'll return it before I leave."

Quinn shrugged. "I'll think about it."

"What are you doing in Washington that keeps you here for a week?" I asked.

"Meeting with my East Coast distributors. On Thursday and Friday, I'm at a conference for Custodei Fidei, the Guardians of Faith, at Catholic University," he said. Then he added, like it was an afterthought, "The Italian prime minister is in town and there's a state dinner at the White House tomorrow, so I'll be going to that."

"Dinner at the White House," I said. "That ought to be nice."

"Yeah," he said. "It ought to."

I thought he sounded the teensiest bit smug about dining with the president. But Quinn had latched on to something else. "The Guardians of Faith? I forgot you were mixed up with that bunch of right-wing fanatics."

I knew I shouldn't wade into this one, considering the level of combustibility in the room, but I did anyway. "Who are they?"

Before Gino could answer, Quinn said, "A bunch of neoconservative Catholics who took over the old Angwin Winery in Napa and formed an evangelical think tank. They're worried the world's going to hell in a handbasket and it's their duty to prevent that from happening."

"The Custodei Fidei," Gino said in a clipped, tight voice, "brings together senior business, government, and religious leaders to have a thoughtful dialogue on topical social and moral issues viewed through the lens of the Catholic faith."

"What that means in English," Quinn said to me, "is that they take their name seriously as guardians of the true faith, keeping the wicked world at bay. When I was in California last year, I saw articles in the *Mercury News* about their annual conference at the winery over the summer. The people who show up there believe it's their sacred mission to do something about the decline of modern society by upholding traditional family values, which are also in the toilet." He turned to Gino. "Which is why this blackmail couldn't come at a worse time, airing all the Tomassi family's dirty laundry, could it? I heard that you're in line to become the next president. How do you think the board of trustees, which includes a couple of bishops, if I remember right, would feel about appointing you as their next leader if they knew your little secret?"

Gino's face turned that mottled shade of red again, as if his blood pressure was off the chart. "Don't you screw with me. Do you understand?"

"In addition"—Quinn continued talking to me, as if Gino hadn't spoken—"there's the Bellagio deal. I heard rumors when I was in California and then I saw the article in the latest issue of *Decanter*. Gino and Dante Bellagio are planning on going into partnership together, looking to buy a vineyard in Napa and start a new label like Bob Mondavi and Philippe Rothschild did with

Opus. Another Tomassi heir in the picture would complicate that deal, too."

Dante Bellagio was a wealthy Italian count who owned the largest winemaking conglomerate in Italy. One of his relatives was an influential cardinal at the Vatican. A daughter owned a fashion house with her own label in Milan. If Bellagio and Tomassi established a vineyard together in California, it would be an especially sweet deal for Gino, since Italian wines already made up the largest share of American wine imports. Plus, thanks to Dante's reputation and clout, Tomassi wines would gain name recognition in Italy.

"I am through here." Gino stood and pulled on his coat with sharp, angry motions. "The two of you will treat this conversation with the sanctity of the confessional. Do you understand? Because if you ever—I mean *ever*—repeat a word of what was said in this room, I will personally make you sorry you did."

"I'm already sorry," Quinn said.

"Please leave," I said.

"You heard her," Quinn told him. "Get out."

Gino slammed the door, and the room reverberated with the sound. A moment later his footsteps clattered down the metal staircase, followed by the *whomp* of the heavy barrel room door as it closed. I picked up the wineglasses with shaking hands and carried them over to the sink to wash them.

I looked over at Quinn to see if he'd noticed how rattled I was, but he'd thrown himself on the couch and was lying on his back, shielding his eyes with the back of his hand.

When I finished the dishes, I dried my hands on a dish towel and leaned against the counter. I felt calmer, but I was still angry.

Gino was gone. Good riddance.

"Hey," I said, "are you all right?"

"Are you kidding me?" Quinn uncovered his eyes and sat up, swinging his legs around so his work boots hit the floor. "I'm sorry you had to witness that. Gino's a real piece of work."

"It's okay," I said. "I had no idea you were related to the Tomassis. Why didn't you tell me?"

He gave me a warning look. "Aw, come on. Don't go there, Lucie."

"Why not?"

"Just—don't."

"Quinn—"

"Then tell me this," he said, his eyes challenging. "Would it have mattered, made a difference to you in any way about my competence in this job?"

I took too long to answer.

"I thought so," he said, getting up. "Now you know why I didn't tell you."

I walked over and stood in front of him. "I don't want to get into an argument with you over this," I said. "*Please.* Especially after that awful scene with Gino."

"Then forget about it. Forget Gino, forget Zara and Johnny and Angelica. Forget my family. I'm sure as hell going to."

"No you're not." We were venturing into territory that always got us in trouble, but I couldn't stop. "You can't keep running away from things . . . from people. Including your family." I took a deep breath. "From people who care about you."

He gave me a searing look. "Are we still talking about Gino? In case you hadn't noticed, neither he nor I would spit if the other one was on fire."

"Yes. No. I don't know." I turned to go, and he grabbed my arm. "I'm going over to the villa to take care of some paperwork. I need to talk to Frankie. Let's drop this conversation, okay? I shouldn't have brought it up."

He released my arm. "Fine by me," he said. "Whatever you say."

I turned and walked out of the office. When I got to the stairs, I was so upset that I nearly missed the step again, grabbing the railing before I stumbled. It wasn't fine by Quinn. None of this was fine. Gino Tomassi's visit here had opened up a Pandora's box of trouble for all of us, and somehow I knew there would be more to come.

Much more.

FOUR

I chose the longer route to the villa, under the shelter of a trellised portico, rather than walking across the windblown courtyard. In summer it would be fragrant with the scent of wisteria twining through a lattice screen, and geraniums, impatiens, and fuchsia would spill out of old halved wine barrels and hanging baskets. My mother had designed the space to connect the barrel room and the villa, creating a central gathering place like the charming village squares she had known growing up in France. Often at the end of the day, if the weather was nice, Quinn and I would take a bottle of wine over to the low stone wall at the far end of the courtyard, where we could watch the sun slowly turn the vines bronze-colored before disappearing behind the Blue Ridge Mountains.

But today the wind cut like a knife and the air had the unmistakable smell of snow, so I was glad for the protection of the colonnaded walkway. There was only one car in the visitors' parking lot, which wasn't unusual for a Monday morning after the hustle and bustle of the weekend, but I doubted it was Gino's. He didn't seem like the type to rent a dark blue Toyota Corolla with a dented fender.

A heart-shaped grapevine wreath decorated with

red and pink silk flowers, variegated ivy, and sprays of berries hung on the front door to the villa in honor of Valentine's Day and the Roaring Twenties "Anything Goes" dinner dance fund-raiser coming up on Saturday to support Veronica House. Frankie would have put it there, and knowing her, she'd made the wreath herself, probably woven it with our own grapevines. She was like that.

It had nearly taken an act of God to persuade her a few months ago that her responsibilities at the Montgomery Estate Vineyard—she was now de facto running the entire retail side of our operation—were too much for one person to handle, even someone who, on her worst day, could make Superwoman look geriatric. Besides managing the tasting room and hiring all the staff we needed—not many people see pouring wine as a career-making commitment, so there is a lot of turnover—she organized our events, took care of off-site sales, and handled the ever-increasing need for publicity and promotion.

We hired four new full-time people in quick succession, and now the offices that Quinn and I used to occupy in the back corridor behind the small library, as well as the old kitchen, had been taken over by an accountant with a lot of tattoos, two sweet-faced motherly women who handled our Internet orders, newsletters, and social net-working, and a new assistant manager, who had relocated to Virginia after spending several years in public relations in the sports world. Frankie moved into my old office off the library and Eli had handled the renovation, modernizing the offices and taking care of getting the place rewired for high-speed Internet. It was part of a deal the two of us had made when he and Hope moved in with me last year after his brutal divorce. His job had gone up in smoke, along with the marriage, so he'd set up his own architectural business in what used to be our old carriage house. In return for free rent, any design work needed at the vineyard or the house would be pro bono, along with supervising the construction.

Frankie was standing at the bar, deep in conversation with Skylar Cohen, one of the social workers from Veronica House, as I walked into the tasting room. Skye, who had her back to me, turned around and flashed a warm smile.

"There you are, Lucie," Frankie said. "I was going to call you and let you know Gino Tomassi was on his way over to see you, but Skye dropped by and I'm afraid I got sidetracked. He did find you and Quinn, obviously?"

Of course Frankie would have seen Gino. How else would he have known where we were?

"He did," I said in a noncommittal voice, ignoring her inquisitive look. "Thanks. Hi, Skye. Nice to see you."

"You, too, Lucie," she said. "I can't tell you how

grateful we are for what you're doing for us on Saturday. Plus collecting all these winter coats." She gestured to two full carrier bags next to her on the floor.

Skye's wardrobe was usually an eclectic combination of Goth and army surplus, which intimidated some people until they discovered her big, compassionate heart and gift for connecting with the more mentally challenged clients at Veronica House. Today she had on a knit orange cap that let only a fringe of bright purple hair show, a camouflage jacket over a gray hoodie, a spiked leather neck collar, jeans with ripped knees that showed off black fishnet tights, and combat boots.

"Don't thank me," I said. "It's all Frankie's idea. And I'm happy to be helping."

Skye picked up the carrier bags. "I'd better get back to the center. Father Niall's a little flipped out with that audit coming up next week."

"Is everything all right?" Frankie asked.

"You know how he is about paperwork."

"If I can help . . ." Frankie said.

"Well, you're on our board, so I'm sure you could talk to him about it."

"I'll call him this afternoon."

"Sure," Skye said. "Do that."

After she left, Frankie said, "Let's go into my office and I'll make us some tea. I've got the space heater on in there. It's warmer."

The office still looked much as it had when it had been mine, and my mother's before that, except for the collection of framed pictures of Frankie's photogenic family—her good-looking husband, and a son and daughter who were both in college—which filled the credenza behind her desk. She sat down in what was now her chair and I took the wing chair across from her. It still felt a bit weird.

"Before Skye showed up," Frankie said, hitting a key on her computer keyboard so the screen flickered to life, "I was going over the final numbers for Saturday night with Dominique. We've sold every single ticket. The fire marshal won't allow any more people in the room." She sighed. "I'd give my right arm for another server, or someone else to pour drinks. Dominique can't spare anyone else from the Inn, since it's Valentine's Day and they've got a waiting list for reservations from here to D.C."

Dominique Gosselin was my cousin on my mother's side and the owner of the Goose Creek Inn, a local restaurant that had won every major dining award in the region for its imaginative menus and romantic setting. Fortunately for us, the Inn also handled the catering for all our events, since the vineyard didn't have the necessary license to prepare and serve food.

Dominique had moved here from France to help take care of my wild kid sister after my mother died, and she, like Frankie, had been born without an off switch. When Frankie took over the job of planning our events from me, I had wondered whether putting together two obsessively organized, detail-minded women who each liked to do things her way would be like mixing oil and water. Instead, it was like a chemical experiment in which you create something even more powerful than the components, or as Quinn said, like combining nitroglycerin and diatomite to get dynamite.

"How many people have we got coming on Saturday? Just how big has this gotten?" I asked Frankie. For events on this scale, she still wanted to be the general running the show; her assistant manager had been demoted to lieutenant.

"Two hundred and fifty as of this morning. And speaking of big, I didn't know you knew Gino Tomassi. He owns the biggest winery in the country. I recognized him the minute he walked through the front door, especially that gorgeous mane of silver hair," she said. "What brought him here to see you and Quinn, if you don't mind my asking?"

She gave me an innocent smile, but nothing got by Frankie.

"Quinn knows him from California," I said in a bland voice. "He just happened to be in the area, so he dropped by."

"Really?" She picked up a mug with *World*

Domination Through Vinification stenciled on it over a grape-colored globe. "You'll have tea, won't you?"

"I'll get it," I said. "Give me your mug."

She moved it out of my reach. "We both know you just ducked my question. And something's bothering you. Does it have to do with Gino Tomassi?"

After that scene in our office, I doubted Quinn wanted Frankie—or anyone else—to know he and Gino were related, and neither of us wanted anyone to know the real reason for Gino's visit, especially after his parting shot about what he'd do if we talked.

So I shrugged and said, "Nope. It's nothing."

She narrowed her eyes. "Nice try."

"Okay, Quinn and I had a little disagreement. No big deal."

Frankie sat back and stared at me, twisting her shoulder-length strawberry blond hair into a knot and stabbing a pencil through it to keep it in place. "Of course. Saturday is Valentine's Day, so why am I not surprised that he wants to hibernate in a cave? Lucie, he's a good winemaker . . . a great winemaker, but he's just going to keep breaking your heart."

"It was professional, Frankie, not personal."

"Sure it was." She shook her head. "Tell me it's none of my business, tell me to butt out of your life, but, honey, move on."

"It's none of your business. Butt out of my life."

She stood up. "I'll get our tea. Stay put."

As she left, I called after her, "Where did I get the idea that I own this vineyard and so I'm the boss?"

When she returned, she said, "It is an open secret, from everyone here down to the day laborers, that Quinn chickened out of moving in with you after he came back from California." She set down a mug in front of me. "All of us love you, Lucie. No one wants to see you hurt."

I drank some tea. *Chickened out.* I hadn't heard that one.

"Thank you all for your concern, but I'm fine." I gave her a defiant look. "After five years of working with Quinn every day, don't you think I've figured him out by now? Besides, with Eli and Hope living with me, it worked out better that he stayed in the winemaker's cottage."

Frankie arched an eyebrow. "Huh."

She wasn't going to back down. Frankie had an innate Noah's ark view of the world and felt that we were all meant to go through life in pairs, each of us with a mate.

"Look, I've got a full life, a busy life, doing what I love. I live on land that has been in my family for two hundred years, working with people I love and care about. Now that Eli converted the old barn into a duplex and Benny and his family and Jesús and his girlfriend are living there, plus the fact that Antonio's fiancée has moved into his cottage, it's like we're becoming a big extended family. And there's you, of course, and all the new staff we hired. Between our own events and all the community activities I'm involved in, I'm busier than ever," I said. "I have a good life, Frankie. I'm happy."

She picked up her mug and blew on her tea. "You didn't mention Quinn."

She was right. I hadn't. I gave her a cross look and said, "Well, obviously he's part of everything that goes on. We're together constantly."

"Huh," she said again in that unconvinced way. She leaned across her desk and picked up a book—*The Great Gatsby.* "I just finished rereading this. For the dozenth time at least. I love this book, but it breaks my heart every time I read it. Why don't you borrow it?"

"I read it in high school," I said. "Like everyone did."

"Read it again." She pushed it over to me. "I love the description of the parties. You know Fitzgerald spent time in Middleburg, don't you?"

I nodded. "I'd forgotten until you mentioned it, but, yes, I did know."

Frankie gave the book one more nudge. "So read it, already." She sipped her tea and gave me a Cheshire cat smile. "I have a favor to ask."

And something up her sleeve. "What?"

"I've got most of the decorations for Saturday

figured out. . . . We're going to turn the villa into a speakeasy," she said. "Everything will be black, red, and silver."

I nodded. We'd talked about this already.

"I happened to run into Mick Dunne at the Cuppa Giddyup the other day when we were both getting coffee," she said. "Did you know he's got an old photo album that the Studebakers left behind when they sold him their place? According to Mick, they used to have some fabulous parties back in the 1920s." She pointed to *The Great Gatsby.* "Like something Gatsby would throw . . . oceans of champagne, food fit for a sultan, a band with a sultry chanteuse from one of the new jazz clubs in Washington, guests dancing on the lawn, partying until dawn." Her blue eyes were sparkling. "Mick said we could borrow the album. Maybe get some ideas or inspiration. I thought you could drop by his place and pick it up."

Sure she did. Frankie made no bones about the fact that she'd always thought I'd made a mistake breaking off my romance with Mick a few years ago, but I'd learned my lesson, and ended up a sadder but wiser girl. He had a wandering eye and he could be fickle.

In every way, Mick was the complete opposite of Quinn. A wealthy, urbane Englishman, he'd owned a pharmaceutical company in Florida, which he sold for multimillions, then moved to Virginia with the romantic notion of buying a farm and becoming a gentleman of leisure. He admitted later he'd watched *Gone With the Wind* one too many times, especially the party scene at Twelve Oaks before the war.

He bought the place next door to mine, the old Studebaker estate, with its parklike gardens, elegant Georgian manor house, and stables that were known for horses that had been Derby and Olympic champions. Before long, Mick had his own string of thoroughbreds, half a dozen polo ponies, and a few foxhunters. He was a regular player in the summer twilight games on the old polo field and, just recently, became the new master of the Goose Creek Hunt, the oldest foxhunting club in the region.

He'd also decided he wanted his own vineyard, though to be honest, he was what we call around here a "trophy winemaker." What he really wanted was a wine label with his name on it to show off at dinner parties. Quinn and I had advised him over the years, since we shared a common property line, but increasingly I'd watched him become less interested in the business of growing grapes and making wine and more involved with the horses.

I gave Frankie a challenging look. "Maybe you're the one who should pick up that photo album, since you talked to him."

"I told him you'd be by," she said, putting on a pair of glasses and peering at me over the top of the fire engine red frame like a schoolteacher regarding a difficult pupil. "He'll think there's something wrong if you don't go. Maybe that you're avoiding him."

"I'm not avoiding him."

"So what's the big deal, then?"

"Stop matchmaking. We're friends now. Nothing more."

"Then go see a friend," she said. "Please?"

"Oh all right." I picked up her book and reached for my cane. "I was planning to drop by Foxhall Manor to visit Faith Eastman this afternoon and then pick up a few things at the General Store before the snow starts tonight. I suppose I can stop by Mick's, since he's just next door."

Frankie gave me a coy smile. "See you when you get back."

I left, already regretting my decision.

FIVE

I never would have made it through the year my mother was killed if it hadn't been for Faith Eastman. The mother of my best and oldest friend, Faith had been the one I'd gone to for comfort during the dark days when everything was going to hell at home and no one was coping well with the shock of my mom's death. My father, who never cared much for his three children and no longer had her as a buffer between us, fought constantly with my older brother, Eli, who began staying out all night and showing up the next morning sullen and hungover, and my younger sister, Mia, who started hanging out with friends who looked like they'd done time in juvie. My salvation from the family dysfunction was fleeing to Faith's happy, loving home.

Faith's daughter, Kit, was her only child and she had raised her as a single parent after Kit's dad walked out on them when Kit was a baby. In spite of a big age difference—Faith was forty-eight when Kit was born—the two of them were as inseparable as peanut butter and jelly. Three years ago, after Faith suffered a stroke, Kit, a journalist whose star was ascending at the *Washington Tribune*, walked away from a senior editor's job and the offer of an overseas assignment and asked for a transfer to the *Trib*'s sleepy Loudoun County bureau so she could take care of her mother. It wasn't exactly like being exiled to Siberia, but it wasn't far off.

A year ago, when it became clear Faith needed more skilled care than Kit could provide, Kit moved Faith to Foxhall Manor, a luxurious assisted living community that reminded me more of a hotel filled with pampered guests. I never asked Kit how she'd scraped together the money to afford the fees, but it wouldn't have surprised me if she'd gone into debt to manage it. Or robbed a bank.

Foxhall Manor was an elegant mansion built as a labor of love by an eccentric English colonel for his American wife after they left India at the end of the British rule in 1947. Today it was the main building for the entire complex. Set on one hundred acres of rolling hills, manicured gardens, and wooded land that backed up to a panoramic view of the Blue Ridge Mountains, the 220-room home was a quirky architectural combination of Palladian symmetry juxtaposed with Indian-style pavilions, elaborate carved stonework, and tucked-away interior courtyards. Its most distinctive feature consisted of four small rooftop domes, each mounted on four columns, which sat atop the corners of the two wings of the pale peach sandstone house. Eli told me the architectural name for the smaller domes was *chhatri*, which literally means "umbrella," and that they were common additions to Indian palaces and wealthy homes.

After the colonel's wife died, a local family bought the estate and renamed it Foxhall Manor, a tribute to the regal-looking bronze fox they installed on a plinth in front of a fountain in the central courtyard. Eventually, the new owners ran out of money, and there were stories about the mansion being haunted, so it had been abandoned for years, until a group of entrepreneurs bought it, restored it, and turned it into an upscale assisted living community. The pavilions had been glassed in and connected to the main house, making the place even more sprawling, and the entire complex now housed community rooms, a library, offices, and a restaurant, as well as forty small apartments. Two more low-rise apartment buildings and twenty semidetached bungalows had been built on land directly behind the manor house, all of which were connected by flagstone paths and a series of culs-de-sac.

I drove through the gated entrance and found a parking place not far from the main building. The courtyard fountain had been turned off for the winter and was filled with snow. Someone had hung a wreath of red and pink artificial flowers around the neck of the haughty-looking bronze fox, obviously in anticipation of Valentine's Day. Next month it would wear a bright green fedora for Saint Patrick's Day.

I stopped at the desk in the main lobby, where a cut-glass vase filled with long-stemmed red roses sat next to a heart-shaped bowl of wrapped candies with their tiny messages stamped in silver on the foil. *Be mine. True love. Cutie-pie.*

"Can I help you, miss?"

I looked up into the eyes of a young woman sitting behind the desk.

"Yes, please. I'm Lucie Montgomery. I'm here to see Mrs. Eastman in two oh five."

"Let me see if she's in her apartment. I didn't see her at breakfast this morning." The woman picked up the phone and dialed Faith's number. "Lucie Montgomery is downstairs to see you, Mrs. Eastman. . . . Very good. I'll tell her." When she hung up, she said, "The maid just finished her rooms, so you can go right on up."

A cleaning cart stood in the hallway two doors down from Faith's apartment and a vacuum droned through her neighbor's open door. I used the brass knocker and rapped loudly. A silver-framed wedding photo of Kit and Bobby Noland, a detective with the Loudoun County Sheriff's Department, taken last fall at my winery, sat on a small shelf outside the door. Next to it a plush white bear clutched a red satin heart with *True Love* embroidered on it. A moment later, Faith's familiar voice called out that the door was open and to come in.

Pale winter-morning sunlight streamed through the windows of a cheerful sitting room furnished with items I remembered so well from her home. It was still a jolt to see them here and not be overwhelmed by memories. Not everything had come with her when she moved—the new apartment was smaller—and I had to fight the urge to look around, feeling the way they say amputees do when they sense the limb they lost is still somehow there.

Faith sat in her favorite recliner, bundled up in a bright pink cardigan over a turtleneck, baggy blue jeans, and fur-lined moccasin slippers. Her snow-white hair was done up in a bun and bristled with hairpins. An afghan she'd crocheted lay across her lap, and the television was blaring with the morning news from CNN. Her oversized walker, which she'd nicknamed "Big Blue," was parked next to her chair.

"Lucie, darling, how nice to see you." She smiled and picked up the remote, muting the television. "I wasn't expecting you today, with that blizzard we're supposed to get."

I went over and gave her weathered cheek a kiss. As always, she smelled of Shalimar, her signature scent.

I took a white bakery box out of a canvas bag with the winery logo on it. "It's not supposed to start until tonight. I stopped at the Upper Crust and bought two slices of French apple pie for us. Shall I warm them up in the microwave?"

She flashed me a grateful look and said, "Please do. What a dear you are."

I walked into the tiny galley kitchen and found plates in one of the cabinets.

"The woman at the front desk said you didn't go downstairs for breakfast this morning." I set the pie on the plates, put them in the microwave, and punched buttons. "Are you feeling all right? Kit said you finally got over the flu, but you look like you've lost weight."

"I'm fine," she said. "I decided to have breakfast in my room."

The kitchen looked immaculate and there were no dirty dishes. "What did you eat?"

"A granola bar and a banana." She sounded defensive.

"That's not breakfast; that's a snack." The microwave beeped. "Where did you hide your trays? Can I make you some coffee or tea?"

"The trays are in the bottom drawer next to the fridge. And I'd love a cup of tea, if you'll have one. There's Earl Grey. You know where I keep it."

Faith had an old-fashioned kettle that whistled. I filled it with water, got out two of her favorite Spode china cups and saucers, and found the tea. I carried the tray with her pie over to her.

Ten days ago, Roxanna Willoughby, who'd lived in the apartment next door to Faith, had passed away, and Faith had taken it hard. The death of one of the residents in a place like this happened all the time, though it still shocked me how matter-of-fact everyone could be about it. There was even a table in the lobby where framed photos of the recently deceased were placed in memoriam for a few weeks—part shrine, part information desk. I had walked by it on my way upstairs and wondered if I would be as calm and accepting about the end of my own life. If I even made it to my eighties or nineties.

Some of the photographs had been taken recently, others during another lifetime, when the future lay ahead, full of hope and promise. Roxy Willoughby's picture was still there, a black-and-white World War II photo in her pilot's uniform. One of the first women aviators to fly noncombat missions, she was standing next to a British Spitfire with a cocky, confident look in her eyes, like she was ready to take on the Germans single-handedly if they'd let her.

Faith had been too ill to attend Roxy's funeral, but I'd gone with Kit. Roxy had been cremated, so it had been a memorial service, a full Catholic Mass at St. Michael the Archangel in Middleburg, followed by a luncheon in the parish hall. Though I hadn't known Roxy well, her nephew, Mac MacDonald, who owned an antiques shop in Middleburg, had been one of my parents' oldest friends. Growing up, I'd called him "Uncle Mac."

"You're still upset about Roxy's death, aren't you?" I said, kneeling next to Faith. "I'm so sorry. I know you were good friends."

"Lucie." She took one of my hands in both of hers. They felt cold and clammy. "I need to tell you something about Roxy."

"What is it?" I asked.

Faith looked into my eyes and said in a deceptively calm voice, "She was murdered."

The kettle gave off a wild shriek. "Pardon?"

"You heard me," she said. "Katherine thinks I'm nuts and Bobby doesn't believe me, either. I know *you* won't think I'm losing my mind. You'll believe me."

The whistling noise from the kitchen grew louder, like an approaching train. "Let me get the kettle and then you can tell me about it."

I retreated to the kitchen and fixed our tea. The medical examiner had said Roxy died in her sleep. Her heart just stopped beating. Where had Faith gotten the idea that someone had murdered her?

When we were both settled with our trays, I said, "Tell me why you think Roxy was murdered."

Faith shook her fork at me. "I don't think so. I *know* so."

"Okay, how do you know so?"

"I heard something," she said, her mouth set in a determined line. "Roxy had a visitor and they got into a terrible argument. The maid was here cleaning my apartment and she had to leave to get something. She forgot to close my door and left it ajar, so I heard them shouting."

"Who was shouting? About what?"

"Roxy and a man. He was speaking more quietly than she was . . . like he was trying to reason with her, I'd say. Roxy was the one who was shouting," she said. "I don't know about what."

"And you don't know who the man was, either?"

"You're starting to sound like Katherine." She gave me an irritated look. "I know what I heard. An argument and then two days later Roxy was dead. Something happened to her, Lucie. I think the man she was arguing with killed her. He managed to put something into her food and that's how he did it. He poisoned her."

It is profoundly disturbing to have a conversation with someone you love and respect, listening to the account of a completely illogical story that you are assured in the most earnest way is God's truth, and not wonder if that person is starting to lose it.

"The medical examiner didn't find anything, Faith."

"Because he wasn't looking for anything," she said, exasperated. "Roxy was ninety-two, for heaven's sake."

"All right, why would someone kill her? She was beloved; you know that. At her funeral, every pew in the church was full."

Faith picked up her teacup and drank. "That was before her will was read and people found out she'd changed it just before she died. In favor of a granddaughter in England no one knew existed."

The revelation, which came out along with the news about her new will, had floored everybody. It seemed that Roxy, a devout Catholic with the upright morals and pristine virtues of a Victorian, had had an affair with an RAF pilot when she was stationed in England during the war. Unfortunately, he was killed on a mission over Germany, and when Roxy found out she was pregnant, she decided to give the child, a daughter, to his sister and her husband and never told anyone about the baby. The daughter passed away a few years ago, leaving behind an adult daughter of her own—Roxy's never-before-heard-of granddaughter.

"The one person who lost out when Roxy changed her will was her nephew," I said to Faith. "Mac MacDonald. He still got the house and the art collection and the antiques, but her granddaughter inherited the money. Are you saying you believe Mac killed his aunt?"

"Oh, dear Lord, of course not. Mac adored Roxy, took care of her the way Katherine looks after me. I've known him for ages. No, Mac wouldn't have harmed a hair on Roxy's head."

"Then who did it? Who are the other possible suspects?"

Faith stared at the muted television, where a man and a woman dressed like chickens were holding hands and jumping up and down on *Let's Make a Deal*.

"Well, she had loads of visitors; you know that," she said. "Roxy helped so many people. I couldn't even begin to tell you who came by. Everyone stopped in to see her, especially folks from her charities. She was always writing checks."

I looked at her, dismayed. "Well, that doesn't narrow the field down much, does it?"

"I'm afraid not." Faith finished the last bite of pie and looked around for a place to set the tray.

"Here, I'll take that." She handed it to me and I took it into the kitchen.

"Leave the dishes," she said. "The maid will take care of them tomorrow."

"I'll wash them now and save her the trouble. Did you ask Roxy about that argument? Or talk to her afterward and find out why she was upset?"

"I would never do anything like that." She sounded horrified. "She was a very private woman. I was as surprised as anyone to learn she had a granddaughter in England. Roxy never spoke about her. Never. I don't think anybody knew, to be honest."

"Including Mac," I said. "Though obviously Sam Constantine knew. He was her lawyer."

"And probably Father O'Malley. Or so I would imagine. He used to come over from Veronica House regularly to hear her confession and bring her Communion after it became too difficult for her to go out to church."

I finished our dishes and wiped my hands on a towel hanging over the dishwasher's door handle. "Neither Father O'Malley nor Sam could ever talk about anything Roxy told them in confidence. A priest and a lawyer. They're both sworn to secrecy."

I went back into the sitting room and pulled up an ottoman so that I was facing Faith. "What is it?" I asked, taking her hands in mine and rubbing my thumbs across the tops of her bony knuckles. "What's bothering you?"

"I told you my door was ajar," she said. "I didn't see who they were, you understand, but they must have realized I heard everything. I'm worried that I'm next after Roxy. I'm worried that someone is going to poison me, too."

Big clanging alarm bells went off in my head.

"Wait a minute." I gave her hands a gentle squeeze. "First of all, who are 'they'? I thought you said there was only one person in Roxy's room. A man."

"Two men walked past my door," she said. "I heard the door to her apartment close and then someone walked down the hall, the man I heard her shouting at, I suppose. Then about half a minute later, someone else walked by."

"Were they together?"

"I don't know. I guess I assumed they were. Now you've got me a bit confused."

"What day was this?"

"Roxy died on a Friday. It was the Tuesday before." She looked at me with fearful eyes. "She started taking her meals in her apartment those last few days instead of going downstairs to the restaurant. It would have been so easy to slip something into her food, you see. Who would ever know?"

"Are you saying someone from Foxhall Manor poisoned her?"

"I think someone who was *at* Foxhall Manor put something into her food and poisoned her. It fits, don't you think?"

What I thought was that she had looped a story around and around itself, twisted it into a pretzeled knot until it seemed logical in her mind, and then persuaded herself of its veracity: Roxy Willoughby had been poisoned because of an argument she'd had with a mystery man a few days before she died.

Right now I agreed with Kit and Bobby. None of this made sense. But I didn't want to upset Faith even more than she already was.

"You know we've always been honest with each other," I said. "We've always told each other the truth."

Faith gave a faint moan and turned pale. "Oh, my God, Lucie. That's it. That's what she said."

"What who said? Roxy?"

She nodded. "I'd forgotten until just now. She kept saying it over and over. 'I want to know the truth. I want to know the truth.'"

"The truth about what?"

"I don't know." She gave me a despairing look. "I'm so sorry. I just don't know. But whatever it was, it's the reason she's dead."

"Faith—"

"You have to believe me, Lucie. I'm not crazy."

"Of course you're not—"

"Then promise me you'll try to find out why

Roxy was so upset and who came to visit her that day. No one will suspect anything if you ask a few questions."

"I don't know—"

"My darling child, I never turned my back on you when you needed me." Faith sat up and gave me a steely look. "Now I need you and I'm asking you to do this favor for me. Katherine won't, so you must."

I closed my eyes. Emotional blackmail. I opened them and took a deep breath. She was watching me like a hawk.

"Okay," I said. "I'll do it."

SIX

I made Faith another cup of tea before I left, and she finally calmed down, apparently convinced I was going to find out who had murdered Roxy Willoughby. When I got back to my car, I called Kit. Maybe she knew something I didn't. Maybe Faith's doctor had changed her medication and she was having problems adjusting.

Kit's phone went to voice mail, so I left a "Hey, call me" message and didn't say why. Then I drove to the General Store. What I really hoped Kit wouldn't tell me was that her mother was starting to lose her grasp on what was real and what she imagined. That I couldn't bear.

• • •

In every small town in America there is always a place that is the beating heart of the community, where everyone gathers to find out the news—who got their garden in early, how the morning hack went with the horses, whose five-alarm chili really should have won first place at the community center cook-off, who got engaged, divorced, married, fired, arrested, promoted, buried—the big and little life events that stitch us together, sometimes a little too intimately. In Atoka, that pulsing nexus was the General Store, which Thelma Johnson had owned since the days when God was a boy. Though she looked like a sweet, slightly befuddled grandmother, Thelma could extract your darkest, most private secrets with the surgical precision of the marines and the unabashed glee of a reality television show host. Usually within five minutes after you walked into the store. Attempting to resist her gentle but persistent questioning—though you'd sworn on your mother's grave that you wouldn't succumb—was like trying to avoid gravity. Then there was this: What happened in the General Store *never* stayed in the General Store, especially if the Romeos, a somewhat cantankerous group of senior citizens whose name stood for Retired Old Men Eating Out, had already been by for morning coffee and pastries, chewing over the latest gossip, which refueled them until they reached their next watering hole.

Thelma's parking lot—which had space for precisely four cars—was empty when I pulled in fifteen minutes after I left Foxhall Manor. Hopefully, that didn't mean Thelma was out of everything and that I'd missed the stampede to get what she liked to call "the white stuff you need when the other white stuff covers the ground"— milk, toilet paper, and bread. I parked next to the entrance to the white clapboard building with its peeling paint, hipped tin roof, and large picture window with the neon OPEN sign that had read OPE for years.

A television blared from the back room as I walked through the front door, which meant Thelma was watching one of her beloved soap operas. A moment later, a reedy voice called, "Coming! I'm coming," and she emerged with the drama and verve of an aging movie star making an entrance at the Oscars, certain there will be a standing ovation.

Thelma dressed for maximum impact—always from head to toe in a color so strong, it seemed to vibrate. Today she wore royal purple: a knit minidress with matching open-toed stiletto heels, two propeller-shaped bows in her carrot red hair, and so much purple eye shadow, her eyes looked like two bruises behind her trifocals.

The minute she saw me, her face lit up. "Why, Lucille," she said, "do come on in, child. My goodness, I haven't seen you for an age and here I was just thinking about you."

That gravitational pull kicked in and I walked over to her, taking a quick mental inventory of anything in my life that might have come under her microscope and drawing a blank. I pasted on a smile and said, "Were you really? How interesting."

Thelma took off her glasses and wiped them on the sleeve of her dress. "Oh, my, yes. And, of course, I knew you'd come in after that." She tapped the side of her head with her index finger and the multiple bracelets on her wrist jingled like sleigh bells. "It's my God-given psychotic powers. I just *know* things. Don't ask me how."

"Well, it's true nothing in Atoka seems to happen without your finding out about it."

She beamed. "I do try to keep my oar in. And, of course, I feel such personal emphasis for folks."

I wasn't sure where she was going with that, but I nodded anyway.

She put her glasses back on and peered at me. "What can I do for you?"

"I need milk, if you've still got it. And bread. And batteries, size D."

"I got chocolate milk is all," she said. "And the Romeos were in this morning like a herd of grazing buffalo, wiping out all my cross-ants and bread. All I've got are doughnuts. But you're in luck with batteries. Right around the corner next to ammunition and greeting cards."

"I'll take the chocolate milk and doughnuts. Hope will think she's died and gone to heaven."

Thelma had a little of everything as long as you didn't mind the lack of variety. Though I could have driven into town to the Middleburg Safeway and found everything I needed there, her little store was a dying breed. If Safeway closed, it wouldn't hurt their bottom line, I was sure. But the village of Atoka wouldn't recover if we lost Thelma. I wondered how long she'd keep the store—and if there was anyone in line who would buy it from her when she decided she wanted to spend all her time watching her soaps and communing with the spirits on her Ouija board.

She got the chocolate milk and put the doughnuts in a white bakery bag while I found the batteries. When I joined her at the cash register, she gave me a sly look. "So, do tell. Who was that good-looking man who paid you a visit this morning? He looked familiar, but I know I've never seen him in these parts before." She placed a hand over her heart. "My, but wasn't he the handsome devil. Looked like a real Hollywood type, a movie director or something."

I said with a straight face, "I'm not sure who you're talking about."

She gave me a stern look. "Course you are, Lucille. He stopped in here about ten-fifteen this morning because he was having trouble with his PMS."

"His—pardon?"

"You know, that map thing in folks' cars that talks to them. He said his PMS couldn't figure out the small roads around here. He was looking for Sycamore Lane, and I knew that was you." She folded her arms across her chest. "So . . . aren't you going to tell me who he was?"

I'd been there all of about five minutes. How did she always know?

"His name is Gino Tomassi. He owns a vineyard in California. A rather large vineyard. He knows Quinn from way back."

"Tomassi? Are you talking about the Tomassi Family Vineyard?" I nodded and her eyes grew wide. "Why, my goodness, I used to drink their Chianti red wine pretty regular years ago. It came in those nice bottles that looked like a jug and they put 'em in a sweet little straw basket. I used 'em for candleholders afterward. Looked real pretty with lots of different colors of wax dripping down the sides."

"I've heard about those raffia-wrapped bottles," I said. "Unfortunately, they don't make them anymore."

"Now that you mention it, I haven't seen them for an age." She pressed the fold in the bakery bag until it was as flat as if it had been ironed and gave me an innocent smile. "Isn't that nice, Quinn inviting an old friend to come for a visit all the way out here from California?"

"Uh . . . yes. It is, isn't it?" Eli always says I'm the world's worst liar, but there was no way I was going to tell her the truth about Gino. "I guess I'm done here. Thanks, Thelma. Take care of yourself and have a nice day."

"Not so fast, missy. You're looking a mite tired, Lucille. How about a nice cup of coffee? On the house. Pep you right up. Besides, I thought you'd be interested in hearing who dropped by this morning. And I don't mean Gino Tomassi, either. It's someone else. I'm sure you'll never guess."

You'd never want to play three-card monte with Thelma. She'd strip you down to your underwear in minutes.

I took the bait. "Who?"

"Uma Lawrence, that's who." She saw the expression on my face and smirked. "Knew I'd surprise you."

She had. Uma Lawrence was Roxy Willoughby's long-lost granddaughter.

"She's in town?"

"Yes indeedy. How Roxy managed to keep that child a secret all these years is beyond me." Thelma put her hands on her hips in a way that said she meant to get to the bottom of that mystery. "She arrived today and, don't you know, she stopped in here just like Gino did, because she was lost. Except she was asking for directions to Mac MacDonald's house instead of yours."

Roxy hadn't confided in anyone that she had a granddaughter, but I wondered if Uma Lawrence had known about her grandmother. If anybody could worm that information out of her, it would be Thelma. Like everyone else in town, I was curious, too.

"I suppose I have time for a quick cup," I said. "What's today's Fancy?"

Thelma always kept three pots of fresh-brewed coffee, labeled Plain, Fancy, and Decaf, on a table near the glass vitrine where her bakery goods were displayed.

She arched a heavily penciled-in eyebrow and it disappeared under her lacquered helmet of red bangs. "It's a peppy one. Brewed Awakening. Perks you right up like a double-double espresso."

I'd just had tea with Faith Eastman, but I said, "I'll try it."

She poured two coffees and gave one to me. "You know where the milk and sugar are."

I fixed my coffee and followed her to a corner of the store where a pair of Lincoln rocking chairs faced each other next to a woodstove. After we sat down, I said, "So, what's Uma Lawrence like?"

Thelma sipped her coffee. "Nothing like Roxy, I can tell you that."

"What do you mean?"

"She's not very friendly. And I don't think she likes it here."

82

"She only just arrived."

"I know," Thelma said. "Though she's quite a beauty. A redhead, like Roxy used to be, probably around your age, Lucille, pushing thirty. One of those English rose complexions, and when she talks, I swear she sounds so British."

"She is British," I said. "She lives in London."

Thelma gave me an irritated look. "I know that. It's just such a surprise to think that Roxy had another family in England all this time and none of us had a clue. Mac told me he was pretty sure Roxy's husband never knew, either. Otherwise, he probably never would have married her, the two of them being such devout Catholics and her breaking that commandment about not committing adulthood."

I nodded. "Right."

After the war, Roxy had worked as a commercial pilot for a charter company that flew wealthy individuals—mostly rich businessmen and their wives and girlfriends—all over the world. She'd married Bruce Willoughby, one of her clients, who was forty years her senior and had made his fortune in international real estate. He passed away shortly after they were married and Roxy ended up a young and very rich widow.

"I still can't get over the fact that Mac didn't know," I said. "He's Roxy's nephew. They were always so close."

"He had no clue, Lucille. And he's right touchy

about it, too," she said. "Once he found out about the new will, he asked a friend who owns an antiques store in London to help track down Uma. Uma was the one told him both her parents were dead, her mother from alcoholism when she was a little girl and her father of a heart attack a few years ago."

Thelma seemed to have acquired an encyclopedic knowledge of Roxy's family in a matter of days. "You certainly have all the information, Thelma."

"Oh, you know me. I'm a regular Orifice of Delphi. People come to me all the time for advice or whatever," she said. "And they want to share their stories, too, so I listen. I have a mind for remembering like a steel trapdoor, you know."

"I do know that," I said. "Did Roxy ever meet Uma or see her daughter again after the war?"

Thelma shook her head. "Uma didn't remember meeting Roxy and she says her mother never mentioned her grandmother, either. But who knows?"

"I guess it doesn't really matter anymore, since everyone involved is dead."

Thelma set her coffee cup down on a stack of soap opera magazines that were piled on table next to the rocking chair.

"It's just so peculiar the way she changed her will right before she died," she said, shaking her head as if she was still trying to work it out. "Let me tell you, Mac is madder 'n a wet hornet at Sam Constantine for keeping quiet about that."

"You know very well Sam couldn't talk about Roxy's will to Mac," I said. "It's lawyer-client confidentiality."

She raised an eyebrow. "Even so, it's been pretty tense between him and Mac lately when they both show up here at the same time for their morning coffee. Mac feels like Sam double-crossed him, because a few weeks ago he sold Sam two oil paintings he picked up at an estate sale in Georgetown. They were real valuable, too. Not like the *Mona Lisa* by that da Vinci Code painter, but still worth a lot of money. Mac said he gave Sam 'the family discount' on account of them being such old friends and now he thinks the least Sam could have done was give him a hint about what was happening."

"It was Roxy's place to tell Mac, not Sam's. Maybe she meant to and she died before she got around to it," I said. "I don't suppose you have any idea why she changed her will?"

A few years ago, Thelma had confided to me that she had lost a baby when she was much younger and, like Roxy, she and the father had never married. It had broken her heart. "Maybe," she said, and her voice was soft with memory, "Roxy woke up one day and realized she'd completely missed out on her daughter's life but that she still had a chance with her granddaughter."

85

She took off her glasses and wiped the corner of an eye.

"Oh, Thelma, I'm so sorry—"

"It's okay, Lucille. Really. But if it was me, I think that would be reason enough."

"Sam Constantine always says that a will is the last time in someone's life that you get to make amends, to put things right," I said. "Maybe you're right and that's what happened to Roxy."

"I just wish the Lawrence girl was a little nicer, that's all." Thelma put her glasses back on and blinked at me. "When she sashayed in here, she acted like she was the queen of England, all high-and-mighty. I don't think she was much impressed with the store, or with Atoka, for that matter. I heard her talking on the phone when she was standing in one of the aisles. Either she didn't think I could hear what she said or she didn't care."

"What was she saying?"

Thelma waved a hand. "That she wanted to get back to England to take care of her dog."

"Her dog? Are you sure?"

"Course I'm sure. She was yakking on the phone, carrying on about some woman making her dog's dinner and that she didn't want her to make a hash this time." Thelma made a clicking sound with her tongue. "A dog that gets fed hash. I never. But it was the other thing she said, Lucille, that got me all riled up. As clear as a bell, I heard her. 'I'm not sticking around for long. As soon as it's sorted, I'm clearing off.' Her very words. Just wants to get what's coming to her and skedaddle."

"That's rather harsh," I said. "Although she never met her grandmother and technically there's nothing to keep her here. Mac's got the house. I guess you can't blame her."

"Oh, I don't blame her. I blame Mercury. It's in retrograde all week long," Thelma said in an ominous voice. "You know what that means, don't you? Trouble. Never do anything important when Mercury is in retrograde, Lucille. You'll just have to fix the mess later." She ticked items off on her fingers. "Relationships go to hell in a bandwagon because people just can't communicate proper, say what they really mean. And you should never, ever make travel plans or sign important papers, both of which Uma Lawrence is planning to do. She'll regret it, just you wait and see. Mark my words, when Mercury starts spinning backward, there's always trouble." She gave me a dark look. "And this time won't be any different."

SEVEN

By the time I left Thelma's, the clouds had thickened and the sky matched the dirty dishrag white of the rest of the landscape, a sure sign that the snow would come soon. In a month this would be a distant memory as we raced to get ready for bud break in the vineyard and the flowering trees burst into bloom at the beginning of spring. But today the potholey roads were bleached with crisscrossing white streaks already laid down by salt trucks over the last few months, and the curbs were edged with drifts of dirty sand. My Jeep and the other cars I passed on Atoka Road as I drove home were coated with swaths of dried-on road spray kicked up from piles of blackened roadside snow or graceless heaps that overran parking lots.

A small convoy of plows drove by in the other direction, heading toward town, and I knew the salt trucks would already be congregating on Mosby's Highway on the outskirts of Middleburg. The predictions were all over the place about how much we were going to get. But no one disputed that we would be hammered by a fast-moving clipper of intense swirling snow that would come up from the south, barge through the metropolitan Washington area like a rude guest, and then continue up the East Coast. We could get six inches, or maybe ten, or possibly a foot on top of the five inches that had fallen a few days ago. Since it was so bone-chillingly cold, at least it would only be snow that fell, rather than sleet or ice, which would be far worse.

I had promised Frankie I would stop by Mick Dunne's to pick up a photo album he'd agreed to loan her. For a moment, I debated going directly home from Thelma's before the snow began, but Frankie really wanted the album and I was driving right past Mick's place anyway. I slowed down and turned onto his private road. This wouldn't take long.

The lane had been plowed out from last week's snowstorm and the saucer magnolias and dogwoods that grew like sentries on either side were winter-bare. In spring, thousands of tulips and daffodils bloomed underneath the flowering trees, and the sight was breathtaking. But today there was nothing but dirty churned-up snow lining an ice-rutted road, just like everywhere else in this eternal, relentless winter.

I pulled into the circular drive and parked the Jeep. Mick's housekeeper, a pretty dark-haired Hispanic woman, answered the door and invited me in, promising to tell Mick I was there and asking if I could wait in the enormous marble-floored foyer.

A mutual friend of Mick's and mine had redecorated the house a few years ago and Mick had given her carte blanche with the place while he threw his attention into the stables and his horses. The result was too grandiose for my taste—acres of dark woodwork, rich saturated colors on the walls, oil paintings in heavy rococo frames of bearded men in uniform or hunting scenes, brocaded curtains, English and American antiques—but Mick liked the masculine baronial splendor and, to be honest, it suited him.

The housekeeper returned, gesturing to a set of double doors down the hall. "He's in the library. And he's having tea. Can I bring you something, as well?"

"No, thank you, I just had coffee."

She smiled and I headed for the library. It was probably my favorite room in the house, the one that seemed the least museumlike. Mick collected rare first editions and the most valuable books were here, rows of beautiful leather-bound volumes lining the shelves of dark-paneled floor-to-ceiling bookcases, the old gilt titles gleaming in the soft light of table and floor lamps scattered around the room. A fire burned in the stone fireplace and the salmon-colored pages of the *Financial Times* lay creased and folded on a dark green leather sofa.

He was standing with his back to me, bent over an antique trestle table covered with an untidy collection of old photographs and news clippings. He must have heard me walk in, because he straightened up and turned around.

"Hello, darling." He crossed the room and gave me a breezy kiss on the lips. "How lovely to see you. You're looking quite gorgeous today."

I had swapped the wine-stained sweatshirt for a thick white ribbed turtleneck, but I was still dressed in old work clothes. No makeup. "Flattery will get you whatever you want," I said. "I presume you need help with something, since I look anything but gorgeous."

He grinned and put an arm around my shoulder. "Come take a look at this." He walked me over to the trestle table.

"What are you working on?"

"The history of the Goose Creek Hunt," he said. "This year's our centenary. I finally got all the photographs and newspaper clippings and fixture cards and the like together in one place. Now we just need to sort through them and put them in chronological order . . . which, as you can see, is going to be a hell of a job."

I picked up a yellowed newspaper clipping of a triumphant owner at the Upperville Colt & Horse Show, holding an enormous silver platter, a ribbon pinned to the horse's bridle. There was no mention of what year it was.

"Good luck," I said.

We both turned as the housekeeper appeared carrying a tray with a silver tea service on it, two Portmeirion cups and saucers, and a plate of butter cookies. She set the tray on a coffee table and said, "I thought you might change your mind about having tea, Ms. Montgomery, so I brought another cup and saucer."

When we were alone again, Mick said, "Join me in a cuppa?"

I nodded. "Just half, please. What are you going

to do with all your pictures and clippings once you get them organized?"

He fixed my tea and brought it over to me. "Turn it into a book for our members. Sell copies at the spring steeplechase races and the Hunt Ball. We'll raise funds for the care of the hounds, plus donate a portion to the equine center and the Sporting Museum." He picked up a photograph of a raven-haired woman sailing over a fence on a beautiful bay horse and turned it over. "Bootsie and Sal . . . at least there's an inscription."

"Which one's the horse?" I asked.

"You don't recognize either of them?" he asked as I shook my head. "You're the one whose family has lived here for donkey's years. I was hoping you'd help me figure out some of these. Maybe come by some night for dinner?"

He went over and poured his own tea.

"I'm not sure I'd be much help, since I don't hunt," I said. "And speaking of photos, Frankie said you have an album that belonged to the Studebakers from the days when they threw some of their legendary parties."

"That's right. She was chatting me up the other day in the Cuppa Giddyup. I told her she could borrow it if she wanted to have a look before your big dinner dance on Saturday." He walked across the room and picked up a leather book from a bookshelf and brought it over to me. "Are you going with anybody? And don't think I didn't notice that you didn't answer when I invited you to dinner."

I took the book and traced a finger over the intricate tooled design on the leather cover. My face felt hot. "If you're asking if I have a date for Saturday, I'm going to be busy working, so . . . no. No, I don't."

"Would you like one?" he asked.

"Mick," I said, "we've been down this road before."

"Is that a yes or a no? You might give a fellow a break." He took the album from me and set it on the trestle table. "Besides, the world and his wife will be there, from what I hear, so we'll have loads of chaperones. Come on, darling. It's just a dance."

A dance on Valentine's Day, the most romantic day of the year.

"Quinn," he said, when I still hesitated, "sees you every bloody day. Not to put too fine a point on it, but apparently he didn't ask you. And I just did."

I'd have bet money that Frankie had somehow worked into the conversation at the Cuppa Giddyup that Quinn and I weren't going together. Mick was right. Quinn had had all the time in the world to ask me to go with him.

If he'd wanted to.

"I know you did," I said. "All right, then, yes. I accept."

"Good." He stared into my eyes with a look that should have made my heart flutter.

"Mick?"

"Yes, love?"

"Can I take a look at your photo album?"

He gave me a fake wounded look. "You're a cruel woman, Lucie Montgomery."

"Yes, I know. Heart of stone. The album?"

"Oh, all right. Come and sit down. Actually, there's something I wanted to show you."

We sat on the sofa together and I opened the leather book. Between each set of pages was a protective sheet as thin as tissue paper. Every picture was labeled, white ink on black paper.

I caught my breath. "Will you look at these? They're great. 'Mary & her new roadster' . . . 'Chas on the links' . . . 'Dickie and Mary by the pool' . . . 'Buffy's new pony' . . . I wonder when they were taken."

"I talked to one of Jim Studebaker's sons after I found the album," Mick said. "He reckoned the early 1920s, once I described the pictures to him."

"He didn't want it back?"

"God no. He said he's had to rent a couple of storage units and they're filled with boxes of not only his parents' stuff but also his grandparents' things. It'll take him an age and a half to go through all of it. He told me to keep this one, since it was part of the history of the house."

"What did you want to show me?" I asked.

"This." He leaned over and draped one arm around my shoulder while he flipped through the album. "What do you think?"

It was a group photo of a good-looking man surrounded by a dozen or so beautiful young women dressed to the nines in flapper dresses, laughing and hoisting flutes of champagne, an uninhibited, giddy group bent toward him, a sultan surrounded by his harem. A stunning young woman who looked like she couldn't have been more than nineteen or twenty sat on his lap, wearing a gauzy décolleté dress with a high side slit. One of her arms was wrapped around the man's neck, and she held her glass of champagne tilted crazily, as if she had already spilled it and didn't care. His glass was upright, his grin lascivious, and his other hand rested possessively on her exposed thigh.

I read the caption out loud. " 'Warren Harding and friends, September 1920.' " I looked up at Mick. "*The* Warren Harding? As in President Warren Harding?"

He nodded. "The very one. I did some checking. In 1920, Harding was still a senator, though he would have been running for president, two months away from being elected. He didn't take office until 1921."

"Maybe he was out in Middleburg taking advantage of the fact that women had just gotten the right to vote," I said. "Though most of the women in that group don't look old enough to use it. And I don't think that sweet young thing on his lap is Florence Harding."

"She was considerably older and didn't look anything like that gorgeous creature," Mick said. "Harding was a notorious womanizer, slipped out without his wife for a little something on the side all the time. . . . Lucie? What's wrong? Did I say something to upset you?"

"No," I said. "It's just that I recognize one of the women in that photo."

Actually, what had caught my eye was her dress—the exquisite flapper dress I'd found in the attic, the one I was planning to wear to the party on Saturday. Smiling, with a vampy, flirtatious look in her eye, was a woman who made me feel as if I were looking in a mirror.

I pointed. "Her."

"Good God." Mick sounded startled. "She's the absolute portrait of you, love. Who is she?"

My voice sounded as if it came from far away. "Leland's great-aunt, my great-grandmother's sister. Her name was Lucy Montgomery." I looked up at him. "But everyone called her 'Lucky.'"

EIGHT

So now I knew who had owned that exquisite dress. Lucy Montgomery, a woman whose nickname—Lucky—fit her perfectly. Someone whose legacy I had never been sure was something to be lived up to—or lived down. Leland named me for her, his much beloved great-aunt—actually, his favorite person in the world. My French mother changed the *y* to *ie,* but otherwise, I was her namesake.

She died when I was three, and even though my memories could only have come from old black-and-white photographs and remembered family stories, she had always seemed flesh-and-blood real to me, as vivid as Technicolor. My father adored her, a kindred spirit whose dazzling good looks and dangerous charm—so they said—could seduce you into betraying your own true self. My mother told me once in a fit of anger that in spite of the difference in their generations, Leland and Lucky were as alike as two peas in a pod, always expecting their tiny lies and little lapses of honesty to be forgiven or overlooked because they weren't accountable to the same standards and morals as the rest of us.

"Are you all right, Lucie?" Mick asked. "You've gone very pale."

"Yes," I said. "It's just such a shock to see her."

"How did she get the name 'Lucky'?"

"Like you'd imagine," I said. "She was a happy-go-lucky person, a real free spirit. Or maybe a hell raiser, depending on your opinion. Look at the date when that photo was taken—it was the beginning of the Roaring Twenties, when women suddenly had so much more freedom. Sex, alcohol, cigarettes. Unchaperoned dates and petting parties. From what I heard, she was in her element. If she'd lived in the sixties, she probably would have been a hippie. Instead, I guess you'd call her 'bohemian.'"

Mick stared at the photo and then at me in an intense, curious way. "It's uncanny how much you two look alike. What happened to her?"

I turned red. "She went to England after her debutante season and fell in love with a married earl. It was pretty intense, a torrid affair, and, of course, eventually he went back to his wife and all of her money, which broke Lucky's heart," I said. "But the worst of it was that because of the affair, she changed her mind about going home and gave a girlfriend her ticket to sail back to New York."

"What do you mean, 'the worst of it'?"

"The ship was the *Titanic.*"

"God, how awful."

"Lucky never forgave herself, even though everyone said she really deserved her nickname after that. From then on, she carried on sort of a gypsy life, traveling all over the world, living in hotels for months at a time or staying with the latest boyfriend she'd pick up somewhere. Inevitably, he owned a villa in Cannes overlooking the Mediterranean or a ruined castle in Umbria . . . a poet, some minor royal, a bad-boy heir to a shipping fortune."

"Obviously she spent time here in Atoka." Mick glanced down at the picture again. "She must have stayed at Highland House for a while."

I shook my head. "It was too quiet for her, too provincial. In those days, there was still a lot of poverty here after all the destruction from the Civil War. Besides, Lucky had money, an inheritance from her mother's family, so she could afford her nomadic life. The only time she worked was as an artist's model when she lived in Paris and hung around with Hemingway, the Fitzgeralds, Gertrude Stein, Picasso . . . all the Paris writers and artists of that generation."

"I would have liked to have known her." Mick spoke with such passion that I felt a sudden unwelcome twinge of jealousy. Lucky had been dead for nearly thirty years, but she was still a seductress.

"Lucky fascinated everyone," I said in a mild voice. "She had loads of admirers and lovers."

"I wonder if Warren Harding was one of them. Just because he had that gorgeous woman on his lap didn't mean she was the only one he was screwing around with," Mick said. "He really was Jack the Lad, having his way with women in hotels, at the White House, even a place on H Street called 'the Love Nest.' I don't know how he got away with it."

"I do believe you're jealous."

He gave me an evil grin. "Not jealous. Curious."

"Those were different times. He wouldn't get away with it today," I said. "How come you know so much about Warren Harding—and his sex life? Our most undistinguished president, and the most corrupt administration in American history, and all you talk about are his women."

"That picture." Mick tapped it with his finger. "There's something about it. The way all those beautiful women are crowded around Harding and that gorgeous creature he's feeling up . . . it's so intimate. You shouldn't look, but you can't turn away." He groped my thigh, but it was more brotherly than lustful.

"Down, boy." I removed his hand and let it flop on the couch. "The Studebakers' parties must have been pretty wild and uninhibited. I heard a story that there was even a duel once. Over a woman."

"There was," Mick said. "Jim's son told me about it when we discussed the album. A lot of blood, but nobody was killed. They were all too drunk."

I turned more pages. "I don't see Lucky or Warren Harding in any other pictures."

"That's the only photo of Harding," he said. "I

couldn't tell you about Lucky, since I didn't know who she was until you pointed her out. Take the album home and have a better look. No rush to get it back."

"Thank you. And now I really should be going. Thanks for the tea." I closed the book and stood up. "Will I see you tomorrow for the hunt, or did you call it off?"

Highland Farm had been part of the Goose Creek Hunt's territory ever since it had been founded a century ago. Once a season, they hunted on my farm; the date had been set for months and I'd received a fixture card with their schedule. After my father died, my neighbors on the other side had tried to pressure me into blocking the hunt from using my land, on the grounds that blood sports were cruel and inhumane. It would have meant turning my back on my heritage, my own family, and a way of life that was woven into the warp and weft of this part of Virginia, so I'd said no and that the Goose Creek Hunt was welcome to ride through my farm as it had always done.

Mick groaned. "Oh, God, sorry, I should have called, but yes, I canceled on account of the snow. Another call came in and I got sidetracked." He shook his head. "Crikey, I'm so ready for this winter to be over."

"Me, too," I said. "We were supposed to start pruning the south vineyard tomorrow. Now

Quinn's probably going to have to plow it out, clear a path so the guys can get to the vines. They hate working in the snow because it's so cold and it really slows them down. I wish we didn't have to do it, but we can't afford to fall behind schedule before bud break."

He walked me to the front door and helped me on with my coat. "My winemaker tells me we'll be doing the same thing," he said, leaning in for a good-bye kiss. "So is it true we're supposed to dress up for this party? Am I expected to look like Al Capone?"

I grinned. "Of course. That's half the fun."

"What are you wearing?"

"I'm not telling. Although, actually, you've already seen it."

"I have?" He gave me a puzzled look. "When?"

"No hints. You'll have to be surprised."

He stood under the portico until I got in the Jeep and started the engine, then went inside. What would he say when he saw me in Lucky's fabulous dress and realized where he'd seen it before? In a picture of a woman who had captivated him, my mirror image twin who had worn it nearly a century ago?

One more time the dress had worked its magic. This time it had bewitched Mick Dunne.

By the time I turned onto Sycamore Lane at the entrance to the vineyard, a few fat flakes had landed on the Jeep's windshield. A harbinger of what was to come. I drove first to the house to leave the groceries with Persia Fleming, the widowed Jamaican woman I'd hired last fall as our housekeeper after Eli and Hope moved in. Before long, Eli poached her as Hope's daytime caregiver when Hopie wasn't in preschool, and she'd moved into a cozy little apartment that Eli had remodeled above the carriage house, where he had his architecture studio. By Christmas, I couldn't imagine how we'd ever managed without someone as capable as Persia, who ran the house like a dream and cared for Hope with such devotion.

She met me at the door, holding a pink wand with a silver star on it and wearing an aluminum foil tiara on top of her silver-streaked cornrow braids, the ends of which she'd wound up in a loose bun. There was a smear of flour on her face like war paint and the house smelled fragrantly of baking.

"I was hoping you were Prince Charming," she said in her lilting accent, taking the bag from me. "With a glass slipper."

"*Cinderella*?" I said. "Again?"

"It was either that or *Finding Nemo*. Which I can recite by heart. And I'd rather be a fairy godmother than a fish, let me tell you."

"Well, have fun." I grinned. "We won't be late tonight. Eli's coming over to help with the blending trials for the new sparkling wine and then Dominique's bringing dinner. With the snow on its way, it'll be quick, so everyone can get home. Sure you don't want to join us for dinner?"

She shook her head. "Hope wants hot dogs and macaroni and cheese. Comfort food before the blizzard. My little angel and I will be fine here, don't you worry. You go make your wine." Persia waved her wand at me, smiling. "Any wishes you need granted before I go?"

I had a laundry list. "No, not really. Mercury is in retrograde. I think it's a bad time to make wishes."

Her smile evaporated. "Oh, Lordy. I'd completely forgotten. Mercury in retrograde is bad. So many things go wrong. I'll need to light some candles when I get home tonight."

I drove over to the villa and wondered if both Thelma, with her Ouija board, and Persia, who dabbled a bit in the Jamaican version of voodoo, were right. Then I remembered my argument with Quinn that morning and what Thelma had said about relationships going to hell.

I, too, would be glad when this week was over and the planets were aligned properly and spinning around the sun as they should be once again.

Someone—probably Frankie—had put a bag of ice melt outside the front door to the villa for when we'd need it later. She was standing behind the mosaic-tiled bar my mother had designed, head bent over something that absorbed her attention, glasses perched low on her nose. Mosby, the silver-gray barn cat that had adopted us a few months ago, lay stretched out in front of the fireplace, where a fire still blazed cheerfully. I bent to scratch his head and he rolled over and began washing himself.

Frankie finally looked up. "Oh, gosh, sorry, I didn't hear you come in."

"Is everything all right?" I walked over to the bar and set down the canvas bag with Mick's photo album in it.

"I'm not sure." She took off her glasses and chewed on one of the stems. "I'm just going over a report on Veronica House. We've got a board meeting the day after tomorrow. Father Niall wants to expand the homeless shelter. He says we need more space." She frowned again. "It's just that our financial situation seems to be a bit precarious. I talked to another member of the board who is helping to get ready for our diocesan audit. She says there's some money that can't be accounted for."

"Oh?"

"We'll straighten it out, don't worry. Niall's so generous, he can't say no to anyone in need, especially when they're desperate. He'll help someone out, and then look for the money later.

He has a good heart, that man. He wants to use the money from the 'Anything Goes' party for the food pantry, since we're so low on supplies. I can't tell you how grateful I am to you for having this fund-raiser."

"I'm glad we're doing it. A lot of people would go hungry or sleep on the streets if it weren't for Veronica House. And Father Niall O'Malley." I opened the bag and pulled out the album. "I brought you something. The Studebaker album on loan from Mick. It's got some great pictures."

"That's nice." She ran her hand over the elaborately embossed leather as I had done, but she didn't open the album. She still seemed distracted. "Thanks."

"Are you all right, Frankie?"

"Me? Sure." She looked over at the wall of French doors that led to a large deck with a view of the snow-covered Blue Ridge Mountains. "It looks like it's already started to snow."

"If you or anyone else wants to take off early, go ahead. We'll still have enough people for the blend sampling. The rest of us live here."

"No one's leaving," she said. "I already told everyone they were done for the day, but all of us want to stay. I think it's because your cousin made carbonnade for dinner. Personally, I would walk a mile barefoot in whatever snow we get tonight for Dominique's amazing beer and beef stew."

I grinned. "Then let's start the tasting early

instead of waiting until five. Dominique's coming over at four anyway. I'll text Eli and let him know."

"You'd better text Kit, as well," Frankie said. "She's still coming, and she's bringing someone. A reporter who's interested in working here on weekends to pick up some extra money. I was thinking of asking her if she's free Saturday to help out with the party."

"Kit doesn't need to come tonight," I said. "Or her friend. We can manage without them. She doesn't need to drive all the way over from Leesburg in this weather."

"She's at Foxhall Manor, visiting her mother, so she'll be passing by on her way home. She phoned earlier, while you were out, to make sure we hadn't canceled," Frankie said. "Apparently, she left you a voice mail and a couple of texts but never heard back from you. And she knows about the carbonnade. You won't be able to keep her away, either."

I pulled my phone out of my jeans pocket, pushed a button, and got nothing. "It's dead. I think I need a new phone. My battery doesn't hold a charge anymore, especially if it's outside in the cold. Can you text everyone for me? Quinn, too?"

"Quinn," she said, "barely spoke to me when he brought the tasting samples over and left them in the library a while ago. Something's bothering him. What's going on? Is it that argument you had this morning?"

I shrugged. Quinn had Gino Tomassi on his mind; that was why he was upset and moody. If he hadn't told anybody he was related to the Tomassis before today, he sure wasn't going to start admitting it now, especially after Gino's visit and his parting threat this morning.

"Lucie?" Frankie gave me a quizzical look. "You know I can keep my mouth shut if there's something you'd like to tell me."

I trusted Frankie completely, but this wasn't my secret.

"No," I said, "there isn't."

She scooped up Mick's album. "In that case, I'll put this in my office for safekeeping. Then I'll let everyone know about the change of plans."

She swept out of the room, her heels making sharp little clicks on the tile floor, her way of letting me know she knew I was lying. But there was nothing I could do about it, so I let her go.

Quinn found me eating Brie and crackers in the kitchen. "Can I talk to you for a minute? In the library, where we've got some privacy." There was an odd glint in his eye.

I followed him through the tasting room and into the library, where we held informal talks and hosted small group tastings. Quinn closed the door behind us. Eight bottles, the samples for tonight's blind tasting, were hidden in paper bags and lined up on a tray on an oak console table next to an arrangement of red and white Valentine's Day mums and carnations. An assortment of wine-related magazines also lay fanned out on the table for guests to peruse.

Quinn picked up the latest issue of *Decanter* magazine, which was on top of the pile, and thumbed through it. When he found what he wanted, he held the magazine out to me so I could see the jagged edges of a missing page. "Did you rip out the page with the news of Gino's deal with Dante Bellagio?"

"Nope."

"Someone did."

I took the magazine. "It was in the 'Heard It Through the Grapevine' column. There was also a story about celebrities who wanted to buy vineyards, especially in Virginia. Maybe someone wanted that article . . . though they shouldn't have ripped it out of our magazine." I set it back on the table. "What are you getting at?"

"I don't know. I just think it's odd, especially after today."

"Maybe Gino took it. He came here before he showed up in the barrel room. Frankie gave him directions how to find it."

'Maybe," Quinn said, but he didn't sound convinced. "There's something else. I've been making some calls to friends in California. The land Gino and Dante want for their joint venture? They've got their eye on a couple of midsize vineyards over near Angwin, on Mount Howell. The thing is, the owners don't want to sell. So guess what Gino's doing?" He took the magazine and rolled it up, smacking it against his hand as if someone was about to get a thrashing.

"Based on the look on your face, I'd say he's doing something to force them to sell."

He nodded.

Clearly we had moved on from our argument this morning. But I still didn't have a good feeling about what was coming next, especially when a muscle twitched in his jaw, a sure sign he was angry.

"The little wineries in California do most of their business from tourists who buy wine in the tasting room," he said. "But the midsize vineyards compete with the big guys like Gino because they sell their wine through distributors. What I heard is that Gino is squeezing those middlemen not to take their wine, not to sell it. And since no one wants to alienate a guy with the clout and market share Gino has, the distributors are falling in line."

"That's horrible. He'll ruin those vineyards. They won't be able to survive."

"And he'll pick them off for a fire sale price when they do start to go under. I told you what he was like." He smacked the magazine against the palm of his hand again. "So I've been thinking."

"You want to stop him?"

"I'd like to try. I'm tired of watching him bully people."

"How do you plan to do this?"

"I plan to find out if the blackmailer is right that Zara Tomassi did have a kid. Do it before Gino or his private eye does. As you so correctly pointed out this morning, they are still my family. Unfortunately. And my grandparents were not the only ones Gino's family has screwed over."

"Quinn, that could be dangerous. Someone's blackmailing him."

"The enemy of my enemy is my friend."

Oh, brother. "Blackmail," I said, "is a crime. In case you forgot."

"Gino's not going to involve the cops, so . . ." He shrugged. "It's just a little family matter, some money changing hands in return for a document Gino wants."

"I don't like this."

"Look," he said, "what do you think is going to happen if Gino does find a descendant—or descendants—of Zara's still alive and well somewhere? That he's going to be like some benevolent fairy godfather, waving a wand and all of a sudden whoever it is becomes a multimillionaire, part of the family business?" His voice rose as he spoke, and I put a finger to my lips. For all either of us knew, Frankie was outside the door, wondering what all the shouting was about.

He nodded and said more quietly, "He's going to do to that person the same thing his old man did to my grandmother. He's going to screw him royally, tie him up in so many legal knots and make him settle for whatever kind of deal it is he wants. Gino's got lawyers, armies of lawyers." He swept his hand as if encompassing the entire vineyard, all of Virginia even. "He wants to airbrush Zara's descendants out of his life and our family. But he won't be able to do that if I know about it, too."

"So what's your plan?" I fiddled with the wine bags, straightening them like a row of tan soldiers, even though they didn't need straightening. I still didn't like his idea.

"It wouldn't surprise me if whoever is behind this is in the wine business and it's a personal vendetta. A lot of Napa and Sonoma wine families go back generations. I'm going to make some more calls. And Lucie?"

I stopped fiddling with the bags. "What?"

"I thought you might want to help."

"What did you have in mind?"

"Zara grew up in Washington and she still has relatives in D.C.," he said. "If she had the baby, where would the logical place be for the kid to end up?"

"Washington."

"Exactly."

"You want me to try to find out what happened to Zara's child? If he or she is still alive?"

"Her father was a big-shot congressman—Ingrasso, remember? There had to have been stories written about him and his family in the paper—you know, society stuff like weddings or fancy parties. I thought you could talk Kit into getting access to the *Trib*'s database of old stories." He gave me a sideways look. "Without telling her why."

"Lie to my best friend. You don't ask much, do you?" I said. "Don't you think Gino's private eye is beating a path to the same doors?"

"Maybe," he said. "Maybe not. And who's to say we won't get there before he does?"

"All right," I said. "I'll talk to her. She'll be here tonight."

Frankly, I was curious, too. If we were nimble enough to stay under the radar, maybe we could find out what had happened to Zara's child and who was behind the blackmail. But what worried me more than Gino, his investigator, or even the blackmailer was Quinn. He nursed a grievance that had festered for three generations and I feared it could bring us to grief. Because revenge, as they say, is a dish best served cold.

And Quinn's anger was still white-hot.

NINE

My cousin Dominique was the first to arrive for the wine tasting shortly after four o'clock. She walked through the front door of the villa holding a large flame-colored Dutch oven with a pair of yellow oven mitts, as if she were carrying the Holy Grail.

"Can I help with that?" I asked. "Or get something from your car?"

She expertly elbowed the door shut and stomped the snow from her feet on a braided oval rug in the entryway. "I met Eli in the parking lot, so he's bringing in everything else," she said. "You can get the kitchen door for me, though."

After setting down the last two wineglasses at the long oak table we used for tastings when the bar was too crowded, I opened the door.

"It smells terrific," I said.

"Thanks." She placed the pot on the stove and turned the burner on low. "I brought potatoes, salad, a *quatre-quarts* for dessert, and those extra baguettes you asked me to bring to cut up for the tasting."

Quatre-quarts was a French pound cake that our mothers and our grandmother had made. It required only four ingredients, which had to be weighed and used in exactly equal amounts:

butter, flour, eggs, and sugar. Hence the name: four-fourths.

My cousin unwound a red-and-white pashmina shawl from around her neck and unbuttoned her coat. There were dark circles under her eyes.

"Thanks for the baguettes," I said. "The real reason everyone's coming for the tasting is your carbonnade, not my wine, you know."

She smiled, but it was a tired one, and her mind was clearly somewhere else.

"Are you okay?" I asked. "You look exhausted."

Her smile morphed into a grimace. "I quit smoking." She dropped the coat and shawl on a chair. "Or at least I'm trying to quit."

Dominique had smoked since she was twelve, filching cigarettes from her parents when she was growing up in France. This winter, a debilitating case of bronchitis and a hacking cough that lingered for weeks had taken a toll on her. I wondered if being so sick was what had finally motivated her to stop.

"I'm glad," I said. "If I can do anything to keep you on the straight and narrow, let me know. It's about time you quit."

She pushed a spiky fringe of auburn bangs off her forehead with the back of her hand and reached into the pocket of her jeans.

"You sound like my doctor. *Mon Dieu*, it's making me so stressed and irritable, I think half the staff at the Inn is ready to put tar on my

115

feathers." She pulled out a package of nicotine gum and shoved a piece in her mouth, chewing furiously.

When Dominique got excited or upset, her English generally went out the window. Idioms, especially, still seemed to baffle her.

"They love you," I said. "I'm sure everyone understands. You're like a family over there, all of you."

She gave me an anguished look and took a wooden spoon from a stone jar filled with kitchen utensils that was sitting on the counter. "I know that." She stirred the carbonnade with intense concentration.

"What is it?" I said. "There's something else besides the smoking."

She set the spoon down and turned to me. "I've been offered a job."

I started to laugh, but her expression stopped me. "You already have a job. You own the Goose Creek Inn, one of the top restaurants in the Washington, D.C., area. You win heaps of awards every year. Your heart, your soul, your blood, sweat, and tears, your life, and your fortune are poured into that place. What other job in the world could—"

She was still watching me with that same fierce intensity, and all of a sudden the air seemed to go out of the room.

"It must be pretty spectacular," I said in a calm

voice, though my mind was leaping ahead to what could tempt her to leave, what it would mean to our family, the vineyard, the town. "Because I have a feeling you're actually thinking about taking it."

She nodded. "Executive chef," she said. "At the White House."

A moment ago, the idea of her giving up the Goose Creek Inn to take a position anywhere else seemed as unlikely as the moon spinning away from Earth to revolve around a different planet. Now it seemed not only likely but perhaps a fait accompli. I wondered whether she'd already accepted it and hadn't wanted to break the news to me yet.

"Are you serious? When? How?"

From the other room, we could hear Eli singing "In the Bleak Midwinter" in a loud, hammy voice as the front door slammed shut.

"Don't tell anyone." She put a finger to her lips and said in a conspiratorial whisper, "I haven't met the First Lady yet, and that's the last interview. I shouldn't have told you. I was asked not to say anything, because they don't want any press leaks."

"Don't worry, I won't say a word," I whispered back, crossing my heart with a finger, though it felt as if I were slicing it open with a knife. "Are you going to accept?"

"It would be such a feather in my nest."

"Avoiding the question, Your Honor."

Her cheeks turned pink. "There's a state dinner for the Italian prime minister tomorrow night. Everything's on hold until after that."

I already knew about the state dinner. The kitchen door swung open and Eli came in carrying a cooler and a large plastic shopping bag.

"Snow on snoooow on snooooow . . . in the bleeeeak . . ." He quit singing abruptly. "You two look guilty as hell. What's going on? Everything's on hold until after what?"

I glanced at my cousin. "Until—"

"After Valentine's Day." Dominique gave him a bright smile. "At the Inn, we have more reservations than you can shake a leg at, and there's your party on Saturday, as well. Eli, *mon ange*, set the cooler and that bag on the counter. Lucie, the baguettes are in the carrier bag. You probably want to cut them up before everyone gets here."

"Sure," I said. "Eli, help me with that, will you?"

Later, when almost everyone had arrived, he walked by me on his way to add another log to the fire.

"Are you going to tell me what was really going on when I showed up in the kitchen?" he asked.

"She quit smoking." I straightened a pencil next to one of the pads of paper Frankie had set out so people could make notes during the tasting. "She doesn't want to make a big deal over it. Don't say anything, okay?"

"Sure," he said, looking doubtful. "Mum's the word."

From the other side of the room, Quinn said, "I'd like to get started, but we're still waiting for Kit, right, Lucie?"

He gave me a meaningful look.

"She's on her way and she's bringing a reporter from the *Trib* who's interested in helping us out on weekends," I said.

The log Eli had just put on the fire hissed and popped, sending a shower of sparks up the chimney. My brother leaned in so only I could hear what he said.

"You didn't tell me Kit was coming. That woman will be late to her own funeral. Why should she keep everyone else waiting?"

Years ago, Kit and Eli had dated, and it had been serious. Then Eli met Brandi, now his ex-wife, and the breakup with Kit had been acrimonious and painful to watch. After that, Kit and Eli had never really gotten along, and it seemed that her recent marriage and his bruising divorce had only stirred up some of the old hostility.

I usually tried to ignore it. "She'll be here any minute," I said. "Cut her some slack, Eli. She's visiting Faith, for Pete's sake. You can't avoid her forever, you know. Especially now that she married one of your old friends."

The front door opened and Kit burst in with a plain-looking dark-haired girl who looked like she was about sixteen. They were laughing and breathless, as though they'd been running. A spotlight above the front door caught the two of them in a pool of light, so the snowflakes that clung to their coats and hair made them look like a pair of snow angels.

"Hey, everybody, sorry we're late." Kit shrugged out of her coat and dumped it on one of the sofas, gesturing for her friend to do the same. She riffled a hand through her short hair, bleached Marilyn Monroe blond, so it looked like a cloud of yellow frizz.

Kit and I had been on the cross-country team in high school, but she had given up running in college, and over the years the pounds had started to pile on. Now she was always on some crazy yo-yo diet that never worked. She'd also begun dressing with edgy flair, choosing clothes better suited to an overly thin runway model, like now. She had on clinging black leggings, a red-and-black-striped tunic, and stiletto ankle boots.

"No one," she told me once, "misses me at a press conference when I raise my hand to ask a question."

She sailed over to the table and indicated her companion. "This is Vivienne Baron, gang. She's been working in the Loudoun bureau of the *Trib* since the beginning of the year, one of my rising stars."

Vivienne Baron flushed pink, looking pleased and embarrassed as she fiddled with a long straight braid that fell over her shoulder. Kit swept her hand in a broad gesture that included all of us and added, "Viv, meet everybody. Everybody, Viv."

She gave me an air kiss and Dominique and Frankie a quick hug while the introductions went on around the table. Then she looked over my brother like merchandise you wouldn't buy even at a deep discount and said, "Hello, Eli. I didn't know you were going to be here. Always such a pleasure."

He gave her a tight-lipped smile. "Only for you, Katherine, darling."

"All right, you two," I said. "Play nice. Kit and Vivienne, why don't you sit down here by me? Eli, I'm sure Quinn could use some help pouring, so maybe you could take the empty seat next to him."

I got the we'll-talk-about-this-later look from my brother, but he walked to the other end of the table and sat down beside Quinn.

"For the benefit of our newcomers, let me explain what we want you to do," Quinn said. "We have eight wine samples—a combination of Chardonnay and Pinot Noir in different proportions, from different parts of the vineyard, picked at different times—one of which we want to use to make sparkling wine. We won't be calling it champagne, of course, because the only place in the world that can do that is the Champagne region of France."

He was talking to Vivienne and Kit, who were nodding, since the rest of us worked here. Journalists that they were, both were taking notes.

"What we're doing tonight is figuring out which sample you all like best," he said. "After that's sorted out, we'll make that blend in larger quantities and put it in one of the tanks downstairs, where it will chill for a couple of weeks before we filter it and then bottle it. Once the wine is in the bottles, we begin the process of turning it into sparkling. Essentially, we're making the wine twice—first the blend, then the fizz and bubbles. What we want to know from you tonight is which one is your favorite."

He looked directly at Vivienne. "Whatever you do, spit, don't swallow, or you'll be drunk before we're done. Drink water between each sample and eat a piece of bread. After the work is finished, you can drink when we have dinner."

Vivienne blushed again and said in her quiet voice, "I understand."

"Go with your instincts and don't overthink it," I said to her under my breath. "All we want to know is which one you like best. Unlike other wines, champagne—or sparkling, as we call it—is all about the blend, what combination of wines you put together to create it. It's an art, not a science."

She nodded as Eli and Quinn began moving along the table, pouring wine into our glasses.

Whether it was the steadily falling snow, which everyone could see through the French patio doors as it swirled like a kid's snow globe in the wash of the outside lights, or just that it was the end of the day, so we were quiet and focused, the tasting took less than half an hour. There was an almost unanimous vote for the blend that had been our private favorite.

Quinn's eyes met mine across the table. "I guess it's settled. Thank you all," he said. "Time to eat."

Dominique and Frankie brought the food from the kitchen while the rest of us cleared the table of glasses, bread baskets, and everyone's notes. Vivienne took her dinner plate and sat by herself on one of the sofas next to the fire.

I caught Kit's eye. "I need to talk to you privately for a few minutes before you go, but we should probably join Vivienne so that she won't feel left out."

"Sure." Kit bit into a piece of baguette. "Mom said you stopped by today. I have a feeling I know what you want to talk about."

We exchanged looks. "That and something else."

We sat down on either side of Vivienne and I asked if she'd enjoyed the tasting.

"I think what you do is fascinating," she said. "Frankie asked if I was available on Saturday night to help with your party, which sounds like a lot of fun. She said if I drop by after work during the week, she'll go over everything with me."

I wondered how this quiet, sweet girl was going to manage a job that was all about being gregarious and social and interacting with people.

"That's great," I said. "We could really use the help."

"I'll ask my husband if he's interested, as well. He's coming to pick me up when we're done here."

"Vivienne doesn't drive," Kit said. "At least not in snow."

Vivienne smiled. "I drive. But we never got snow in San Diego. Or ice."

"It won't be winter forever," I said. "At least that's what we're hoping."

"It's hard on the folks at the Manor," Kit said. "A lot of them like to go for walks, and it's just too dangerous with the snow and ice."

"Especially people like your mom who have to use walkers or canes," Vivienne said to Kit.

"You know Faith?" I asked her.

"I met her when I interviewed Roxy Willoughby for a story on the first female pilots to fly during World War Two," she said.

"You're writing a story about Roxy?"

She nodded. "I'm trying to find as many local

women from her squadron as I can before there's no one left to tell their story. Fortunately, I finished interviewing her before she passed away."

"We're running the piece in the weekend magazine," Kit said. "I'll need your corrected version first thing in the morning, Viv."

"You'll have it. I just needed to check a few facts with Olivia Cohen."

"Olivia Cohen?" I said. "Any relation to Skye Cohen?"

"Olivia is Skye's grandmother," Kit said.

"Skye was just in here this morning," I said. "Picking up winter coats for Veronica House. I didn't know her grandmother had been a pilot. She and Roxy must have been friends."

Vivienne shook her head. "Apparently the friendship broke up years ago."

"What happened?"

"I think it had something to do with Roxy's getting pregnant when they were in England together," she said. "Olivia mentioned it during the interview and then she looked like she wanted to bite her tongue out. She asked me to forget she'd brought it up. I didn't exactly promise, but I did say I would be discreet."

"I didn't know Olivia told you about that," Kit said. "Go on. You know we're dying of curiosity."

"Well, I asked Roxy about the baby. At first she was upset—actually, she was angry—but then it seemed as if she felt better telling someone after keeping it a secret for so long. And I did say I wouldn't use any of it in the story, since it's not really relevant."

"You must be the only person besides Sam Constantine, Roxy's lawyer, and maybe Father Niall O'Malley, if she confided in him, who knew before Roxy passed away that she'd had a daughter," I told her. "No one else had a clue she had a family in England, not even Mac MacDonald, and he's her nephew."

"Roxy told me she'd never spoken about it to anyone," Vivienne said. "And since the golden rule of journalism is 'Never burn a source,' I think she knew I would keep her secret, as well. It probably helped that I was a total stranger; plus, she said I was the same age as her grand-daughter. She talked about her, too, how she wished she'd known her."

"Uma Lawrence," Kit said. "I saw her today as I was leaving Mom's apartment."

"Thelma said she was in town. What was she doing at the Manor?" I asked.

"Probably checking out her inheritance." Kit made a face like she'd eaten something she wanted to spit out. "Roxy's apartment is nearly cleaned out of all the furniture and it's going to be up for rent soon. It won't take more than a couple of days, you wait and see. There's a huge demand for those places. I hope Mom gets another nice neighbor."

"Did you talk to her?" I asked. "Uma, I mean."

"Just condolences. She was a bit standoffish, I thought. Maybe it's that English reserve."

"What are you three talking about that's so engrossing?" Frankie came over to us, holding a plate with a slice of *quatre-quarts* on it. "We're serving dessert, which you seem to have missed. If you don't hurry, the rest of the vultures will devour what's left before you get a piece."

Kit stood up. "Over my dead body. And we were just talking about Roxy Willoughby."

"Her granddaughter's in town," Frankie said, passing the plate to Vivienne and sitting down with her. "She arrived today from England. I guess she's here because of the will. The mailman told me when he brought the mail. He'd just come from the General Store."

"Why do we even bother putting out a newspaper?" Kit said as I gave her a plate with an extra-generous slice of cake. "I swear, Thelma knows things even before they happen. Her 'extrasensory psychotic perception,' as she calls it."

I laughed, and she said, "So, let me guess what you wanted to talk to me about. Mom's been after you to find out who poisoned Roxy, hasn't she?"

I nodded. "Is she all right? Did her doctor switch her meds or something?"

"No, it's nothing like that. But she's got this obsession that Roxy had an argument with someone right before she died and that person killed her. It's crazy."

"What does Bobby say?"

"He adores Mom—you know that—but he says there's nothing to investigate. The medical examiner said Roxy died of natural causes. End of story. And there's no one with a so-called motive, unless you count Mac. He's the one who lost out when Roxy changed her will," she said. "Do you really think Mac MacDonald murdered his beloved aunt?"

"God no," I said. "And neither does your mom. I asked her the same thing."

Kit shrugged and said through a mouthful of *quatre-quarts*, "Well, then. There's your answer."

"Maybe I'll talk to Mac," I said.

"And ask him if he's a murderer?" Kit gave me an incredulous look. "Good luck with that."

"Don't be silly. I'm not going to ask if he poisoned Roxy. But if I could find out who Faith overheard arguing with Roxy and what it was about, that might calm your mom down."

"Better you than me. You're the one who called him 'Uncle Mac' growing up. He might tell you something." She scraped her plate with her fork and ate the few last crumbs. "What was the other thing you wanted to ask me about?"

"A favor," I said. "Something from the *Trib*'s archives."

Before dinner, I'd done an Internet search on

Congressman Victor Ingrasso. He'd served for nineteen terms—from 1890 to 1928—retiring just before the stock market crashed. Quinn had been vague about when Angelica and Johnny had gotten married, but he thought it was in the mid-1920s. So if the Ingrasso family had taken Zara's child, it would have happened in that same rough time frame. It seemed like a long shot to find some mention of the baby in the press, but it was a place to start, and we didn't have much time. Gino had to deliver the money by Friday, and this was Monday night.

Kit set her plate on the table. "What is it?"

I told her, and, predictably, she said, "May I ask why?"

I'd thought this through. "His name came up while I was doing some research on Prohibition for the party on Friday. I've got a relative—named Lucy Montgomery—who lived around the same time. Just trying to figure out if there was a connection between the two of them."

It was a bald-faced lie. Kit frowned. "Someone named Lucy Montgomery, the same as you? Are you talking about an affair?"

"Spelled with a *y,* not an *ie,* but yes, the same name. As for the affair, I'm not sure. What I'm looking for would be in the society pages, nothing to do with legislation he was involved with or anything like that," I said. "Hopefully, that will narrow down the search."

She was still giving me a suspicious look. "I've got a lot going on at work at the moment, but I could try to get to it next week."

"I need it sooner than that."

"How much sooner?"

"Tomorrow would be good."

" 'Tomorrow would be good.' " She folded her arms across her chest. "You want to tell me what's really going on?"

"I can't."

"Oh, brother," she said. "I should have figured."

"I'm sorry. Can't you just trust me?"

She looked exasperated. "Don't I always?"

"You're an angel."

"Yeah, right," she said. "What I am is a pushover. Though if you can calm Mom down after you talk to Mac, I suppose it will be an even exchange."

"I'll go see Mac tomorrow," I said. "If we don't get snowed in tonight."

"And I'll see what I can dig up about your Congressman Ingrasso," she said, giving me a dark look. "Too bad I don't know what I'm looking for. Because I have a feeling you do."

TEN

We had finished clearing the dishes and the party was starting to break up when the front door opened. Later I would remember that it seemed as though everyone stopped mid-motion, frozen, like in a kid's game of statue, to stare at the tall, handsome man who walked in. He took off a brightly colored cap with earflaps and two long strings and shook the hat and himself, shedding the snow that had settled on his clothing, seemingly oblivious that a dozen people were watching him. When he finally looked up from under a mop of dark brown hair, his eyes locked on mine and his smile was dazzling.

"Will, you're here." Vivienne's face lit up with such joy and love that I felt a tiny tug of envy. "Come, darling, I want you to meet everyone."

She ran across the room and grabbed her husband's hand. He smiled and let her lead him over to our group, looking like an indulgent parent who has come to fetch a child at school.

"This is my husband, Will Baron," she said with shy pride as she quickly rattled off everyone's names to him.

Quinn shook Will's hand and said, "I think I've seen you in Middleburg once or twice. Do you work around here?"

"Will's studying for the bar exam," Vivienne said before he could answer. "He graduated from UVA law school in December. He's going to be a brilliant lawyer with heaps of offers once he passes. We moved to Leesburg because of my job at the *Tribune*."

Will Baron flashed that heart-stopping smile at us again and said, "My one-woman cheering squad. Vivienne gets a bit carried away sometimes."

"I do not. Someday you'll be arguing cases before the Supreme Court. Wait and see."

He tugged her braid, and Vivienne grinned. "In the meantime," he said to Quinn, "I'm a lowly delivery guy when I'm not hitting the books. A long way from the Supreme Court. We still have to pay bills."

"He just got hired at the Goose Creek Inn," Vivienne said. "He's not just a lowly delivery guy."

"Right, I'm a lowly part-time bartender, too." He smiled at me. "I understand your cousin owns that place?"

"Dominique," I said. "That's right."

"We could always use help around here if you're interested," Quinn said. "We're bottling wine on Thursday. You'd be quite an asset, since there's heavy lifting involved. We'd feed you and give you a few bottles to take home."

"I'd like to help with that," Vivienne said. "What do you think, Will?"

"Unfortunately, I'm not free Thursday, but I'll send my second," he said to Quinn, putting an arm around his wife and pulling her close. "If that's okay."

Quinn nodded. "Sure, we can use Vivienne, too. She can check labels, make sure the bottles are filled properly, that sort of thing. We start at nine."

"Can you drive me?" Vivienne asked, looking up at Will. "Thursday's one of my days off this week. And I almost forgot. Saturday night they're having a charity fund-raiser here, a dinner dance. I said I'd work then, too. I know it's Valentine's Day, but I thought we could do it together. It's for a good cause, for Veronica House, the homeless shelter in Leesburg."

Will gave her a look, as though she had broken some private marital rule, and her cheeks turned pink.

"I'll drop you here Thursday morning," he said in an even voice. "And maybe we can talk about Saturday night another time, okay, sweetie?" He paused. "It is Valentine's Day, after all."

"Sorry. I should have talked to you first," she said, her face now scarlet with embarrassment. To Frankie and me, she said, "Can I let you know about the party when I see you on Thursday?"

"Of course you can," I said, and Frankie nodded.

After they were gone, I walked Kit to the front

door. "What do you make of Vivienne and Will?" I asked.

"She's gaga over him, that's for sure. Who wouldn't be, a hunk like that?" She shrugged. "He may be gorgeous, but she's the brainy one. I think it took him an extra semester to finish law school, because he flunked two courses; plus, he's at least ten years older than she is, probably around our age. I hope, for her sake, he passes the bar." She gave me a hug. "I'd better get going, or my hunk of a husband will send a patrol car looking for me. I guess we'll be talking tomorrow."

I nodded. "Thanks," I said. "I owe you."

"Don't you worry," she said. "I plan to collect. In full."

I woke up, as I always did, a minute before my alarm went off, shut it off, and lay in bed until the quiet explosion of the heating system kicking on at 6:00 A.M. sounded reassuringly from the basement. My feet touched the icy floor before I found my slippers and pulled on my bathrobe. The weather forecast had called for snow all night. I walked over and pushed open the curtains. Fluffy flour-sifter flakes still fell fast and thick on an already-deep carpet of snow. In the fading starlight, the blue-tinged backyard looked like a lunar landscape, amorphous lumps and shapes that were bushes and flower beds buried in snow, their soft contours silver-edged against the cobalt sky.

I dressed in a sweatshirt and jeans and took the back staircase down to the kitchen, avoiding the creaky treads so I wouldn't wake Hope or Eli. When I opened the door, the kitchen, which always stayed warmer than the rest of the house, still smelled of Persia's baking—homemade applesauce bread made with apples we had canned last fall from our orchard. I switched on the radio to the all-news station and made a pot of coffee while a male announcer struggled to keep up with the growing list of schools, businesses, and other places that were announcing cancellations or closures.

"If you can hear my voice," he finally said, sounding weary, "wherever you were planning to go today, you can take my word for it that it's closed. Everything's closed."

Eli showed up just after seven, his hair caveman wild from sleeping on it, and poured himself a cup of coffee. "I guess I won't be meeting my client at our job site in an hour." He cut a hefty slab of applesauce bread. "What time is it supposed to stop snowing?"

"Ten or ten-thirty. Which piece are you eating? The big one or the less big one? You might leave something for your daughter and me, you know?"

"There's plenty left. You two eat like birds." He went over to the refrigerator and took out the butter. "Persia is one amazing cook."

I swiped the plate with the larger piece and

poked him in the stomach. "You do appear to be enjoying her cooking."

He quit spreading butter on his bread and gave me a suspicious look. "Hey, is that a dig?"

He sounded aggrieved, but I noticed one hand moved surreptitiously to shield his protruding belly.

I tugged his belt. "I hear you downstairs at night raiding the refrigerator, even if you think you're being sneaky."

"Look, just because you can eat your entire body weight every day and not gain an ounce thanks to your hummingbird metabolism or whatever it is, you don't need to be snarky," he said. "This is my winter coat, that's all. I'll get rid of it in spring. Plus, work is keeping me so busy, I don't have time to exercise anymore. I would if I could, you know."

"Then once it stops snowing, we can shovel out together," I said, "since you're not meeting your client."

He gave me a martyred look. "I thought Quinn and Antonio were coming through with the plows."

"Eventually. They've got all of Sycamore Lane and the villa parking lot to do first. We'll get out faster if we start shoveling ourselves." I paused. "If I can shovel, you can shovel."

Even an oblique reference to my disability makes Eli squirm, since it means we are venturing into land mine territory. To this day, neither of us alludes to the rain-wrecked night a car driven by an ex-boyfriend, who was also Eli's good friend, plowed into the stone wall at the vineyard entrance because we were arguing over whether the rumors he'd slept with Eli's ex-wife were true.

My brother's eyes slid away from mine. "Oh, all right. I'll call Persia and ask if I can take Hope over to her place until we get a path cleared to the house."

"Thank you." I walked over to the pantry and opened the door. "Have you seen the flashlight? The one that's supposed to be here for when we lose power?"

"It's in my office," he said. "I took it when I needed it one night. Sorry. I'll bring it back. Why do you need a flashlight?"

"I want to get something in the basement for Quinn from his mother's trunk."

Eli cut another slice of bread, and I glared at him. "It's just a little piece. There's plenty left. What's in Quinn's mother's trunk?"

"An old photo album."

Quinn had asked me to find out if there was anything in the *Trib* archives about the Ingrasso family's having adopted a child at approximately the same time Zara had died, and Gino seemed to think Angelica could have left something having to do either with Zara or her baby in the old trunk. Though Quinn was certain all it contained now were keepsakes belonging to him and his mother—except for Angelica's photo album, which Gino wanted—I still thought I'd check it out.

Besides, ever since I'd seen that photo of Lucky at Mick's place yesterday, I'd been thinking about Angelica Tomassi. What kind of woman would burn her husband's late wife's possessions and forbid any mention of Zara ever again? She must have been jealous as hell. By my calculations, Angelica's album, which chronicled the early years of the Tomassi Family Vineyard, dated from the same years as the Studebaker album.

"Before the wine-tasting session last night, Frankie showed me a photo album that Mick Dunne loaned you from Prohibition days, when the Studebakers held some bacchanalian orgies," Eli said.

A sharp little zing went down my spine, as I thought of Lucky at one of those parties. *Orgy* conjured up images of debauched revelry and raunchy, voyeuristic drunken acts that no one admitted to later—if they remembered them at all.

"They weren't orgies," I said with some heat. "What makes you say that?"

"What makes you say they weren't?" he said, giving me a surprised look. "I remember Granny Montgomery talking about parties that went on for days, where all the guests got drunk as skunks and had sex in the upstairs bedrooms with everyone except the person they came with. She used to say that Satan himself partied there."

"Granny Montgomery was a teetotaler," I said. "She used to go to the picnics on the old temperance grounds with her mother, so she grew up believing that demon alcohol sent you straight down the road to hell."

"And now her relatives own a vineyard. Go figure." He licked butter off his thumb. "So what's in Quinn's photo album?"

"I have no idea. I just thought I'd get it for him."

Eli gave me the look. "Man, you never could lie, Luce. You've got something up your sleeve."

When Hamish Montgomery built Highland House in 1787, the kitchen had occupied the entire stone- and earth-walled basement, as was the custom in those days. Later, in the mid-1800s, another Montgomery added two symmetrical wings to the boxy Federal-style house: a first-floor kitchen on one end and a light-filled conservatory on the other. We called the conservatory "the sunroom," and it was where the grand piano now sat.

The original basement kitchen had been left intact except for shoring up the earthen walls with more fieldstone quarried from our land. No twentieth-century conversions to a subterranean kids' playroom with cast-off furniture, beanbag chairs, and a Ping-Pong table for us. The blackened stone hearth, which still smelled faintly of the greasy smoke of long-ago cooking, took up an entire wall, and the whole place was dark, cob-webby, and as wildly atmospheric as a dungeon. The biggest change had been the addition of built-in shelving and storage for Leland's now much-depleted wine cellar.

Quinn's mother's trunk sat near the bottom of the old wooden staircase, in the spot where the deliverymen had deposited it after I bribed them with an exorbitant tip. Like the attic, the basement was lit by bare bulbs that gave off a watery light, but I had left the door open at the top of the stairs so that a wedge of brighter light illuminated the trunk. Unfortunately, when I knelt in front of it to unlock the padlock, I blocked most of the shaft of light and everything was in shadow again.

It was a grand old steamer trunk, dull black metal with a high dome top and scuffed wooden slats joined together by tarnished brass clasps. All in all, it was in surprisingly good condition except for the leather handles, which had long since become so stiff and brittle, I was afraid they'd break if I tugged on them. I laid my hands on the lid, as though the dust and sunlight and sounds of long-ago rail stations and harbors and grand hotels would seep through my fingers and transport me to a time when the voyage itself had been a sublime luxury and passage on the *Queen Mary* or the Orient Express had been the dream trip of a lifetime.

The brass key stuck, so I had to fiddle before it would turn in the lock. I lifted the lid and sneezed as dust motes floated in the air. Pasted to the domed lid was a hand-colored lithograph of a ravishing long-necked Gibson girl, her luxurious dark hair piled on her head, her gaze serene and confident as she looked over her shoulder with a teasing air of mystery. The rest of the trunk's contents were deeply in shadow. If I wanted to see what was inside, I needed either to get the flashlight Eli had pinched or to move the trunk so it would be better situated in light from upstairs. I knelt and gave it a good shove, since I didn't want to use the fragile handles, and heard a scraping sound, probably one of the brass clasps catching on the uneven floor. Too late I also heard the dry crack of wood snapping. I closed my eyes and heard myself telling Quinn, "I'm so sorry, but honestly, it was an accident," and imagining the look on his face.

The sound had come from underneath the trunk. I checked the wooden slats for cracks and tipped the trunk on its edge, running my fingers along the bottom, but nothing felt damaged. The noise must have come from inside, though I couldn't figure out how or what.

Inside the trunk, a shallow tray covered in faded pink-and-white floral paper held a yellowed christening gown and a delicate crocheted baby's blanket. I lifted out the tray and set it on the floor next to me. What lay underneath had clearly been tossed around during the move from California to Virginia, the jumbled-up memorabilia of Quinn's life and his mother's—report cards tied together with twine; Quinn's high school diploma in a severe black frame; an elaborate hand-embroidered linen tablecloth with matching napkins; a silver-framed photo of Quinn when he graduated from high school, mortarboard askew and looking as uncomfortable as hell; and another photo of a beautiful raven-haired girl holding a chubby-cheeked baby—obviously Quinn and his mother. It was the first time I'd seen a picture of her, and I felt a quick pang of guilt to have stumbled on it this way, rather than having him choose to show it to me.

Angelica's photo album lay at the bottom. It looked almost exactly like the tooled leather album Mick Dunne had loaned me, except this one was blood-colored, the deep red of a good Chianti, with the gilt initials *A* and *G*—the latter for Gianluca, not *J* for Johnny—intertwined around a regal-looking *T.*

I put the album with the other items and sat back on my haunches, staring at the bottom of the empty trunk. Nothing appeared damaged there, either. I reached inside and began feeling along the seam between the sides and the bottom. At one of the corners, something gave way under my fingers, as though it were spring-loaded.

Now that I looked closer, the bottom of the trunk—also covered in that busy floral-print paper—was not a seamless piece as I had thought. The section I'd pushed on, roughly nine by nine, had popped up and I could easily slide it to one side. What it revealed was a long, narrow compartment in the false bottom.

I reached in and touched something dry and dusty that felt like a packet of letters that had been tied together. They snagged on something as I started to pull them out at the same moment Hope's sweet chirpy voice came from upstairs, calling Eli and me.

If I had known the child was awake and had come downstairs from her bedroom, I would never have left the basement door open. Eli and I had put reinforcing the steep, rickety stairs— old wooden boards and a flimsy railing with no balusters, a sheer drop to the floor if you lost your footing—on the list of things around the house that needed fixing, but it hadn't been an urgent project.

"Hope?" I tried to keep the anxiety from creeping into my voice so I wouldn't scare her. "Where's Daddy?"

"Aunt Wucie? Where are you?"

"Hopie, don't come near the basement door, okay, sweetie? Stay right where you are. I'm coming upstairs, so wait there for me. Promise?"

She appeared in the doorway, backlit by the

hall light, sweet as a sugarplum in a fuzzy pink bathrobe, Sleeping Beauty pajamas, and bunny rabbit slippers.

I pushed the letters back into the compartment and slid the lid back into place. It clicked shut as smoothly and seamlessly as a Chinese puzzle box. If you didn't know it was there, you'd think it was merely a seam in the floral paper.

"Aunt Wuuucie, where are you?" Hope's high-pitched voice was now a plaintive wail.

I looked upstairs at my niece, who had started to reach for the railing and was swaying slightly. My heart caught in my throat.

"I'm right here, angel. I'm coming. You just stay put, okay? Don't touch the railing. Do you hear me?" My voice was sharp with fear, and she dropped her hand, stepping back from the edge of the stairs. "That's better. Stay right there, okay? Did you have breakfast yet?"

"Daddy gave me Pop-Tarts," she said in a sing-song voice.

"Did he really?" Probably because he'd polished off the applesauce bread.

I picked up the photo album and got up. As soon as I took care of Hope, I'd come back and retrieve those letters and anything else that was in that compartment.

"Yup." Hope nodded her head so hard that her dark curls shook. "Strawberry. With frosting."

I reached the top of the stairs and knelt down,

pulling her close and kissing the top of her head. "Let's get you dressed, pumpkin."

She touched the photo album with a plump finger. "What's that?"

"A picture book," I said. "I got it for Quinn. We'll look at it later, okay?"

I set it on the demilune table in the foyer and climbed the sweeping spiral staircase with her to the second floor.

The photo album was Angelica's. That I knew from Quinn.

And so were the buried secrets in the hidden compartment of her trunk.

ELEVEN

I called Quinn after I finished getting Hope dressed and brought her Barbie dollhouse downstairs to the parlor so she could play in front of the fire Eli had made in the fireplace. He'd gone off to the kitchen to get another cup of coffee and reconnoiter with his client, so it was just the two of us in the room. Hope lay on the Oriental rug and crooned happily to her doll, lost in the innocent imaginary world of a little girl.

I reached Quinn on his way outside with Antonio to start plowing. "What's wrong?" he asked. "Did something happen?"

"I decided to get your family's photo album

from Angelica's trunk after breakfast this morning on the off chance Gino was right that she'd left some clue behind about Zara's child."

There was a moment of silence while he digested that, and then he said, "Don't tell me you found something?"

"Not in the album. I haven't looked at it yet." I told him about the secret compartment and the letters. "Did you know about the hiding place?"

"Nope."

"Do you think your mother knew about it?"

He sucked in his breath. "No idea. If she did, maybe the letters belonged to her. Did you see who they were addressed to?"

"I couldn't get them out without tearing what was underneath. So, no, I didn't. Not yet."

"My old man wrote letters to my mom and me after he left us. I wouldn't read them. If that's what's there, I want you to take them out and burn them."

"Quinn—"

"I mean it."

The tension hung in the air between us, as thick as smoke.

"Okay," I said. "I'll do it."

"And don't read them, either."

"I'm not even going to dignify that with an answer."

"Yeah, well, if it's something else, call me, okay? Otherwise, I don't want to know."

"I'll do that," I said, "if it's something else."

He disconnected and I sat there staring at the phone. Eli hollered down from the second floor. "Hey, I just talked to Persia. She said to bring Hope over and she'll give her lunch at her place and we can get a start on shoveling. Can you put her snowsuit on her? It's on a hook in the mudroom."

"Sure, no problem," I hollered back. I went over and scooped up my niece. "Let's go visit Persia, sweet pea."

The letters in that compartment had been there for decades, maybe even a century if they had belonged to Angelica. A few more hours wouldn't matter. But the moment we were shoveled out, I was heading straight back to the basement to retrieve them and whatever else was hidden there.

Eli and I spent the next two hours clearing the driveway and called it quits around twelve-thirty, when most of the shoveling was done and my brother announced that if he didn't eat, he would keel over from hunger.

"You want lunch, too, don't you? Aren't you starved?" he asked as we hung our wet jackets, hats, and gloves in the mudroom outside the kitchen.

"I'm okay for now. You go ahead." I sat down on a ladder-back chair and pulled off my boots. "I need to get something in the basement."

"Again?"

"I forgot it this morning."

He shrugged. "Want me to wait for you to eat?"

"That's okay, I know you're hungry. This might take a while."

He gave me a curious look. "Are you all right? You seem kind of preoccupied."

"I'm fine."

"I'll make you a sandwich and leave it on the counter, then head over to the studio." He pinched my arm. "You're wasting away, you know that? No flesh on those bones."

I waited until he was in the kitchen and I heard the clatter of dishes and drawers being opened and shut before I went back downstairs. This time, the spring wouldn't give when I pressed the panel. I kept on pushing, trying to duplicate what I had done before, until finally it groaned and the panel popped up. I retrieved the packet of letters, but whatever was stuck underneath them was jammed at the back of the compartment. My index finger caught on something sharp and I yanked my hand out. A wood splinter had torn the top layer of skin off like a peeled piece of fruit. I sucked on my finger to stop the bleeding and reached in with my other hand, taking care to avoid that lethal shard of wood.

After a few minutes of wiggling it like a loose tooth that needed to come out, I pulled out a cardboard envelope. Nothing was written on it and the flap was secured by a string wound around two cardboard disks.

"Hey!" Eli's voice startled me from the top of the stairs. "Luce, are you all right? You've been down there so long, I was getting worried you had fallen or passed out."

"I'm fine. Just finishing up."

"What are you doing?" He shielded his eyes with a hand and stared down the staircase. "How can you see anything in that dim light? Want some help?"

"Just wrapping up. I can see fine when you're not standing in the doorway blocking the light, and I would see even better if I had the flashlight that's supposed to be in the pantry. And thank you anyway, but I don't need help."

"Okay, okay, I'll return it. I promise. Your sandwich is sitting on the counter. I wasn't sure what you'd like, so I made you the same thing I had. A slice of leftover meat loaf with provolone cheese on a sourdough roll. I thought ranch dressing would be overkill for yours, but I did put ketchup on it."

"Uh . . . thank you. That sounds hearty."

"It'll stick to your ribs. I'm going over to the studio and I'll check in on Persia and Hope. See if they want to stay at her place or come back here."

"Great," I said. "I'm going to take care of some paperwork and then I'll probably head over to the villa once Sycamore Lane is all plowed out."

"It is. I heard a truck drive by while I was eating. Twice," he said. "You coming up now? I can wait."

"I need to tidy up first. You go on."

After a moment, he said, "What'd you find down there, a dead body? You obviously can't wait to get rid of me."

"That's exactly what I found," I said. "See you later."

I carried everything upstairs and sat at the kitchen table with Eli's monster sandwich, untying the frayed blue satin ribbon that held the letters together. There were at least a dozen, almost all in business-size envelopes addressed to Zara Tomassi at Bel Paradiso, Calistoga, California. The last three were addressed to Zara Ingrasso at 309 East Capitol Street, Northeast, Washington, D.C. Some had no return address and the others had simply 341 Senate in the upper left-hand corner. Gino had said Zara's father was a congressman, not a senator.

I slipped the top one out of the envelope and started reading. By the time I finished, I could feel the heat in my cheeks after reading an explicit letter to Zara written by her lover. It was addressed to "My dearest darling" and was signed "Your ever-loving Warren."

I thought about the photo Mick had shown me yesterday of Warren Harding—Senator Warren Harding, before he became president—with his arm wrapped around a young woman who sat on his lap and looked like she was already half in the bag. Were these letters from the same man? It took less than a minute of checking on my phone to find a match for the return address.

Warren Harding—*the* Warren Harding—had had an affair with Zara Ingrasso Tomassi.

Half an hour later, I had looked through the entire bundle of letters and knew more than I wished I did about what appeared to be a passionate, long-standing affair between Harding and Zara that had begun before she married Johnny Tomassi, when she was still living in Washington, and continued after her marriage.

Had Angelica kept these as blackmail, or was it more for insurance? Maybe she wanted to make sure Johnny didn't stray from her side again, or maybe she wanted to remind him just how unfaithful Zara had been. She must have found the letters when she had gone through Zara's things before she burned them on the funeral pyre Gino had stumbled over in the woods near the Bel Paradiso chapel. Back then, an affair between a married woman—especially a married Catholic woman—and the president of the United States would have been a much bigger scandal than it would be today. The kind of scandal that could ruin reputations or even cause a governmental crisis.

There were four more envelopes, which I hadn't

looked at; they were smaller, the size of a social note, and the handwriting was different. All were addressed to Zara at Bel Paradiso, with no return address and a Washington, D.C., postmark. I pulled out the first one and started to read. It appeared to be from a girlfriend of Zara's or maybe her sister, catching her up on all the latest news in Washington, a chatty, gossipy note. It was signed "Your Adoring Izzy." I slipped it back into the envelope and wondered why Angelica had kept these letters in addition to the others.

I put them aside and picked up the cardboard envelope. Inside were two professionally taken photographs of a stunning young girl who looked about sixteen or seventeen. A watermark on the back of the pictures had the name of a photography studio and a D.C. address.

This had to be Zara Ingrasso Tomassi. As Gino had said, she was gorgeous. Then there was this bombshell realization: I had seen her before.

Yesterday in the photo of Warren Harding surrounded by a group of beautiful young women, including my namesake Lucy Montgomery. Unless I was mistaken—and I didn't think so— Zara Tomassi was the drop-dead gorgeous vixen who had been sitting on Warren Harding's lap at the Studebakers' party.

TWELVE

For the longest time I sat there and stared at the photos of Zara Tomassi when she'd been a teenager. Had Johnny known about the affair? And what about the baby? Could it have been the love child of Zara and Warren Harding? If Johnny knew about any of this, had he finally become so outraged and furious at Zara that it had driven him to murder?

Maybe this was what Gino had been so worried about. Maybe he knew about Zara's affair with Harding. If Harding had been the father of Zara's child, the revelation could bring all kinds of unwelcome attention—everyone from historians to gossip magazines, and even the mainstream press, would be interested—to someone who was in line to become the next president of a prestigious conservative Catholic think tank.

I wrapped up Eli's sandwich—I couldn't eat, not now—and put it in the refrigerator. Then I retied the packet of letters with the blue ribbon and slipped the photographs of Zara back in the envelope after I took pictures of them with my phone. For safekeeping, I put everything in the bottom drawer of the antique secretary that had belonged to my mother and was now in the study off my bedroom.

Quinn needed to know what I'd found. But before I told him anything, I wanted to get my hands on the Studebaker album, which was still in Frankie's office at the villa. Though I was almost certain I wasn't mistaken about Zara's being the woman on Harding's lap, I wanted to look at that photograph again.

And then there was the bizarre coincidence that one of my relatives had been partying with Quinn's great-grandfather's first wife right here in Atoka. Wait until Quinn heard about that, not to mention learning whom Zara had been sleeping with—the president of the United States—when she was married to Johnny Tomassi.

I drove over to the villa and thought about the six degrees of separation that supposedly connect any two people in the world. In Atoka, it had shrunk to only two degrees. Maybe even one.

Now that the snowstorm had moved up the East Coast, the sun had come out, brilliant and blinding. Against the deep azure of a cloudless sky, the sunlight reflecting off the snow was so dazzling, my eyes hurt. By tomorrow the pristine whiteness would be churned up and dirty, but today the vineyard, draped in a fresh blanket of snow, looked like a glittering winter fairyland.

The plowed-out parking lot was empty when I pulled in. Like everyone else, we had announced we would be closed for the day. I unlocked the front door, let myself in, and turned off the alarm.

The place was hushed and quiet, just odd little noises, which I finally realized were the sound of melting snow dripping off the roof. From behind the bar, Mosby, the barn cat, came padding out, stretching and yawning as he flopped over in a patch of sunshine.

"Hey, buddy, how'd you manage in the storm? Did you keep the mice at bay?" I scratched him behind his ear. "Let's find you something to eat."

In the kitchen, I opened a can of cat food, gave Mosby fresh water, and fixed myself a cup of green tea, which I took into Frankie's office. The album was sitting on the credenza behind her desk. I got it, sat in her chair, and found the page I was looking for. It was the same woman all right. I checked the pictures on my phone. The black-and-white studio photographs were of a demure young girl—dark shoulder-length hair framing her face in soft curls, a discreet amount of makeup, a high-necked white blouse trimmed in lace. She looked like she belonged in an old-fashioned advertisement for shampoo or bath soap, an all-American beauty.

The woman sitting on Warren Harding's lap could not have looked more different. By then she'd cut her hair—bobbed it, as they said in those days—and her clothes and makeup were anything but demure. Harding's hand rested on her exposed thigh through the slit in her dress. She was leaning forward to show off a provocative amount of cleavage, and one long, slender arm held a tilted glass of champagne in the air, as if she didn't care whom she spilled it on. Based on her glassy-eyed expression, she was probably drunk, as well. What a difference a few years had made.

I went back to the beginning of the album and started over, this time looking for more pictures of Zara and Lucky. Too bad I didn't know what her friend—or her sister—Izzy looked like, or even her full name. What were the odds Izzy was in that group photo as well, and that maybe Lucky had known her, too? I had nearly come to the end of the album when I heard the beep of the security system, someone coming in through the front door.

Whoever it was would have seen my car and known I was here. I slammed the album shut and had just turned around to set it back on the credenza when Frankie said, "Were you looking for something?"

I spun around. "Just looking at Mick's photo album."

We had not gotten around to talking about it yesterday, though I knew she must have gone through it, since she had shown it to Eli before the tasting party.

"Oh." She seemed puzzled. "You drove over here just for that?"

"I thought I'd feed Mosby and check on things,"

I said. "What about you? Why aren't you taking a well-deserved day off?"

"I've still got heaps to do to get ready for Saturday." She sat down in the wing chair across from the desk. "I thought I'd take advantage of the quiet to get some work done. I think Father Niall might stop by later, as well. I hope you don't mind, but I invited him over for a glass of wine at the end of the day, since we're closed and there wouldn't be anyone around."

Somehow I didn't think she had expected me to be here in the villa, either.

"I don't mind at all." I stood. "I ought to be going."

She gave me a curious look. "Was there something in particular you were looking for in Mick's album?"

There was only so long I could keep putting her off. Frankie wasn't stupid. I picked up the album again and found the Harding picture, turning it around so she could see it. "Recognize anyone? I mean, besides Warren Harding."

She gave me a crooked smile. "Yes, I saw that picture, as well. Obviously not Mrs. Harding on his lap. Whoever she is, she's stunning."

I pointed to the picture of Lucky. "Look at her. Look what she's wearing."

Frankie's hand flew to her mouth. "My God, it's your dress. How sensational. Who is she? Good Lord, she's the portrait of you, Lucie."

I told her about Lucky, the same stories I'd told Mick. When I was done, Frankie's eyes were enormous.

"That's quite incredible. We should . . . we should *do* something about that photo." Her eyes darted around the room, as if she were searching for inspiration.

"I don't think so, Frankie. The future president of the United States is partying with a bunch of young women—one of whom is my namesake—and his wife isn't anywhere to be seen."

"Oh, come on. Harding's affairs were common knowledge," she said. "The Library of Congress owns a collection of steamy love letters he wrote to one of his mistresses. Her family donated it or something. I read about it a while back, when the letters were first released to the public. You can read them on the Internet. . . . Let me tell you, some of what he wrote was X-rated stuff." She gestured to the photo. "This is pretty tame."

Based on what I'd read at my kitchen table an hour ago, I could believe the letters were explicit. Harding even had a name for his penis: Mount Jerry.

"It's Mick's picture—" I said, but she cut me off.

"Oh, Mick will say yes. Don't worry about that. We could copy it and blow it up, make it into a poster for the party. It is the 'Anything Goes' party, after all. It'll add some spice, plus, it's local history . . . and then there's your dress."

"I don't want to use it, Frankie. I'm sorry. I just don't." With everything I knew now about Zara, Harding, and Quinn's family, it just seemed like a bad idea.

She looked surprised and a little hurt. "You're the boss." She gestured to my mug. "Can I get you another cup of tea?"

"Thanks. I'm still good."

"I'll make myself a cup, then," she said. "Excuse me."

She left the room, and for the second time in two days I knew she was irked with me. I followed her into the kitchen. "I need to find Quinn," I said. "We've got some things to sort out."

She put a mug in the microwave and slammed the door. "He's over in the south vineyard. He and Antonio are plowing so the guys can get in to prune. I drove by them on my way here." She got the milk out of the refrigerator and said, without looking at me, "If there's anything I can do about whatever's on your mind, you have only to ask. You know that."

"I do," I said. "And thank you, but I'm afraid I really can't talk about it."

"I see." She didn't. The microwave dinged and she got her tea.

"Would it help if I said that Mercury's in retrograde and that's part of the reason? It's a lousy time for communicating and not good for relationships, either. Nothing turns out right."

She gave me a look like I'd lost all my marbles. "Not really," she said, and splashed milk in her mug. "But I guess it will have to do."

Quinn stopped plowing when he saw the Jeep pull up to where he'd cleared a path at the edge of the Chardonnay block. I grabbed my cane off the passenger seat and got out as he came over. He wore mirrored wraparound sunglasses against the brilliant sunshine and snow, and when he got close, I saw a fun-house version of myself in them.

He studied me and said, "You look upset. The letters were from my old man, weren't they?"

I wished I could see his eyes behind those glasses.

"I don't know an easy way to tell you this, so I'll just say it straight out," I said. "Zara was having an affair with Warren Harding. *The* Warren Harding, as in President Harding. The letters were love letters from him to Zara and, let me tell you, they were pretty explicit. I also found an envelope with two photos of her, probably taken when she was a teenager."

I don't think he could have looked more stunned if I'd told him I'd seen the Gray Ghost in the vineyard last night, Colonel John Singleton Mosby, the Confederate Army's legendary guerrilla commander, who folks said still roamed our area on moonless nights looking for Yankee soldiers.

The wind picked up, blowing snow around us

like a mini-tornado. A frigid blast of air caught the ends of my scarf and whipped it in my face. Quinn moved so he stood in front of me, shielding me from the buffeting wind.

"There's more." I grabbed my scarf and knotted it tighter around my neck, tucking in the ends.

He took off his sunglasses, squinting in the harsh brightness. His expression was grim. "I can't wait to hear."

I told him about borrowing Mick's photo album for Frankie, who wanted it as inspiration for our party. "Apparently, Harding came to one of the Studebakers' parties," I said. "And after I saw the photos of Zara that had been in the trunk, I realized that I had also seen a picture of her in Mick's album."

"Zara was *here?* At a party at the Studebakers'? You've got to be kidding."

"She grew up in Washington and her father was a prominent congressman, so that's probably how she met Harding. She was beautiful, Quinn. Gino was right. A real knockout. No wonder Johnny fell for her. And so did Warren Harding."

There would be time later to tell him about Lucky Montgomery. He still looked like someone had just slapped him.

"So Gino was right," he said. "Angelica did leave something behind in her trunk."

"What do you want to do?"

He looked over at the snow-covered vines. "I

161

need some time to deal with this," he said. "And I want to finish the plowing myself. That way, I can be sure there'll be no damage to the vines."

"You ought to read the letters."

He put on the sunglasses, so I couldn't see his eyes again. "I know."

"Come over for dinner tonight. Eli will be taking care of Hope afterward, putting her to bed, so we'll have some privacy. You can look at them then."

My phone rang and I pulled it out of my pocket. "It's Kit. Last night I asked her to see what she could find out about Zara's family in the *Trib* archives. She's probably calling about that."

I hit Accept and said, "Hey, what's up?"

"You tell me," she said. "I did some research on your Congressman Ingrasso and his family. Personal life only, since that's what you asked."

"Uh-huh." I held the phone away from my ear so Quinn could listen, as well. He bent his face close to mine.

"So it seems his daughter Zara married a guy named Gianluca Tomassi, the founder of Tomassi Family Vineyard in California. The wedding was a big deal, a couple of hundred people, with a huge reception at the Willard Hotel. The cardinal married them in St. Matthew's Cathedral and President and Mrs. Warren Harding were among the guests."

"Really?"

"Yeah," she said, "but you already knew that,

didn't you? Maybe from Gino Tomassi, who came by to pay you a visit yesterday? Bobby stopped in at the General Store this morning and got an earful from Thelma."

Quinn's eyes met mine. I hadn't told him about Gino dropping into the General Store and my getting the third degree from Thelma about him. Quinn made a slashing motion across his throat.

"I didn't know the Hardings were at the wedding," I said to Kit, which was the truth. "Did you find anything else?"

I heard the noisy sound of a straw sucking up the last of a drink and the rattle of ice cubes in an empty cup. "Obviously, the marriage didn't last long," she said. "The next thing that turned up is her obit, two years later. It's funny, though. The article about her wedding took up two columns in what used to be the society section. Her obit was one short paragraph. She died after suffering head trauma from a fall on the family estate in California. Survived by her husband, no children. A private burial, no funeral Mass. That's weird, don't you think?"

Quinn and I glanced at each other. "Can you send me those articles?" I asked.

I heard the whoosh of an e-mail being sent, and she said, "I just did. You want to tell me what this is all about? You weren't looking for information about Congressman Ingrasso. It was his daughter, wasn't it?"

163

"I wasn't sure what you'd find," I said. That, actually, was true. "Thanks for doing this, Kit. I really appreciate it."

"Well, when you can explain what 'this' is, I'll be all ears," she said in a tart voice. "In the meantime, Mom called again and bent my ear about Roxy Willoughby and how she was poisoned. I was on the phone for over half an hour trying to calm her down."

"I'll call Mac after I hang up with you," I said, "and see what I can find out. I'll bet he was the one Faith heard arguing with Roxy and that will be the end of it. She knows Mac didn't poison his aunt."

"Well," she said, sounding mollified. "I suppose that's the least you could do, since you aren't going to tell me why you're so interested in the Ingrasso family and Zara Tomassi."

She hung up, and I said to Quinn, "I knew she'd suspect something. I shouldn't have asked her to go through the archives for old stories on Ingrasso. Obviously, it was going to lead to Zara. We're no nearer knowing anything about her baby."

"Yeah, but we did learn something," he said. "Her obituary confirms what Gino told us. An accidental death at Bel Paradiso."

"Actually, it confirms what Johnny and Angelica said. What we did learn was that there was no funeral Mass for Zara. I think that's odd, with the

Ingrassos being such staunch Catholics. They'd at least have had a memorial Mass."

"Maybe not, if the baby was Harding's," Quinn said. "A nice Catholic family would want everything hushed up, just like Johnny and Angelica did."

"I guess so." But it still sounded odd to me. "I'd better call Mac. See you tonight?"

"Okay." He leaned over and kissed me on the cheek. "Thanks."

"Are you all right?"

"Dandy." He gave me a twisted smile. "I'm just freakin' dandy." Then he stomped back to the Gator.

I watched him until he lowered the plow with a sharp jerk and started plowing again before I went over to the Jeep. He was more upset than I'd ever seen him, even the time he left to go to California. And once again, it had something to do with his family.

My heart ached for him and I hoped he'd figure this out, make peace with himself and the ghost of his father, because if he didn't, it would haunt him forever. I got into the Jeep, turned on the motor, and blasted heat through the vents with a loud roar that filled my head. When it was warm again, I turned it down and phoned Mac.

"Why, Lucie darling, how nice to hear from you," he said in his broad drawl. "Though I have to say, I was rather expecting your call."

"You were?"

"I figured it wouldn't take you long to find out, the way news travels in this town," he said. "I'm so glad you called before I sold it to anyone else."

"Sold what?"

"Your grandfather clock. Isn't that why you're calling? I just had it brought here yesterday from the Georgetown store. With the storm, no one's been in to see it yet. It's a splendid one, sugar, in perfect condition. English, from the 1850s, just like the one you sold me."

"Actually," I said, "I didn't know about it."

When I first moved home from France, my father had so many debts that, out of desperation, I'd sold Mac several pieces of furniture, all family antiques, and begged him to give me a good price. Eli and Mia had been furious when they found out, but it wasn't as if we'd had a choice. We couldn't even afford to pay Quinn's salary; we were that tapped out.

The hardest thing to let go was a beautiful English tall case clock that had been in our family for generations. I couldn't bear to be in the house when Mac's movers had come to take it because it had been so upsetting. And later when I got home and saw the empty space in the foyer where it had been, I felt as if the heartbeat of the house had stopped and someone beloved had died.

"I know it broke your heart to sell that clock," Mac said. "I never felt quite right about taking it, but preferred you sell to me rather than to someone who didn't know its history. I know you never asked, but I made sure the right person bought it."

"Thank you," I said. "I had no idea."

"We haven't spoken about it, but I've been on the lookout for something to replace it ever since. Now that you're back on your feet again financially, I thought maybe it was time. Excuse my little pun." He chuckled at his own joke. "Do come by and see it, Lucie, honey. I'm keeping it for you, but I know someone else is going to fall in love with it the moment they set eyes on it."

I was touched by his concern, but I also knew Mac. He was baiting the hook and now he meant to reel me in. I knew why, too.

A few years ago, he and several of the Romeos had lost their shirts when they discovered that a financier they trusted had been suckered into a Ponzi scheme into which he had poured all their money. It had been a devastating blow for everyone, but it had been especially hard on Mac, whose only income now came from his two antiques stores in Middleburg and Georgetown.

The silver lining, so to speak, was that as Roxy Willoughby's nephew, he was her sole heir, her only surviving relative, and the assumption around town had been that he would inherit her considerable estate one day and be back on his feet. Then Roxy changed her will shortly before she died, and everyone—including Mac, according to Thelma—learned she had an estranged granddaughter in England named Uma Lawrence.

"I'm in the store today," he said to me now, "even though we're closed on account of the snow. You could stop by this afternoon and have a look before anyone else gets a chance to see it. I wouldn't want someone to outbid you, sugar, and have you disappointed all over again."

Another tug on the line, but he was right. If he'd found a clock like the one I'd sold him, I was definitely interested. Plus, it gave me a legitimate excuse to see him and work the conversation around to whether he'd been the one Faith overheard arguing with Roxy.

"All right," I said. "I'll be there in twenty minutes."

I could practically hear him beaming through the phone. "Knock on the door and I'll let you in. You might have to knock real hard, since I could be in the back."

Or he'd be hovering nearby, waiting for me, which I figured was the more likely scenario.

I drove over to Mac's down freshly plowed streets and thought about everything I'd learned about Quinn's extended family in the past twenty-four hours, including the fact that he had an extended family.

Why would a *testa dura* like Angelica Tomassi have hidden love letters from Warren Harding to

Johnny's first wife? It couldn't have been to protect Johnny, or she would have burned them along with the rest of Zara's things. Maybe I was right and they were some kind of insurance policy to keep Johnny in line so his eye wouldn't wander to another woman again, to remind him how unfaithful Zara had been.

Then there was the matter of Zara's death, whether it was an accident or possibly murder.

Now that I knew Warren Harding had also been involved, it could explain why Zara's own family—who had been devout Catholics, and her father, a prominent Washington congressman who probably wouldn't have wanted word to get out that his daughter had been sleeping with the president of the United States—had been willing to go along with the conspiracy of silence surrounding her death.

Which meant that if it was murder, everyone involved—Johnny, Angelica, and the Ingrasso family—had had a motive for covering up something that then had remained a secret for nearly a century.

Until now. Someone apparently had discovered that Zara's baby had lived after all, found the child's birth certificate.

But why now, after so much time? And who was foolish enough to take on Gino Tomassi? It was like kicking a hornets' nest and figuring you wouldn't get stung.

Because Gino—and I was sure of this—would go to any lengths to keep this family scandal a secret. And he had the friends in the right places who knew how to shut someone up for good.

THIRTEEN

I found a place to park across the street from Mac's store on Liberty Street and pulled in next to a snowbank left behind by a plow. As I got out of my car, a tan-and-gold Loudoun County Sheriff's Department cruiser pulled up alongside the Jeep and Bobby Noland powered down his passenger window.

"Hey, Lucie, glad I ran into you. Looks like you're all plowed out," he said, leaning across the seat so he could talk to me through the window. "How are you doing?"

I'd known Bobby since I was a kid. He hadn't stopped his car in the middle of Liberty Street just for a little social chitchat.

"I'm doing fine, Bobby," I said. "How about you?"

Bobby was Eli's age and the two of them had been friends and classmates, though by the time they got to high school, Bobby had drifted into being a regular at detention hall, struggling with his studies and skipping class whenever he could get away with it. No one expected to see him end up in law enforcement, except on the wrong side of the jailhouse bars. Instead, he became one of the county's senior detectives, thanks to an uncanny knack for solving crimes—almost as if he could read the minds of the guilty—and especially a talent for knowing when someone was lying.

"Good," he said. "Doing real good. Kit said she had fun at your wine-tasting party last night."

"I'm glad. She really helped. Sorry you couldn't make it."

"Yeah, I was working late."

He still hadn't gotten around to the real reason for this impromptu tête-à-tête. "So we'll see you and Kit on Saturday for the 'Anything Goes' party, right?" I said.

"We'll be there." He nodded. "Hey, there's something I want to ask you, if you don't mind."

Here it was. "Sure. Shoot."

"What was Gino Tomassi doing at your vineyard yesterday?"

At least I wasn't caught completely off guard, since Kit had told me Thelma had mentioned to him that Gino had dropped by. "He and Quinn know each other from California," I said. "And Gino's in town for that state dinner at the White House tonight with the Italian prime minister. He stopped in to say hi."

"I see."

I had a feeling Bobby already knew that Gino

was going to the White House dinner. Had he found out somehow about the blackmail? "Why are you asking about Gino?"

"Oh, I like to know who comes and goes in the county," he said. "Make sure they behave themselves, obey the law."

"You're worried about Gino Tomassi obeying the law?"

"Not him," he said. "But he's got some interesting friends. Just checking up on him."

"Right."

A car pulled up behind Bobby, but the driver obviously wasn't going to honk at a police cruiser.

"Course it's not surprising he stopped by to see Quinn, is it?" Bobby said, giving me a bland look. "I'd better get going. I'm holding up traffic. See you Saturday, Lucie."

He closed his window before I could say anything and drove off. I stared after him, my brain whirring. Bobby knew Gino and Quinn were related. He had to. And Kit had probably told him about my clumsy request that she look into the *Tribune*'s archives for any information on the Ingrasso family.

Bobby had deliberately put me on alert, asking about Gino for a reason.

I wondered what it really was and what he knew.

As I'd figured, Mac was waiting in the front of the store, so there was no need to knock on the door.

I waved through the window. He let me in and gave me a friendly kiss on the cheek.

MacDonald's Fine Antiques was always carefully curated, reminding me of a slightly cluttered English country house drawing room where every piece of furniture, every Oriental rug, every oil painting had some intriguing tale to explain its provenance. By the time you made a purchase, you felt you were the next steward entrusted with a legacy item that had played a role of some significance in American or English history.

The first thing I did was look around for my clock—I had already started thinking of it as mine—but Mac must have left it in the back of the store, because all I saw were two mantel clocks, a sweet beehive clock, and a grandfather clock with a pagoda-shaped hood and the phases of the moon on its painted dial that had been there the last time I was in.

"Come in, darling, come in." Mac shut the door behind me. "My Lord, but it's bitter cold today. That wind is wicked. It cuts you like a knife."

I pulled off my gloves and hat and unbuttoned my coat. "It's the polar vortex. The temperature on the outdoor thermometer at the vineyard read five degrees."

Mac gave a little shudder, as if the wind had just blasted through the store. Usually, he was impeccably dressed in a suit, tie, and a silk pocket handkerchief, but today, with the store closed because of the snow, he had on a pair of worn tan corduroys, a turtleneck, and a Fair Isle sweater with a stretched-out hem, which made him look rumpled and frumpy. He also looked like he hadn't had a decent night's sleep in a while.

"Too cold for man or beast," he said, shaking his head. "When I was over at Thelma's a while ago, she mentioned Skye Cohen had stopped in for a cup of hot cocoa to warm up. She was driving around trying to round up anyone who might be sleeping rough and get them to come over to Veronica House. Keep 'em from literally freezing to death."

Mac was an old-school Southern gentleman who never brought up business without first chatting about something on a completely different topic. Eventually, he circled around to the reason you were in the store: that there was something that had struck your fancy, or, in my case, something you hadn't known you were interested in buying . . . yet. Last but not least was the money discussion. The longer he took to get around to that topic, the higher the price tag.

"Are you all right?" I asked. "You look tired."

It was the first time I'd seen him since Roxy's funeral. What he really looked like was someone who'd aged a couple of years in a couple of days.

"The last two weeks have been difficult, with

the funeral and all. I just didn't expect to lose her when we did, even though she was in her nineties. I'm still getting used to it."

He had just given me the perfect opening. "I know you loved Roxy, Mac. You took such good care of her. But you've been through a lot, especially the way things worked out."

He knew what I meant. The new will.

"Thank you for that." He gave me a grateful look. "I wouldn't mind as much if that granddaughter of hers wasn't so unpleasant. She may look like Aunt Roxy when she was that age, but let me tell you, that child is nothing like her grandmother. Fortunately, she isn't planning to stick around town for long."

"At least you inherited the house, her furniture, the art collection . . . the things she really loved."

"I know, and I'll be fine. Don't you worry about me," he said. "Not quite what I imagined financially, but no one put a gun to my head and made me invest with that crook of an investment adviser a few years back. That was my own stupidity and greed. And it was all the money I had from my share of selling my mother's family's home in Washington." He pressed his lips together, as if the memory still pained him. "What's done is done. It's the same with Aunt Roxy's will—no use crying over it. Obviously, she changed her mind and decided she wanted to make it up to the daughter she'd abandoned in

England. I can't fault her for that. I just wasn't expecting it is all."

"That's very generous of you."

"Oh, I'm no saint. I was angry with her when I found out, and at Sammy Constantine for not telling me she did it. Especially after I gave Sam such a good deal on a pair of paintings he wanted for his office, even having them delivered for free and all." His smile was sad. "You know what Father Niall said to me the other day? 'Let it go, Mac. It's only money. God will always see to it that you have everything you need and you'll be just fine. Don't harbor any resentment over what could have been or should have been, because not forgiving someone is like drinking rat poison and waiting for the rat to die.' "

"That sounds like Father Niall," I said, smiling.

"He's right," he said. "That kind of bitterness is corrosive."

"Can I ask you something?"

He tilted his head and considered the question. "I guess I should say that I may not answer. But go ahead, ask away."

He walked over to a large picture window with its beautifully arranged display of winter items from the store—brass andirons and an ornate set of fireplace tools, an oil painting of a snowy rural landscape, a woolen throw draped over the seat of a bowed-back Windsor rocking chair—and placed his hands behind his back, posture ramrod straight as he surveyed the snowy street like the captain on the bridge of a ship assessing what lay ahead. Across from us, some of the other shops had begun opening for what was left of the day. A couple of snow-covered cars drove by and a group of teenagers who had an unexpected school holiday ran past the store, lobbing snowballs at one another and laughing. Life in Middleburg returning to normal after the blizzard.

I went over and joined him. "Faith Eastman said she heard Roxy arguing with someone in her apartment a few days before she died, shouting in a loud voice about wanting to know the truth about something. Faith's quite upset, especially because Roxy died so soon after that argument. I was wondering if that person might have been you."

He turned to me and said in a curt voice, "I have no idea what you're talking about, and no, it was not me."

"I'm sorry. I didn't mean to upset you, Mac."

"Well, you have. Why are you asking about this?"

"Just trying to put Faith's mind at ease."

"Faith Eastman should stay out of other people's business."

"She meant no harm. She was Roxy's friend, too, you know."

He caught himself—I was still a prospective customer, after all—and said, "Of course she was.

Well, I will say that Roxy could be testy from time to time. Maybe Faith heard her get cross with the maid over how her room was cleaned or perhaps she told the waiter who brought her meal that it was cold or some minor infraction. It could be just that simple."

"I didn't know she had a temper."

"She tried to curb it, especially in public. But, oh my, yes," he said, "especially when she was younger. My mother always talked about how Aunt Roxy was the rebellious older sister growing up, headstrong and acting before she thought about the consequences. She argued with Granny Chase constantly—my mother said they had terrible fights. It got so bad Roxy left home as soon as she was old enough, running off to learn how to fly an airplane. Then during the war—well, you know what happened when she was in England. That rebellious streak got her in a pack of trouble."

"You mean the baby?"

He nodded and, sounding reflective, said, "Granny Chase took it hard. What really broke her heart was that she never reconciled with her elder daughter. After she died and Roxy's husband died, that's when Roxy changed. Realized sowing all those wild oats caused so much heartache and pain, not just for herself but for others. That's when she decided to use the money she'd inherited from her husband to do good."

"And she did. St. Mike's was packed for her

funeral," I said. "That's why it seems so odd that Faith heard her arguing with someone. Everyone loved her."

He gave me a stony look. "It also could have been the television, sugar, turned up real loud. Did Faith ever consider that?"

"No, she seemed positive it was a visitor, not the television."

He put his hands on his hips. "The next time you talk to her, tell her she's got the wrong end of the stick about this. Tell her I said so. Now, shall we go take a look at your clock?"

He was done talking about Roxy. I wasn't going to get anything more out of him.

"I just have one more question." He started to cut me off, but I said, "It's not about Roxy or Faith."

"All right." He sounded grudging. "Go ahead, then."

"Do you remember if your grandmother knew the woman I was named for? Lucy Montgomery, Leland's great-aunt. Everyone called her Lucky."

"I couldn't say," he said after a moment. "Why do you ask?"

"I came across something of hers recently and it got me wondering about her. We lost all our photo albums in that fire a few years ago. I'd like to know more about her. Apparently, she stayed here back in the 1920s, came for a visit. She was kind of a gypsy."

"All the Chase and MacDonald family photo

albums are at the house," he said. "Uma's staying there now. I've moved into the little apartment I've got above the store. It's easier, since being around her gets me in a state. But I can look for you the next time I'm there. . . . I'm quite sure Uma is planning to be gone by the weekend, once the money matters are settled."

"Thank you," I said. "I'd appreciate that."

From the back of the store, a bell sounded as a door opened and closed. "That you, Will? I'm out here," Mac called. To me, he said, "I've hired a nice young man who's handling my deliveries now. Come and meet him."

"I believe I already have," I said as Will Baron walked into the room carrying two Styrofoam cups and wearing the colorful hat he'd had on the night before. He had the same catch-your-breath effect on me he'd had then, a dark, dangerous charm that he seemed all too well aware he possessed.

His handsome face broke into a smile when he recognized me. "Hey, Lucie, nice to see you again. I just picked up a coffee for Mac. If I'd known you were here, I would have gotten you one, too."

"Thanks, I'm just fine."

"Thoughtful, isn't he?" Mac said with a smile, accepting the coffee from Will. "I don't know how I ever got along without him." He reached into his pocket and pulled out his wallet.

"Forget it." Will waved the money away. "I

appreciate your letting me use the apartment upstairs to study. I get a lot done up there. Before I forget, I took the last of your aunt's furniture from Foxhall Manor over to the storage barn. Here are your keys."

"Thanks, son." Mac put his wallet back in his pocket and took the keys. "Speaking of deliveries, I'm hoping Lucie here will buy that grandfather clock you brought from the Georgetown store yesterday."

Will turned to me. "Mac said he thought of you when he bought it. It's in perfect condition, not a scratch or a nick. English oak, with a hand-painted Roman numeral dial and landscape scenes in the corners. Mac has the paperwork about the original owner, the earl of Lancashire, who had it made in 1810. His descendants finally sold it, so it'd been in the same house for over two hundred years. Like the one you sold Mac."

"I think I should hire Will as a salesman," Mac said, "and look for someone else to take care of deliveries."

"You seem to know a lot about antiques," I said to Will. "And about me."

That mesmerizing smile again. "I like old things, anything with history or a story to it. And Mac's a good teacher. As for knowing about you, that's thanks to Vivienne. After she met you yesterday, she went home and looked you up on the Internet." He gave me a mischievous look. "You'd be surprised the things I learned."

I felt my cheeks go hot. "Really?"

He nodded. "Vivienne admires anyone who runs their own show the way you do, especially a successful woman in what's mostly a man's world." Will indicated Mac with his cup. "That's what got her so interested in Roxy Willoughby. She read something about the first squadron of women pilots who flew in World War Two. Next thing you know, she's tracking 'em all down, interviewing everybody."

"I'd like to see what she writes about Roxy before it comes out in that article of hers." Mac looked fretful. "The time Roxy spent in England was . . ." He seemed to be searching for a word. "Complicated. Roxy kept that part of her life to herself for as long as she lived. Now that she's gone, I'd like to preserve her dignity . . . her legacy, if you know what I mean. I want people to remember her charity work, her philanthropy, rather than a youthful indiscretion. Not everything that happens in a person's life needs to be printed in the newspaper."

"I'll talk to Vivienne," Will said, "and have her get in touch with you."

"I'm sure you can persuade her there's no need to sully a good woman's reputation without getting me in the middle of it." Mac sounded peevish. "That wife of yours adores you, Will. She'll do it if you ask her."

"I'm a lucky man." He bowed his head, acknowledging the compliment. "And I'll talk to her. It'll be fine, Mac, don't worry."

"I appreciate that." He nodded, apparently mollified. "Let's go have a look at Lucie's clock, shall we?"

The three of us walked to the back of the store. It was, as they both had said, a real beauty. I let out a long breath and fell in love.

"How much?" I asked, but we both knew that giveaway reaction had cost me leverage in bargaining over the price.

Mac flashed a look at Will, who said, "I believe I ought to do some brushing up on torts. I'll be upstairs, Mac, if you'll excuse me."

"That'd be fine, son." Mac nodded. "We can have it delivered as early as tomorrow, sugar," he said to me. "You're here tomorrow, right, Will?"

"I've got the evening shift at the Goose Creek Inn tomorrow, so I thought I'd hit the books during the day, but I can come in for a few hours if you need me," he said. "Lucie, Mac will give me your number and we can coordinate when it's convenient for me to come by."

"You're both presuming I'm going to buy this clock," I said.

"We're not presuming anything." Will flashed that smile again. "We know you're going to buy it."

After he left, Mac and I dickered for a while, and he told me, as I knew he would, that he wasn't even going to recoup the cost of paying Will for delivering the clock if he gave it to me for the price I wanted. We finally settled on a number and I sat down in the Queen Anne chair next to the oak partners desk, where he wrote out all his transactions, while he finished the paperwork.

"I'll have Will call you," he said, handing me the bill of sale. "And I'll take a look through the family albums next chance I get. See if I can find any photos of your namesake."

He let me out the front door after planting a good-bye kiss on my cheek. Instinctively, I glanced up at the windows above the store to Mac's apartment, where Will Baron was now studying torts for the bar exam. For a moment, I could have sworn I saw the quick ghost of Will's face in the window, watching me, and I nearly raised my hand to wave at him. But then my cane hit a patch of ice on the sidewalk and I looked down to steady myself. When I looked up again, there was no one, not even the flutter of a curtain being released.

I crossed Liberty Street and wondered about Mac's stubborn insistence that Faith was wrong and that Roxy had either been scolding a maid or else had the television turned up too loud. I didn't believe either explanation. Whether or not Mac had been the person Roxy had been arguing with,

I had a feeling he knew what had upset his aunt.

Which meant maybe the man I'd spent much of my life calling "Uncle Mac" had just lied to me about not knowing that Roxy had changed her will.

FOURTEEN

By the time I turned the corner at the entrance to the vineyard, it was going on four o'clock. The brilliant noontime sunshine had faded, and in the colorless winter light, the snow-covered landscape looked duller and more somber. I took a left at the fork in the road where the two-hundred-year-old lightning-cleaved tree that had given Sycamore Lane its name still stood, heading toward the villa, rather than home to Highland House. If Quinn was coming over tonight for dinner, I wanted to show him Mick's photo album, which was still in Frankie's office.

When I pulled into the parking lot, her red BMW was where it had been when I'd left. Next to it was Father Niall O'Malley's car, a black SUV with tinted windows, now gritty with salt and road spray.

I saw them through the window as I went up the walk. They were sitting side by side on one of the leather sofas next to the fire. Frankie's legs were tucked up under her, an elbow resting on the back of the sofa and her fingers twirling a lock of strawberry blond hair, a wineglass in her other hand as she sat facing Father Niall. He kept nodding, apparently at something she was saying, as he stared into the fire, his head bowed, arms resting loosely on his knees, wineglass in both hands, as if he were holding a Communion chalice.

When he was at Veronica House, Father Niall dressed like everyone else who worked or volunteered there, usually in jeans, or shorts in the summer. Everyone still knew he was a priest, though; there was something about him that set him apart, even without the Roman collar. Frankie joked that it was his Irish charm and a poetic way with words that captivated what she referred to as "the Holy Harem," the many women who had crushes on him.

The only time I saw him in his black clerical attire was at the hospital while visiting the sick or at a community meeting or some formal occasion. Today, though, he had on a plaid lumberjack shirt with the sleeves rolled up to the elbows over a turtleneck, jeans, and work boots.

For a moment, I debated whether I should intrude on what looked like an intense conversation, but Frankie must have sensed she was being watched or caught a flash of movement through the window, because she looked up and waved, swinging her feet to the ground and standing up. Father Niall got to his feet as well and ran a hand through his short white hair in a way that made me think he'd been mulling over something that preoccupied him.

My French mother had been a lapsed Catholic and Leland was a practicing atheist, so Mia, Eli, and I grew up believing, with the blissful innocence of children, that at Easter a bunny brought you chocolate eggs in pastel-colored straw baskets and Christmas was when Santa and his reindeer left the North Pole to fly all over the world delivering gifts to good boys and girls. Eli wised up about the real identity of Santa and the bunny (and the tooth fairy) by the time he was nine and ruined the magic for me as soon as he knew. When my mother found out, she made death threats if we spoiled anything for Mia, who believed—or pretended to—until she was ready for middle school. Over the years, though, I secretly envied my friends who dressed up in their best clothes at Christmas and Easter and went to church with their families, a special rite that bound them together, conferring a mystical grace my family would never know.

But my unrequited wish to be like my church-going friends hadn't been strong enough to make me consider exploring my mother's Catholic faith and possibly joining the Church myself, even when I'd discovered that she'd sought out Father Niall for spiritual guidance during a rocky period in her marriage when both she and my father were having affairs. Whatever he had told her had obviously comforted her, because, by accident, I'd found a book on forgiveness with his name written on the flyleaf, a rosary, and a Catholic book of prayers, also with his name on it, when I was looking for something in her desk after she died. The next time I checked, the drawer was empty.

Either Leland had returned everything to Father Niall or, more likely, he'd gotten rid of it. I never asked, since I wasn't supposed to know about any of it, especially the affairs.

"Lucie," Frankie said when I walked in. "Niall and I were just having an end-of-the-day drink. Won't you join us?"

Something unsettling definitely hung in the air between them—the tension I thought I'd sensed through the window—and I knew Frankie was lying about it being just a happy-hour drink. Father Niall's deep blue eyes met mine, but in his business he was a master at keeping secrets and poker faces, and his gave nothing away.

So I smiled and said, "Thanks, but don't let me interrupt. I just stopped in to get something and I'll be out of here. Nice to see you, Father."

"And it's nice seein' you, too, Lucie," he said. Though he'd left Ireland forty years ago and moved here as a newly ordained priest, he still spoke with the burr of an accent, and I wondered, occasionally, if the brogue wasn't a wee bit of blarney he could turn on for charm and effect. "I can't thank you enough for what you're doin' for Veronica House with your fund-raiser. I hope you know how much I appreciate it."

"It was all Frankie's idea," I said. "I'm glad we can help."

Frankie pointed to the wine bottle. "Sure you won't have a quick one with us? I'll get a glass."

I shook my head. "I've got to get home. I just need to get Mick's photo album. It's still in your office, isn't it?"

"It is," she said.

The album was on her desk, rather than on the credenza, where I'd found it that morning, so I guessed she had spent some time looking through it again herself. I picked it up and walked back into the tasting room.

In the brief time that I'd been gone, someone else had come in. A tall, slender woman stood in the entryway, wearing a bottle green parka with a fur-trimmed hood pulled over her head, so it partially hid her face, black ski pants, and fashionable high-heeled black boots. She pushed the hood back, revealing flaming red hair, porcelain skin, and dark winged eyebrows above almond-shaped eyes.

When she spoke, she had a cut-glass English accent. "I hope I'm not too late and you haven't closed for the day. But I was told I could buy a bottle or two of champagne here."

Frankie and I exchanged looks. So this was Uma Lawrence. As everyone said, she did resemble a young version of Roxy—the same Titian-colored hair, high, sculpted cheekbones, English rose complexion—but no one had mentioned she was beautiful enough to take your breath away.

"I'm sorry, but I'm afraid you were misinformed," I said. "We don't sell champagne here. This is a farm winery; we're not a retail store."

Quinn and I had agreed to keep quiet about our decision to make sparkling wine until we were further along in the process, since so few vineyards in Virginia were doing it. Someone must have spilled the beans. I wondered who it was.

Frankie gave her a friendly smile. "But we do sell our own wines, and I'd be happy to show you the wine list. I'm sure we can find something you'll like," she said. "I'm Frankie Merchant. I run the tasting room at Montgomery Vineyard. This is Lucie Montgomery, who owns the winery, and this is a friend of ours, Father Niall O'Malley."

"How do you do. I'm Uma Lawrence." She walked into the room and pulled off a pair of leather gloves. "I'm in town for a few days. Visiting . . . family." She stumbled over the last word.

"You're Roxy's granddaughter," Father Niall

said, and I noticed that he had not taken his eyes off her. "My deepest sympathy for your loss. You were missed at her funeral. It was quite a tribute to a very fine lady."

"Are you the priest who took care of her funeral service?" she asked.

"I said the memorial Mass," he said. "As she wished. Roxy planned the funeral herself, you know, right down to the readings and the hymns. As I said, she was a great lady. I miss her sorely as a dear friend. It's a shame you never had the chance to know her."

Uma's cheeks turned pink, but she lifted her chin and gave him a cool look. "I didn't know her, but I certainly knew all about her."

"I should hope so," he said. "You have quite a legacy to live up to, Miss Lawrence. Roxy was generous and good-hearted, always thinking about those less fortunate than she was. Those are grand shoes you'll be filling."

"Thank you, Father, but you can skip the sermon," she said. "I was told that everyone in this town knew everyone else's business. I may have been here only a day, but I do know that my grandmother's will came as a surprise to many people. Especially those who thought they might be rewarded by her good-hearted generosity." She emphasized *rewarded* and gave Father Niall a pointed look.

For a long moment, no one spoke. The impact

of what she'd all but said outright went through the room, as if she'd just touched a high-voltage electrical wire. It was true Roxy had left her money and her possessions to the only two people in the world who were her living relatives, Mac and Uma. She had been abundantly generous to her charities when she was alive, but blood was blood and she had chosen to care for family—and only family—in her final bequest.

Frankie had mentioned money problems in the financial report she'd been reading about Veronica House. Had Father Niall expected to be rewarded, as Uma so crassly put it, in Roxy's will and been as surprised as everyone else when his charity had been left out?

Father Niall's eyes narrowed and he picked up a black wool coat that had been lying on the sofa. "I think I'd best be getting back before our guests arrive for dinner. I want to check on a few things, make sure we've got everything set up, since we have so many people spending the night in this dreadful cold." He shrugged into his coat and wound a tan-and-red plaid Burberry scarf around his neck. "Thank you for the drink, Frankie. I'll be seeing the pair of you Saturday night for the gala, won't I now?" He smiled at both of us, but his eyes were grave.

"Absolutely," Frankie said.

He glanced over at Uma. "Miss Lawrence, I'd quite like to speak with you again, get to know the granddaughter of a woman I loved and admired," he said. "Perhaps you could come by Veronica House and we could have tea while you're still in Atoka."

Uma shot him a look, as if he'd just suggested they meet so he could perform an exorcism. Frankie and I traded uneasy glances.

Finally, Uma said with chilly finality, "I'm terribly sorry, but I'm sure I won't have any free time while I'm here, Father O'Malley. I'm leaving this weekend, and I have a lot on my plate between now and then."

Father Niall slipped his wallet out of his back pocket and pulled out a card. "Take this. My contact information if you change your mind. Call anytime."

He held it out, and for a long moment Uma stood there with her arms folded across her chest like a belligerent child defying a parent. But Father Niall didn't move, either, his hand still outstretched as he waited her out. Finally, she threw him a sulky look and took the card and shoved it into her jacket pocket.

"Well," he said in a soft voice, as if to himself, "I guess that's that, then." He pulled on a fire engine red knit hat that had been in the pocket of his coat. "Good afternoon, everyone, and God bless."

"I'll walk you to your car, Father," I said. "I'm leaving, too."

"Uma," Frankie said, as if nothing unpleasant had just happened, "why don't you come over to the bar and let me pour you a glass of wine? I'm sure we'll find something you might like to purchase, since you've come all this way." She turned to Father Niall. "I'll call you about the other matter, okay?" She kissed him on the cheek and gave his arm an affectionate squeeze.

"It'll all be fine, Frankie, don't you worry. God will provide. He always does," he said.

I waited until Father Niall and I were outside before I said, "That was terribly rude of her, don't you think?"

The wintery afternoon light had faded, softening the landscape like an out-of-focus picture, and the wind blasted a heartless assault that caught us both in the face like a hard slap. We both pulled our collars tighter.

"I'd say it was a bit of good old Catholic guilt at work, even if she's not Catholic." Father Niall flashed a brief half smile. "All of a sudden she has more money than she's ever had in her life and she doesn't know how to handle it . . . not just the money but how different her life will be because of it."

"Money isn't going to buy her happiness. I wish her luck, or at least I'd like to be charitable enough to wish her luck," I said. "I'm not sure I do."

He gave me a self-deprecating grin. "There's no

shame in being honest, Lucie. Maybe in time she'll open her heart, help others the way Roxy did. That's why I was hoping to get her over to Veronica House. The people I deal with every day have nothing. No home, no job, all their worldly possessions in a couple of carrier bags from Safeway. Sure and you're right about money not buying happiness, but a bit of it would go a long way toward making their lives easier. There's nothing romantic about poverty."

"I don't know that kind of poverty," I said. "And I know how lucky I am. But after Leland died, we were so broke, I was afraid we'd lose everything. We had to climb out from under the mountain of debts he left behind, but I paid every one of them back. I hope I never have to do something like that again."

"I remember," he said. "And I admire you for it."

"We never talked about this," I said, "but I know you helped my mother when she was going through a rough time years ago. I found out about it after she was gone. I just wanted to say thank you."

We reached the parking lot and he pulled his car keys out of his pocket, hitting the Unlock button on the SUV.

"She was a lovely woman, Chantal," he said. "Did you know she was thinking about returning to the Church? We had just started talking about it before she died."

Somehow that news didn't surprise me, and I wondered if he was giving me an opening to say something about my own spiritual life. Or lack of one.

"No, I didn't. We never talked about religion at all when I was growing up," I said. "One last thing, Father. Do you know anything about an argument Roxy Willoughby might have had with someone a few days before she died? Faith Eastman, her next-door neighbor, is my best friend's mother and she's been like a second mother to me. She's taken Roxy's death terribly hard, especially that argument."

"Do you know what it was about?"

"Roxy wanted to know the truth about something. That's all Faith heard."

"I'm afraid I can't help you. And even if I did know something"—he pointed to the sky—"I'm bound by that fellow up there to take anything I was told in the sanctity of the confessional to my grave." The wind gusted hard again and he held on to his car door to keep it from slamming into me. "Even murder."

I nodded, wondering how many confessions he'd kept to himself that could have sent someone to jail. A lot of the homeless people who came to his shelter lived on the outside edge of the law—many had done jail time—so I guessed the answer was that he'd heard his fair share. How did he deal with the morality of something like that? How could it not warp his sense of right and wrong?

He patted my shoulder. "You ought to get out of this wind. It's bitter."

We said good-bye again and I got into my car, watching him pull out of the parking lot and put on his blinker as he turned on to Sycamore Lane. His taillights disappeared, and I had an uneasy feeling in the pit of my stomach. Father Niall O'Malley knew more than he'd let on just now. Just like Mac.

I drove home to get dinner sorted out before Quinn came over and we finally got to talk about the letters from Warren Harding to Zara Tomassi and I told him about Lucky Montgomery.

The evening was just getting started.

FIFTEEN

Dinner later that evening—Persia's homemade chicken potpie—was a quiet occasion, with Eli, Quinn, and me talking about the work still to be done around the vineyard and Hope entertaining us with stories about her Barbie doll's life as a circus performer, which seemed to involve mostly hopping up and down. Afterward, Quinn and I did the dishes while Eli put Hope to bed. We were nearly done cleaning up when Eli came back into the kitchen, bundled up to go outside.

"Are you staying in tonight?" he asked. "I was wondering if you'd mind baby-sitting Hope."

It was a rhetorical question. He was definitely going out and he already knew I was staying home, since Quinn was still there.

"Yes to staying here and no, I don't mind baby-sitting," I said. "Can I ask where you're going?"

"Just meeting a friend for a quick drink at the Inn." He tried to look me in the eye, but his glance skittered sideways and he and Quinn exchanged looks. "I'll have my phone on, of course. Call if you need me."

"Sure," I said. "Have fun. Does Hope know you're going out?"

"Ah . . . not exactly. She'll be okay, though. She was nearly asleep when I left her. Thanks a bunch, Luce. Don't wait up. I might be late." He gave me a quick kiss on the cheek and bolted.

I hung the damp dish towel over the oven door handle and said to Quinn, "Are you going to tell me what that was all about?"

Quinn reached for the half-filled bottle of Cab that we'd been drinking at dinner. "Refill?"

I nodded. "You were saying?"

He got two clean wineglasses from a cupboard. "He met someone. And before you get on your high horse, I only found out because I was having a drink the other night at the Inn when they walked in. Will Baron was there, by the way."

"Don't change the subject. Eli met someone and you didn't tell me?"

"Of course not. Where do you want to read these X-rated letters? The parlor?"

I nodded. "They're upstairs in my study. I'll get them if you'll make a fire. And why not?"

"Why not what?"

"Why didn't you tell me about Eli's new girlfriend?"

"Because it's not my place and you know it. Eli should have told you."

I gestured to the doorway through which my brother had vanished. "Well, you saw that. He didn't."

"Maybe he didn't want to upset you, since he doesn't have the best track record with women. Brandi." He shook his head in disgust. "Man, I wouldn't have lasted thirty seconds with her."

"Too late for that. I am upset. He should trust me, you know? I mean, he's living here, he and Hope . . ." I looked up at the ceiling. "I give up. Whatever."

"Lucie." Quinn put the wineglasses and the bottle on the counter and pulled me into his arms. "Calm down, sweetheart. He'll tell you when he's ready. You know that." He kissed my forehead. "Go get the steamy letters, okay? Everything's gonna be fine. I'll meet you in the parlor."

He was still tucking kindling between the logs when I came downstairs with the letters and the two photo albums, Angelica's and the Studebakers'. I set everything on the coffee table while he lit the fire.

I untied the ribbon from the letters and he joined me on the sofa, pulling his reading glasses out of his pocket. "I think it makes the most sense to read them in chronological order," I said. "Oldest first, when Zara was still living in Washington, before she got married. You read one and I'll read one; then we'll swap."

Considering their racy content, I thought it was a good idea for him to read them to himself. I had skimmed the letters earlier, but now I took my time and read more carefully. Every so often, I could feel Quinn squirm next to me.

"I told you they were explicit," I said.

"I feel like I'm reading porn." He refilled our wineglasses. I'd hardly touched mine, but he'd drained his. "You didn't tell me Warren Harding had a name for his—" He turned red.

"Are you referring to Mount Jerry?"

"Well." He scratched the back of his neck, still beet red. "Yes, actually, I am. I mean, who does that?"

"Obviously he did. I wonder if Zara's letters to him were as graphic. It must have been quite a torrid correspondence, not to mention a passionate relationship. Listen to this: 'I cannot wait to bury my face in your milky breasts.'"

"Okay, okay." Quinn shook his head, still

200

flustered. "I guess Zara's congressman father introduced her to Harding before she married Johnny and that's when they started seeing each other. But then she moved to California and he was in Washington. So they must not have slept together after that. Just wrote letters about how crazy they were about each other and how great the sex had been. He was poetic, I'll give him that."

I picked up the last four letters, which I had set apart from the others. "These are from someone named Izzy. Either her sister or a friend. I read only one of them and it's a lot of gossipy stuff, written after Zara married Johnny. Whoever she was, she knew about the affair."

He held out a hand. "Let's do this. May as well read 'em all."

"I wonder why Angelica kept them." I passed him a letter.

By the second letter, I knew the answer to that question. "Izzy knew about the baby," I said. "This was written May 27, 1923. She was planning to go out to California to be with Zara in the summer and stay until the baby was born. And don't ask me why, but she seems like a friend, not her sister."

"The one I'm reading was written earlier." Quinn sounded ominous. "October 18, 1922. Zara planned to come home for the holidays. Back to Washington for Thanksgiving and stay through Christmas and New Year's."

"She was here for the entire month of December?" I counted months on my fingers. "If she got pregnant in Washington, the baby would have been due sometime in August." I looked at him. "Oh my God. What if it really was Harding's child?"

He got up. "I'm getting that bottle of brandy I saw on the dining room sideboard. I need another drink. Want one?"

He left the room before I could answer, and I picked up the last letter from Izzy. It was dated July 4, 1923, and was unlike the others—only one short paragraph, no gossip or gushing.

> Zee, my dearest darling, you should have nothing more to do with him. I told you he would break your heart, didn't I? As you said, he and the Duchess will be staying at the Palace when they're in San Francisco, but he won't be in town for long. You mustn't even think of trying to see him, especially not in your condition—it's far too dangerous. Before long I will be with you and then I can hold you in my arms again and comfort you. I so wish the child were mine, as you well know, and I am longing to see you again. Your loving Izzy

Quinn walked into the room, holding two glasses and the bottle of brandy. He took one look at my face. "What?"

"Pour first. Then read."

After he poured our brandies, I handed him the letter. A moment later, he said, "It almost sounds like they were—" He set the letter down.

"Lovers?"

"Maybe." He looked around the room as if searching for the nearest exit so he could bolt through it. "I mean, why else would Izzy wish the child were hers? Jesus, this is weird. Do you think Izzy was jealous of Zara's relationship with Harding? Maybe Izzy wanted Zara for herself."

"I don't know. But the letter is so . . ." I searched for the right word. "Possessive."

"Do you think Zara was having an affair with this Izzy? *And* Warren Harding? *And* she was married to Johnny." When I didn't answer, he said in a soft voice, "No wonder Johnny—" He stopped.

"Killed her?" I said.

"I shouldn't have said that. I have no idea what happened."

"Do you think Gino knows?"

He blew out a long breath, like air leaving a tire. "He knows something. That's why he's trying to keep a lid on this."

I drank my brandy and let the fiery taste burn my throat. Then I picked up Izzy's last letter and read it again. "I wonder who the Duchess is and what Palace in San Francisco Izzy's talking about."

"The Palace is a hotel downtown," Quinn said.

"It's one of those old-world places, and it does remind you of a palace. It's a few blocks up from the Embarcadero on Market Street. Been around since the late 1800s." He set down his glass. "You know what? Warren Harding died there. The hotel's got a scrapbook full of newspaper clippings about his death and Calvin Coolidge taking over as president. A friend of mine who worked there showed it to me once."

He picked up his phone, thumbed it on, and started typing. After a moment, he said, "I knew it. Harding was on a West Coast trip after a visit to Alaska. It was the first time any president had visited that state. He got sick while he and Florence Harding—whose nickname was 'the Duchess'—were staying at the Palace Hotel. He died quite unexpectedly."

"When?"

"August 2, 1923."

"Kit e-mailed me Zara's obituary." I reached for my phone and found it. I enlarged the screen and read. "Oh my God."

"What?"

"Zara died the next day. August 3, 1923. I wonder if she saw Harding when he was in San Francisco. Maybe Johnny found out and he was so furious, he . . . did something about it."

"No." Quinn sounded adamant. "She was about to have a baby. Maybe Harding's baby. You think a woman in her condition would take off on her own, make the trip from Calistoga to San Francisco, especially back in those days, when it took a lot longer to travel?"

"Izzy could have gone with her."

"Izzy didn't want her to go, according to the letter." Quinn reawakened his phone and started scrolling. "The story about Harding's death is pretty murky. After he died, Florence Harding refused to allow an autopsy and there was talk that maybe she got so tired of her husband's shenanigans that she might have poisoned him."

"Good Lord. I didn't know that."

"It was disproved later, obviously. If the First Lady had murdered the president, every school kid who studied American history would remember something like that. But still, a lot of stuff was swept under the carpet. And it's true Florence Harding refused to allow anyone near Warren after he died. She had him embalmed and then she burned loads and loads of his letters and papers after she got back to Washington."

"Like Angelica did with Zara's things," I said. "I wonder if that was a coincidence."

"I don't believe in coincidences," Quinn said. "I wonder if Gino knows about these letters."

"I doubt it. I think he would have said something."

"He wanted Angelica's family photo album, remember? Maybe he thought he'd find something tucked away in there." He slid the album over and picked it up, setting it between us on our laps. As in the album Mick had inherited from the Studebakers, the photos were labeled, but Angelica had also added the dates they were taken.

"These look like happy family pictures from the early days, after Johnny and Angelica were married." Quinn turned pages quickly. "That's Gino's father and my grandmother." He pointed to two dark-haired, chubby children who sat on their parents' laps, serious expressions on their faces as they stared at the camera.

He started flipping faster. "These are all of the Tomassi clan after Zara was airbrushed out of the family. We won't find anything about her here."

He closed the album and started to set it back on the coffee table, but the pages, which were laced together by a slender silk cord, suddenly shifted and their weight caused them to fan out, as if they were going to tear. Quinn caught the album in time, but a newspaper clipping fell out and landed on the carpet. I picked it up and unfolded it.

It was the front page of the August 3, 1923, *San Francisco Chronicle.* The headline, of course, announced the death of President Warren Gamaliel Harding, the twenty-ninth president of the United States, who died of "a stroke of apoplexy" at 7:30 in the evening of August 2 in San Francisco, after traveling to Alaska and the western states on a "Voyage of Understanding." The article went on to say that while the president had been unwell, no one had expected that he was so seriously ill; in fact, he had received visitors in the hotel's eighth-floor Presidential Suite, where he was staying with Mrs. Harding.

Quinn drained the last of his brandy and set his glass on the table. "Maybe you were right and Zara was one of his visitors."

"I'm afraid there's more." I reached for Mick's album. "There's something else I need to show you."

He gave me a look, as if I'd just asked him what he wanted for his last meal before the execution.

"Zara was here. In Middleburg." I slipped the studio pictures of Zara as a young woman out of the envelope and showed them to him. "You should see these first. They were with the letters in Angelica's trunk. Zara, as she was."

I waited until he had studied them before opening the album to the page with her sitting flirtatiously on Harding's lap. "And here she is at a party at the Studebaker place in the 1920s."

I heard his breath catch as he took stock of his great-grandfather's first wife. He whistled softly and said, "Gino was right. She was a knockout."

"I wonder if one of the other women in the picture is Izzy," I said. "Too bad we don't know anything about her, not even a last name. And none of her letters has a return address, just a Washington, D.C., postmark."

"Yeah." He seemed to be only half-listening.

"Hey," he said after a moment, "the woman in the back row, second from left."

He had just zeroed in on Lucky. I stopped breathing as he looked more closely at her picture, then turned his head and stared at me.

"Her name is Lucy Montgomery," I said before he could ask. "But everyone called her Lucky. She was Leland's great-aunt, a real free spirit who lived all over the world, which is why he adored her. My mother used to say they were cut from the same bolt of cloth."

"Your father's great-aunt knew Zara. And Warren Harding." He sounded like someone had just knocked the wind out of him. "And you could be her identical twin."

He stared hard at me again, as though he were trying to imprint Lucky's face over mine, see if there were any tiny differences between the two of us, or maybe this was some kind of crazy Photoshopped prank and it was really me after all.

"I recognized Lucky when I saw the album at Mick's house yesterday. But I didn't realize the woman on Harding's lap was Zara until this morning, when I found the other pictures of her. Of course, she was younger then," I said. "And you can't say for sure Lucky and Zara knew each other just because they were at the same party."

"Why not?"

"Because Warren Harding was probably the most famous guy there, and who wouldn't want a photo op with him? 'Look, Ma, me and the president.' Just like today, except now it would be someone's camera phone and a group selfie posted on the Internet two minutes later."

"Maybe."

"Lucky was visiting her family, my family, who lived next door to the Studebakers, so it would have been logical for her to be at that party. Who knows where Zara was staying, maybe with her family in Washington, maybe with Izzy. And we know where Warren Harding lived."

"What are you getting at?" he asked.

"That neither of us knows if they were friends or just showed up together in a photo. I think the key to the puzzle is Izzy. Who was she?" I pointed to the picture. "Maybe she's right here smiling at us. Maybe Gino knows who she is."

"Maybe," he said. "And believe me, he's got plenty of explaining to do when I get hold of him."

"You're going to see him again?"

"You bet I am." He tapped the letters. "Leverage. Now I've got some leverage over him."

"Do you think he'll tell you the truth?"

"He'd better not lie to me this time, or I'll make him sorry he ever showed up here."

That sounded like something Gino would have said, and now I wondered if there was more of the Tomassi side of the family in Quinn than he admitted. Because his threat sounded an awful lot like *omertà*.

SIXTEEN

Quinn called Gino after that—it was going on eleven—and, as expected, his phone went to voice mail, since he was probably still at the White House dinner. He left a noncommittal message, asking Gino to return the call anytime and saying he had new information "concerning the matter we were discussing yesterday." Plus, he had a few questions.

It all sounded very matter-of-fact, no hint of what we'd uncovered.

"What do you bet you get a return call as soon as he listens to his messages?" I said. "Maybe he'll even call back tonight."

"Wouldn't surprise me if he did. I'm convinced Gino knows what really happened to Zara. He'll want to know what we found out, deal with it, and get control of the situation as soon as possible." He reached for the bottle of brandy again and held it out to me.

"I've had enough," I said. "Actually, we've both had a lot."

He filled his glass anyway. "I'll pay for this tomorrow, but right now I don't give a damn."

"Quinn—"

The logs on the fire suddenly pancaked into a heap, sending a shower of sparks up the chimney.

He got up and took the poker, prodding the glowing wood so the fire would burn more evenly before it finally died down. Then he sat down and pulled me to him.

I laid my head on his chest and listened to the slow, steady beat of his heart. He tilted my face for a kiss. It had been a while since we'd kissed like this, deep and slow and sweet. Too long.

"I don't want to talk about Gino anymore. What're you wearin' to the party Saturday night?" he asked as I felt him relax against me. His mouth was next to my ear and his breath was hot with brandy. He had started to slur his words. "Do I hafta wear some Roarin' Twenties gangster suit?"

Mick had asked me practically the same question when he asked me to be his date.

"We can talk about that later," I said. "Not tonight."

He mumbled something incomprehensible and turned so his other arm lay across my waist, trapping me like a prisoner. Thirty seconds later, his eyes were closed and his brandy glass started to tilt. I extricated it from his hand before he dumped brandy on the sofa, and he murmured something else I didn't understand.

I set the glass on the coffee table as the front door opened and closed. A moment later, Eli poked his head through the doorway and gave me the what's-up look. I put a finger to my lips, untangling myself from Quinn and letting him slump over on the sofa.

I grabbed the bottle and our glasses and joined Eli in the foyer. He took one look at the bottle and said, "Did you two really polish off half a bottle of brandy tonight? Plus the dinner wine? What's going on? Jeez, Luce, it's not like you to get wasted, especially on a weeknight. Or Quinn."

"Nothing's going on, and I only had one glass of brandy."

He followed me into the dining room, where I set the bottle back on the sideboard, and then we went into the kitchen, where I left the glasses in the sink.

"Quinn looked like he was down for the count," Eli said as we climbed the back stairs to the second floor. "I presume he's staying over?"

"I'm going to get him a quilt from the hope chest so he doesn't freeze when the thermostat drops to sixty for the rest of the night. It's even colder downstairs than upstairs, but I think he's better off sleeping where he is."

"Is everything all right with you two?"

There were a million ways to answer that. "Everything's fine."

He gave me a disbelieving look and said, "Right. Is Hope okay?"

"An angel. How was your evening with your friend?"

"Fine," he said. "Very nice."

We said good night and he went to check on Hope. Quinn didn't stir when I moved his legs off the floor and placed them on the sofa before laying an old Flying Geese quilt over him. Then I tidied up the letters and the photo albums and put them in a drawer in one of the side tables next to the sofa.

After that, I went back upstairs, got undressed, and climbed into bed. Frankie's copy of *The Great Gatsby* was on my nightstand. I picked it up and opened it to chapter 1, page 1.

> In my younger and more vulnerable years my father gave me some advice that I've been turning over in my mind ever since.
>
> "Whenever you feel like criticizing any one," he told me, "just remember that all the people in this world haven't had the advantages that you've had."

I had nearly forgotten the plot, but it wasn't long before I was completely engrossed in the story of working-class Jimmy Gatz who reinvented himself as the fabulously wealthy Jay Gatsby to impress a woman he was desperately in love with.

The last thought I had before I fell asleep was how complicated life can be when you fall in love with the wrong person. Like Zara Tomassi and Warren Harding.

· · ·

By the time I came downstairs the next morning, Quinn was already in the kitchen, cooking up a storm. Though he looked like something someone had forgotten to shoot, he'd made coffee and was busy flipping eggs and a couple of mystery ingredients in a skillet.

"Good morning," he said. "You're just in time for breakfast."

"What are you making?"

"Omelet surprise. I found the odds and ends in your refrigerator and put them all together. I hope you're hungry. The only milk you had was chocolate."

I stared into the frying pan. "I never heard of adding macaroni and cheese to an omelet. Or soy sauce." I picked up the bottle. It was nearly empty.

He kissed my hair, still smelling rough, and said, "I'm sorry about last night. I think I had too much to drink."

"You said so last night and that it was because of all the family stuff you're dealing with." I went over to the coffeepot and poured myself a cup while he got two plates from a cabinet. "We could talk about it, you know. You don't have to keep it bottled up like the Great Sphinx."

"Thanks, but I don't need therapy. Just Gino out of my life. Then I'll be fine."

That's how he was. Bury everything deep inside

214

and immerse himself in work. I sipped the coffee and coughed. He'd made his usual rocket fuel brew.

"I wonder when you'll hear from him," I said.

"Gino? Three A.M." He put our plates on the worn oak table. "Come and get it."

"Pardon?" I sat down and he joined me.

"He called at three A.M., when he got back to the Hay-Adams after carousing with a bunch of *paesans* from the old country once the White House dinner was over. He sounded a bit in his cups. You want ketchup?"

"Uh, no, thanks." I wondered how he could tell Gino was drunk, since he would have been fairly inebriated himself. "What did you say?"

"At that hour? I told him something had turned up in Angelica's trunk that he'd be interested in looking at, more than the photo album, and that he was welcome to drive out here and I'd show it to him."

"What did he say?"

"He said he needed to clear his calendar in the morning and that he figured he could be to Middleburg by ten-thirty or thereabouts, so I told him to meet us at the Goose Creek Inn. If he couldn't make it, let me know. Otherwise, we'd see him there."

I was glad he'd said "we." I wanted to be in on this, too.

"Your omelet is pretty good," I said. "And the

Goose Creek Inn doesn't open until eleven-thirty—for lunch."

"Sticks to your ribs, and I know it doesn't open until eleven-thirty. After Gino stopped by on Monday, I got questioned six ways from Sunday by everyone around here, all wanting to know if I was planning to quit and move back to Napa because he'd offered me a job. Plus, as you so helpfully informed me, Gino stopped by the General Store to get directions to the winery from Thelma, the Mouth That Roared, and now she and the Romeos have been busy getting out the word that Gino Tomassi of the world-class Tomassi Family Vineyard paid me a visit," he said, stabbing the air with his fork to emphasize each word. "To avoid being the number-one topic of conversation around Thelma's coffeepot this morning, I texted your cousin at three-ten A.M. and asked if she'd be willing to let you, me, and another person meet privately at the Inn."

One of the reasons the Goose Creek Inn was so popular was my cousin's well-known reputation for discretion. Washington power brokers who dined there over the years knew she'd whisk them away to a table in a secluded corner or a special room when they showed up with their "secretaries" or "nieces." Dominique probably knew more secrets than the CIA and FBI combined about who was seeing whom on the side. But she also knew how to keep her mouth shut and guarantee the privacy of her famous guests, which is why they kept coming back.

"Did you really text Dominique at three in the morning?" I asked.

"You bet I did. She keeps worse hours than Gino does. She texted right back and said no problem, just knock on the front door and someone would let us in. No one will see us or know we're there and we'll be gone before the place is open."

Quinn had finished breakfast and was long gone by the time Eli came into the kitchen at eight o'clock, a trace of arctic cold clinging to his clothes.

"It is so cold, your words could freeze in little speech bubbles," he said, setting the *Washington Tribune* on the table. "I don't remember a winter this bad."

I pulled the paper over and looked at the front page. The lead story was the White House state dinner last night. "I think the high temperature for the day is going to be twelve degrees."

I read the headlines: LA DOLCE VITA AT THE WHITE HOUSE AS PRESIDENT AND FIRST LADY HOST ITALIAN PRIME MINISTER. The subheading read "Warm Welcome in Spite of Frigid Weather and Snowstorm." Above the story was a picture of the smiling trio, the men in tuxedos and the First Lady in a stunning gown,

217

standing under the White House portico, with a caption about how *bellissima* she looked in Versace.

Eli walked over to the coffeepot and said, "I smell mac and cheese."

"Quinn made an omelet with our leftovers."

I flipped to the "Lifestyle" section, which had a more gossipy account of the evening, along with a photo gallery. I skimmed the article and, sure enough, there was a photo of Gino, dapper in a well-cut tux, walking alongside a diminutive man in the clerical attire of a bishop or maybe a cardinal—black cassock with violet buttons down the front, short elbow-length cape, wide fringed violet sash around his waist, enormous silver cross, and a violet biretta on his head. I looked down at the caption. Gino's companion was the papal nuncio.

Eli sipped his coffee. "Obviously, Quinn made the coffee, as well. I ought to bottle the rest of it so we can use it to strip floors." He got bread out of the bread box and stuck a couple of pieces in the toaster. "What's so fascinating in the *Trib*?"

"The story about the White House state dinner last night. Someday I'd like our wine to be served at one of those."

"Yeah . . . Hey, that's Gino Tomassi." He pointed to the picture. "Frankie told me he stopped by here the other day to see Quinn. She said they know each other from California. I guess this explains why he's in town."

"Yup." I closed the paper and folded it up. "Can I ask you something?"

"Shoot."

"When were you going to tell me you met someone new?"

He gave me a knowing look. "I knew you wormed it out of Quinn as soon as I left. Sasha's nice, Luce. You'll like her. I'm bringing her to the party Saturday night."

Valentine's Day.

"I'm sure I'll like her. And I'll look forward to meeting her," I said in a neutral voice. "Does Hope know?"

He gave me a nervous look. "Ixnay to that. One thing at a time. I don't want to upset her."

"So it's serious?"

"It's the first relationship I've had since Brandi walked out. That doesn't make it serious." The toaster bell dinged and he got his toast.

"I'm not prying."

"Of course you're prying. You wouldn't be you if you didn't pry."

"I'm only asking because I'm worried about Hope, how she'll take it."

He raised an eyebrow. "Is that all?"

"And you, of course," I added. "I'm worried about you, too. I don't want you to get hurt again."

"You don't need to be worried. I'm a big boy, remember?"

I set my coffee cup in the sink. "I'd better get going, or I'll be late."

"Something happening at the winery?"

"Bottling tomorrow," I said. "Don't forget."

"Sure." He spread Persia's homemade blackberry jam in a thick layer on his toast. "What about today?"

I didn't want to tell him about meeting Gino at the Inn later on.

"First thing, I'm going to drop by Foxhall Manor and check in on Faith. I'm taking her the last piece of Persia's apple pie, so do not polish it off for breakfast, under penalty of death."

"Okay, okay. Want me to wrap it for you while you get ready?"

"No, because you'll lop off a corner."

"You have no faith in me," he said. "And for the record, I'm not the only one who's not being very forthcoming. Care to tell me what's going on around here?"

He gave me a level look and I faltered. "Everything's fine. Really."

"Sure it is." He folded his arms across his chest. "You know what they say about secrets and lies, don't you? 'What you can't say owns you. What you hide controls you.' "

"I'd better go," I said. "I'm going to be late."

I parked next to a blue Toyota with a dented bumper in the parking lot at Foxhall Manor. It looked a lot like Skye Cohen's car. Sure enough, I ran into Skye in the lobby, on her way out. She was carrying two small Japanese porcelain table lamps, one in each hand, like they were war trophies.

"Can I get the door for you?" I asked.

"Thanks," she said. "A friend of my grandmother's who lives here told me they were getting ready to give these away. Nice, aren't they?"

"Very. What do you mean 'give them away'?"

"You know they have kind of a thrift shop in the basement, don't you?"

"I didn't."

She nodded. "The Manor tries to sell whatever furniture people give them when someone dies or donates something. The profits go toward their medical center. Anything still hanging around after six months gets donated to charity or tossed, since they run out of space. So we pick it up for Veronica House to furnish homes for some of our people."

"What a good idea."

"I'm also taking a dining room set and a sofa," she said. "But they're being delivered straight to the new condo we're furnishing. I met a guy whose wife interviewed my grandma a few weeks ago for a newspaper article. He's got a big truck and he's doing it for us real cheap."

"Are you talking about Will Baron?"

She blinked, surprised. "How did you know that? You know Will?"

"I do," I said. "And I know his wife. Where does he get the truck?"

"Oh, MacDonald's Antiques lets him use it. He just drives the furniture to where we need it. Our guys take care of loading and unloading."

I wondered if Mac knew about Will's moonlighting, and then figured he didn't, because Mac kept a close eye on expenses. He wouldn't like paying for gas and the extra wear and tear on his truck just so Will could pick up some additional money on the side, even if he was helping a local charity. Then I decided none of this was my business.

"That's great," I said. "I'd better be going."

"Sure," she said. "Be seeing you."

I held the door and she left.

"I'm positive it was a man I heard in Roxy's apartment," Faith said a few minutes later when I was up in her apartment and she was greedily wolfing down the last slice of Persia's home-made apple pie. "It wasn't the television."

"How can you be sure?"

She gave me a look, like I'd just asked the world's dumbest question. "Because if it was the television, everyone would have been shouting." She raised her voice to make sure I got the message. "Roxy was the only one who was shouting. *He* was trying to calm her down."

"Oh," I said as someone knocked on her door. "Shall I get that?"

"It'll be the maid. Yes, please."

A sturdy young Hispanic woman in a pale blue uniform stood in the doorway, next to a well-equipped cleaning cart. "I come to clean," she said with a heavy accent.

"Pilar," Faith called to her, "can you please come back in half an hour, after my guest leaves?"

"Of course." Her head bobbed up and down. "I go cleaning next door. Then I come back."

She left and I went back to Faith. "Do you have the same maid every day?" I asked.

"Yes. Pilar does a good job."

"If she was the one who left your door ajar the day Roxy had her visitor, maybe she ran into him in the hall on her way back to your room."

"I don't think so. She didn't come back until after they'd left."

"Then perhaps she heard something as she was leaving."

"She speaks almost no English. I doubt she'd have understood."

I took Faith's plate, which she'd scraped clean, into the kitchen. "Well, Mac says it wasn't him," I said as I washed it. "Do you want another cup of tea?"

"Yes, please. Did you actually ask him?" Faith sounded horrified. "Good Lord, Lucie."

"How else was I going to find out?"

"What did he say?"

"What you'd think he'd say. He wasn't happy with me for asking why Roxy was upset and he said it wasn't any of your business. Or mine."

Faith sat up in her chair. "Roxy was my *friend*. I was worried about her."

"I know. That's why I asked." I went back into the living room. "What about Roxy? Did she say anything to you after that argument? Even something that didn't seem significant at the time?"

She lifted her hands from her lap and let them fall again. "If I knew, I'd tell you. But she was upset, I can tell you that."

"What did she talk about?"

"Well, family. I remember she said your flesh-and-blood family are the only people in the world who are never supposed to let you down. With everybody else, it's optional." Faith's mouth twisted in a grimace. "Of course, now I understand why she said it, regretting not being there for her daughter and granddaughter."

"That's so sad."

Faith nodded. "Well, at least now we know it wasn't Mac who upset Roxy," she said. "But it *was* somebody. And I'm still counting on you to find out who it was."

"I know," I said.

Mac had more of a reason to be arguing with his aunt than anyone else did. If it wasn't him, who else could it have been? Someone from one of Roxy's many charities who felt passed over by the new will? And since many of them were local organizations I wondered if it would turn out to be someone I already knew.

SEVENTEEN

Pilar's supply cart was parked outside the apartment next to Faith's and the door to Roxy's apartment was wide open. The place had been cleaned out and the muffled sound of a vacuum came from a back room. The hall was deserted and I knew I wasn't going to walk away without taking a look around. Anyway, I wanted to talk to Pilar.

The nail holes on the walls where Roxy's paintings and photographs had hung were still there, along with matted-down furniture indentation marks in the plush wall-to-wall carpet, except for one set of shallower marks near the entryway, as though someone had moved something recently. The vacuuming continued, an asthmatic, dull whine. As in Faith's apartment, there was a coat closet in the little foyer. I stepped through the doorway and pushed open one of the louvered doors. The closet was empty except for an iron on the top shelf.

Roxy's kitchen was larger than Faith's, but, like

hers, it was adjacent to the sitting room, a half wall with a long marble counter atop it that looked like a bar. Pilar was still vacuuming, so I went into the kitchen and checked the cabinets and drawers, which were all empty. The vacuum cut off and a few seconds later Pilar entered the sitting room. She gave a startled yelp when she saw me. Then she realized who I was and composed herself.

"Why you here?" she asked in a severe voice.

"I'm sorry, Pilar," I said. "I didn't mean to frighten you. You remember me, don't you? I was visiting Mrs. Eastman. I knew Mrs. Willoughby, too."

"*Señora Willoughby murió*," she said, frowning. "Nobody here. You no here. You go." If she'd had a feather duster, she would have shooed me away with it.

Faith had said Pilar spoke almost no English, but I still wanted to ask her about the argument Faith had overheard. "I'll go," I said, "in a minute. First I'd like to ask you something."

She eyed me warily and her gaze kept flicking to my cane. I wasn't getting far with her.

I pointed to the cane. "An accident. Car. *Coche.*"

"*Lo siento.*"

The stilted conversation probably hadn't done much to build trust between us, especially since she'd caught me snooping, but she'd said she was sorry about my accident, so I plowed on. "Do you remember a day—Tuesday—right before

Mrs. Willoughby died when someone visited her and she had an argument with him? Two men, maybe one waiting in the hall?"

Pilar gave me an uncomprehending look. "I don't know," she said.

I had a feeling what she meant was that she didn't understand.

"*Dos hombres. Aquí. Con Señora Willoughby. Martes.* Two men here with Mrs. Willoughby on Tuesday. Before she *murió.* Before she died."

She shook her head. "I don't know," she said again. "You go. I must work. I no want trouble you here."

"Of course," I said. "I'm leaving right now." I reached for my purse, which was slung over my shoulder, and unzipped it, pulling out the leather case that contained my business cards.

She was still watching me, a suspicious look in her dark eyes. I took out a card and held it out to her. "If you remember anything about those men, please call me, okay? Lucie. *Me llamo Lucie. Mi amigo Quinn habla español muy bien.* He speaks Spanish. Very good Spanish. You can talk to him if you call, okay?"

"No," she said. "I no talk. Nothing." She folded her arms across her chest. "Now you go or I call my boss."

"Okay," I said. "I'm going. Have a nice day, Pilar."

She stood there without moving and watched

me walk out the door. But as I turned the corner, I tucked my card between some folded towels in her cart, where she'd be sure to see it. I had a feeling she knew something. Either she'd heard the argument or she'd seen Roxy's visitor. Maybe she'd even recognized him.

It was a long shot.

But right now, it was the only one I had.

The Goose Creek Inn sits on the banks of the creek that gave it its name, tucked into the bend of a winding country road just outside Middleburg. If you aren't expecting it as you come around the sharp right-angle corner, it seems to appear out of nowhere, the way children in fairy tales happen upon the house they've been searching for in the middle of the enchanted forest. In spring, the flowering cherry and dogwood trees that surround the Inn make it seem as if the pretty half-timbered building is floating on a pink-and-white cloud. But on a bitterly cold February day, the tree limbs were bare and stark, and the snow, glittering like crushed diamonds in the brilliant sunshine, was piled high around the edges of the gardens and the gravel parking lot, where a plow had dumped it. The place looked homey and welcoming as a curl of white smoke puffed out of a chimney into the bright blue sky.

Quinn's Camaro was already parked near the entrance, but it was the only car that was there when I pulled in just before 10:30, so Gino hadn't arrived yet. The front door was locked, so I knocked, and a moment later my cousin answered.

I stepped inside to cheery warmth and the smells of lunch being prepared. We exchanged kisses on both cheeks in the French way, and I thought I smelled a faint odor of cigarette smoke. She looked dragged out and tired.

"Thanks for letting us have this meeting here," I said. "What in the world were you doing awake at three in the morning? Quinn said he texted you and you answered right back."

She gave me a wan smile. "My White House interview is tomorrow. They've asked me to prepare a meal for the First Lady and her staff. *Mon Dieu*, I'm driving myself crazy trying to figure out what to make."

"Your interview is tomorrow?" My heart gave a little flutter. "As soon as that? Then they'll let you know?"

Of course they would hire her, give her the job as White House executive chef. They'd be crazy not to. She'd come up with something brilliant and amazing, as she always did, and everyone would be completely wowed.

She nodded and held out her hand for my coat and scarf. "I only found out yesterday afternoon," she said as she hung my things in a cloakroom next to the maître d's stand. "I suppose they want to see how creative I can be on short notice.

Preparation for the way it can be every day at the White House."

"You'll knock 'em dead," I said, then realized what I'd said. "I don't mean literally, of course. Anything you make will be fabulous."

She smiled. "*Merci, chérie.* Quinn's in the bar and there's a fire in the fireplace. If you ask me, he looks like death hungover."

"He probably feels that way, too."

"I asked Hassan to take care of you. Don't worry, he's very discreet, I assure you. He wouldn't be my headwaiter if he weren't. He took one look at Quinn and immediately brought him an espresso." She gave me a sideways look. "Quinn told me the third guest is Gino Tomassi."

I nodded. "He was at the White House last night, a guest at the state dinner with the Italian prime minister. Quinn . . . um, knows Gino from California."

"I'd like to meet him," she said. "We don't serve any Tomassi wines here. Maybe we could work something out—"

"Dominique?" A woman wearing a chef's toque poked her head around the corner. "Can you come right away?"

She nodded as someone knocked on the front door. "That'll be Gino," I said.

"Come get me when your meeting is finished, so I can meet him," she said. "Maybe he and I can do business."

She disappeared and I answered the door. Gino gave me a cool look as I let him in. "I wasn't expecting to see you here," he said. "What's this about?"

"Nice to see you, too," I said. "Quinn's in the bar. We'll have complete privacy there. The Inn doesn't open for an hour. Follow me and you'll find out."

Quinn was sitting in a high-backed chair that faced the fire, reading the newspaper. When we walked in, he got up and folded the paper in half, but not before I saw that it was the "Lifestyle" section of the *Washington Tribune*, with the article mentioning Gino.

"Good morning, Gino," he said. "I see you made it."

"You said it was important," Gino said. "So I came."

"Have a seat." Quinn gestured to two chairs that were pulled up around a scarred oak table.

They were sizing each other up like two wary animals not certain which one was going to start the fight. I hoped neither of them would bait the other.

"Dominique's sending a waiter to take our order," I said, sitting down and giving Quinn a warning glance not to drop any bombshells before we got that out of the way. As if he'd been listening, there was a polite knock and Hassan walked in carrying a full tray.

"I took the liberty of ordering for everyone to save time," Quinn said as Hassan set down three cups of café au lait and a basket of warm croissants with butter and jam.

Quinn pulled out his wallet, and Hassan said, "On the house. Dominique insists."

"At least let me take care of the tip," Quinn said, passing him some money.

Hassan nodded his head, a gesture of thanks. "I won't disturb you again. If you need something, I'll be in the dining room."

After he was gone, Gino said, "Let's get this show on the road." He dropped two lumps of brown sugar in his coffee and stirred it.

Quinn pulled a croissant out of the basket and tore it apart. He spread raspberry jam on one of the pieces and said, without looking up, "Why didn't you tell us Zara was having an affair with Warren Harding?"

Gino's spoon dinged the edge of his coffee cup, sloshing coffee onto the saucer. "How in the hell did you find out about that?"

"Answer the question and then I'll tell you." Quinn bit into his croissant and chewed, watching Gino.

Gino glanced at me. "No comment," I said.

"It didn't seem relevant," he said finally. "It was enough of a goddamn scandal back then as it was. But at least now you know why Angelica forbade any talk of Zara ever again. She was screwing the president of the United States."

"Was Harding the father of Zara's baby?" I asked.

"I don't know." Gino set down his spoon. He leaned back in his chair and crossed one leg over the other. "What else did the two of you find out?"

"Before we get to that," Quinn said, "who murdered Zara?"

Gino's head reared back in surprise. "No one murdered her. Her death was an accident. I told you that."

"No, you wanted us to believe that," Quinn said, licking jam off a finger. "I happen to think she was murdered. I also think you know what really happened to her."

"All I know," Gino said, "is what I told you the other day."

"Not true," Quinn said. "You know more than that."

"Tell me how you found out about the affair and I'll tell you what I do know. But don't hold your breath. It isn't much."

Quinn eyed me and I got up and got a leather satchel off the bar. When I sat down again, I pulled out the parcel of letters and the two photo albums. Gino watched in silence, a puzzled expression on his face, which convinced me he hadn't known about the letters.

"The letters are from Harding to Zara," Quinn said. "Some before she married Johnny, but most of them were written afterward, sent to Bel Paradiso. They're love letters, Gino. They're pretty explicit and there's stuff about inserting part A into receptor B, if you get my meaning. Though it's quite poetic, if you're into that sort of thing."

Gino's face reddened. "I get it."

I thought he might pick up the packet and have a look at the letters, but he didn't touch them.

"They were in a secret compartment in Angelica's trunk," I said. "I found them by accident when I was getting the album. I think they'd been hidden away since Angelica put them there. I had to blow the dust off them."

"And that's the first you knew about them?" Gino said to Quinn. "All these years the trunk was in your family and you had no idea they were there?"

"That's right," Quinn said. "What about you? You wanted to take a look at Angelica's photo album. You suspected she was hiding something, didn't you?"

He shrugged. "I wondered. But I didn't know. I guess Angelica took that secret to her grave."

"I doubt it," Quinn said. "I bet she made sure at least one person knew: Johnny. The letters would keep him in line, wouldn't they? Angelica would make sure she was always his one and only."

"Even if Johnny did know about them, what of it?" Gino asked.

"Angelica keeping those letters sounds like emotional blackmail to me," I said. "I thought you said their marriage was happy and that Angelica adored Johnny."

Gino threw me an irritated look. "She did. But the marriage was complicated."

"Have you ever heard of someone named Izzy?" I asked. "She was a good friend of Zara's, someone Zara knew from when she lived in Washington. Zara obviously trusted her, because Izzy knew about the affair and the baby. She even went to California to be with Zara when the baby was due. Angelica saved four of her letters, along with the Harding letters. She must have had a reason."

"I have no idea who you're talking about," Gino snapped at me. "I never heard of anyone named Izzy."

By now he seemed really rattled, as if Quinn and I had found the map revealing where all the unexploded land mines lay buried, discovering things we weren't supposed to know. Quinn moved the basket of croissants and got Mick's album, opening it to the Harding and harem photograph.

"Warren Harding, Zara Tomassi, and friends." Quinn turned it so it faced Gino. "I presume she was still Zara Ingrasso in that photo."

Gino folded his lips together and breathed in sharply through his nose. "Where did you get this?"

"The album belongs to my next-door neighbor," I said. "The former owners used to give parties at their home all the time."

"So Zara was here?" He sounded as incredulous as both Quinn and I had been. "In Middleburg?"

"Obviously," Quinn said. "Recognize anyone else in that lineup?"

Gino stared at me and pointed to Lucky. "She's the portrait of you."

"She's my great-great aunt," I said, as the heat rushed to my face. "I was named for her."

"I can see why," he said.

"Other than Lucky Montgomery, I meant," Quinn said.

"No. No one else."

Quinn took the folded newspaper with the story of Harding's death out of Angelica's album and opened it, laying it on top of the picture of Harding and Zara. "We found this. Angelica kept it."

Gino glanced down at it without speaking.

"Izzy's last letter to Zara mentioned that she knew Zara planned to visit Warren Harding when he was at the Palace Hotel in San Francisco, right before he died," Quinn said.

"Go on." Gino's face had turned that mottled shade of red that meant he was angry or upset. I caught Quinn's eye. We had struck a nerve. Gino knew about this, too.

"Did Zara ever make it to the Palace?" Quinn

asked. "Harding died August 2, 1923. We have a copy of Zara's obituary from the *Washington Tribune*. She died the next day."

"What are you getting at?" he said.

"What are you covering up? Who murdered Zara?"

"For the last time, all I know is what I told you the other day. She hit her head on a rock and died." He enunciated every word, as if we were dim-witted children.

Maybe he really didn't know anything else. "Did you find out anything from Zara's brother's grandson when you talked to him?" I asked.

For a moment, I thought he wasn't going to answer. Finally, he nodded. "Zara met Harding through her father, Victor Ingrasso," he said. "Her old man hated that Harding was sleeping with his daughter, especially after she was married, but he could hardly make a stink, could he, since by then Harding was the president of the United States? Besides, once Johnny married Zara, Ingrasso worked out a deal to get Johnny's wines served in the White House. It was all highly illegal, since it was Prohibition, but hell, Congress may have passed the Eighteenth Amendment, making the country dry, but they drank like the proverbial fish and goddamn hypocrites they were. Washington was a pretty wet town, if you knew where to go."

"Are you saying Johnny turned a blind eye to the

affair because he was selling wine to the Harding White House?" I asked. "Along with what he sold to the Catholic Church as sacramental wine?"

"At least Johnny got something out of the marriage." Gino sounded bitter, even resentful. "All the while Zara's making a fool out of him. I told you Zara was wild and out of control. Her death—shall we say—solved a lot of problems."

"Not for her," Quinn said.

But Gino was right. Her death had benefited a lot of people. Johnny and Angelica were at the top of the list, followed by Victor Ingrasso. Then there was Warren Harding, though by that time he was dead, as well.

"You know what?" Gino balled his napkin and threw it on the table. "I think we're done here. There's nothing more to discuss. These secrets stay buried with the family. Do you understand?"

"Only if you cooperate, Gino," Quinn said. "Because if I find out that you and Dante Bellagio have forced a sale on those two vineyards in Angwin that you're looking at, I'll sell these letters to some tabloid, I promise you, and the whole sordid story that goes with it. If Zara's death wasn't an accident . . . well, there's no statute of limitations on murder. If you want my silence, find some other land for your joint venture. You don't need to ruin other people's lives and their businesses."

Gino stood up, and I thought he was going to

go after Quinn. Instead, he picked up the letters in one efficient move and strode over to the fireplace. Quinn was across the room in three quick steps, pinning Gino's arms behind his back, but not before Gino tossed the packet on top of the blazing logs. Quinn swore and shoved Gino out of the way as I grabbed a pair of tongs from a fireplace tool stand. I knelt in front of the fire and tried to extract the letters, but the logs underneath gave way as the tongs bumped them, and the fire roared to life.

The dry paper burned in a flash, consumed by the bright blaze and disappearing with a wicked hiss. The three of us watched charred fragments float up the chimney, caught in an updraft. For a few horrified seconds, no one spoke.

When I finally found my voice, I was so angry that it shook. "How dare you? How could you do that? You had no right to burn those letters."

Gino swung on me. "Let me make something very clear. I had every right in the world to protect my family. Do you understand? Nothing and no one is going to stop me. Least of all the two of you."

"Get out, Gino," Quinn said. "I mean it, beat it, before I throw you out of here myself." He picked up Angelica's album from the table and shoved it into Gino's gut. "And take this with you. I made copies of those letters, just so you know. What I said before still stands."

He hadn't. At least I didn't think he'd made copies, though I wished we'd thought to do it. But he was bluffing.

"Let me repeat what I told you both the other day," Gino said. "Neither of you will ever repeat what you know about Zara Tomassi, Warren Harding, or Johnny or Angelica. Anywhere. To anyone. If you do and I find out about it, I will burn you both. I will destroy your business, Lucie Montgomery, make certain you never sell your wine anywhere, not even as vinegar. And Quinn, you'll be even sorrier."

"Leave her out of this, Gino," Quinn said. "You're nothing but a bully."

"I'm not scared of you," I said to him.

Gino's eyes flicked over to where my cane lay propped against a chair. "Then you're both very foolish," he said.

"Get out of here," Quinn said. "While you can still walk out."

Gino left, slamming the door so hard, my teeth rattled in my head. A moment later, the front door to the Goose Creek Inn shut with equal force. The shuddering sound reverberated through the entire building, final and absolute.

Then silence.

EIGHTEEN

Quinn came over and pulled me into his arms, wrapping me in such a tight embrace, I could scarcely breathe. The smokiness of the wood fire had embedded itself in his flannel shirt, and after Gino's disturbing departure and ugly threats, the comforting, homey scent calmed me down.

"I am so, so sorry," he said, his lips against my hair. "I never should have gotten you involved in any of this. If he does anything to harm you or the vineyard, I swear I'll kill him with my bare hands."

I slid my arms around his waist and closed my eyes. "You didn't do anything," I said. "I got myself involved, especially since I'm the one who found those letters. And please don't make threats like that, saying you'll kill Gino, okay? You scare me."

"Gino plays rough," he said. "He has to win and he thrives on being pushed or challenged. He craves it and it's what fuels him. He's a scary guy."

"You never told me you came from a family of pyromaniacs," I said with a shaky laugh. "Getting rid of the evidence by burning it. Both Gino and Angelica. My God, I still can't believe he threw those letters in the fire."

Quinn loosened his grip on my shoulders and stepped back so he could look down into my eyes. "I can fix this, you know? Gino won't touch you if I'm not around. He only cares about hurting me. You'd just be collateral damage."

"No," I said in a firm voice. "We're not having this discussion. I won't listen to you. You're not going anywhere. You're not leaving. Whatever Gino throws at us—if he even bothers doing anything—we'll handle it. Right now all he cares about is not losing Dante Bellagio and the Italian deal. He won't waste time on you and me."

"I wouldn't be so sure about that," he said. "Don't underestimate Gino."

"I don't. Believe me, I don't."

"I'll make you a promise," he said. "I won't talk about leaving unless Gino makes good on his threat and goes after you or the vineyard to get to me."

"No."

"You don't get a vote." He tilted my face and kissed me. "It's almost eleven-thirty. Let's get out of here before the place opens and the Romeos find us. We'll never hear the end of it."

"You go ahead," I said. "I need to see Dominique and break the news that Gino had to leave unexpectedly and so she probably won't be making a deal with him to serve his wines at the Inn. At least not today."

"Or any day, unless it's over my dead body," he said. "And Lucie?"

"What?"

"This business with Gino, what happened to Zara, her baby, the person who's blackmailing him . . . it's over now. Okay? You're out of it," he said. "For good."

"What about you?"

He gave me a searing look that told me he wasn't walking away from Gino, in spite of what he'd just said. That he would make good on his promise if Gino ran those two vineyards out of business.

And that scared me.

I found Dominique sitting at her desk in her office a few minutes later, studying what looked like sheaves of menus. It also looked like she had just slipped a pack of cigarettes underneath a folder.

"Gino Tomassi had to leave unexpectedly, so he can't make your meeting," I said. "He sends regrets."

She gave me an ironic look. "Lucky for you that the walls of the Inn are so thick. Even so, everyone could hear shouting, and Hassan saw Gino leave. He said he looked madder than a nest of wet hens."

"He was."

"Do you want to talk about it?"

"I'm afraid I can't. If I had known it was going to deteriorate into that shouting match, I would have told Quinn that we should meet somewhere else. Like a cave."

She laughed. "No harm done, I'm sure."

I decided to let that one pass. "Have you figured out your White House menu yet?"

She sighed. "No, but I need to decide soon. I'm running out of time, and they want me to submit a grocery list."

"Why don't you just make something you serve here? The food is fabulous."

She considered the idea. "You could be right. Maybe it's better to go with what you know rather than the devil in the deep blue sea."

"I would if I were you." I blew her a kiss. "Good luck. Will you let me know how it goes?"

"Of course."

I was halfway down the hall when I turned around and stuck my head through her doorway again. "And since my secret is safe with you, yours is safe with me. For God's sake, have a cigarette. You can quit after the interview."

"*Merde*," she said. "Everyone's a spy."

Hassan was at the maître d' station and nodded to me as I left the Inn. "I hope everything is all right, Mademoiselle Montgomery," he said.

I smiled. "No broken china or overturned furniture, so it's fine. Thank you for your discretion, Hassan."

He raised an eyebrow. "Believe me," he said, "I've seen it all."

Quinn's car was gone when I got to the parking lot. Either he'd gone back to the vineyard or he'd just taken off for a while to clear his head. Knowing him, it would be the latter. I hit the Unlock button for the Jeep as my phone rang in my coat pocket.

It was Frankie.

"Hey," I said. "What's up?"

"I hate to bother you with this," she said. "Uma Lawrence's credit card was declined. She bought three bottles of the special reserve Cab that Quinn made from the vines your parents planted. Our oldest vines. She said she wanted the most expensive wine in the house. So it was a six-hundred-and-sixty-dollar charge."

The headache that had started behind my eyes after the Gino incident now started to pulse. "Well, isn't that interesting," I said.

We see this more often than I care to admit. Bad checks, credit card fraud, even counterfeit money. It never fails to anger me, especially because we always deal with everyone in good faith—and more often than not, we can't ask them simply to return what they purchased. Usually because they've drunk it.

"I'm sorry, Lucie." Frankie sounded mad, and I didn't blame her.

"It's not your fault," I said.

Maybe it was an honest mistake. But what was surprising was that Uma Lawrence, the town's newest heiress and an overnight multimillionaire, couldn't cover the purchase of a couple of bottles of wine. If her credit card had bounced anywhere else, it wouldn't be long before word got around. Small town.

"I'm at the Inn," I said. "I'll drive by Roxy's house on the way back to the vineyard. Mac told me Uma's staying there while she's here. I'll have a chat with her, and I'm sure she'll make good on what she owes."

"If she doesn't, then get the wine back. We're not a charity."

Frankie wasn't usually this grumpy so I knew it irked her, especially after the way Uma had treated Father Niall yesterday. "I wonder if she knew the card was bad when she gave it to me," she added.

"I guess I'll find out," I said.

Roxy Willoughby's house had been built in the early 1800s, a stately two-story brick mansion with wide steps leading to a white-columned veranda, the kind of graceful antebellum estate where you could imagine Roxy sitting in a wicker rocking chair on a warm summer evening while a ceiling fan turned lazily and she sipped sweet tea laced with bourbon as fireflies danced on the lawn and the moon rose above a weeping willow that dominated her front yard.

Today in the frigid cold, it was hard to think of summer, especially because the long gravel driveway had not been plowed since yesterday's storm, so the Jeep rocked back and forth as I drove over icy ruts left by the multiple tire tracks of previous cars.

A pearl gray Land Rover sat parked in front of the house. I pulled up behind it and noticed the rental sticker on the bumper. Obviously, Uma had used a different credit card if she'd managed to rent that car. At least I knew she was there.

She answered the door on the third ring, dressed in a pair of lime green sweatpants and a matching sweatshirt, which made me think they were her pajamas. Her dark red hair was scraped in a high offside ponytail and she wasn't wearing makeup. Still, she was breathtakingly lovely.

From the expression on her face once she realized who I was it was clear she knew what I was doing on her doorstep. She wound the end of her ponytail around a finger like a corkscrew.

"Hullo," she said. "Can I help you with something?"

"You can," I said. "May I come in?"

I placed the tip of my cane across her threshold in case she got the bright idea that the answer to that question was no. At least she didn't say she was surprised to see me. She opened the door wider and I stepped inside.

"The credit card you used yesterday to make a six-hundred-and-sixty-dollar purchase for the wine you bought at my vineyard was declined," I said. "I'm sure it's some mistake on the company's end. You know how careful credit card companies are these days if you make a purchase that they don't think is really yours. Maybe you forgot to tell your bank you'd be traveling to America."

Her eyes darted back and forth as she seemed to be considering what I'd said. "Oh, my goodness, how dreadfully embarrassing. Yes, that's probably precisely what happened," she said. "I do apolo-gize and, of course, I'll settle this at once. And I shall ring my bank and get to the bottom of what went wrong."

She had said all the right things and it seemed to me she was genuinely upset. Maybe I'd been wrong and it was, after all, just an honest mistake.

"Thank you, I appreciate that," I said. "Then I can be on my way and that will be the end of it. I'm sure you've got enough on your mind as it is."

"That's very kind of you," she said. "My wallet is upstairs. I'll just fetch it. Would cash be all right?"

"Of course."

She ran lightly up the wide-planked staircase and disappeared into a bedroom at the back of the house. While I waited, I looked around. Roxy's house was laid out much like mine, the same kind of symmetry that was common in these old Colonial homes: a wide foyer, a central staircase, and four large rooms downstairs, two on each side of the foyer. Though Roxy hadn't lived here for the last year and a half, Mac had moved in, and I reckoned the place looked exactly as she'd left it—furnished with fine Early American and English antiques—with the exception of whatever she had taken with her to Foxhall Manor.

Uma had obviously made herself at home, and I hope she'd clean up the opened cartons of Chinese food that sat on the enormous inlaid mahogany dining room table before they left grease stains on the beautiful old wood and Mac found out about it. Two of the three bottles she'd bought of Quinn's Montgomery *Vieilles Vignes* Cabernet sat there, as well. A closer look and I saw they were empty. That was a lot of wine to consume in an evening. Though judging by the number of white cardboard boxes littering the table, either she ate like a horse or she'd had company.

I heard footsteps and looked up as Uma came clattering down the stairs clutching a fistful of bills in her hand. She paused mid-step when she realized my attention was directed at the food-strewn table in the dining room.

"Checking up on me?" She bounded down the rest of the stairs, a scowl on her face. "Do I need to give a full report of everything I do while I'm in this bloody town? Doesn't anyone here respect a person's privacy?"

She pronounced *privacy* in the English way, so it rhymed with *privy* rather than *private*. And sounded a lot more accusing.

I held my ground. "I wasn't doing anything other than waiting for you to get the money you owe me for my wine. Which you obviously already enjoyed. It's your business what you do here. I just came to collect an unpaid bill."

Her eyes flashed. "I'm not a lush, if that's what you're implying." She gestured to the table. "My cousin had some of my grandmother's furniture brought back here because he had to clear out her flat at Foxhall Manor, since they want to rent it again. The guy who takes care of his deliveries happened to come by with some of it yesterday evening, so I asked him if he'd care to stay for a take-away meal. We got Chinese and opened your wine."

"Will Baron," I said. "Yes, I know who he is."

"I'll bet you do," she said. "He's rather gorgeous."

I gave her a pointed look. "He's also rather married. I know his wife. She's a lovely person."

Her cheeks turned pink, but she said, "I'm aware that he's married. And his wife, Vivienne, did heaps of research on my grandmother, so over dinner Will told me stories about her, her World War Two squadron and how courageous she was." She gave an impatient shake of her head, which made her ponytail bounce like an angry exclamation point. "This isn't a very hospitable town. To be honest, I feel like some kind of pariah. Will was kind enough to stay and talk to me. I was grateful for his company."

She held out the bills between two fingers like they were contaminated. "Here. This should settle what I owe you."

"I'm sorry you feel that way." I took the money. "Maybe you just haven't gotten to know us. If you're going to be here on Saturday, why don't you come to our Roaring Twenties party at the vineyard? It's a fund-raiser for Veronica House, the local homeless shelter and food pantry that Father Niall runs. You'll meet loads of people." I paused. "Perhaps you should give us another chance."

For a moment, she seemed flustered. "I was planning to go home this weekend."

"What day are you leaving?"

"I'm not sure yet. I haven't decided."

"If you're still here on Saturday, why don't you come by? It's dinner and dancing. Everyone's dressing up in clothes from the Roaring Twenties. It'll be a lot of fun and it's for a good cause," I said. "Your grandmother was a big patron of Veronica House."

She fiddled with her ponytail again. "Yes, so Father O'Malley said yesterday."

I looked at the money in my hand. "You gave me seven one-hundred-dollar bills," I said. "I'm afraid I haven't got change. Not that I'm trying to strong-arm you, but the tickets for the dinner dance are forty dollars. Or else you can stop by the winery and pick up your change."

"Just keep it." She sounded irritated. "I really need to get back to something I was working on."

"I won't hold you up," I said. "But I hope we'll see you Saturday night."

She gave me a coy smile. "I rather doubt it. And please don't think just because you've invited me to your little affair that I'm going to change my mind about supporting my grandmother's charities, because it won't happen. I'm not Roxy, you know. I have my own interests."

I opened the front door. "Yes," I said, "I can certainly see that you aren't Roxy."

When I was halfway down the stairs, she slammed the door behind me. I got into my car, thinking that this was the second time this morning someone had banged a door after a conversation that hadn't gone well. First Gino Tomassi. Now Uma Lawrence.

NINETEEN

Frankie was in her office, eating a sandwich at her desk, when I showed up twenty minutes later.

"From Uma Lawrence." I set the money down in front of her with a little flourish. "With love. Keep the change."

"It went as badly as that?"

"I can't figure her out. At first she seemed

genuinely apologetic for the bad credit card. Then we started talking and she went on about what an unfriendly town this is, so I invited her to the party on Saturday. I told her she'd meet a lot of people and maybe she wouldn't feel so alienated from everyone. We're really pretty nice folks when you get to know us."

Frankie raised an eyebrow. "What'd she say?"

"She assumed I did it because we're trying to get her to keep supporting all of Roxy's charities," I said. "She told me it's her money now and she'll spend it how she likes."

"What a rotten thing to say. And speaking of rotten, Quinn came in this morning looking like he was loaded for bear. He said he'd be in the north vineyard, pruning." She gave me a look over the top of her glasses. "I thought you were starting to prune in the south vineyard."

We were. He just wanted to get away from everyone and take out his anger at Gino on some overgrown grapevines with a pair of secateurs.

"He's trying to get a head start over there," I said. "You know him."

She took an aggressive bite out of her sandwich. "I'll be really glad when whatever is going on around here is over," she said. "Because it's driving me nuts."

I picked up a piece of paper on her desk. It was the menu for Saturday night. "Is this the final menu?" I asked. "It looks terrific."

"We're almost there," she said in a terse voice. "But since Dominique has her interview tomorrow at the White House, I'm taking care of what's left on our list so she can concentrate on that." She caught the surprised expression on my face and said, "She told me you know about the job. In fact, you and I are the only people who do know."

"If she gets it, do you think she'll take it?" I asked.

"We talked about it. She asked me to keep what she told me to myself." She took the menu from me and scanned the page. Without looking up she said, "There are sandwiches in the kitchen, by the way. I ran out to the Upper Crust and picked them up for everyone, since they've been knocking themselves out all week for the party. I also bought butterscotch pecan cow puddles for you, since you love them."

"Thank you," I said. "For everything."

She set down the paper. "I'm sorry for that dig. It was uncalled for," she said. "And you're welcome."

My phone rang at three o'clock, when Antonio and I were in the middle of transferring last year's Cabernet Sauvignon from the barrels where it had been aging into a stainless-steel tank before the bottling truck showed up in the morning. Larger vineyards have their own on-site production line to bottle wine, but smaller places like ours have a hard time justifying the expense and space for equipment that's used only a few days a year. Instead, we hire a mobile unit that comes to the crush pad, an eighteen-wheeler with the whole works on board: an entire automated bottling line inside. And since you pay for their time in addition to a sterile facility, you need to be ready to go when they show up.

Antonio is younger than I am, in his early twenties, with the kind of rugged good looks that turn female heads. Women eye him with lust and longing, much to his girlfriend's consternation. But he is also the dutiful son who goes by the Western Union counter in Safeway every two weeks to send money to his mother and sisters in Mexico because his father is in jail. If I hadn't been here just now, he would have had the radio turned to a Hispanic station, some pulsing danceable beat loud enough to be heard above the pneumatic whine of the pump, and I would never have heard the phone ring.

Instead, I did hear it, and when I looked down, I saw Will Baron's name on the display. Maybe Vivienne wasn't going to be able to help out tomorrow and he was letting me know.

I answered it and said, "Hi, Will. What can I do for you?"

"Actually, it's what I can do for you," he said. "I was wondering if I could come by now."

255

"Uh—"

"To deliver your clock," he said. "Remember?"

"Oh," I said. "My clock."

"Don't tell me you forgot about it." He sounded reproachful. "Especially considering how much money you plunked down, cash on the barrel-head."

I couldn't tell if he was teasing or serious, but to be honest, the clock had slipped my mind completely, with everything that had happened since yesterday afternoon, when I'd bought it in Mac's shop.

"Sorry, but you caught me in the middle of something at work," I said. "Of course I didn't forget."

He seemed to accept my little fib. "One of the guys from the Georgetown store is here with me now, so we could be at your place in about twenty minutes."

I glanced at Antonio, who was switching the hose to a new barrel. After we finished moving over the Cab, we needed to get the Meritage into a tank as well, and it had to be done today. "I'm sorry, but I'm afraid I can't do it right now. Could you come after five? Or maybe another day?"

"It's going to take two people to carry that clock inside and JJ's got to get back to D.C. in an hour," he said. "Now that we've brought more furniture to the Middleburg store, the back room is filled up, so Mac wants this delivery taken care of today."

"In that case, there are plenty of people around here I can ask to help. Don't worry, I'll corral someone. So, would five be okay?"

"Well, it's not rocket science, so I guess that would work if you're okay taking responsibility for your guy," he said, though I thought he sounded peeved. "See you at five."

"I heard that, Lucita," Antonio said when I hung up. "I can help with your delivery, if you need someone. Especially if it's not rocket science."

I grinned. "It's a grandfather clock and I'll pay you. It's above and beyond your responsibilities here."

He waved a hand. "Forget the money. But you could give me some time off. My girlfriend . . . fiancée says we gotta start planning the wedding. She wants it before the baby comes."

It was the first time I'd heard him mention a wedding. "Why don't you work it out with Quinn? And you can have the wedding here, you know."

"Thank you for that. I'll tell her." He walked over to start the pump again and raised his eyes to the ceiling, as if searching for divine intervention. "But *Díos mio*, she's already making me crazy with her mood swings and staying up all hours 'cause she has to have a quesadilla. From Taco Bell." He shook his head. "What did I get myself into?"

The delivery truck from MacDonald's Fine Antiques was waiting in the circular drive outside my house when Antonio and I pulled up in our respective cars at five o'clock. Will got out of the truck and I introduced the two men.

The temperature had been dropping as the afternoon wore on and we could see our breath, puffs of white smoke in the frigid air, when we spoke.

"How about if you show me where you want this clock before we take it inside?" Will said. "So we don't have to move it half a dozen times while you make up your mind."

The flirtatious charm from yesterday had vanished, as though a veneer had been scuffed away. Just now he seemed moody and out of sorts.

"I know exactly where I want it," I said, giving him a cool look. "In the spot where the other clock used to be. Come in and I'll show you."

I opened the front door and the two men stamped their boots on the doormat and followed me inside. The house looked as serene and welcoming as an embrace, and smelled of freshly baked bread and the lavender-scented furniture polish Persia always used. The Tiffany lamp on the demilune console table and the small spotlight in the alcove above the bust of Thomas Jefferson had been lit, and the room glowed with their soft warmth. A vase of red roses and baby's breath sat next to Jefferson—Persia must have put it there earlier—and from upstairs came the unmistakable sound of Persia giving Hope her

258

evening bath, laughter and splashing water, and the two of them singing "Rubber Ducky" loudly and off-key.

Will Baron pulled off his colorful cap and looked around. "Nice place."

"Thank you. This house has been in my family for over two hundred years."

"Ah," he said, a note of disapproval in his voice, "you inherited it. I should have guessed."

"Something wrong with that?"

"No," he said. "Sorry. I didn't mean to imply there was. But what do they say? 'The rich are different from you and me.'" He gave a self-deprecating smile. "Well, different from me, that is. Probably not you."

"F. Scott Fitzgerald said that," I replied, giving him a sharp look. "Now why don't I show you where I want the clock?"

"Sure," he said. "That's right. F. Scott Fitzgerald."

I flipped a light switch and the enormous Waterford chandelier that hung from the second-story ceiling lit up the room. Persia's voice floated downstairs.

"Lucie? Is that you?"

"It is. I meant to tell you that I bought a grand-father clock yesterday," I called up to her. "Antonio and a fellow from Mac's shop are bringing it inside now."

"A clock, you say?" She leaned over the railing, drying her hands on a pink bath towel. "Well, hello there, Antonio. Haven't you been a stranger? Nice to see you."

"You, too, Persia," he said.

"Lucie," she said, "Eli asked me to tell you that he's gone out for the evening. He's having dinner at the Inn with a friend and said not to wait up. I can stay and baby-sit if you have plans, as well."

If Eli was using Persia as a messenger, then he was out with his new girlfriend again and hadn't wanted to tell me himself. "Thanks, Persia, but I'm going to crawl into bed with a book after dinner. You go on home when you're done here. This delivery won't take long."

"I'll keep Hope out of the way upstairs until you're finished," she said, and disappeared.

It took Will and Antonio only a few minutes to bring the clock inside and set it up. "The pendulum seems to be brushing against the back of the case," Will said after a moment. "The wire could be a bit bent, but I think the more likely culprit is your floor. It's probably warped, since it looks original to the house. I can level it with a shim. A small piece of cardboard would do, if you've got something handy."

"I'll take a look in the recycling bin in the mudroom," I said. "Antonio, you don't need to stay for this. I'm sure you'd like to get home. Thanks for the help."

"No problem," he said. "See you in the morning bright and early for bottling, Lucita."

When I came back into the foyer with a torn piece of cardboard, Will was standing next to the console table with his hands behind his back. For some reason, I had a feeling he'd poked his head through every doorway and checked out my home.

"I found this," I said.

He took it and fiddled with placing the cardboard under the clock case for a few minutes. Then he stood up and brushed the dust off his hands. "That should do it," he said, "but if it's not right, call Mac and he'll get someone out to level it properly."

"Thank you," I said as we walked to the front door. "I guess I'll see you in the morning."

He pulled his hat out of his jacket pocket. "Pardon?"

"Aren't you dropping Vivienne off at the barrel room for bottling? If she's still interested in helping out, that is."

"That's right," he said. "We talked about it the other night at your wine tasting. It's volunteer work, isn't it? You don't pay for this."

"We'll feed her and send her off with several bottles of wine," I said, ignoring the reproach in his voice. "So it's more like bartering. If she's willing, of course."

"She'll be there," he said. "Viv likes learning new things. She's always been that way."

I opened the door. "Great. Please let her know

we appreciate her help. Enjoy your evening, Will."

"I'm working until closing tonight at the Goose Creek Inn," he said. "Good night, Lucie."

I closed the door and leaned against it as the movement of the clock settled in a familiar way. A moment later, it sounded the full Westminster chime for the hour and then struck six times, lovely and deep.

Something nagged at the back of my mind about that Fitzgerald quote Will had brought up. There was more to it. "The rich are different from you and me."

Then I remembered.

"Yes, they have more money."

The noise downstairs woke me. Frankie's copy of *The Great Gatsby* lay open on my lap in bed and the last thing I remembered was the grandfather clock chiming ten. I'd fallen asleep with the lights on. Again. I reached over and checked my phone. Ten-forty. Probably Eli coming home from his date. I lay there and waited for him to come upstairs.

Maybe he was in the kitchen having a post-prandial late-night snack. Something to tide him over after dinner and before breakfast. If I ate at this hour, I'd have such bad indigestion, I'd never fall asleep. How did he do it?

I should have heard the creak of the kitchen

door opening and closing if he was fixing himself something to eat. Or else he should have been quietly climbing the stairs, probably with his shoes off and skipping the treads that squeaked so I wouldn't hear him.

I sat up and threw off the blankets, reaching for my robe and sliding my feet into my slippers. Something was wrong, off-kilter. I could feel it, that the house seemed to be gathering itself together against someone who didn't belong here.

Above our front door was the Montgomery clan motto, carved into the stone lintel: *Garde bien.* Watch well. Watch out for us. A warning to beware because the Montgomerys were a warrior clan, a martial clan. Even the land my house was built on had been given as a reward to Hamish Montgomery for fierce fighting in the French and Indian War.

But though there had always been guns in this house, they were all securely locked away in Leland's gun cabinet downstairs in the library. When Eli and Hope moved in, my brother and I agreed they would stay there as long as there was a child living here. We'd left the key in the same spot where Leland had always kept it: on the ledge above the door to the library, far out of the grasp of Hope's chubby fingers.

I reached for my phone. If I called someone—Quinn, maybe, or 911—what would I say? "I have a weird feeling someone is in my house"? Maybe

I should just call Eli. What a laugh when his phone would ring as he was climbing the stairs.

But I didn't think it was Eli. That was my first thought. My second was for Hope, my sweet, innocent niece and the love of my life. Nothing could happen to her. I wouldn't allow it.

I turned off my light and walked quietly in the dark to the landing, where I could look down into the foyer. The space below was wild with shadows cast by the Tiffany lamp, glowing in its corner like a lit jewel. Had I imagined that I'd heard something? It could have just been the unfamiliar sound of the clock movement settling before it chimed each quarter hour, instead of my overactive imagination.

I listened for a moment outside Hope's door until I could hear the faint sound of her deep, steady breathing. Then I went downstairs and called Eli on my cell phone.

He took his sweet time answering. "Luce? I'm on my way home," he said, sounding as if I'd interrupted something. "I was just leaving. Everything okay?"

"Hope's fine, since I know that's what you're asking. Sleeping like an angel," I said. "I thought I heard something downstairs, so I came down to check. It's probably just the grandfather clock, making weird sounds I'm not used to."

"You've got the hearing of a bat, so that's probably exactly what it is," he said. "You know, maybe we ought to start locking the front door again. We've gotten kind of lazy about it."

I walked over to the door and turned the dead bolt.

"That's because you're always running back and forth between the house and your office," I said. "And you never have your keys."

"My bad," he said. His voice sounded different now and I knew he was talking to me through the speakerphone in his car.

"Are you only just leaving? I thought you said you were already on your way home."

"Relax," he said. "I'll be there in fifteen, maybe twenty minutes max. If you're still up, we can have a nightcap."

"Fifteen or twenty minutes? I'll be up," I said, and disconnected.

It was two minutes before eleven. The back door to the kitchen was locked, but just to be sure, I figured I ought to double-check it. I had just started to walk toward the kitchen when a quiet explosion sounded from the basement. For a moment, I thought it was the thermostat kicking in to turn off the furnace for the night, but the Tiffany lamp went out like a snuffed candle and from various parts of the house electronics that had been abruptly cut off squawked in protest.

In the bleak silence that followed, I knew someone had cut the power. I whipped my phone out of my bathrobe pocket, where I had dropped it after talking with Eli, and started punching in the code to unlock it.

He came out of nowhere from deep in the shadows, a tall figure dressed in black with a ski mask covering all but his eyes. His arm came up to knock the phone out of my hand as he kicked my cane away with his boot. Before I could cry out, he grabbed me, covering my mouth with a gloved hand and twisting my right arm up behind my back so hard, it hurt.

"Shut up," he said in a guttural voice, "and I won't hurt the child. You say anything and she's next. Got it?"

I nodded and he removed his hand.

"Please don't hurt me or her," I said. "Just take whatever you want and leave. I won't call the police."

His hand slid down my side, toward the opening of my robe, and I tensed, waiting for what I was sure he would do next. Instead, he yanked on the belt, untying it and pulling it from the loops until it swung free.

Fifteen minutes, Eli had said. Twenty, max. I probably didn't have that long. My intruder frog-marched me into the kitchen in silence and complete darkness.

He knows where he's going. He knows my house.

"Lie down. On your stomach. Don't look at me." This time, I paid attention to the accent. Hispanic. I couldn't tell from what country.

I had to hold on to one of the kitchen chairs for balance, since I didn't have my cane. He bound my hands together behind my back with my bathrobe belt and then used the other end to bind my feet, trussing me like an animal.

Maybe he wasn't going to hurt me after all, just tie me up and rob me. Then I heard him unlock the kitchen door. Was he just going to leave? A blast of cold air assaulted us and he bent down and swept me up in his arms, facedown, as if he were carrying a bundle of logs.

"No," I said. "Please don't."

He dropped me on the veranda on my stomach and slammed the door to the kitchen. The sound reverberated with a terrifying finality. I tasted blood; either my nose was bleeding or I'd split a lip from that fall.

He hit me once, hard, on the back of my head. Before I passed out, I heard the crunching sound of his boots retreating on the icy snow as he walked down my garden path and left me outside in the frigid cold to die.

TWENTY

Wake up, Aunt Wucie. Please . . . pleeeeese wake up. Are you okay? You're bleeding."

I opened my eyes. My sweet niece, who had crouched next to me, was patting my cheek with one of her hands. Her other hand was smeared with blood. My blood.

"Hope." I could barely say her name. How long had I been here? I couldn't feel my limbs. "Call Daddy. My phone."

Somehow, she'd had the presence of mind to put on her winter coat over her nightgown. From her pocket, she pulled out my phone.

"You dropped it," she said. "It's dark inside. I'm cold."

The power was still out.

"The code," I said, and mumbled it. She frowned, concentrating as she typed it in and found the icon for the phone. A picture of Eli holding her on his hip showed up at the top of my list of favorites.

"Push the button, pumpkin. Call Daddy."

I heard his voice on the other end of the line, testy and impatient-sounding. Expecting me to be calling and demanding when he was going to be here.

"Daddy." Hope cut him off with bossy almost-four-year-old authority and indignation. "You come home now. Aunt Wucie is sick. She's lying down in the snow and she's bleeding."

I heard his voice rising in panic. Hope held out my phone. "Daddy wants to say hi."

She put it next to my ear. "Hurry," I said, my voice a croak. "Nine one one. I was attacked. He tied me up and left me outside. I'm frozen."

"Oh my God." Then he disconnected.

"Hope," I said, "do you know where we keep the scissors in the kitchen?"

She nodded. "I'm not allowed to play with them. Only mine, Persia says."

"You can play with them this one time. Do you think you could get them and cut this cord so I can move my hands and feet?"

Another nod. "Stay here," she said. I would have laughed if I could have.

She disappeared inside and I tried to roll back and forth, closer to the warm air I could feel coming from the kitchen. But it felt as though my mind had become disconnected from my limbs and I had no idea if I was moving or just imagining I was.

"I got them." She crouched next to me again. "What do I do?"

"Cut the belt to my bathrobe, sweetie. Make a nice cut right in the middle."

"Okay."

I heard her muttering to herself and grunting as she struggled with the unfamiliar scissors. "You can do it, Hopie. Keep trying. Two hands."

Then without any warning, my arms and legs flopped to the ground. Though they were still bound together and my arms were pinned behind my back, at least I could move.

"I did it."

"Good girl. I know you did. Help me sit up,

269

honey, okay? I'm going to roll on my side first. You push me like a big log. It's a game."

"Okay."

She was stronger than I thought she was. By the time I sat up, a car had roared into the driveway and stopped with a screech of brakes. I heard my brother yelling my name and Hope's.

"Daddy!" she said.

"Get him," I said. "Hurry."

Eli carried me into the darkened house, white-faced with shock and grief, and took me into the library, where he placed me on the sofa and bundled me up in throws from an antique quilt rack next to the fireplace.

"Sit tight," he said. "I'm going to turn the power back on. Hope, honey, you stay with Aunt Lucie."

By now we could hear the wail of sirens coming up Sycamore Lane, followed by more commotion as multiple vehicles pulled up outside. People slamming doors and talking in raised voices. Through the enormous library windows, I could see red and blue lights strobing the night sky. A moment later, the lights in the house blinked on, and suddenly the library was overflowing with noise and people; two men and a woman dressed in bulky parkas with fur-edged hoods over their navy EMT uniforms carrying medical bags, an oxygen tank, and rolling a low stretcher on wheels. I heard Eli talking to someone in the foyer, probably whoever had arrived from the Sheriff's Department, and Hope's little voice chiming in.

One of the men put a blood pressure cuff on my arm and checked my temperature while the woman knelt by my side and asked if I could tell her what had happened. While I talked, she carefully cleaned the crusted blood off my face and neck from the bloody nose I'd gotten when I'd been dropped on the wooden veranda floor.

"Where did he hit you?" she asked.

I raised a hand and touched the place where his blow had landed. "Here."

Her hands were gentle as she felt my skull, but when she came to the spot I'd indicated, I winced.

"We'd like to take you to the hospital," she said. "Make sure you don't have a concussion. You could be suffering from shock after a trauma like this; plus, you were outside in extreme weather conditions. You don't appear to have hypothermia and your temperature is ninety-seven, which is a miracle, but you should still be evaluated. Make sure you're okay."

I knew this was coming. After the car accident and the months and months I'd spent in hospitals, she would have to drag me kicking and screaming before I set foot in one again.

"I'm fine," I said. "My speech isn't slurred and my vision's fine. Except for the time I passed out, I remember everything, so no amnesia. Other than a nasty headache and a bump on the noggin from where he punched me with his fist, I think I got off lucky. I'll rest and do whatever you tell me to do, but no hospital. Please."

What I didn't say was that I wasn't going to leave my home. It would seem as if I'd be letting this guy know he'd won if I did.

The woman looked at her colleagues. "We can't force you," she said, "but we strongly recommend it."

"How about if I agree to see my doctor tomorrow if I feel worse?"

"You will feel worse. You're probably going to have a lot of bruising, especially on your face. And you've already got the start of an award-winning shiner."

"I'll put ice on it. And take ibuprofen."

"No ibuprofen, in case you're bleeding internally, which is what we're worried about."

"*Lucie.* Oh, my poor lamb." Persia stood in the doorway, holding onto the doorjamb with one hand as if her life depended on it. Her hair was in a wild braid that hung over one shoulder and she was dressed in red-and-purple tie-dyed leggings, snakeskin cowboy boots, and a Redskins sweatshirt under her winter coat. Her eyes flashed with righteous fury. "Who did this to you?"

"Ma'am," the paramedic said, giving her a doubtful look. "A little privacy, please?"

"It's okay," I said. "Persia is our housekeeper

272

and my niece's nanny. She's family and she lives next door." To Persia, I said, "I think Eli and I are going to be up for a while. Will you take care of Hope tonight? She saved my life, you know."

She nodded, still agitated. "My little angel. I heard how brave she was. But the blood on her nightgown—"

"It's mine, only mine. Don't worry."

"I'll give her a hot bath," she said. "And I'll stay with her for as long as you need me to be here. Shall I fix you some tea first? You need to get something hot in you, warm your insides up."

Eli appeared next to her, carrying Hope, who clung to him like a little monkey. "I'll get her tea, Persia, if you'll take Hopie. And Luce, if you're up for it, there's a deputy here who wants to talk to you about what happened. Quinn's outside, too. He wants to see you."

"Yes to both," I said as Eli passed his daughter to Persia.

The female paramedic stood up and said, "We'll leave you to talk to the deputy. But I'm going to check in with you afterward, make sure you haven't changed your mind about the hospital."

"Thank you," I said. "I'll be well looked after here. And you have my word about seeing my doctor if I need to."

She gave me an I've-heard-that-before look and waited until a young dark-haired deputy wearing a heavy jacket with the Loudoun County Sheriff's

Department logo stitched on it walked into the room before she and the two men left. He introduced himself and said, "I explained to your friend that he needed to wait outside until I talked to you."

Bobby Noland told me long ago that it's standard procedure in law enforcement to question witnesses separately, keep everyone apart. The minute that two or more people get together to corroborate on their version of what happened, the story gets muddied and details start changing.

I nodded, and he said, "Do you think you could you tell me what happened? From what your brother said, it sounds like you're lucky to be alive."

He wrote down what I told him in a small reporter's notebook. When I was done, he said, "My partner and I checked your doors and windows for signs of forced entry and didn't find anything. Your brother tells me you leave your front door unlocked most days and even at night. My guess is that he just walked in."

"We've gotten out of the habit of locking it," I said, and knew I was letting myself in for a well-deserved lecture on smart people doing stupid things. "I've lived here almost all my life and I've always felt safe here."

"You might want to get *into* the habit of locking it from now on." He gave me a stern look. "It could have been enough of a deterrent tonight to keep this guy out. Your brother says nothing seems to be missing. Either you showed up before he could rob you or he was here to find you."

I hadn't gone down that road yet in my mind, but one thing I did know for sure was that this hadn't been a random burglary.

"He seemed to know the house," I said. "And he knew Hope was upstairs . . . though that could have been because he overheard me talking on the phone to Eli before he cut the power and attacked me."

"Did he have a weapon?"

"I didn't see one."

"Can you describe him?"

"He was so bundled up in a ski parka and heavy pants and boots that I couldn't tell you much of anything about him. Everything he wore was black, including his gloves and his ski mask. I don't even know what color eyes he had. Plus, the house was dark."

He wrote all that down and I heard the hitch in his breath. I'd given him nothing to go on.

"Lucie." Eli stood in the door. "I've got your tea."

The deputy nodded and Eli came in and handed it to me. He waited until my brother had left before he said, "Any enemies we should know about? Disgruntled employees, present or past? Plus, you hire seasonal labor, a lot of 'em Hispanic. You said this guy had an accent."

I sipped my tea and warmed my hands on the mug. "During harvest, yes, we hire a lot of migrant workers. As for the people who work here year-round, almost everyone lives on the property in housing we provide. I've known them and their families for years. It wasn't someone who works here, Deputy. I'm sure of it."

"If I had a nickel for every time I've heard that, I could retire young," he said. "More often than not, it turns out the criminal has some connection with the victim. What makes you so sure it's not a present or former employee?"

"I just don't believe it could be anybody who works here now."

He raised an eyebrow and gave me a disbelieving look. "What about someone who used to work here? Any customers visit your winery and get into an argument? Has anyone threatened you recently?"

The answer to that last question was yes.

Gino Tomassi. *I will burn you both.* Except the guy who did this to me wasn't Gino. Too tall, too slim, and that Spanish accent. Someone sent by Gino? I didn't even want to think about that.

"Ms. Montgomery?" He tapped his pen on his pad. "Can you answer the questions, please? I can't help you if you don't help me."

There was no way I was going to protect Gino, but I needed to think things through and talk to Quinn before I said anything to this officer.

"We had a property manager a few years back. Chance Miller. He's in jail now. At least I think he is. I've lost track of him," I said. "And over the years we've had a couple of seasonal workers who had to be let go for one reason or another."

"Besides Chance Miller, any other names?"

"Right now I'm a bit shaken up," I said, "and I need to talk to my winemaker. He might remember the ones we had problems with better than I do at the moment. Let me get back to you, okay?"

He gave me a look that said he knew I'd ducked the question, then said, "We'll be back in the morning to take a look around outside when it's daylight. Maybe he wore special boots or dropped something when he took off. You didn't hear a car before he showed up?"

I shook my head as he flipped his notebook shut and clicked his pen on the cover like a sharp exclamation point to let me know he didn't appreciate my holding back information.

"If you think of anything," he said, "give me a call. Your brother has my card. Good night, Ms. Montgomery. I hope you feel better."

"Thank you."

He stopped in the doorway and turned around. "We'll be looking for whoever did this, but in the meantime he's still out there. If all he meant to do was give you a warning or scare you, then he did what he came for. But if he intended to kill you, once he learns he wasn't successful, he might try again. So be careful."

"Thank you," I said in a shaken voice. "I will."

"The more you help us," he added, giving me a pointed look, "the sooner we can get this guy."

Then he was gone.

When Quinn and the female EMT came into the room, I was holding an empty mug and staring out the window.

"Are you okay, miss?" the woman asked. "You look quite pale."

She took my temperature again and placed the blood pressure cuff on my arm.

"I'm all right," I said. "I'm afraid I wasn't much help to that deputy, and as he reminded me, that guy is still out there."

I gave Quinn a look that said not to say a word until we were alone. He nodded, barely a twitch of his head, and moved closer to me. I caught the overpowering scent of cologne, as if he'd dumped a whole bottle on himself, and breath mints, a sure sign that he'd been drinking before he showed up here.

The EMT gave him a knowing look and said, "Are *you* all right, sir?"

"No," he said. "I'm not. Someone tried to kill Lucie tonight, so I'm most definitely not all right."

She finished taking my blood pressure and said to me, "You'd be better off in the hospital, you know. At least for observation overnight."

"I'll be fine at home," I said. "Thank you for your concern, but I'll be well taken care of here."

She gave Quinn a look that indicated she wouldn't trust him to care for someone's pet rock and said, "It's your decision."

After she left, Quinn kissed my forehead and took my hands in his. "If this was Gino," he said, "I will kill him."

I shuddered and said, "It wasn't."

"Or one of his goons. Same thing."

"You can't go killing people. They have laws about that kind of thing," I said, and got a slight smile from him. "Do you think it could have been someone who used to work here? We have had a few bad apples over the years. And whoever was here knew the house, knew his way around."

"My money is still on Gino."

"Why me, then? Why not you?"

"To let me know he's serious. That he'll go after someone I love. It's worse than going after me."

Someone he loved. I nodded because there was a lump in my throat suddenly, and he squeezed my hands. "If he wanted you dead, you'd be dead."

"He came pretty damn close," I said. "Though you could be right. I was on the phone with Eli just before he attacked me. He probably heard me say something to Eli about seeing him in a few minutes, when he got home. So he knew I'd be rescued."

We both looked up as Eli walked back into the library. "They've all gone now," he said. "Quinn, can I talk to you for a minute?"

"Sure." Quinn got up.

"Lucie, you want any more tea?" Eli asked.

"Thanks. I'm fine."

"Sit tight," he said. "We'll be right back."

I heard them talking in hushed voices in the foyer, and when they walked into the library a moment later, I knew a plan had been hatched.

"Luce, Quinn's going to stay here tonight," Eli said, "but he's going to sleep downstairs. I'll be upstairs with my bedroom door open. Persia's with Hope. I think she finally managed to get her to sleep. We both thought you'd be more comfortable in your own bed. I'll carry you upstairs, if you're ready."

"Thanks, Eli, but I'm sure I can walk just fine."

"Don't argue."

"I love you, but I can handle this. And I'm taking a shower and getting out of this bloody nightgown before I go to bed."

Someone had propped my cane against the table in the foyer. Whoever did it must have picked it up from where it fell after the intruder kicked it away. I reached for it, and that's when I saw the envelope—white, business-size—lying on the table on top of yesterday's mail. Nothing was written on it. It hadn't been there earlier.

"Anyone know what this is? Or where it came

from?" I picked it up and tore it open before either of them could answer.

The message was spelled out with letters that had been cut from a newspaper and pasted on a piece of plain white paper.

MIND YOUR OWN BUSINESS OR ELSE

Quinn swore under his breath. "I told you it was Gino. He sent his guy to deliver a message, to let you know he could get inside your house if he wanted to. That he could get inside your *head.* You must have surprised him."

I nodded, unable to speak. Or else what?

"Gino—Tomassi? Is that who you're talking about? He attacked Lucie? Are you kidding me?" Eli's gaze swiveled between Quinn and me. "What the hell is going on here? It's about time I know, don't you two think?" He paused and said in a strangled voice, "He could have gone after Hope once he'd finished with Lucie."

I gave him a terrified look. "Don't even think it."

"Look." Quinn held out his hands palms down, like he was trying to tamp down our panic. "I'm getting the bottle of brandy and then we're going to go back into the library and we'll discuss this. Okay?"

I let Quinn do most of the talking while I lay on the sofa. As I figured, he kept it short and filled in only the essential details. By the time he was finished, it was nearly 3:00 A.M. and he and Eli had made a serious dent in what was left of the brandy.

"I'm calling Bobby in the morning. Which will be in a couple of hours," Eli said. "He needs to see that letter." He stood up and gave Quinn a coded look. "And now I think we should go to bed. Luce, I'm taking you upstairs."

Quinn kissed me good night and told me not to show up for bottling in the morning or he'd personally throw me out, no questions asked.

"I'll see how I feel," I said.

"Tie her to the bed, Eli," Quinn said.

"You heard him," Eli said. "You're not going anywhere. Besides, I'm staying here tomorrow so I can keep an eye on you."

He wrapped his arm around my waist and we slowly climbed the big spiral staircase. When we reached the top step, I heard the unmistakable sound of Leland's gun cabinet being unlocked and the squeak of a door as it opened after many months of disuse.

"Eli," I said. "What's going on?"

"Nothing," he said. "Quinn and I have every-thing covered. You just get some sleep. I'll check in on you after you have your shower, make sure you're okay."

He said good night to me at my bedroom door, and after I closed it, I went over and looked out the window, straining my eyes to see if anyone might be out there, lurking in the darkness, watching the house, watching me. I saw no one, but what I did hear was the stealthy sound of footsteps, Eli going downstairs once again.

I knew why, too.

Quinn had gotten guns and ammunition out of Leland's gun cabinet for the two of them. By now, Quinn had probably loaded both weapons.

And he and my brother were ready to use them.

TWENTY-ONE

To my surprise, I slept. My alarm clock, which I'd set a lifetime ago, before a masked intruder left me to freeze outside on my own back porch, went off as usual at 6:00 A.M.

I switched it off and turned on the light on my nightstand. The female EMT who'd treated me last night was right. I felt like the Tin Man from the Wizard of Oz before Dorothy found the oilcan.

The bottling truck would be at the crush pad in an hour and a half. Maybe if I took a hot shower and threw down a couple of Tylenol, some of the aches and stiffness would subside. What I really didn't want to do was look in the mirror. I could tell without even seeing myself that I was more ready for Halloween—without the costume— than Valentine's Day.

I made my way across the bedroom, a slow shuffle into the bathroom, and took a shower. I saved the mirror for last. The woman who stared at me was unrecognizable. No amount of makeup was going to be able to camouflage the Technicolor bruises that ran along my right cheekbone and down the side of my nose, along with my spectacular-looking black eye.

My mother had owned a pair of enormous sunglasses that she had laughingly called her "Jackie O glasses" because they covered so much of her face. After she died, I'd found them in her car and tucked them away in the top drawer of my dresser. Until now, I'd never worn them.

Quinn was finishing a cup of coffee when I walked into the kitchen. He took one look at me and my sunglasses and said, "And just where do you think you're going, Suzy Sunshine?"

"We're bottling today," I said in a bright voice, "if I remember correctly."

"Lucie," he said, "we've got enough people coming to get it done without your being there. Go back to bed, sweetheart." He came over and gently removed the sunglasses, staring at my face. "If I find the son of a bitch who did this to you, I will personally tear him limb from limb."

"What did you do with your gun?" I asked, taking the glasses back. "I heard you and Eli get guns out of Leland's gun cabinet last night."

He poured me a cup of coffee. "I made it weaker than I normally do, just for you, since I know you think I make sludge," he said, passing me the mug. "And, to answer your question, I took the bullets out and put everything back where it belongs. Eli's going to be here with you today, so you'll be all set."

"All set" meant Eli planned to be armed.

"I love you both," I said, "but I'm not going to lie in bed and be waited on. If there's anything I learned after the car accident, it's that the sooner I get up and start moving, the better. Otherwise, everything hardens into concrete. And Eli needs to lock up his gun, too. I'll tell him when he gets up."

The kitchen door swung open and my brother said, "Tell me what?" He was fully dressed, and I wondered if he'd slept that way. He took one look at my face and swallowed hard.

Quinn pointed to the coffeepot and Eli nodded.

"How are you holding up, Luce?" he asked.

"Put the gun back in Leland's cabinet, Eli," I said. "Please. We agreed no weapons in the house that weren't locked up as long as you and Hope live here."

"That was then," he said. "This is now."

"I'm not staying home today," I said. "I took a shower and a couple of Tylenol and I'm feeling better than I thought I would. Which is why I'm going to work, just like I do every day, and live my life just as I always have. This guy isn't going to win. I'm not going to let him."

"Hold on just a second, tiger," Quinn said, glancing at Eli. "Before you take on the world, you need to hang around here for a while. Bobby's coming over this morning to talk to you. It's better if you do it here, rather than at the winery, don't you think? No point upsetting the staff any more than they're already going to be once they find out. And, uh, especially after they get a look at your face."

I slipped on the sunglasses, suddenly self-conscious. Too late, I caught Eli's double take and wished I'd said something to him about where I'd gotten them before he saw me wearing them.

"What about the staff?" I asked, turning to Quinn. "We need to figure out how we're going to tell them about what happened last night, try to keep this contained. There hasn't been any crime worth mentioning in Atoka or Middleburg since someone stole the ox and the ass from the manger outside the Episcopal church at Christmas."

My phone rang in my pocket just as Quinn's phone, which he'd set on the kitchen counter, went off.

"Frankie," I said, looking at mine.

"Antonio," Quinn said.

"So much for keeping things contained," Eli said.

By the time Bobby Noland rang the doorbell at 9:00 A.M., Eli, Quinn, and I had concocted a plan for Hope to spend the day at Persia's, arranged for Antonio to supervise the bottling truck until

Quinn could get over there, and I had the house landline and my cell phone forwarded to the villa, where Frankie would tell anyone who called that everything was just fine and dandy. If they persisted, the official story was that I had stumbled on an intruder before he could rob us and he'd gotten away, but the Sheriff's Department had good leads and would soon catch the guy.

Eli answered the door and let Bobby in. Quinn and I were waiting in the foyer like an official welcoming committee. I held my mother's sunglasses in one hand, figuring it was better to get this over with, let him see me in all my black-and-blue glory, and then we could move on.

"Hey, Eli," I heard Bobby say as Eli opened the door wider and Bobby's eyes fell on me. He paused mid-step, glancing at Eli before he looked back at Quinn and me. "Looks like you went a little heavy on the eye makeup this morning, kiddo."

It was typical of Bobby, that mordant cop sense of humor, but it made me feel better that he was acting normally around me.

"I got dressed in the dark," I said, and put on the sunglasses. "What can I say?"

"Coffee, Bobby?" Eli said. "Before we do this?"

"Thanks, but I'm caffeinated up the wazoo," he said, "and I need to talk to Lucie on her own, guys."

"Actually," Quinn said, "you need to talk to me,

as well. And since Eli knows everything and he lives here, he should hear this, too."

"In that case," Bobby said, "why don't we sit down someplace and do this?"

We adjourned to the parlor, Quinn and me on the sofa and Bobby and Eli in the two wing chairs across from us on opposite sides of the fireplace. With everything that had happened, no one had cleaned the hearth from the fire the night before last, when Quinn and I had pored over the Harding love letters and the photos, so the room smelled of the faint tang of woodsmoke.

It still upset me to think those letters were now themselves ashes, but I held my tongue and didn't interrupt as Quinn told Bobby all of it: Gino's visit and the blackmail, how Gino was trying to cover up the nearly century-old death of Zara Tomassi, her baby, and the now-destroyed love letters written by Warren Harding.

When he was finished, I got the envelope with the pasted-together warning. Bobby pulled a pair of latex gloves out of his back pocket and examined it.

"You think this is from Gino?"

"I do," Quinn said.

"I don't know," I said. "I can't see Gino sitting in his hotel room dressed up in his tuxedo ready to go to a White House state dinner, cutting letters out of the newspaper and gluing them onto a piece of paper. And having it delivered by some thug who tied me up and dumped me on my porch."

"Crude," Quinn said, "but effective."

"You said the guy had a Hispanic accent," Bobby said. "What about your crew or a day laborer with a grudge? We still need to consider the possibility that it might not be Gino. Last night he was at a shindig, some political fund-raiser, at the National Building Museum in D.C. that went past midnight. A buddy of mine moonlights as hired security and he worked that party."

I caught Quinn's look of surprise when Bobby spoke about Gino's whereabouts with such precision, but I hadn't told him about how Bobby had questioned me the other day in front of Mac's shop, asking about Gino's visit to the vineyard. And his cryptic remark implying he knew that Gino and Quinn were related. To be honest, I wasn't sure how much of what Quinn had told Bobby just now about Gino was news to him, either.

"I don't know," Quinn was saying. "I still think it's Gino."

"We'll look into it," Bobby said. "Obviously."

"What about Gino's blackmailer?" I asked.

"What about it?" Bobby said. "If Gino doesn't ask for help from law enforcement, we can't go busting in on what he says is a private matter. The only time we can get involved is if someone breaks the law and we find out about it. And even then, it's not as easy as you think. Last week we answered a nine-one-one call from a woman in Leesburg, half hysterical, reporting a stabbing in her home. We show up and, sure enough, there's a guy lying on a sofa with a knife next to him, a stomach wound, and blood everywhere. You know what she says then?" He gave us a disgusted look. "Horseplay. Her husband and his brother got a little rough. Sorry to bother us over nothing. The two guys backed her up, so we left when the ambulance arrived. It was over. Finito."

"So you can't do anything?"

"Nope. At least now I know why my deputy thought you were holding back something last night, Lucie," Bobby said. "I'm going to need names from you. Anyone who worked here who might have left on bad terms, any unhappy clients. As soon as possible. In the meantime, I think Lucie and I need to finish up this discussion alone. Gentlemen, you're free to go."

"I'll be in the library, getting some work done," Eli said. "Bobby, stop by before you leave, will you?"

"I'll be on the crush pad with the bottling truck," Quinn said.

After they left, I said to Bobby, "You didn't learn one new thing from what Quinn told you about Gino. You already knew all of it."

"Now where did you get that idea?"

"You were already watching Gino Tomassi. And I know you."

Bobby stretched out his legs and crossed one ankle over the other. "Let me play devil's advocate for a moment," he said. "The letter told you to mind your own business. You and Quinn immediately jumped to the conclusion that Gino sent that message."

"Well, he did threaten us."

"True," he said. "But according to Kit, you're also looking into why my mother-in-law believes someone murdered Roxy Willoughby, aren't you?"

I hadn't seen that coming. "Oh, come on, Bobby, are you serious? I'm just trying to placate Faith, find out who might have argued with Roxy before she died. All I did was talk to Mac MacDonald. Don't tell me you think he's behind this?"

He raised an eyebrow. "Mac? No, I can't say I do. Did you talk to anyone else?"

"No—wait. Yes. Father Niall. Another likely suspect?"

He grinned. "Okay, not him, either. That's it?"

"Faith's maid. Pilar. To be honest, I'm not sure she understood what I was asking, since she barely speaks English."

"I'm just covering the bases, kiddo. It's what I do."

"Do you agree that it was probably Gino, then?"

"Gino looks good for this, but I still need a list of people who worked here, anyone who might have it in for you. How about you work on that while I have a chat with Eli? You can give it to me before I go."

By the time Bobby was ready to leave, I'd come up with a short list of the names of former employees and day laborers who hadn't left the vineyard on the best terms. Stealing, falsifying time sheets, and not knowing a ripe grape from an unripe one at harvesttime were the three main reasons we let anyone go. I gave it to him in the foyer after he finished talking with Eli.

"The work is seasonal, Bobby," I said. "These guys come and go. I doubt most of the people on this list are in the area in February."

He shrugged. "It's a place to start. You're sure this guy was Hispanic?"

"He said only a couple of words, but he had an accent."

"My men found boot prints from your back porch over to a place next to the Ruins. They ended at some tire tracks. Seems like this guy knew the lay of your land. He must have just drove out." He waved my list at me. "You keep your doors and windows locked, you hear me?"

"I will."

At the front door, he said, "Though I don't usually get involved in what goes on between you and my wife, I have been ordered to tell you that if you don't call her once I leave here, she is driving over to drag the story out of you. She says you've forwarded all your calls to Frankie."

"I'll call her," I said, adding in a half-joking way, "and she'd better not try to send a photographer if she plans to cover this for the *Trib*."

Bobby gave me a grave look. "Don't worry, no photographer, but she does have to report the story; you know that. You look like you've been to hell and back." He touched my shoulder lightly. "We're both just so glad you're okay. You're lucky, all things considered."

He left and I leaned against the door, thinking about what Bobby had said. If it wasn't Gino or some lackey who worked for him, then what had I done and whom had I angered enough to drive him to break into my house and dump me outside in the frigid cold?

And was the officer who questioned me last night right that it was someone I knew?

TWENTY-TWO

I drove over to the barrel room shortly before noon, after convincing Eli that I felt well enough to do so and that I didn't expect to be attacked by anyone in broad daylight.

"I think it's high time," Eli said, "to install an

alarm system in the house. While you were still talking to Bobby, I called a company I've worked with a couple of times. They're sending over someone this afternoon."

"That's going to be expensive, installing sensors on all the doors and windows. Maybe we just need to start locking the doors."

"We'll all sleep better," my brother said in a don't-argue-with-me voice, "with an alarm."

There is nothing quiet about bottling wine. Being in the vineyard, especially if you're alone, evokes the Zen-like tranquillity and reverential silence of a sacred place, but bottling is raucous and noisy and fast-moving. In spite of the cacophony, it's also incredibly organized. Like a circus performer spinning plates, you can't take your eyes off what you're doing, or the process comes crashing to a halt.

I knew Quinn, Antonio, and the crew would take a lunch break at noon to let everyone warm up after a morning of working outside in below-freezing temperatures, so I planned my arrival to be as near to their quitting time as possible. The first time anyone got a look at my face when I stepped onto the crush pad, I knew I'd be a huge distraction in the midst of an operation that needed to run as smoothly as a Rolls-Royce engine.

Unlike growing grapes or making wine, which

are heavily labor-intensive jobs, the process of bottling wine is totally mechanized. Wine bottles are put one by one on a narrow conveyor belt, which takes them inside the sterile environment of the bottling truck, where they end up on a rack to be steam-cleaned. Then the clean, dry bottles are filled with wine before moving on to the next station, where the cork is inserted. Another piece of equipment puts a foil wrapper, known as a capsule, over the cork and seals it; the last stations are where the front and back labels are put on, and, voilà, you're done.

After that, it's a matter of quality control, with someone checking to make sure the labels are on straight, the corks are inserted correctly, and the bottles are filled to the proper level as the they rattle by in a tidy, precise column. Then they leave the truck and travel down the conveyor belt to where they're packed in cases, upside down to keep the corks wet, by whoever is waiting outside in the cold. Finally, the boxes are sealed, labeled, and placed on a pallet, where they're eventually moved on a forklift to our bonded cellar. On a good day, with no hitches, we can bottle two hundred cases in an hour, or 2,400 bottles of wine. None of this happens without pulse-pounding rock music blaring through the sound system above the din of the truck and the clattering bottles, a sound track chosen by Quinn to motivate you, keep you moving so that you forget just how damn cold it is.

I made sure he saw me before anyone else did when I stepped outside—he was driving the forklift—and watched him signal to Antonio to let everyone inside the truck know it was time for a lunch break. One by one, they all came over to me with condolences and hugs, whispered words of concern and expressions of shocked disbelief as they took in my bruises, until I felt like I was in a receiving line at my own funeral.

"The guys and me," Antonio said in my ear, "we're going to ask around, see if anyone knows anything. I got friends who owe me favors."

I nodded. There was no point telling him or Benny or Jesús not to get involved because they'd just ignore me.

"If you find out anything," I said, "promise me you'll tell Quinn or me, and we'll get Bobby over here, right, Antonio? Let the police handle this."

Antonio gave me a heavy-lidded look that reminded me of Gino Tomassi when he'd stood in the barrel room only a few days ago and I suggested he tell the police about his blackmailer. Later I'd have to remember to ask Quinn what the Spanish version of *omertà* was called.

"*No te preoccupes*, Lucita," he said. "Don't you worry. We'll take care of this."

Frankie hung back until last, her face as white as death when she saw me. "Quinn told me what that man did to you." Her voice vibrated with rage. "I don't have any words for it, except that it's a miracle you're alive."

"The front door was unlocked, which was stupid, and Hope came downstairs and found me almost immediately, which is the reason I'm here," I told her. "Bobby dropped by the house this morning. They're looking for the guy who did it right now."

"Quinn says it might have been someone who worked for us." She gave me a worried look. "The guys are upset, especially that he seems to be Hispanic. It's almost like they feel responsible, and they're taking it personally. It's been a pretty weird morning around here."

Her eyes shifted to Benny and Jesús, who were readying boxes of empty wine bottles for the afternoon session. I followed her gaze. Antonio was somewhere in the barrel room with Quinn, probably getting the hoses ready for the next tank to be emptied.

"I'll help out after lunch," I said. "The best thing to do is get life back to normal."

"Are you out of your ever-loving mind?" Frankie gave me an incredulous look. "You'll do no such thing. We're fine. We've got enough people for this, even without you and Vivienne Baron."

"What happened to Vivienne?" I asked. "I saw Will last night when he came to my house to deliver a grandfather clock I bought from Mac

MacDonald. He said she'd be here and that she was looking forward to it."

"Nope," Frankie said. "He called the villa first thing this morning and said she was sick and wasn't going to be able to make it."

"Sick, huh?" I said. "That's funny, because when we talked about it yesterday he made a point of mentioning how we weren't paying her to help out today. Maybe the sickness was just an excuse for her to gracefully get out of showing up."

"Maybe," Frankie said. "I hope I can count on her for Saturday. She is getting paid for that. I'll call her at the end of the day and see what I can find out."

"Let me know," I said.

"I will. In the meantime, let's get some lunch. I'm starved and it's freezing."

We started to head inside as my phone rang in my pocket. I pulled it out and looked at the display. *Kit Noland.*

"You go ahead," I said to Frankie. "Kit's going to chew me out because I forgot to call her after Bobby left, and I'd just as soon get my head handed to me in private."

Frankie gave me a feeble smile. "For someone who's been through what you have, you're acting surprisingly normal. See you in the villa."

I climbed the stairs from the crush pad to the mezzanine and walked down to our office door, clicking my phone to answer Kit's call.

"Don't yell at me. Please." I opened the door and flipped on the lights. "I know I should have called. It's been a crazy morning."

"Damn straight you should have called. I have been beside myself with worry. Bobby said you look like you went a couple of rounds with the world heavyweight champion before he took you out with a knockout punch. Your right eye is practically swollen shut."

"No, it's not. He exaggerated." I lowered myself onto the sofa. Everything had started to ache again. Time for more Tylenol.

"My husband never exaggerates. If anything, he minimizes things." She still sounded outraged, but I knew it was because she was scared to death about what had almost happened.

"I'm going to be good as new once the bruises heal. At least I didn't need stitches, so there won't be any scars," I said. "Look, Bobby's going to find the guy. You know he is. His people have been all over my house and the vineyard with magnifying glasses and tweezers. They found boot prints on the veranda and traced them to a place by the Ruins, where he probably left his car."

I could hear her shudder through the phone. "Luce, you could have *died*."

"But I didn't. It was a minor miracle that Hope found me so quickly after he dumped me outside and a major miracle that he didn't stick around to wait for me to freeze to death and find her, as well," I said. "So I'm feeling lucky and blessed."

"I need to write about this for the paper," she said. "We'll use a file photo of the vineyard, so we won't be sending anybody over to your place. I'll just do it as a phone interview."

"You're going to write the story?"

"I've got a couple of people out sick. I swear to God, the flu shot this year was like getting a placebo."

"Frankie told me Will Baron called her this morning and said Vivienne was sick, too. So she didn't show up for bottling."

Kit groaned. "Please God, not Vivienne. She's my best reporter. Wait until you read her piece on the history of the women pilots in World War Two, in the Sunday magazine. She did a terrific job. I'm going to submit it for a Pulitzer; it's that good."

"Are you serious?"

"Yup. Her interviews with Roxy Willoughby and Olivia Cohen were outstanding. Mac gave me a photo of Roxy in her pilot's uniform, sitting in the cockpit of a British Spitfire, and Viv got a photo of Olivia. We're using them on the cover."

"You know," I said, "Mac said Roxy wasn't arguing with him before she died, but your mom is absolutely certain she was arguing with someone, claiming she wanted to know the truth. I wonder if it had anything to do with her baby and the affair. She changed her will not long before she died in favor of her granddaughter. If anybody would know about that period in Roxy's life, it would be Olivia."

"Viv said Olivia clammed up after she mentioned Roxy's affair during the war. I doubt she'd say anything more on the subject."

"Roxy was still alive when Vivienne talked to Olivia," I said. "Now she's not. What's to lose by trying to talk to her again if it could bring peace of mind to your mom? Look, I've been banned from my own vineyard today as walking wounded, so I'm going to call her and ask if I can drop by."

"Bobby says you look kind of scary at the moment," she said. "How are you going to handle that?"

"I'm going to be my most charming self," I said. "Beauty is only skin-deep anyway."

"Good luck with that," she said. "Lay the charm on really thick."

Skye Cohen answered the phone when I called a short while later and explained that I wanted to talk to her grandmother about Roxy Willoughby.

"I don't know, Lucie," Skye said. "Grandma and Roxy had a falling-out years ago and they never patched it up. I don't think she wants to talk about her to anyone anymore."

"Couldn't I just ask her myself? Please?"

I could hear Skye sigh through the phone. "I can

put her on," she said. "But I don't think she'll agree."

Olivia Cohen had a high, querulous voice and seemed to think I was Vivienne Baron calling back.

"Please, Mrs. Cohen, wouldn't you just reconsider? I'm asking for a dear friend who was Roxy's next-door neighbor. She's worried Roxy died with something weighing on her conscience. Whatever you say would be private, but it might help my friend to be a little more at peace."

"If you're not a reporter like the other one," she said, "then who are you?"

"My name is Lucie Montgomery," I said for the third time. "I own a vineyard."

"A vineyard?" she said, brightening up. "You mean you make wine?"

"I do."

"Is it any good?"

"It's very good," I said, surprised. "A lot of our wines have won awards."

"Would you bring me some?"

Now we were getting somewhere. "Absolutely," I said. "What do you prefer, red or white?"

"Bring 'em all," she said. "Especially the award-winning ones. And I'll talk to you about Roxy."

Olivia Cohen lived in a one-story stone cottage on Wirt Street in the historic district of Leesburg.

Frankie packed up a gift box of wine for me after I told her I was taking it to Skye's grandmother. Half an hour later, I parked on the street in front of Olivia's house and put on the sunglasses before I got out of the car.

Skye met me at the door. She had added a few streaks of red to the purple hair, and her bloodred lipstick had left a big kiss mark on the rim of the coffee mug she was holding.

"I heard about your intruder last night," she said. "I'm glad you're okay."

"Word travels fast," I said. "Who told you?"

"Frankie called Veronica House this morning and told Niall. I heard from him. Come on in," she said. "And tell me how you persuaded Grandma to talk to you."

I held up the box of wine. "This."

She smiled and shook her head. "I should have guessed."

"Do you live with her?"

"No, but I come by and help out my mom from time to time if she needs to get out and the home helper isn't available," she said. "Let me tell her you're here. I'd also better warn her about your accident before she sees you, so she won't be freaked-out. Wait here a minute."

She disappeared down a narrow hallway to the back of the house. When she returned, she gave me a wry look. "You may approach. She's ready for you." As I followed her down the hall, she said, "And I hope you're ready for her. Grandma's a pistol."

Olivia Cohen sat in an enormous carved Victorian throne chair, wearing a brilliant magenta, saffron, and violet silk kimono, an orange turban, and gold brocade elf slippers with curled-up toes. She looked like a dowager empress awaiting the arrival of her subjects. Half a dozen rings glittered on her fingers, her long nails were gold-tipped and painted the color of old blood, and a gold and amethyst amulet hung around her birdlike neck. Her face was deeply lined and her makeup made me think of Japanese Kabuki. It would not have seemed out of place to curtsy.

The walls of the room were a deep burgundy, and the small space was cluttered with fussy furniture, framed photos, and antique collectibles on every tabletop and filling two curio cabinets. She had eclectic taste—colorful glass paperweights, snow globes with elaborate scenes, Lladro figurines, Wedgwood candy dishes—and a particular fondness for carved pigs and roosters. It was also as hot as the inside of a clothes dryer.

"Mrs. Cohen," I said, taking off my jacket and wishing I hadn't worn a heavy turtleneck, "I'm Lucie Montgomery."

"I know," she said. "You've brought the wine."

As if she had been waiting outside the door, Skye appeared with a tray, two wineglasses, and a corkscrew. "Grandma likes a little drink in the afternoon," she said. "She believes it has medicinal benefits. Enjoy."

"Why don't you pour, Lucie?" Olivia said. "Red, of course, since I presume the white isn't chilled. And then we'll talk. You'll drink with me, of course?"

It was a command, not a request. I poured her a small glass of Merlot and an even smaller one for myself.

"To Roxy," Olivia said, holding up her glass. "May she finally rest in peace." We drank to Roxy, and she said, "This is rather nice. You *do* make good wine, dear."

"Thank you," I said, "and what did you mean about Roxy finally resting in peace?"

"Why, her affair, of course," she said. "I think it haunted her all her life. She loved him, you know. I believe he was the great love of her life. She married Willoughby on the rebound. Of course it didn't hurt that he was as rich as Midas and old enough to be her grandfather."

"Did you know the man she had the affair with?"

She nodded. "Before the Americans let women fly noncombat missions during the war, the Brits were allowing it. A couple of us who were determined to do our bit went to England and volunteered for the ATA, the Air Transport Auxiliary. They trained us, you see, and we flew the Royal Air Force's frontline aircraft." She paused to drink more wine and her voice grew dreamy with memory. "Those were incredible times, so exciting. You have no idea."

"What was Roxy's pilot like?"

"Group Captain Thomas Van Allen. Tommy. My God, but wasn't he a dreamboat. He and Roxy were such a gorgeous couple. There wasn't a girl in the squadron who didn't envy her. And, of course, you could guess how it was going to end up."

"With Roxy getting pregnant?"

Olivia drank more wine. "Pregnant and scared what could happen to her if the word got out. We were good friends back then—roommates, actually. I was the only one she told, and between us, we managed to camouflage her baby bump so no one guessed. She was a little bit of a thing anyway. Never really looked pregnant. Later I think that was the reason she dropped me, because I knew her secret, knew she gave the baby to Tommy's sister and her husband after Tommy was killed."

"You never kept in touch?"

Olive gave me a tight smile. "Roxy moved on. She was that kind of girl. Ambitious, you see. And then she married a very rich man and started moving in different circles."

"When was the last time you saw her?" I asked.

She fingered her amulet. The light of a nearby

table lamp caught the amethyst as she turned the stone, and it flashed like a sly, winking eye. "To talk to? It was years ago. At a charity dinner dance in Washington. She was with her husband and, ho-ho, let me tell you, she wasn't pleased to see me."

"Because you knew about the affair?"

"And what happened to the child." She sat up straighter in her regal chair. "She never wanted anyone to know about it."

"My friend's mother was her next-door neighbor at Foxhall Manor," I said. "She overheard Roxy talking to a man shortly before she died. According to Faith, Roxy kept insisting that she wanted to know the truth. Do you think that might have had something to do with her affair? Or something that happened in England?"

Olivia laid an index finger against her lips and sat there for a moment as if lost in old memories. Finally, she sighed and said, "If it does, I'm afraid I couldn't help you with that. Roxy was a wild one when I knew her. She'd had a bad time with her family back home, terrible arguments with her mother. I'm fairly sure she went to England to get away from them."

Mac had said something similar the other day, how his grandmother and Roxy had fought constantly.

"Did she ever talk about her family?"

"Never," she said. "But when she found out she

was pregnant, it made things even more difficult for her. She was Catholic and she had no one to turn to in America. I think it only hardened her will to give the child away, because she knew what would happen if she went back as an unwed mother."

She reached over and picked up an envelope on a small table next to her chair. It had been sandwiched between a Lladro ballerina and a brass piggy bank. "Would you pour us a drop more wine, dear?"

I filled her glass and added another splash to mine. She appeared not to have noticed that I hadn't really drunk anything.

Olivia waved the envelope at me. "Have a look."

The envelope contained a black-and-white photograph of Roxy with a man who had to be Group Captain Tommy Van Allen, and a third person, a curly-haired blonde vamping for the camera, who, I realized with a shock, was Olivia. They were standing in front of what looked like a stone plinth with two enormous signs wrapped around it. I could just make out what they said: CARRY ON LONDON and SALUTE THE SOLDIER. Though the three of them had their arms around one another, you could tell there was something special between Roxy and Tommy, the way she was tucked into his arm and the tilt of their heads together.

But what struck me the most was the uncanny

resemblance between Roxy and Uma Lawrence. Anyone who'd seen the photo of Lucky Montgomery in Mick's album had noticed how alike we were, but looking at Roxy was eerily like looking at Uma.

"What a wonderful picture," I said. "You all look so happy."

"We had a rare day off and the weather was glorious," Olivia said with a smile. "So we walked from the Embankment and the Houses of Parliament down Whitehall to Trafalgar Square. That picture was taken at the base of Nelson's Column. As you can see, there were patriotic signs everywhere. . . . The Blitz was such an awful ime in London, bombing and destruction everywhere. And, of course, later we found out that if the Germans had invaded London, Hitler would have carted the column off to Berlin as a war trophy."

"I didn't know that," I said. "Where did you get the photograph?"

"One of Tommy's friends took it," she said. "He and I were dating at the time, but it never came to anything. He sent it to me about twenty years ago, along with the one I gave that reporter. He figured I'd know how to get in touch with Roxy, and that I'd be the best person to pass the pictures along to her." She shrugged. "By then I'd seen her at that fund-raiser and she'd snubbed me every time she saw me after that, so I just kept them."

"You gave Vivienne Baron another photo like this? With the three of you in it?"

She nodded. "She promised to return it when she finished writing her story. I said she could borrow it as long as she didn't mention Roxy's affair with Tommy, and she gave her word."

Though Kit had told me Vivienne's story was appearing in the *Trib*'s Sunday magazine, I figured it was Vivienne's place to tell Olivia that news, not mine.

"I heard," Olivia went on, "that Roxy's granddaughter is in town and that Roxy left her quite a generous inheritance."

"How did you find out about that?" I asked.

"Skye heard from Father Niall. I gather he met her."

"That's right, he did. Her name is Uma Lawrence. She and Father Niall met at my vineyard, actually," I said. "She looks so much like her grandmother, especially that red hair."

"Funny," she said. "Because Roxy's daughter—Uma's mother—was the portrait of Tommy. Nothing of Roxy in her. Mind you, I only saw her when she was an infant, but still, you could tell." She waved a bejeweled hand at me. "Give it to Uma. If anyone should have it now, it's Roxy's granddaughter. I'll keep the other picture as a souvenir, but Uma should have this one of her grandmother and grandfather together."

"She's leaving for London this weekend," I said,

"but I'm sure I can get in touch with her. Or Mac MacDonald can."

"Yes, see to it, won't you? And now I'm tired and it's time for you to go." She said it unceremoniously and in such an abrupt manner, I wasn't sure if I'd heard correctly. "My granddaughter will show you out."

Either Olivia had a hidden buzzer somewhere or Skye had been listening on the other side of the door, because it suddenly opened and she walked in.

"I hope you two had a good chat," she said.

I slipped the photo into the envelope and stood up, pulling on my coat. When I looked over at Olivia Cohen to bid her farewell, her head was lolling against the back of her chair and her eyes were closed. In the past thirty seconds, she had fallen asleep and was now snoring gently.

At the front door, Skye said, "Don't say I didn't warn you about Grandma. Wine always puts her to sleep. It's like a knockout drug."

"I won't," I said. "When she wakes up, please tell her I said thanks and good-bye."

"My mom should be back any minute, and I need to get back to Veronica House," she said. "I'll tell Mom to pass on your message to Grandma. Good-bye, Lucie. See you Saturday night at your party."

I decided to take the back roads home to Atoka, something I always did when I needed time to think. Though the plows had been through since the storm two days ago, the smaller country lanes weren't as well cleared as the highways, so there were icy patches where the road dipped or ran through the woods. But the Jeep had four-wheel drive and I knew what to do if I went into a skid.

At the intersection of Lime Kiln Road and Delta Farm Lane, the road made a sharp right-angle turn around a blind corner. I hadn't seen a car for the last seven or eight miles, so the red Subaru, flipped over and jutting into the road like a crooked tooth, seemed to come out of nowhere. I swerved and slammed on the brakes—the worst thing to do, but there wasn't time to avoid hitting it—and spun onto the shoulder. The other driver must have taken the corner too fast and lost control. It looked like the Subaru had also spun around—more than once, judging by the skid marks on the road—and then flipped over before landing on its side. At some point, it had crossed the road, where it had struck a large oak tree and plowed into a low stacked-stone wall. The hood was so badly smashed in, the car looked like a crumpled soda can, and most of the windshield was missing.

I grabbed my phone and got my cane from the backseat, picking my way across the ice-rutted road. There was a gaping hole in the windshield.

Vivienne Baron, who didn't drive in snow or ice because she was too inexperienced, who needed her husband to pick her up and drop her off everywhere she went, and who had been too sick today to show up at the vineyard, lay slumped over the steering wheel, her hands still clenched tightly around it. Her long dark hair was loose and covered her face. I reached through the windshield and said her name, brushing her hair away from her pale cheek. For a moment, I thought she was wearing bright red lipstick, until I realized her mouth was covered with blood. She lay in what looked like a crystal pool of pebble-size pieces of glass from the shattered windshield, and her eyes were wide open, as though something had startled her.

I turned away, afraid I was going to throw up right there, and called 911. But I already knew it was too late. Vivienne Baron was dead.

TWENTY-THREE

A female 911 dispatcher took down my information and promised that someone would be on the way soon. I admire anyone who works at a hot-line crisis center, the way they remain unruffled while they help you hold it together so you can tell them about a tragedy unfolding in real time. The woman I spoke to had endless patience and a soothing voice.

But the wind had picked up, whipping my words away, so she had to ask me to repeat myself more than once. Finally, she said, "Is there someplace where you can get out of that wind so I can hear you?"

I went over to the Jeep and got inside.

"That's better," she said. "I'm sorry to ask this, but are you certain she's dead?"

"I can't really get to her because the door on the driver's side is jammed shut and there's broken glass all over the place, but I'm as certain as I can be," I said. "She's not moving or breathing. Her eyes are open and she's just . . . staring."

"Okay," she said. "I know it must be tough. I need you to stay on the scene until someone arrives, hon. You going to be okay with that?"

"I know her," I said, and for the first time my voice was shaky. "I'm not going to leave her out here by herself."

"Hang in there," she said. "You're doing a great job. Someone's coming as soon as they can get to the both of you."

She disconnected and I wondered what to do next. Vivienne was beyond any help I could give her and I knew well enough not to try to move her before someone from the Sheriff's Department and the EMTs arrived. I took a deep breath and called Bobby.

"I heard and I know you're the one who called it in," he said. "I'm on my way there now. What happened?"

"She's dead, Bobby. The car flipped over. She's

lying in a lot of broken glass from the windshield and it looks like she was going pretty fast when she took the corner," I said. "First of all, she was supposed to be at the vineyard today, helping with bottling. Second, her husband called and said she was too sick to come by. And third, she doesn't drive."

"What do you mean, doesn't drive?"

"She does drive. I mean, she knows how. But the other night when Kit brought her over to our tasting party, she said she was from Southern California and didn't know how to drive in snow and ice. Her husband drove her everywhere."

"Do you recognize the car? What's the plate number?" he asked.

"I've never seen Will driving anything other than Mac's van," I said. The car had spun around, so I could see the Virginia license plate, now upside down, on the rear bumper. I read the numbers to him.

After a moment he said, "Registered to William Baron."

"I've got his phone number stored on my phone because he called me yesterday before he dropped off a clock at my house," I said.

"You don't have to notify him," Bobby said. "We can take care of that."

"I feel like I ought to," I said. "I'm the one who found her. Maybe you could tell Kit. She's going to be devastated."

"I know," he said, and for the first time I heard a tremor of emotion in his voice. "She'll take this really hard."

He clicked off and I found Will's number on my phone. I hit Call and got his voice mail.

"Hey, you've reached Will. You know what to do. So do it and I'll call you."

I stammered a message, asking him to call me because there was something urgent I needed to tell him about his wife. My phone rang as I was finishing up and the display flashed an incoming call from Kit.

She'd been crying. "Oh my God," she said. "What in the blue bloody *hell* was she doing behind the wheel of a car?"

"I don't know." I glanced over at the Subaru again. From where I was, I couldn't see Vivienne lying among all that broken glass, her hair fanned out like Hamlet's Ophelia floating in a pool of water. "I thought she was sick today."

"Can you hang on?" she said, sniffling. "Mom's calling my office number. I'd better take this."

I said sure, and the line went silent while she put me on hold. In the distance, I could hear sirens for the second time in less than twenty-four hours. A moment later, Kit was back.

"I don't know what's going on, but Mom said Viv was late for an appointment to come by and see her." She sounded perplexed. "So now Mom's all upset because Viv's not there and she figured

I'd know where she was. She says Viv called her this morning and told her it was important—no, wait, Mom said 'urgent'—that she come by today." She made an exasperated noise, like air leaving a tire. "This whole thing is crazy."

"Maybe she was on her way to Foxhall Manor when her car went off the road. And if it was urgent, maybe she was speeding," I said. "What did you tell your mom?"

"Not the truth, that's for sure. I said something came up and Vivienne wasn't going to be able to stop by this afternoon. I'll explain about the accident in person. . . . In fact, I think I'm going to drive over there now. Mom's not feeling that great."

"I hope it's not flu."

"I don't know what it is. That's why I'm going over."

"Let me know, okay? I left a message for Will. I didn't tell him, of course, just asked him to call me back. The only other person I can think of to call is Mac. Maybe he knows where Will is."

"Maybe." Her mind was someplace else.

"What was so important that Vivienne had to see your mother today, enough to make her get behind the wheel of a car?" I asked. "I wonder if it has something to do with whatever was upsetting Roxy before she died, that argument your mother overheard?"

"God knows. What did Olivia Cohen say?"

"Unfortunately, she had no idea what it was." The sirens grew louder. I stuck my finger in my ear so I could still hear Kit. "I'd better go. I'll talk to you later."

"Sure," she said, her voice catching on another ragged sob. "That poor kid."

Bobby told me he didn't think I ought to stay around and wait until they extricated Vivienne from the passenger seat of the car. "You don't need to freeze your butt off waiting in this cold," he said. "Go home, warm up, and take care of yourself. You're shivering and you've been through enough lately. Besides, there's nothing anyone can do for her now."

His eyes met mine and I knew the real reason he was telling me to get lost was because he didn't want me reliving another occasion when the fire department had to use the Jaws of Life to get a woman out of a car that had been totaled after crashing into a stone wall: me. I had been unconscious when they'd rescued me. Watching Vivienne, who hadn't survived, would be like watching the horror movie of my own accident— something that, until now, existed only in my imagination—happening for real.

"If you don't mind, I think I will take off," I said. "I left a message on her husband's voice mail. So he still doesn't know."

"We'll get hold of him," Bobby said. "Don't you

worry about it anymore. He and Vivienne rented a cottage on Sam Fred Road, so I'll drive over there when we're done here and see if he's home. This isn't the kind of news you tell someone over the phone anyway."

"No," I said. "It isn't. You might try Mac's if you don't find him at home. Or the Inn. He works there tending bar some nights."

He walked me to the Jeep. "I'm afraid we don't have any leads on your intruder yet. I'll keep you posted. But in the meantime"—he gave me a stern look—"you lock up, you hear?"

"I will," I said. "Don't worry."

Unexpectedly, he put his arms around me and mine went around him. "Even I have a hard time dealing with something like this, Lucie," he said into my hair. "You'd think it would get easier, but it doesn't. Take care of yourself, kiddo."

I drove home, more slowly than usual, and wondered why Will Baron hadn't driven his wife to Foxhall Manor to see Faith Eastman. Unless she'd chosen not to tell him what she was doing and took their car without telling him.

What had Vivienne wanted to talk about with Faith? I drove home through the gathering gray dusk and wondered what it was and why she had risked her life for it.

The news about Vivienne Baron's fatal accident went around Atoka like lightning. My cell phone rang nonstop until I finally put it on mute and let the calls from neighbors and friends go to voice mail. The only exception I planned to make was if Will Baron called. Or Kit.

Neither of them did.

Quinn joined us for dinner—Persia had made enough lasagna to feed Lee's army—and I soon realized he and Eli had already discussed sleeping arrangements for the night. Persia was spending the night in Hope's room again and Eli and Quinn planned to sleep downstairs. Antonio, Benny, and Jesús had different shifts throughout the night to patrol the property.

The phone in the foyer rang after dinner, when we were all in the parlor, sitting in front of a fire that Eli had made. The men were drinking what was left of the brandy and Persia had fixed me a cup of chamomile tea before she took Hope upstairs for her bath.

I got up. "I'll see who it is."

It was Mac. I sat down in the Queen Anne chair next to the table and took the call. I hoped he had news about Will, who still hadn't called back. Plus, I had the picture of Roxy that Olivia Cohen had given me. I needed to tell him about that, too.

"I heard you're the one who found Vivienne, sugar," he said. "And I heard about that break-in at your place last night. Are you all right?"

"I'm okay," I said. "Mac, have you talked to

Will? Bobby Noland was trying to find him this afternoon to tell him about Vivienne."

"His cell phone battery had died. Apparently, he was outside doing some chores and the cold drained the battery," Mac said. "Bobby finally tracked him down at his place. Will called me later to tell me the news. The poor boy sounded so distraught. He quit his job here on the spot, said he couldn't bear to stick around Middleburg without his wife."

"He's leaving town?"

"He's got a brother somewhere. I'm not sure where. He said he was going to stay with him once he buried Vivienne."

"I guess he'll be going to California for the burial, since that's where she was from."

"I don't know. He didn't say," Mac said. "He asked if he could borrow the truck for a few days, since they had only the one car and he's got a lot to do. I told him he could use Roxy's car. It's been sitting in the garage ever since she moved to the Manor, but I take it out often enough that it still runs. I'm taking him over there tomorrow morning to pick it up."

"You're a good soul, Mac."

"You do what you can," he said. "By the way, part of the reason I'm calling is because of Will. He said to tell you he got your voice mail on his phone and once he talked to Bobby, he put two and two together and figured out why you'd called. He's not up to calling you back, said he hoped you'd understand."

"Of course," I said. "When you see him tomorrow, please give him my sympathy."

"I'll do that," he said. "I must say, he sounded surprised that you were the one who found her. Said he hoped you were doing okay. 'Night, sugar."

"Before you go," I said, "I have one more question. I was wondering if you know a woman named Olivia Cohen?"

"The name sounds familiar, but I can't place it. Why?"

"She's Skye Cohen's grandmother. Skye works over at Veronica House."

"Can't say I really know her, either. Why do you ask?"

"Olivia was a member of Roxy's squadron in England, another of the first women pilots during the war. They were roommates. She's living in Leesburg now," I said. "I went to see her today and she gave me a picture of herself with Roxy in London. Roxy's pilot—Group Captain Thomas Van Allen—is also in the picture. She wants Uma to have it, but I thought you might like to see it, as well."

"How did you find this out?" His voice was sharp with annoyance.

"From Vivienne Baron. She interviewed Olivia for the feature story she wrote on women pilots in World War Two."

"I can understand Vivienne's reason for seeing her," he said, still cross. "What was yours?"

"I wondered if Roxy was so upset before she died because of what happened to her in England."

"Are you referring to the conversation Faith Eastman thinks she overheard?" He said *thinks* as if Faith was living in la-la land.

"She doesn't think she did. She knows she did."

"You are meddling, sugar, in matters that don't concern you."

The rebuke stung, but I held my ground. "I did it for Faith," I said. "You told me you had no idea why Roxy was so upset. I thought it was worth a shot to ask Olivia. Who, for the record, has no idea, either."

"For the record"—Mac repeated my words, and I could hear the taut anger as he emphasized each one—"I'm going to tell you something that is none of your business. But if it will put a stop to this nonsense, then so be it. And you will drop this once I say what I have to say. Is that clear?"

What was clear was that he was finally going to admit that Faith hadn't been making this up.

"Yes," I said. "Please go on."

"I was the one Faith overheard talking to Roxy that day," he said, as if it pained him to admit it. "Faith must have the hearing of a bat."

"She said you were shouting."

"Be that as it may," he said, "I have never told this to anyone, not a blessed soul, but Aunt Roxy

323

was adopted." He paused to clear his throat. "She never knew the truth until a few weeks ago. She was devastated, particularly once she discovered I'd known for years because my mother had confided in me before she died. The conversation Faith overheard—Aunt Roxy shouting—was the day she realized she was the only one in the family who'd been kept in the dark, that my grandparents weren't her real parents, and my mother wasn't her blood sister. She felt . . . betrayed, I guess you'd say."

"Didn't Roxy do practically the same thing herself? Keep her own child a secret from your mother and your grandmother . . . and you? You had no idea Uma Lawrence even existed," I said. "It seems odd she'd feel betrayed, under the circumstances."

"You're right, of course," he said. "But this news changed her. She felt it was time to acknowledge her own blood relatives. Her daughter was dead, but it wasn't too late for Uma."

"Is that why she changed her will so suddenly?"

"Yes, it was," he said in a tight voice. "My parents and grandparents were dead, which left me as the only living relative from the Chases, her adopted family. But she also had a grand-daughter, the daughter of the love child she had to give up in England. Suddenly, Uma mattered very much to Aunt Roxy, so she acted accordingly."

"I'm sorry, Mac. Really."

"Don't feel sorry for me. She was quite generous, leaving me the house and its contents. I have no complaints. I'll be very well-off."

"Thank you for telling me this," I said. "But why did you lie to me the day I was in your store? You said that the shouting Faith heard must have been the television turned up too loud. Roxy's dead now. What harm could it do to tell the truth?"

"Roxy was not at peace when she died," he said in a way that made me think he wasn't at peace, either. "All of a sudden, she didn't know who she was anymore. The family she'd believed were her blood relatives had lied to her, or at least kept the truth from her. It haunted her that she might have inflicted that same punishment on her own daughter and granddaughter."

"I won't say anything, Mac. Don't worry."

"What about Faith? What are you going to tell her?"

"I'll think of something. But not that story."

"Thank you." He sounded grudging. "As for that photo, I would quite like to see it. And since I'm driving out to the house tomorrow anyway with Will, maybe you could find your way to coming by the gallery in the morning. I'll give it to Uma myself. It would be fitting."

I owed him that much. Olivia wouldn't mind who gave it to Uma.

"Of course," I said. "But Mac, there were two photographs. Olivia loaned the other one to

Vivienne. She wanted it back after her story came out in the paper. You might want to ask Will about it. Eventually, he's going to have to go through Vivienne's things."

"I'll do that." He sounded surprised. "And I'll see you in the morning. Ten-thirty would be convenient."

When I finally walked back into the parlor, Quinn was alone, kneeling in front of the fire. I sat down on the sofa and picked up my tea. It was tepid.

"Who called?" he asked. "You were gone awhile."

"Mac. He talked to Will and wanted to fill me in. He said Will took the news hard, quit his job, and he's leaving Middleburg."

"That's rough."

I nodded. "Where's Eli?"

As I spoke, we heard the piano from the sunroom, a great crash of melancholy chords and sweeping arpeggios.

"What is that piece of music?" Quinn asked, turning around.

"'*Dies Irae.*' 'Day of Wrath,' by Verdi. Eli always plays it when he's upset."

"I guess it fits," he said.

"It's been a long day," I said. "I think I'm going to turn in. You two don't need to sleep down-stairs, you know. Nothing's going to happen tonight. The guy's long gone."

Quinn poured more brandy into his glass with an unsteady hand. "You don't know that," he said. "I called Gino, by the way. Told him the police are looking into whoever broke in here last night. If they trace it to him, he'll have more problems than a blackmailer to deal with."

"You called him? What did he say?"

He sighed, sounding weary. "What do you think? He had no idea what I was talking about."

"He wouldn't admit it if it even if it had been him," I said. "It's also possible he was telling the truth."

"So if it wasn't Gino," Quinn said, "then who was it? Who told you to mind your own business?"

"I'm not sure." I gave him a worried look. "I guess it could be the devil I don't know."

The screams woke me in the middle of the night. I bolted upright in bed, listening to the blood-curdling sound of high-pitched shrieking, like a woman in distress outside in the woods near the house. My first crazy thought was that I was back on Lime Kiln Road again and I'd gotten to Vivienne in time. She was still alive and she needed my help.

A moment later, I heard Hope's anxious cries, followed by Persia's soothing voice murmuring to her until she got the child to calm down.

I made my rabbiting heart slow down. I knew

that sound as well as I knew my own voice. Not human. A fox.

There was movement downstairs, too. By the sound of it, both Eli and Quinn were up. I went to the top of the stairs and called their names. Quinn appeared in the foyer.

"Eli's checking, but I think it's just a fox," he said. The moonlight streaming through the windows limned his silhouette, turning him into a ghostly apparition. "Probably another animal got it."

"There's a den behind the springhouse," I said. "Two adorable baby cubs. I hope it's not one of them."

"We'll see in the morning," he said. "Go back to bed."

I took more Tylenol for my aches and pains and tried to fall asleep again. But I was too wide-awake and too wired. I picked up Frankie's copy of *The Great Gatsby* and read to the end. About the murder of Jay Gatsby, the millionaire so obsessed by Daisy Buchanan, his dream girl, that to let Daisy off the hook, he pretended to be the driver of the car that killed her husband's mistress. The book broke my heart, as Frankie said it would.

I set it on my nightstand, but it wasn't long before my thoughts returned to the intruder last night and who he might have been.

What did I know that was threatening enough for someone to break in and leave that note? And why didn't I know what he was talking about?

TWENTY-FOUR

By the time I got downstairs the next morning, Quinn was gone and Eli was in the kitchen finishing breakfast.

"How much sleep did you get?" I asked. "Because you look like you were up all night."

He gave me a weary look. "Not much. I've got a meeting with a client at eight-thirty, the one I never got to the day of the snowstorm. I might come back here when I'm done and get a nap. Someone from the alarm company is coming by later, too. I'll handle it, okay?"

"Do you really think we need an alarm?"

"All I have to do is look at your face and know we do."

Though he said it calmly, it sent a shock through me that straightened my spine. I touched my bruised cheekbone. When I'd looked in the mirror earlier, not much had changed. I still looked like something from the set of a horror movie.

Our eyes met and I said, "Okay. I give in. We'll probably all sleep better. Once this week is over, though, I think everything will settle down and life will get back to normal. Tomorrow night's 'Anything Goes' party is going to be fun and hopefully we can put all this behind us."

"There's still today." He gave me an ominous look. "It's Friday the thirteenth."

"Oh, come on. Don't tell me you're that superstitious."

"This from the woman who won't get involved in any business deals or make travel plans when Mercury's in retrograde?"

"Oh God. It still is. With everything that's happened, I nearly forgot about it."

"Don't walk under any ladders or break any mirrors," he said.

I gave him a rueful grin. "Everything's going to be just fine, you wait and see. I can feel it in my bones."

He passed me the saltshaker. "You might want to hang on to this," he said. "We'll talk tonight at dinner. And you can tell me then how great your day went."

We left the house together. Eli was headed for his client meeting, and I wanted to stop by the villa before the staff arrived. Frankie's red Mercedes was already there when I pulled into the parking lot at eight o'clock. She wasn't due in until nine; knowing her, she was tackling her to-do list for tomorrow's party.

I found her on one of the leather sofas by the fireplace, still wearing her winter coat. Her face was blotchy and her eyes had the rheumy look of someone who had been crying. Mosby was rubbing against her legs, but she was ignoring him. I had never, ever seen Frankie cry.

She stood up when she saw me and dabbed her eyes with a tissue. "Sorry, my allergies are acting up. What are you doing here at this hour?"

"I own the place," I said. "What's your excuse? And I'm not as dumb as I look. You're only allergic to tree pollen."

She made a face. "It might be Mosby, then. Cat fur."

"You want to tell me what's going on? Is Tom okay? Is it one of the kids?"

She waved the tissue as if it were a white flag. "No, it's nothing like that. Everyone's fine. I'm sorry. I didn't expect you to be here so early. Give me a minute to fix my makeup. . . ."

"Sit down," I said. "I'm going to start a fire because it's cold enough to see your breath in here and then I'm going to fix us both a cup of coffee. You can tell me about it then."

She sat down and pulled Mosby onto her lap, stroking his silky fur. I made a fire in the large stone fireplace, and when I came back from the kitchen a few minutes later with our coffees, she was walking out of one of the bathrooms. Her makeup was now freshly reapplied, but her eyes were still red.

I sat down and passed her a mug. "What happened?"

She drew a ragged breath. "You can't tell anyone."

There was a lot of that going around. I made an *X* over my heart with my index finger. "Go on."

"Remember I told you the other day that there might be some money missing from the Veronica House bank account?" I nodded, and she said, "We've got that diocesan audit coming up next week, so we're trying to get everything in order before then."

"Was that what you and Father Niall were talking about when I walked in on you having a drink the day Uma Lawrence dropped by?"

She gave me a worried look. "Yes. I had a long talk with the chairman of the board yesterday afternoon. We don't actually know how much is missing, but it's starting to look like it could be a lot. Maybe six figures. We're still digging through the old financial ledgers."

"The accounts aren't computerized?"

"'Fraid not. No fancy bells and whistles for us. Just a regular old-fashioned accounting book to keep track of deposits and withdrawals. And a checkbook."

"Maybe it's just a math error. Or cumulative math errors."

"I wish it were. But the money is gone." She snapped her fingers. "Poof. Vanished."

"How?" I said. "And who?"

"God knows. Niall just runs the place, you

know? He's a priest, not a CPA. He was more worried about the food pantry being stocked than the checkbook being balanced. A couple of people who are involved with Veronica House and a few of us on the board can write or sign checks, me included. As long as there was money in the account, we just carried on."

"So maybe someone wrote themselves a couple of checks and recorded it in the ledger as something else," I said. "It wouldn't be the first time. Especially if he or she knows no one is paying attention."

Her eyes flashed. "Niall's utterly devastated. He believes the best of everyone. When his office was broken into last year and someone took his bicycle, you know what he said? 'Whoever did it needed it more than I do. We mustn't get attached to things, to material possessions.'"

I couldn't tell whether she was angry or frustrated. But I did know that more than anything, she was heartbroken that a charity she'd thrown herself into heart and soul could turn out to be run by people with the most human of foibles: greed. Stealing money from a program that helped homeless people, people who had nothing.

"What about your audit?" I asked. "Are you going to get this sorted out in time?"

"I don't know. That's what started the whole thing. It's the first time in years we've had a thorough audit like this. I drove into Washington to see Niall last night. He's going to take the blame for all of it. He's the director of Veronica House, so he says there's no way he's going to pass the buck and claim he wasn't paying attention." She swiped her eyes with the back of her hand. "Once the bishop finds out, he'll probably get sacked, which is so unfair. They're already not on the best of terms because Niall's such a rebel, standing up to the bishop on a couple of issues. If it weren't for Father Niall O'Malley, Veronica House wouldn't be what it is today. He holds that place together by sheer force of will. He's the reason—his charm and charisma—that people give so much money."

"I'm sure," I said. "What was he doing in Washington?"

"Oh." She looked flustered. "Sometimes he spends the night in D.C."

"Spends the night? You mean at a seminary or a church rectory?"

Now she reddened. "I shouldn't have said anything. Niall owns a town house on Capitol Hill. He drives into D.C. and stays there when he needs a bit of space, when he doesn't have to be out here at the center. Please don't mention it, he'd rather no one at the center know he's got such a posh place. . . . Only a few people he trusts know about it. A former parishioner he helped through a really bad time left it to him in her will."

"A woman who wasn't a relative gave him a town house? On Capitol Hill? It must be worth a fortune. I thought priests were supposed to take a vow of poverty."

"Those in religious orders do that. Diocesan priests don't. They're allowed to have personal wealth, especially since they don't have a community to take care of them like religious do once they retire. At least now Niall has a home where he can eventually live when he needs it. His friend left him all her furniture, the dishes, linens . . . everything."

"Lucky him."

Her eyes flashed anger. "Who's going to care for him when he's too old and they make him retire, Lucie? He doesn't have any family left in Ireland. I say good for him."

"Sorry. I didn't mean to sound flip. But what about the party tomorrow, the fund-raiser for Veronica House? What are we going to do about that now?"

"We're not going to say anything. Mum's the word." She grabbed my hand and squeezed it. "So far, only four people know about this. Five, counting you. Niall, me, the chairman of the board, the current treasurer, and now you. Niall's going to be there tomorrow night, give the speech he planned to give, thanking everyone for their generosity, and we're just going to carry on like nothing has happened. He doesn't want to ruin the party or do anything to discourage people from supporting Veronica House. With or without him, it's going to go on. We still need it in the community."

"Are you serious?"

"What other choice is there?" She gave me an anguished look. "We'll get our house in order, straighten this out. Once Niall finds out who's behind this, he'll probably want it handled as quietly as possible anyway. Besides, I think he's still hoping for a miracle and that the money will turn up somehow. Veronica House doesn't need a scandal like this. You know that."

"No, it doesn't," I said. "But it's got one. You can't hide this. How many other scandals has the Catholic Church swept under the carpet? It's going to look terrible."

"Lucie—" She gave me a warning look.

"I mean it, Frankie. If the Montgomery Estate Vineyard is throwing a party to raise money for Veronica House, Father Niall needs to be honest with the people who are going to be here and give their hard-earned money to a charity they believe in. If he doesn't, they'll feel betrayed. I'll feel betrayed. In the short run folks may be upset and he'll lose some support, but in the long run people will appreciate his candor and honesty," I said. "I'll tell him how I feel about this, if you don't want to."

She pursed her lips and I thought she was ready to fight back on this, challenge me.

"No," she said finally, sounding resigned. "I'll tell him."

"You'll get to the bottom of it, Frankie, put things right. It will all work out."

"Yeah. Sure." She finished her coffee and set her mug on the coffee table. After a moment she said, "I know you were the one who found Vivienne Baron. The news is everywhere. I'm sorry, Lucie. If I hadn't been at Niall's and so caught up in everything with Veronica House, I would have called you last night. It really has been a hell of a few days for you, hasn't it?"

I set my mug next to hers. "It has," I said.

I decided to leave early for my ten-thirty meeting with Mac so I could stop by the General Store. Frankie said the news about Vivienne was all over town. What I still couldn't figure out was why Vivienne had been behind the wheel of that car yesterday: a woman who didn't drive in bad weather and supposedly was too ill to come by the winery, at least according to her husband, who had called Frankie to say Vivienne wouldn't be helping out with bottling. Had Will refused to drive her to Faith's, or had she taken the keys to the car without telling him because she needed to speak to Faith so urgently that she couldn't—or wouldn't—wait for her husband?

Either way, it had to mean something had gone wrong between Vivienne and Will. If anybody had learned anything new, Thelma would know about it by now.

She was cleaning the shelves of the glass vitrine where she kept her pastries and doughnuts when I walked in wearing my mother's sunglasses and a baseball cap with the Washington Nationals logo on it. There wasn't going to be an easy way to brazen this out once she saw my bruises.

She looked up as I walked in, and for a moment I could tell she didn't recognize me. Then she froze, clutching her cleaning cloth with one hand while the other went over her heart, as if she couldn't catch her breath.

"It's okay, Thelma," I said. "It's not as bad as it looks."

"Lucille." It came out like a croak. "Oh my poor, poor child. Come over here right now and let me see you. No, wait. You go sit down in that rocking chair next to mine and I'll fix you a nice cup of coffee and get you the last doughnut. We can't have you walking around when you're wounded like that."

I did as I was told and let her fuss. Finally, she sat down in her own rocking chair after handing me the coffee and a jelly doughnut and said, "I gave you today's Fancy. Black Cat Brew-ha-ha, being as today is Friday the thirteenth." She gave me a worried look. "How are you doing, child? It's a miracle you're sitting right here with me. I heard all about it."

338

"I'm sure you did," I said. "I guess you probably also heard that I was the one who found Vivienne Baron yesterday when her car went off the road."

"Oh, my Lord, yes, I heard that, too. You've had a couple of turrible days recently, haven't you?"

I nodded and took a bite of the jelly doughnut. Once you start eating those things, you can't stop or the jelly leaks all over the place. I mumbled "Mmm" through a mouthful of doughnut and waited for her to continue telling me what she knew.

"Mighty peculiar that she was driving without her husband. Supposedly, he took her everywhere," she said, and I nodded again. "He was in here just yesterday morning, all by himself, buying a couple of cans of chicken soup and asking me what he should take for that awful cold and cough he picked up."

I wiped jelly off my mouth with the paper napkin she'd given me and said, "He bought medicine for himself?"

"Well, after I told him what to get," Thelma said. "I may not have taken the hypocritical oath like a doctor does, but I do know how to fix what ails folks sometimes."

"Did Will say anything about his wife being sick, too?"

She shook her head. "He said he hoped she wouldn't catch his germs, or some such thing. Though I guess when you have congenital relations with the person you're married to, it's pretty difficult to keep that from happening."

"Right." Frankie said Will had told her Vivienne was the one who was sick.

"And, of course, he's leaving town, poor thing, now that she's gone," she said. "Mac told me he's all torn up with grief."

"I can imagine."

"Course, Mac's upset, too, wondering where he'll find a replacement as talented and clever as Will is," she went on. "He was counting on Will to help bring some of the furniture he's had in storage from the house he sold in Georgetown years ago out to Middleburg. Now that Roxy left him her place, I think he wants a few things there from the Islington side of the family, not just the Chases."

I bolted upright in my chair so fast, I sloshed coffee on myself. "Pardon? The who?" I dabbed at a wet spot on my sweater with my paper napkin.

"The Chases and the Islingtons," she said. "Mac's grandmother was Pauline Islington before she married into the Chases. They were a big society family in Washington." She cocked her head. "Didn't you know that?"

"No," I said. "I did not."

"Oh, my, yes. She was quite a catch for Mac's grandfather. A real beauty."

"I don't suppose you know whether anybody

ever called her Izzy because her last name was Islington?"

"Oh, honey, that was before my time. You'll have to ask Mac," she said.

"I'll do that." I stood up. "In fact, I'm on my way there right now."

All this time, I'd assumed Zara Tomassi's good friend's nickname was short for Isabel or Isabella. A woman's first name. Could "Izzy" have been a nickname for Pauline Islington, before she married Mac's grandfather and became Pauline Chase? I did some quick mental math. Zara and Pauline would have been about the same age.

Thelma said that Mac's grandmother came from a well-connected D.C. family, which meant it was likely she would have known Zara, a prominent congressman's daughter. Washington may be the capital of the United States, but it's always been a small town with only one business: the govern-ment. A century ago, it would have been an even smaller town.

If Pauline Islington Chase was Zara's Izzy—*if*— then Pauline probably knew what had happened to Zara's baby. Though by now, I was starting to think that maybe I had a glimmer of an idea what had become of the child, as well.

I needed to talk to Mac about Pauline, his grandmother, and Roxy, Pauline's daughter and his aunt, and maybe then I'd know for sure.

TWENTY-FIVE

I parked near the Episcopal church and walked over to MacDonald's Fine Antiques. The Windsor rocking chair that had been in the window when I bought my clock was gone and the artwork had changed. Mac must have had a busy few days.

I could see him through the large glass window, hunched over something at the partners desk where he did his bookkeeping and paperwork. He looked up when he heard the door chime as I walked in.

"Hello, Lucie," he said. "Thanks for coming by."

Lucie. Usually it was "sugar" or "honey." Lucie was for when he was upset.

"Hi, Mac." I was still wearing the sunglasses.

Under other circumstances, he would have gotten up and given me a friendly kiss, but today we both were acting unnaturally stiff and formal toward each other. His behavior was probably due to last night's conversation. Mine, because of what I was about to ask him, which I knew he wasn't going to like one bit. Maybe even tell me to *mind my own business*.

Could I have been wrong about Mac? He couldn't have been my intruder, but had he sent someone to deliver the message to stay out of his family's affairs? Bobby and I had dismissed him as a possibility when we spoke yesterday at the house, but as Eli had said earlier, that was then.

Now I knew things I hadn't known a day ago. Or thought I knew them.

"Come on over here and have a seat." He sounded grudging. "I presume you brought the photo?"

I took off my sunglasses. "I did."

His eyes grew wide with shock. "Dear Lord. You poor child. Have they found who did this?"

"Not yet. Can I ask you something before I give you the photo?" I sat in the chair next to his desk.

"About what?"

"Your grandmother, Granny Chase. Pauline Islington Chase."

"What about her?" He leaned back in his chair and folded his hands in his lap, still visibly distressed by my big black eye. Maybe I should cross him off my list of suspects after all.

"Did she ever go by Izzy? And was she friends with a woman named Zara Tomassi?"

I so wish the child were mine. Not an affair between Zara and Izzy. Izzy, who didn't have a child of her own at that point but desperately wanted one, and Zara, who didn't want her own baby, an anchor to tie her down and keep her from being the fun-loving party girl she'd always been. So when Zara died, it was simple: Izzy took her friend's baby and raised the child as her own.

343

The look in Mac's eyes told me everything I needed to know. "How did you find out? Who told you?"

"No one told me. I guessed once Thelma mentioned your grandmother's maiden name was Islington. All this time I thought Zara Tomassi's best friend, Izzy, was a nickname for someone named Isabel. Your aunt Roxy was Zara's daughter, wasn't she? Your grandmother adopted her and raised her as her own child after Zara died."

The color drained from his face and he reached out to support himself against his desk, as if the floor had tilted sideways. "Who else knows about this besides you?"

"Right now, no one," I said. "Do you know what happened to Zara, Mac? How did she die? Was she murdered?"

"You have no right to be asking these questions," he said, still pale, but his voice crackled with anger.

"Maybe not." I held my ground. "But I know two people who do. Quinn and Gino Tomassi. They have the right to know."

"Is that why Gino's in town?" Mac asked. "To see his cousin?"

It was my turn to be caught off guard. If Mac knew that Gino and Quinn were related, did he also know about the blackmail? Could he have been the one who found a copy of Roxy's birth certificate, which proved she was Zara's daughter?

Was *Mac* blackmailing Gino?

"Gino was invited to the White House state dinner for the Italian prime minister. So he stopped by to see Quinn," I said. It was a truthful, if incomplete, answer. "I didn't realize you knew they were related."

"Of course I knew," he said in a testy voice. "I made it my business to find out everything about Roxy once I learned who she really was."

"Last night on the phone, you said Roxy found out she was adopted a few weeks ago," I said. "Either someone told her or she came across something that proved it—a letter or a document. I was wondering which it was."

He glared at me. "You're so good at guessing, you tell me."

I picked up a pen and spun it around on his desk like a compass needle while I thought about it. The pen stopped, the tip aimed at Mac's heart. "Not a person. Not someone. She found something."

"What makes you say that?"

"Well, who knew, besides you? Everyone else is dead, right?"

He gave a jerky nod of assent. "My grandparents kept Roxy's adoption a secret while she and my mother were growing up. Even Mother didn't learn the truth until Pauline was on her deathbed."

"So Roxy must have come across a document,"

I said. "A letter or something else she found. Her birth certificate?"

His eyes flickered. "It was a letter. Taped to the top of a drawer of a small Queen Anne chest that used to be in the front hall of her home. Roxy suddenly decided she wanted it moved to Foxhall Manor. So I had Will take it over."

That explained the indentations I'd noticed in Roxy's carpet from a relatively new piece of furniture. And if it wasn't Roxy's birth certificate, then Mac wasn't the one threatening Gino. In fact, I was starting to doubt he was even aware that Gino was being blackmailed. Which meant at least one other person did know Roxy was Zara's daughter: whoever had the birth certificate.

"What was in the letter?"

One of the wall clocks chimed the quarter hour, out of sync with all the others in the store. Mac looked as if he still didn't want to discuss this, but I waited him out.

"Roxy's adoption papers," he said finally.

"Then why did Faith hear Roxy shouting that she wanted to know the truth? Did she mean the truth about who her birth parents were?"

"Yes."

"Did you tell her?"

"I told her I didn't know."

"But you do know. Maybe you didn't want to tell her because of the circumstances surrounding Zara's death?"

"I refuse to discuss that subject."

"You know what happened to Zara, don't you?" I said. "And if you do, you're the only one who does. Gino Tomassi has no idea about any of this. Zara's name was banned forever from all family conversation once Johnny Tomassi married his second wife, Angelica."

His eyes narrowed. "Gino coming to town has something to do with Roxy, doesn't it?"

"Gino doesn't know that Roxy was the daughter of his grandfather's first wife. He has no clue."

He gave me a shrewd look. "Gino may not know about Roxy, but I'll bet he does know about Zara," he said. "He came to see Quinn because he's trying to find out what happened to Zara's daughter. Am I right?"

He deserved an answer to that after what he'd just told me. "Gino never knew Zara's baby lived, so, yes, he was trying to find out about her."

"Why?" he said. "Did he think he'd inherit any money from Roxy's estate?"

"Good Lord, no. Gino's worth millions. He doesn't need her money."

"Then what is it?"

There wasn't any way to avoid telling him. Besides, this conversation had just eliminated any reason for Gino to pay the blackmailer. Mac could tell Gino what he needed to know and save him a quarter of a million dollars.

"Someone found Roxy's birth certificate and

that complicates matters for Gino because now Uma might be a potential heir to the Tomassi Family Vineyard," I said. "For enough money, the blackmailer will hand over the birth certificate."

"Someone has Roxy's birth certificate?" He seemed stunned.

I nodded. "I think you and Gino and Uma and Quinn need to sit down and talk this through. Gino always thought Zara's baby didn't survive her mother's accident, so he had no idea there were any other potential heirs to the Tomassi Vineyard. It's time to get everything out in the open."

"No. I've done all the talking I want to do."

I reached over and took his hands in mine. "Mac, this has to end. I can set something up at the winery where you'll have complete privacy. I'm sure I can get Gino and Quinn there. I can probably even get Uma to come, if you don't want to ask her. But you have all the answers. You need to do this."

For a long time, he didn't speak, but his shoulders grew more stooped. I guessed it might be the weariness of carrying around the burden of what he had known for so long. Izzy, his grandmother, must have known the truth about what happened to Zara—whether her death was really an accident or a murder that had been covered up.

"Fine." He gave a tired shrug. "If they agree to a meeting and you make the arrangements, I'll do it."

"Thank you."

He jerked his hands from mine. "Don't thank me. It's not going to be the comforting balm you seem to think it will be."

"Do you know who Roxy's father was?" I asked. "I assume you know that Zara was having an affair with Warren Harding. It sounded . . . complicated."

"My God," he said. "How did you find out about *that?* From something Lucky left behind?"

"Lucky Montgomery?" I was dumbfounded. "She was involved in this, too?"

He gave me a smug look that sent a shiver up my spine. "You didn't know about your own family's role in this? Well, isn't that rich? I told you, not everyone will be happy with what I have to say. You ought to be at this meeting, too, Lucie."

"Oh, I'll be there," I said. "Don't worry."

"I need to go pick up Will," he said. "And now if you have the photo of Roxy and Tommy Van Allen, I'd quite like to have it. I'll give it to Uma when I'm at the house."

I got it out of my purse and gave him the envelope. I already knew he would wait until I was gone before he looked at it.

"Before I go, I have one more question," I said, putting on my sunglasses.

"I might not answer it."

"Come on, Mac. I don't understand how everyone involved managed to keep this quiet for so long," I said. "Someone had to forge documents that listed your grandparents as Roxy's mother and father, since no one was supposed to know who her birth parents were."

He gave a one-shoulder shrug. "Apparently, it was quite easy. The Tomassis and Zara's family were well connected in the Catholic Church. Johnny Tomassi even made sacramental wine for the Church during Prohibition, and there was a priest who became a close family friend and also served on the board of the Tomassi Family Vineyard. Roxy was born at home, not in a hospital. It was easy to falsify the documents."

"A Catholic priest helped them?" I said.

"That's what my mother told me," he said. "Why, is something wrong?"

"No," I said. "You just reminded me of something. We have some more winter coats that Frankie collected at the vineyard. I need to take them over to Veronica House, so I'd better get going. I don't want to miss seeing Father Niall. I'll call you later, Mac."

I left before he even said good-bye, my mind reeling with what he had just said. Mac wouldn't tell Roxy the truth about her birth parents, so who else would she have confided in, asked for help?

Her priest and confessor, Father Niall O'Malley, perhaps? He would keep her secret. His vows bound him to do so, even—as he told me—if someone confessed a murder.

Could it be that Father Niall figured out how to get hold of Roxy's birth certificate . . . and then blackmailed Gino Tomassi once he realized who she was? *Would he?*

Uma Lawrence had crudely implied that Roxy might have slighted her charities in leaving all of her money to her granddaughter, but maybe her comment hadn't been too far off the mark. Had Father Niall been expecting money from Roxy's estate to help him bail Veronica House out of its financial problems caused by the missing money? And then when he didn't get it, did he resort to plan B? Get it from a member of the family that had given up Roxy as a baby?

I got into my car and called Quinn. "I know who Zara's daughter was. And her granddaughter. And I think I might know who is blackmailing Gino. I'm driving back to the vineyard from Mac's place right now to pick you up. Can you get the carrier bag of winter coats Frankie collected for Veronica House? We're going to pay Father Niall a visit."

The silence on his end of the phone went on forever. Then he said in a grim voice, "Does visiting Father Niall have something to do with what you just told me?"

"I don't know," I said. "That's what we're going to find out."

TWENTY-SIX

On the drive back to the vineyard, I kept thinking over and over that I couldn't be right. Father Niall O'Malley could not be the one blackmailing Gino Tomassi. If he was, it would be like the ground opening up under Veronica House and swallowing it without a trace. He *was* Veronica House, as Frankie had said, thanks to the sheer force of his personality: the way he bullied, cajoled, charmed, and occasionally shamed everyone in the community into acknowledging a shared responsibility for the people he served. Gently reminded us we were all our brother's keepers and that there was no excuse for poverty and homelessness in a region of so much easy affluence and abundant wealth. Frankie thought he walked on water. If what I suspected was true, I couldn't bear to think how she would take the news.

I had also asked Quinn to bring the copy of *Decanter* magazine with the page torn out about the Tomassi-Bellagio deal. Father Niall had been over at the vineyard more than usual lately because of the fund-raiser coming up. Maybe he'd been waiting for Frankie and killed some time by looking through the magazines in the library, found that page, and saw an opportunity.

Or maybe I was completely wrong.

After I spoke to Quinn, I had called Veronica House. The woman who answered the phone said Father Niall was busy with some of the guests in the day shelter but that she'd be glad to take a message.

"It's Lucie Montgomery," I said. "We're hosting a fund-raiser for your center tomorrow night. Something has come up and I really need to talk to Father Niall. Could you please tell him I'm calling about a financial matter?"

"Give me a moment," she said, and put me on hold.

He came on the line, probably because I'd mentioned money, as I figured he might, and my heart sank.

"Lucie," he said, "lovely to hear from you, my dear. What can I do for you?"

Maybe I was listening for it, but I thought he sounded tense and ill at ease.

"I need to talk to you about something, Father," I said. "It would be better to do this face-to-face. In fact, I'm on my way over there now. I'd be grateful if you could spare a few minutes for me."

"Is anything the matter?"

"I hope not," I said. "I'll be there in about half an hour. We can talk about it then."

"I know you spoke to Frankie," he said in a grave voice. "She called me about an hour ago. I hope you're not reconsidering about tomorrow night, donating the money you raise to Veronica House. We're just so terribly grateful for what you're doing for us. And we'll get our financial house in order, sure and we will."

"That's what Frankie said," I said, wondering what, exactly, Frankie had told him. "But I still have a few questions. And we're bringing more coats for the shelter. I'm sure you can use them with this frigid weather."

" 'We'?"

"Quinn Santori is coming with me," I said. "We'll see you soon."

By the time we pulled into the parking lot at Veronica House, I'd told Quinn about Pauline Islington Chase—Izzy—and how she'd adopted her best friend's daughter and kept it a secret after Zara died. And that Roxy Willoughby was that child. He'd been floored.

"And now you think Father Niall is blackmailing Gino because he's got the birth certificate?"

"Mac told Roxy he didn't know who her real parents were," I said, "which was a lie. But apparently Roxy was determined to find out. Father Niall visited her all the time; plus, he was her spiritual adviser. He'd keep her secrets. Maybe he used the adoption papers to work backward to find out who had given her up. It was a priest who forged the documents to begin with. Mac said the adoption papers came with a letter, so Father Niall would have had a place to start."

We pulled into the parking lot at Veronica House and Quinn said, "I can't believe you're actually going to ask him if he's blackmailing Gino."

"I'm not," I said. "You are."

"Me?"

"It's your family. You didn't think I was going to do this, did you?"

Father Niall's mouth was set in a grim line and there was a tightening around his clear blue eyes when Quinn and I met him in the lobby of the day shelter a few minutes later. But when I took off my glasses, his face registered such shock and dismay that I wondered if we were making a mistake, that I had gotten this completely wrong.

I really didn't want it to be him.

"How are you doing, Lucie?" he asked, putting an arm around my shoulder and giving it a squeeze. "I hope they catch whoever did this to you. And I'm ever so glad you're all right. God was really looking out for you, I think."

"Thank you," I said. "I'm a lot better today than I was yesterday. Father, could Quinn and I talk to you for a moment? In private?"

"Of course," he said. "Unfortunately, my office is full of people, since we're getting the books in order before the diocesan audit. But we can talk in the chapel without being disturbed. Follow me."

The chapel was a rustic one-room structure that

looked like a log cabin and was connected to the rest of the rambling center by a corridor that seemed to slope downhill. Father Niall pushed open one of the double doors and stepped back so Quinn and I could enter first.

It was as plain inside as it was outside, and I'd always loved its beautiful simplicity on the occasions I'd visited the center. The pews were wooden benches and the unadorned crucifix above the rough barn-wood altar was made of more reclaimed barn wood, with tree branches overlaid on top of it. The two stained-glass windows provided the only light in the room and were equally primitive: simple modern depictions of Jesus holding his hand out to a man and a woman in one, and surrounded by little children in the other. Each had a quote from the Bible carved in another piece of wood, the letters stained black to stand out.

Sunlight streamed through the window where Jesus stood among the children, lighting a swath of pews, which glowed with a light that almost seemed celestial. Father Niall pointed to the benches and said, "Shall we sit over there? It's very peaceful."

Quinn and I took one pew; Father Niall sat by himself on another and turned so he faced us. "What can I do for you?"

"I believe you have something that belongs to my family," Quinn said to him.

I should have known Quinn wouldn't beat around the bush. Father Niall didn't even blink.

"And what is that?" he asked.

"Roxy Willoughby's birth certificate. Not the fake one some monsignor in California doctored for Pauline Islington, but the one with her real birth mother listed on it: Zara Tomassi, Johnny Tomassi's first wife. Johnny is my great-grandfather, by the way."

Even in the warm shaft of light from the stained glass, I could see the color leave Father Niall's face. "I'm not sure what you're talking about, Quinn. I'm sorry."

Quinn and I exchanged glances. "Mac MacDonald has family papers and correspondence that prove all this," I said. "That Roxy was Zara's daughter."

That wasn't exactly true, but I figured it wouldn't hurt to let him think it was.

Father Niall folded his hands together in his lap as if he were praying and said, "And why are you telling me?"

"Because you're blackmailing Gino Tomassi," Quinn said. "Roxy gave you her adoption papers and asked you to find out who her birth parents were. Once you got hold of her birth certificate, you knew who she really was. But maybe by then she had died and you'd learned about her new will, along with everybody else. The only ones who inherited anything were Mac,

Roxy's nephew, and Uma, her granddaughter. Had she promised you something, Father, that you were surprised not to get?"

Father Niall gave an abrupt laugh. "We're always needing money for Veronica House and I'm not shy about asking for it to help God's poorest children, as you well know. But I don't resort to blackmail, son."

Quinn leaned over so that his face was inches from the priest's. "I'm not enjoying this one bit. But you've got two choices. You can give me the birth certificate and I'll call off Gino. Or you can try to get your money from him and see how far you get. He's got a private detective looking for you, an ex-cop, and friends you wouldn't want to meet in a dark alley. His best friend is the head of the biggest Mafia family on the West Coast. Good luck with that." He stood up. "Come on, Lucie. We're done here. We warned him."

I wasn't ready to go, not just yet. The copy of *Decanter* was in my purse. I pulled it out and flipped it open to the place where the page had been torn out, then set it down on the pew. Father Niall said nothing, but something flickered behind his eyes.

"I think you might know where the missing page is," I said, "with the article about the proposed deal between Gino Tomassi and Dante Bellagio." When he didn't answer, I said, "I'm really sorry about this."

"Lucie." Quinn reached for my hand. "It's okay. Come on, let's get out of here."

I picked up my cane. "Good-bye, Father."

He let us get all the way to the double doors before he said, "Wait."

Neither of us turned around.

"Please come back and sit down again. Both of you."

I glanced at Quinn, who nodded. We went back and took our seats.

He held up his hands in a sign of surrender. "I meant no harm. I did it for the center. But you're right: An opportunity presented itself when Roxy asked me to find out who her birth mother was once she'd learned she was adopted. Unfor-tunately, she passed away before I could tell her," he said. "And I realized I was sitting on an unexploded time bomb."

"So you blackmailed Gino."

"The Tomassi family turned its back on Roxy when she was born. And Gino is a multi-millionaire. Roxy was going to help the center, leave me—us—money in her will, until she found out she was adopted," he said in a bitter voice. "Once I learned the identity of her birth mother, it seemed only fitting to get the money Roxy would have given us—*should* have given us—from the family that abandoned her. Besides, what's two hundred and fifty thou-sand dollars to Gino Tomassi? Especially if it will help the poor, the homeless, who have nothing?"

"You're right. It's pocket money," Quinn said. "Gino said as much. But Father, the nuns taught me the Ten Commandments in Sunday school, including 'You shall not steal' and 'You shall not covet your neighbor's goods.' They were written on stone, not rubber. You don't bend them to make them work for you."

"What happened to the money that's missing from Veronica House?" I asked.

Father Niall stared out the window. "It's probably a series of careless mistakes. We—I—should have paid more careful attention to the books, but there's always so much to do here, I'm afraid I let it go. Anyway, I already told Frankie I plan to take full responsibility for anything that can't be accounted for."

"Frankie said it's probably going to end up being in six figures," I said. "That's a lot of bad math and careless mistakes, don't you think?"

"I couldn't say." He still hadn't looked at either Quinn or me.

"Did you know the money was missing before your staff started getting your finances ready for the auditors?" I asked.

"Don't be daft," he snapped, swinging his gaze to us now. "Of course I didn't."

In the painful silence that followed, one thing became crystal clear: Father Niall O'Malley was lying. He'd known about the missing money all along.

"Did you take it?" Quinn asked him.

"I'm done answering your questions. I'd like you both to leave."

"You didn't answer that last question," I said. "Did you take the money? Is it gone? What did you do with it? Spend it?"

His eyes flashed, but he remained silent, and I thought about Frankie's comment about the posh town house he owned on Capitol Hill, left to him by a wealthy former parishioner, how he didn't want people to know about his bolt-hole in Washington. A house like that required upkeep and maintenance; there were property taxes. Where had Father Niall found the money to pay for those expenses?

"Forget it, Lucie," Quinn said. "It won't be too hard to find out where the money went once the auditors finish going over the books. If you didn't have any twinge of conscience over blackmailing Gino, Father, I suspect you've got a few other secrets buried somewhere in your life."

The light shifted and a shaft of blue light from the stained glass caught Father Niall's face and hands, freezing him as if he had turned to stone.

"What do you plan to do now?" he asked finally. "Turn me over to the police?"

"I'll call off Gino for you once I leave here. That's my gift to you," Quinn said, sounding disgusted. "And maybe you could do yourself a favor and get out in front of this before the auditors figure out what happened to the missing money. Because they will. What did Saint Matthew say in the Bible? 'No one can serve two masters, God and money.' Not even you, Father. The real question is what do *you* plan to do now?"

TWENTY-SEVEN

When we got back to the Jeep, I said to Quinn, "When did you become a biblical scholar, quoting Saint Matthew?"

He gave me an ironic look as a gust of wind rattled the car windows, then said, "I'm just full of surprises. Give me your keys. I'll drive so you can call Gino."

"Me call Gino? No way, buddy. He's your cousin."

"I just accused a Catholic priest of blackmail and embezzling money from a charity for the homeless. That's my good deed for the day. It's your turn. You're the one who figured it all out. You tell Gino everything and get him to call off his Mafia buddies from retaliating against Father Niall. If I call, he'll hang up before I get to the end of *hello*."

We sat in the parking lot while I called Gino, who sounded like he was at a raucous party. He told me he'd call back when he got some privacy, so I told him it was urgent and had to do with the blackmailer.

"How'd he sound?" Quinn asked. He started the engine and pulled out of the parking lot.

"Surprised. And shocked, I think," I said. "Mac promised he would come to a meeting if I could set it up with you, Gino, and Uma. I'm going to ask Gino to come out to the vineyard tomorrow morning, say ten o'clock. We can confirm the time with Mac and get him to tell Uma. But I think Gino should talk to Mac before Uma shows up. It's going to be quite a shock when Gino meets Roxy's granddaughter for the first time."

"Fine by me," he said as the phone rang.

"I'm putting this call on speakerphone," I said. "You need to be part of the conversation, too."

I hit Accept on my phone and said, "Hello, Gino. Good of you to call back."

"You said it was important," he said. "So I called."

The money had never mattered to him, $250,000. Telling him we'd saved him that expense, that he didn't have to pay off the blackmailer, just washed over him. What he cared about was the birth certificate, the realization that Zara's child—a baby girl—had lived after all. That was the lure to get him to come to the vineyard on Saturday morning. Along with the promise he would meet Zara's great-granddaughter.

Then he wanted to know the identity of the blackmailer.

"How in the hell did you figure it out before my guy did?" he said. "It must have been one of the Ingrassos, Zara's family, or someone from her new family."

"Neither," I said. "It was a Catholic priest who was close to Zara's daughter. Under the circumstances, we'd like you to call off your guy . . . your private detective."

"A priest. Are you kidding me? Who is he? What's his name?"

"We'll tell you everything tomorrow morning. It's complicated."

Gino snorted. "Fine. We'll do this your way for now, but tomorrow is another story. I'm the one who was threatened and this is about my family. You make sure whoever is supposed to be there shows up. Understand?"

"You bet," I said. "And you're welcome."

Quinn dropped me off at the barrel room when we got back to the vineyard.

"What are you going to do?" I asked before he drove off.

"Check the pruning in the south vineyard," he said. "I'll probably be gone all afternoon. You're going to call Mac and set up the meeting, right?"

I eyed him. "Or you could do it."

"You're better at this than I am. Besides—"

"Yeah, yeah. I'm the one who figured everything out."

He left, and I knew the real reason he didn't want to hang around. He still needed to blow off steam after the session with Father Niall and the conversation with Gino.

My first call was to Mac. He didn't sound surprised to hear from me, but he wasn't happy about it, either.

"It would be better if Uma arrived after you've had a chance to talk to Gino about Roxy," I said to him. "The two of you have a lot to discuss."

Like whether Mac's grandmother, Pauline—Izzy—knew anything about how Zara died. The real story behind her so-called accident.

"If you want Uma to be there, you call her," Mac said in a snippy voice. "She's done listening to me. When I gave her that photo from Olivia Cohen today, it didn't seem as if she cared much about it one way or the other. She's planning to leave town tomorrow, by the way."

"Thelma overheard her talking on her cell phone about her dog back in England and worrying about whoever is feeding it, so maybe that's why she's in such a rush to get home," I said. "I'll call her. Don't worry, she'll be there."

"Good luck trying to persuade her," he said. "I think she's met all the family she wants to meet."

"I have my ways. See you here tomorrow morning at ten-thirty."

Uma answered on the third ring, and when she realized who was calling, she turned sulky. After talking to Gino and Mac, I was ready for her.

"No, I am not coming to your bloody party tomorrow," she said. "And I already told you to keep the money you owe me. I don't want it."

"I'm not going to waste your time," I said. "Or mine. Your grandmother was adopted and she died before she learned anything about the family that gave her up. As it turns out, someone from that family had been looking for her and now he'd like to meet you—Roxy's granddaughter—before he flies home to California and you go back to London."

"I'm not interested in meeting any more relatives I never knew," she said. "Or someone who didn't know about me until five minutes ago."

"You'd be interested in meeting this man," I said.

"I doubt that."

"There's another inheritance involved," I said. "A great deal more money than your grandmother left you, in fact. You want to walk away from that kind of money, fine by me. I'll let him know. He'll be here tomorrow."

She was silent.

"Good-bye, Uma. Have a nice trip back to England."

"Wait," she said. "How much money are you talking about?"

"I have no idea," I said. "But the family business is worth hundreds of millions."

"What time do I have to be there?"

Hook, line, and sinker. "Eleven. You already know the way."

I disconnected.

Quinn came back to the office at the end of the day and held out his hand to me, pulling me up from my desk chair.

"We're going out tonight," he said. "Dinner at the Inn. Go home and change and I'll pick you up in half an hour."

"What's the occasion?" I asked, surprised.

"Making it through this day."

"I'd like that very much," I said. "But it's not over yet."

He groaned. "Now what?"

"Frankie. I've been avoiding her ever since we got back from Veronica House. Before she goes home, I need to see her."

"Are you going to tell her anything?"

"I don't know. I think I'm going to make it up as I go along. You want to come with me for moral support?"

He gave me a nervous look. "No, you handle this stuff better than I do. You go ahead and talk to her."

"Thanks," I said. "You're all heart."

I found Frankie in the supply room off the kitchen, counting tablecloths and surrounded by boxes of plates, cutlery, and table decorations in red, black, and silver.

"I'll get here early tomorrow and start setting up," she said, looking up and blowing a strand of hair off her face. "Thank God we decided to close early. There's so much to do."

But her smile was halfhearted and her eyes had a defeated look I'd never seen before.

"It'll be great," I said. "Everyone's going to have a fabulous time, thanks to you."

"Yeah. Thanks." She waved a hand, brushing away the compliment. "You saw Niall today, didn't you?"

"Yes."

"He called." She sounded pained. "He's asked a couple of us to stop by his office tonight because he wants to talk about the audit." She gave me a long look. "I don't know how you know this, but you know something about the money that's missing from Veronica House."

"Yes."

"Care to tell me?"

I wondered what Father Niall was going to say to her later, whether he'd have the guts to come clean about all of it or whether he'd take advantage of her unswerving loyalty and devotion to help justify what he'd done.

"It's probably better if you hear it from him."

"As bad as that?" She said it lightly, but she wasn't joking.

The e-mails Father Niall sent Gino could be recovered on his computer even if he'd deleted them. It would only be a matter of time before the paper trail of the audit led whoever was looking into the missing money to the blackmail threats.

In the end, it would all come out.

"Niall said he was feeling under the weather, so he thought it would be a good idea for him to skip the party tomorrow," she said, still in that hurt, pained way. "He doesn't want anybody to get sick."

"I'm really sorry, Frankie."

She lifted her chin, defiant. "He'll get through this. Whatever it is. He has a lot of friends, you know. He's a good man, Lucie. You don't know him like I do."

I didn't want to tell her the truth. That he'd kept another life from her, hidden it so well that she didn't really know him, either.

"I'll see you tomorrow," I said. "Don't stay too late."

I closed the door quietly, and as I walked away, I heard her start to cry.

TWENTY-EIGHT

As soon as Quinn and I walked into the Goose Creek Inn, I remembered that Dominique's interview at the White House had been yesterday. With everything that had happened, it had completely slipped my mind. I suspected Frankie, who usually never forgot anything, hadn't remembered, either, because she, too, had been preoccupied by the events concerning Father Niall and Veronica House. Dominique hadn't called me, but that didn't mean she hadn't been offered the job. More likely, she *had* gotten it and was trying to figure out a way to tell everyone.

Hassan gave us a table in my favorite dining room next to the fireplace, where a bright fire blazed, and told us a waiter would be with us shortly. Quinn thanked him, and I said, "Is Dominique here tonight?"

"Not yet," he said. "She said she might come by later. Shall I ask her to stop by if she arrives while you're still here?"

"That would be great," I said. "Thanks."

"Everything okay with Dominique?" Quinn asked when Hassan left.

"Sure. Fine. Why?"

His eyes flickered. "Okay," he said. "You'll tell me what it is when you want to."

I opened my menu. "I don't know what you're talking about."

"Secrets," he said. "In the end, they get us all in so damn much trouble."

He was right. Like Eli had said the other day: "What you can't say owns you. What you hide controls you." Wasn't that the truth?

• • •

Dinner was nice, but subdued. Neither of us talked much and Quinn seemed more preoccupied than usual. Every so often I would catch him stealing a glance at me when he thought I wasn't looking, until I finally said, "Do I have food in my teeth, or is it the bruises you're staring at?"

He turned red. "Sorry. I'm not staring."

We saw Dominique at the maître d's station as Quinn was helping me on with my coat after dinner. "Give me a minute?" I said.

"Sure."

My cousin and I exchanged kisses and I said under my breath, "I'm so sorry. I should have called yesterday to ask how it went."

"I got in at midnight," she said, "and passed out. You wouldn't have reached me."

"Well?"

She gave a self-conscious shrug. "The chief usher called this afternoon and asked me if I'd like to be the next White House executive chef."

I had known they would offer it to her; she was talented, creative, unflappable, and a workaholic, all essential qualities for anyone who worked in the pressure-cooker/goldfish-bowl setting of the White House. Still, her news took my breath away.

"That's fabulous. Congratulations, I'm so thrilled for you." I hugged her and tried to sound like I meant it. Working at the White House would be like disappearing into a black hole. Anyone I knew who'd worked there said the price you paid was giving up family, friends, and a personal life. "We'll have a party for you at the villa once it's officially announced. It's terrific news, Dominique. You ought to be so proud. . . . *What?*"

She was watching me, sober-eyed and serious.

"You didn't turn it down," I said, "did you?"

"I think you're letting the horse close the barn door after it's gone," she said. "I haven't given them an answer yet."

"Why not?"

"They gave me twenty-four hours to think about it."

I gave her an assessing look. "You're just playing hard to get. If I know you, you've already got the first week's menus figured out and you're thinking about how you're going to rearrange the White House kitchen."

She smiled. "Perhaps. But I am going to think about it." She put her finger to her lips. "Don't say anything to anyone, okay?"

"Don't worry," I said. "Your secret is safe with me."

On the drive home, Quinn said, "I thought I might spend the night at your place again tonight. Maybe upstairs with you this time. Would that be okay?"

For the last three nights, he'd slept downstairs on the living room sofa. Once with a gun. We'd had a hell of a week, argued like cats and dogs about his family, Mercury was in retrograde, so it was a horrible time for relationships, and today was Friday the thirteenth.

Now he wanted to spend the night in my bed.

"Of course it would be okay," I said. "It's always been okay. Ever since you came back from California, when I thought you wanted to move in for good, it's been okay."

He gave me a guilty look. "I know. You've been great about that. . . . I mean, that I didn't move in."

It's an open secret, from everyone here down to the day laborers, that he chickened out. Frankie had said that just the other day.

"If you want to spend the night, I have one condition."

"I have to move in?"

"No guns in the bedroom."

He laughed. "I'm sure we can figure out something creative to do that doesn't involve firearms."

It was good with him, as it always was. I'd nearly forgotten how passionate and tender he could be. But the day had been emotionally exhausting—my confrontation with Mac in his store, the session with Father Niall, the calls to Gino and Mac and Uma, plus Dominique's news—so I fell asleep in his arms, and the last thing I remember was his voice in my ear, whispering things I had wanted him to say to me for a long time.

· · ·

The quiet sound of footsteps outside my bedroom door woke me. Quinn had been with me when I'd fallen asleep. Now I was alone. And naked.

I started to look for my clothes, which I'd scattered across the floor as we'd undressed, when the door opened and he came in carrying my mother's heavy silver tray. On it was a wine bucket with a chilled bottle of champagne, two Waterford champagne flutes, a red rose in a cut-crystal vase, and my grandmother's silver candelabra with two lighted candles.

"What in the world—"

"Happy Valentine's Day."

I pulled the covers around me, trying to mask my astonishment. "Happy Valentine's Day to you, too."

He set the tray on my bedside table and kissed me. "I figured I'd get an early start."

"You did," I said as the rich sound of the grandfather clock chiming the hour sounded downstairs. "It's just turned midnight."

He opened the champagne. "I was considering *sabrage*, but you said no weapons in the bedroom."

Sabrage is the art of beheading a bottle of champagne with a sword. It dates back to the era of Napoléon's cavalry, the Hussars, who celebrated their many conquests and victories by slicing open champagne bottles with their sabers. I'd seen it performed once when I was living in France. It was as dramatic as it sounds.

I laughed. "I would have made an exception if I'd known."

He handed me a glass. "To us."

"To us."

After we drank, I said, "You're full of surprises. Champagne, roses, and candlelight at midnight. I'm afraid I didn't even get you a card."

Mostly because I hadn't thought we would be celebrating Valentine's Day together, based on the way our week had gone. Besides, I was going to tomorrow night's—no, tonight's—party with Mick Dunne.

"You'll pay for that," he was saying. "I'll collect at the party."

I had to tell him about Mick. "Quinn—"

"Wait," he said. "Before you say anything, there's something I need to tell you. The other night when I got here and saw you beat-up and bruised after that guy attacked you, I just about died. I don't know what I would have done if anything had happened to you." He was staring into his glass, rubbing a thumb over the pattern in the cut-glass flute.

"It's okay. I'm okay."

He looked up. "Don't stop me. You know how hard it is for me to talk about this stuff. Besides, I know everyone who works at the vineyard thinks when I came off the assembly line, I bypassed the station where they give you a heart."

"That's not true—"

"You know it is," he said. "Frankie thinks my outsides are made of rubber and my insides are made of cast iron. Nothing sticks to me and I'm coldhearted."

He set my champagne glass on the bedside table and reached for my hands.

"Lucie Montgomery," he said, "I love you and I'm asking you to be my Valentine. Will you?"

When I could speak, I said, "Of course I will. And I love you, too."

Quinn was already awake when I opened my eyes the next morning. He was propped up on an elbow and watching me with an intense, serious look, as if he had been studying me while I slept. For a moment, I wondered if I had dreamed last night. Then I wondered if I *hadn't* dreamed last night, but maybe he had regrets or morning-after remorse about what he'd said and what we'd done. It wouldn't be the first time.

As if reading my mind, he leaned down and kissed me. Before long we were making love again in the soft gray dawn and it was as good and sweet and satisfying as it had been the night before. We showered together without saying much, partly because we didn't want to wake Eli or Hope and partly because by now I knew he was preparing himself for the upcoming meeting with Gino.

Eli walked into the kitchen while we were eating breakfast. His eyes went from Quinn to me to the silver tray on the counter, where Quinn had left it with the remnants of our romantic evening.

"Well, well, well," he said. "Love is in the air. Happy Valentine's Day, you two."

"Shut up, Eli," I said, unperturbed.

He helped himself to a cup of coffee and said, "So what's on for today?"

"Frankie could use a hand at the villa setting up for tonight," I said. "Maybe you and Hope could drop by and help out."

"Sure, no problem," he said. "What about you two?"

Quinn and I cut a look at each other. "We've got something to take care of in the barrel room," he said.

Eli shoved two pieces of bread in the toaster. He hadn't missed a thing. "Well, good luck with whatever it is."

"Thanks," I said as Quinn said, "We'll need it."

I don't know what I expected from the meeting with Gino, how it would go after we told him about Father Niall's blackmail and then introduced him to Mac and Uma. It didn't help that relations between Mac and Uma were already tense; between Gino and Quinn, they were downright combustible. And Mac had warned that what he knew wouldn't make everyone happy, including me. How many more land mines could there be?

At least the weather wasn't going to give us any heartache, because it was already turning out to be a spectacular day with hard, bright sunshine and skies the cloudless cobalt blue of a van Gogh painting. For the first time in weeks, temperatures were expected to rise above freezing to a tropical forty degrees.

We had the winery to ourselves, since everyone else was at the villa helping set up for the party, so I was pretty sure nobody saw Gino Tomassi slip in through the door he'd used that first day when he'd barged in on us, accusing Quinn of blackmail. He gave Quinn a curt nod and turned to me, his eyes widening as he took in my bruises, which had faded from vivid purple to an unflattering shade of puce.

"You thought I was responsible for that?" he said to Quinn, pointing to my face. "Why you—"

"What?" Quinn said, his fists already balled up.

"No fighting." I stepped between the two of them. "Stop it, both of you. Why don't we adjourn to the office, where it's warmer. And maybe everyone could calm down a little. This is hard enough as it is."

We took the same seats we'd taken the other day, Gino on the sofa and Quinn and I on the two club chairs across from him.

"I could use something to wet my whistle," Gino said.

"We can make coffee," Quinn said.

"Something stronger."

I got up before Quinn could say anything more and said, "Red okay?"

Gino nodded, so I got a glass and found an open bottle of Bordeaux. After I gave him his wine, I put a filter and coffee in the coffeepot and filled the carafe with water. Then I hit the brew button and sat down.

Quinn and I had agreed that he would do most of the talking, but before he began, I said to Gino, "Mac MacDonald, the nephew of Roxy Willoughby, the woman who was Zara's daughter, is going to be here in about twenty minutes. Mac is aware someone was blackmailing you, but he doesn't know we learned the identity of the person behind it, and Uma Lawrence, Roxy's granddaughter, doesn't know anything about it at all. We didn't think there was any reason for either of them to find out, so that's why you're here by yourself right now."

Gino took a sip of his wine and crossed one leg over the other. "Go on."

Quinn took him through everything, explaining about Izzy and Roxy and how Mac's comment about a priest forging the original documents when Zara's baby was born had led to Father Niall, Roxy's confessor and good friend, as the blackmailer. Gino's head kept swiveling in my direction as Quinn talked, but I kept my mouth shut and got up when the coffeepot beeped so that I could busy myself with fixing two coffees.

"I don't know what's going to happen to Father Niall," Quinn said, "whether he's going to do jail time because he embezzled the money. But in the short term, the scandal is probably going to hurt Veronica House."

Gino set his empty glass down on the coffee table. "I'm sorry to hear about that."

"I'm glad you are," Quinn said, "because Lucie and I were thinking it might be nice if you made a donation to Veronica House before you leave town. We're hosting a fund-raiser for the place tonight. A generous check from you would be a big help."

I hadn't known that was on the table, but Quinn went on. "Then there are those two vineyards you and Dante Bellagio are looking at buying out in Angwin for your joint venture. The owners don't want to sell. If I find out they do and that you're behind it, I guarantee you that I will sell the whole sordid story of Zara and Warren Harding and Johnny to the highest-paying tabloid out there. No skin off my nose, but I bet you wouldn't be too happy about it."

"You wouldn't."

"Try me."

"That's blackmail."

"I don't think of it that way," Quinn said. "You don't run your neighbors out of business. And as for the donation to Veronica House, Roxy would have given that money to the shelter if she hadn't found out she was adopted right before she died. I think it's more a Tomassi family debt of honor, to finally right old wrongs."

I avoided looking at him. He didn't know what had been in Roxy's original will, any more than I did.

"You said you had the birth certificate," Gino said. "So far, all this is just talk."

"I do have it," Quinn told him. "But I'm not going to give it to you."

Gino got to his feet. "I've had enough—"

"Calm down, Gino, and sit down, will you? I haven't finished."

Gino glared at him, but he sat.

"I've been in touch with Father Niall," Quinn said. "Now that he's had some time to think through what happened, he's decided he wants to meet you face-to-face. Tell you how sorry he is, ask your forgiveness. We're going to see him when we're done here. I thought he should give you the birth certificate, since he's the one who found it. And you can tell him about your donation to Veronica House."

I had to work to keep a poker face. When had Quinn found time to talk to Father Niall? We'd been together every single moment since going to bed together last night, except when he'd gotten up to get the champagne some time before midnight. I wondered who had gotten in touch with whom.

"That's probably Mac," I said as footsteps clattered on the metal staircase a moment later.

"Mac MacDonald is Roxy's nephew," Quinn said to Gino. "He's the son of her younger sister."

Mac knocked and I got up and opened the door. He walked in carrying a leather satchel under his arm and a chip on his shoulder. His eyes immediately went to Gino as he said to me with uncharacteristic formality, "Good morning, Lucie. I trust I'm not arriving too early? Hello, Quinn."

Quinn introduced Gino and Mac, pulling up his desk chair for himself so Mac could take the seat next to me. I fixed him a cup of coffee while Quinn eased him into telling Gino the life story of the woman he'd believed was his aunt until he'd found out differently, her stormy relationship with his grandmother, and the secret Roxy had kept about giving birth to a daughter in England. I saw Gino exchange looks with Quinn and knew what he was thinking: that history, unknowingly, had repeated itself, two unplanned pregnancies, two daughters raised by different mothers, and the life-changing consequences that had rippled through generations.

When Mac was done, I said, "Do you know what really happened to Zara, Mac? Izzy went to

California to be there for the birth of the baby, so presumably she was there when Zara died."

He looked down into his coffee mug as though he would find the answer in the bottom of it.

"I don't know everything," he said. "But I do know things that I'm quite certain have never come to light."

Gino gave him a skeptical look. "And how would you know these 'things'?"

"Because Pauline Chase, my grandmother—Izzy—kept a journal."

The remark dropped into chilling silence like a stain polluting a clear pool of water.

Gino leaned toward him. "Where is this journal?"

"My mother destroyed it. She never wanted Roxy to learn the truth about what had happened to Zara."

"What did happen, Mac?" Quinn asked. "You've been beating around the bush ever since you got here."

"Oh, come on, folks." Mac threw up his hands. "Don't tell me you haven't figured it out by now. Zara's death wasn't an accident. Just planned to look like one."

I caught my breath. Quinn and Gino exchanged looks.

"Who killed her?" Gino asked. "Was it Johnny?"

Mac pursed his lips in a tight smile. "Have any of you ever read *Murder on the Orient Express*, by Agatha Christie?"

"What the hell are you talking about?" Gino said as Quinn shook his head. "Can't you just answer the question?"

"He did answer it," I said after a moment. "Everyone did it. A murder was committed on board a train—the Orient Express—when it was stranded in the snow for a few days after it left Istanbul. Hercule Poirot, Agatha Christie's detective, figured out that either a total stranger on board the train had killed the man and then slipped away or else all the other passengers were in on it together. As it turned out, each of them had a motive, so Poirot concluded that everyone had to be guilty."

Mac's smile tightened. "Precisely."

"Zara fell into a ravine while she was out walking at Bel Paradiso," Quinn said. "Are you saying more than one person pushed her?"

"I'm not saying anything of the kind." Mac sounded irritated. "She wasn't out *walking* anywhere."

"What did happen?" I asked.

"Zara wanted to take the train down to San Francisco," he said, "to pay a visit to President Harding at the Palace Hotel when he was in town on his western trip. Apparently, she was desperate to see him. Johnny wouldn't let her out of the house—her baby was due any day—and Pauline backed him up. According to Pauline's diary, Johnny and Zara had a huge fight,

384

screaming at each other, even throwing things. By that time, Zara's father—Congressman Ingrasso—had gotten involved, too. He told Johnny to keep Zara away from the president, do whatever it took, because the affair had become such a political embarrass-ment to him." Mac glanced at me. "Lucie, I told you yesterday that Lucky Montgomery was involved, as well. What I didn't tell you was that she was a good friend of both Pauline and Zara, and that she was also seeing Warren Harding, if you know what I mean. Pauline knew about Lucky's affair, but Zara didn't. At least not at first."

I heard Gino's sharp intake of breath. He hadn't heard about Lucky's being in the picture. For that matter, Quinn didn't know, either.

Two women, two friends, sleeping with the same man. A love triangle. I swallowed hard and said, "I see."

"Lucky had come to San Francisco for the same reason Zara wanted to travel there," Mac said. "To see the president. But by that time, Harding was so sick that his wife, the First Lady, made it clear they wouldn't be welcome. So Pauline persuaded Lucky to go to Bel Paradiso and help her baby-sit Zara instead."

He sipped his coffee. "This has gone a bit cold. Do you think you could warm it up, Lucie?"

"Sure." I got up, dumped the coffee in the sink, and poured him a new cup.

When I handed it to him, he blew on it and said, "Where was I?"

"Lucky went to Bel Paradiso to baby-sit Zara," Quinn said in a tense voice.

Mac nodded. "That's right. She arrived on August second, the night Warren Harding died in his hotel room and Zara gave birth to a daughter at Bel Paradiso. The next morning, Zara over-heard one of the maids crying because Harding was dead. She became hysterical." He set his mug on the table and folded his hands together. "This is where it becomes complicated."

"Why am I not surprised," Gino said.

"Please." Mac gave him a pained look. "This is difficult enough."

I frowned at Gino, who shrugged. Mac drank more coffee, but it seemed like a stalling tactic while he pulled himself together.

Finally, he said, "Lucky was so upset about Harding's death that Zara put two and two together and guessed that he'd been sleeping with her, as well. There was another shouting match and Zara left the house, left the baby with one of the maids and just ran off. Lucky told Johnny and Pauline, but by then Johnny was so fed up, he said to let her go."

"That's when she fell?" Quinn asked.

"No," Mac said. "Eventually, Pauline and Lucky decided they'd better go look for her—she'd just had a child, after all—so they got the keys to

Johnny's car and took off. I don't know who was driving, since Pauline left that out of her account of what happened, but Johnny saw them leave, so he ran after them, chased them down. They stopped the car and he got in."

He sighed again, his shoulders slumping. "Zara hadn't gotten very far and she hadn't reached the entrance to Bel Paradiso, but she was heading that way. When she heard the car, she started running."

I felt my heart constrict. "They hit her? Deliberately?"

"They ran her over," he said in a strangled voice. "That wasn't in the diary. My grandmother told my mother right before she died."

"Good God, who was driving? Whoever was behind the wheel is the one who actually killed her." Gino sounded stricken. "Didn't Pauline tell your mother who it was?"

Quinn's mouth hung open. I felt sick to my stomach. Each of us was related to someone who had participated in the murder of a woman in cold blood nearly a century ago. And then had covered it up.

All I could think of at that moment was how Jay Gatsby claimed he'd been driving the car that killed Myrtle Wilson, rather than letting Daisy Buchanan, the woman he adored, take the blame. No one—not Johnny, Pauline, or Lucky— had taken responsibility for killing Zara.

"I don't know who was driving," Mac was

saying. "But Pauline wrote that they were all in a complete panic, terrified. That's when they came up with the idea that she had fallen down a ravine. And that's where she was found, so to speak, a few hours later. By then she was dead."

The silence in the room went on for a long time, broken only by the noise of Gino refilling his glass with the last of the Bordeaux.

"I don't suppose Pauline knew who Zara's baby's father was," he said to Mac in a dull voice.

"Even Zara herself wasn't sure. Apparently, there were a couple of possibilities."

Gino threw back his wine and set the glass down hard. "Great," he said. "Just great."

"She would have gotten pregnant in December if the baby was born in August," I said. "She came back to Washington for Thanksgiving and the Christmas holidays, so it must have happened here. In other words, it's possible the father could have been Warren Harding."

"Possibly, but Johnny came to Washington for Christmas, as well," Gino said. "He and Zara stayed with the Ingrassos and all of them dined at the White House on more than one occasion. Johnny always took care of the wine."

"So that doesn't rule Johnny out as the father," Quinn said.

"No," Gino said, "but at least we have a way to find out—Zara's great-granddaughter."

"Who should be here," I said, glancing at my watch as Quinn's phone rang.

"It's Frankie," he said, and answered the call. "Hey, what's up? Oh yeah? Well, can you give her directions to the office? Thanks." He hung up. "Uma Lawrence is on her way. She got lost."

He got up to get a new bottle of wine and more glasses. Then he gave us all a mirthless smile. "Showtime," he said.

TWENTY-NINE

The meeting between Uma Lawrence and Gino Tomassi did not go at all as I had expected and lasted less than fifteen minutes. By the time she walked into our office, I figured she'd either been drinking or she was on something. Or else she was extremely nervous.

We were running out of places to sit, so she joined Gino on the sofa after I introduced her to him and to Quinn, who had also never met her. She was wearing jeans, boots, and a light gray formfitting sweater, unbuttoned to reveal a lacy black camisole. Today she wore her luxuriant red hair loose, though she pulled it to one side, so it fell against one shoulder.

She refused coffee or wine, so Gino, who had not taken his eyes off her since she arrived, finally cleared his throat and got down to business.

"Miss Lawrence . . . Uma," he said, "you're here today because it's very possible we are related. In fact, forgive me for staring, but it's uncanny how much you resemble photographs of my grandfather's first wife, a woman named Zara Tomassi. Your grandmother, Roxy Willoughby, was Zara's daughter. Unfortunately, Zara died in childbirth, so Roxy was adopted by a good friend of hers."

"Pauline Chase," Mac said. "My grandmother."

Uma had clasped her hands together so tightly that her knuckles were white. "Sorry. I don't understand. Are you saying we might not be related because Roxy was adopted?"

Gino gave her an indulgent smile. "Adoption doesn't change genetics. I'm not sure there is an easy way to say this, but it's not certain that the father of Zara's child—your grandmother Roxy—was Johnny Tomassi, my grandfather. After Zara died, Johnny remarried. His second wife, Angelica, was my grandmother. My father and Quinn's grandmother were their children. So, yes, we might be related. Or we might not."

"But if we are, I could inherit a lot of money."

"Not so fast," Gino said. "What we need to determine, before this discussion goes any further, is whether you are indeed Johnny Tomassi's great-granddaughter."

"And how will you do that?" she asked. "Roxy's dead. She's been cremated."

Gino gave her a tolerant look, though I think he was surprised that she didn't understand what he was talking about. "Well," he said, "there's you, of course."

"What do you mean?"

"My dear, don't tell me you've never heard of DNA testing? If you're related to Johnny, we'll know immediately."

"No." She turned pale. "No one's going to poke and prod me."

"All you need to do is let someone swab the inside of your cheek," I said. "It takes five seconds."

"Forget it." She stood up, her knee banging against the coffee table and rattling everything on it. Quinn reached for the bottle of wine before it fell over.

"The results would be completely confidential, I assure you," Gino said. "But at least we'd be certain—"

"I said no." Uma shook her head. "I have enough money to live on for the rest of my life, thanks to my grandmother, someone I never knew. No one is going to test my DNA and find out whether I'm related by blood to more people I don't know. I don't care, Mr. Tomassi, whether I'm your long-lost cousin or not. If my great-grandmother slept around, then so be it. I don't want to know."

The blower kicked in and the heat came on

with a dull roar, but otherwise the room was silent. Gino looked stunned. Mac just shook his head, and Quinn cut a glance at me. I gave him an imperceptible shrug. *Go figure.*

"If you're sure," Gino said.

"I just said I was."

"Fine," Gino said. "I hope you understand that I would like you to put this in writing. For you to sign a legal document stating you relinquish any claim on the Tomassi Family Vineyard should you ever decide to change your mind and submit to genetic testing."

"Sure, whatever. Just mail me the papers. I'll sign them."

He pulled an envelope out of the pocket of his jacket. "As it happens, I took the liberty of having my lawyers draw up a document—"

"If you have a pen, show me where to sign." She sounded impatient. "Then I need to go. My flight leaves this evening and I have a lot to do."

Gino slid his business card across the table when she was done. "You're still related to Johnny's first wife, my dear," he said. "I would like to stay in touch with you."

"Sorry, I'm not good at staying in touch." She got up without picking up his card. "Good-bye, everyone."

"I certainly don't plan to stay in touch with her," Mac said after we heard the barrel room door slam. "Good riddance, I say."

He picked up his satchel, which was leaning against his chair, and took out a small packet of letters. "For you, Lucie. Lucky's letters to Pauline. I don't want them back. Keep them."

"Are you sure?" I asked.

He gave me a pained look, and I knew if I didn't take the letters, he was going to get rid of them and their unhappy memories now that the whole sordid story was out in the open.

"Quite sure. Their friendship never recovered after Zara died. You won't find any correspondence after that happened." He glanced at Gino. "I have to hand it to you, Gino. That was well played. Of course it helped that she's not terribly bright."

Gino gave him a bland smile. "What are you talking about?"

"You know what I'm talking about." Mac stood and tucked his satchel under his arm. "I'd best be going. The store's closed, and there's no one to help out now that Will's gone, so I need to get back. Lucie, I might not make it to your party tonight. It's been a rough week."

After he left, Quinn said, "And that's why they call you the Silver Fox, right, Gino?"

"You can find Roxy's DNA in the house she lived in for years and years, obviously," I said. "You don't need Uma to swab her cheek."

"But you just got her to sign away any right to a claim on the Tomassi family fortune, whether she's related or not," Quinn said.

Gino gave him an unrepentant look. "So what? I didn't need to twist her arm, did I? She signed those papers willingly. You saw that."

Quinn snorted. "Let's get out of here. It's time to go meet Father Niall. And then you and me, Gino, we're done."

We split up in the parking lot, Quinn and Gino leaving in two cars to drive over to Veronica House, while I headed to the villa to see how Frankie was holding up. The place, which had been made over into a Prohibition speakeasy, looked fabulous. She looked utterly defeated.

"I went to Mass at St. Mike's this morning. Niall said it," she said. "Then I took him out for breakfast. He confessed to borrowing the money." She sounded resentful. "Though I suppose you already know that."

"I didn't know, but I did guess he might have. I'm sorry."

"He always meant to pay it back. To be honest, he was expecting Roxy to leave him something."

"And she didn't," I said. "What in the world did he do with it?"

She shrugged. "The town house in D.C. needed repairs and some renovations."

"A quarter of a million dollars' worth?"

"He . . . also bought a small condo in Palm Beach."

"A condo in Palm Beach? Frankie—"

"I know," she said. "There's no justification for that. He's going to sell it and repay what he owes. He said real estate is crazy expensive there and he'll make a good profit."

"Why?" I said. "Why did he do it?"

"He said he was just trying to take care of his future. It wasn't about the money or being rich."

"'The rich are different from you and me,'" I said. "According to your friend Scott Fitzgerald."

Frankie gave me a twisted smile. "'They think, deep in their hearts, that they are better than we are . . .'" She shook her head. "I don't think Niall thought that. He's not jealous or resentful that there's so much wealth and affluence around here, if that's what you're implying."

I frowned. "I thought the next line was 'They have more money.'"

"Nope. It's from a short story Fitzgerald wrote called 'The Rich Boy.' Look it up," she said. "I'm pretty sure I'm right."

My phone rang and I pulled it out of my pocket, expecting the call to be from Quinn. Instead, the display read *M. Dunne.* Mick, probably calling about tonight.

"Sorry, I'd better take this."

"Go ahead."

I hit Accept and walked into the kitchen. "Mick," I said. "I'm glad you called. There's something I need to talk to you about."

"Before you say anything, love, I'm afraid I'm

going to have to cancel our date tonight. I'm terribly sorry."

"It's okay," I said, and hoped the relief didn't show in my voice. "You sound upset. Is anything the matter?"

"A business deal I'm involved in has turned into a complete dog's dinner. I'm flying to Florida tonight."

"Turned into a what?"

"Sorry. Weird British expression. It means an utter mess, a total hash of things," he said. "I'll ring you when I get back, okay? Have fun tonight, darling."

A dog's dinner. Thelma had overheard Uma talking about a dog's dinner on her phone and took it literally, thinking that she was referring to a woman who cared for her dog in England, feeding it hash for dinner.

Uma wasn't talking about a dog at all. She was telling the person she was speaking to that she didn't want someone—a woman, presumably—making a mess of things. And that she was leaving town as soon as she got her money.

Then this morning, she had walked away from Gino Tomassi's offer of a DNA test to find out if she was a potential heir to the Tomassi Family Vineyard, which made no sense. Even Gino had been stunned at how easily Uma had signed the paperwork relinquishing any claim on a possible inheritance.

After Mick hung up, I called Mac. He answered, sounding peeved. "I don't want to talk about those letters I gave you, if that's why you're calling."

"It's not," I said. "Did you send Will Baron to your house the other day to drop off some of Roxy's furniture from Foxhall Manor?"

"He picked the last of Roxy's furniture up from the Manor, but I had him put it in storage," he said. "Why do you ask?"

"Just trying to figure something out."

"Lucie? What's going on?"

"I'm not sure," I said. "I'll get back to you."

Uma had lied about the reason Will dropped by Mac's house, but she hadn't lied about having dinner with him. And she had just flatly turned down Gino when he wanted her to undergo a DNA test to find out if she was related to Johnny Tomassi.

I was starting to wonder whether the reason was that she knew she'd fail the test. Not only would it prove she wasn't related to Johnny Tomassi; it would also reveal that she wasn't related to Zara Tomassi, either.

No one in town had ever met Uma Lawrence before she showed up here the other day. How hard would it be to fake her identity if she knew enough about Uma's family history and a few salient facts about Roxy Willoughby? The only person who had delved into Roxy's background with any thoroughness was Vivienne Baron, and now she had died under suspicious circumstances that possibly involved her husband. Vivienne had even had a photo of Roxy that had been taken when she was in England during the war, given to her by Olivia Cohen, which she had no doubt shown to Will.

Now the woman who claimed to be Uma Lawrence was leaving town for good, and so was Will Baron, supposedly because he was so cut up with grief about his wife's death. Same day, same time.

The only thing I couldn't figure out was how Will Baron had known that Roxy Willoughby had changed her will in favor of Uma, cutting out Mac and her charities. Otherwise, I was fairly certain I was right: Uma Lawrence was an imposter and Will Baron had orchestrated the scam for her to show up in Middleburg and collect Roxy's granddaughter's share of her inheritance money.

And they were about to get away with it.

Almost.

THIRTY

I picked up my phone again and this time I called Bobby.

"I just hung up from talking to Kit," he said. "She says her mom isn't feeling too good. I think she—"

"Bobby, there's something I need to tell you," I said, cutting him off. "I think Uma Lawrence and Will Baron knew each other before she came to Middleburg. I also don't think her name is really Uma Lawrence. I think she's an imposter and that Will Baron helped her fake Uma's identity so she could collect Roxy's inheritance."

His silence went on for a long time. Then he asked, "Why do you think that?"

I told him, explaining how Will could have passed along information to the fake Uma so she'd know enough about her "relatives" to seem authentic. A bottle of hair color to turn her into a redhead, if she wasn't one already, and she could pass as Roxy's long-lost granddaughter. Though everyone in town said Uma was the spitting image of Roxy, we were also expecting her to look like her grandmother sixty years ago, so we'd made it that much easier for her to pull off the con.

When I had finished talking, Bobby said in a grim voice, "I think I'll go have a talk with her. In the meantime, we're looking for Will Baron. We just found out someone cut the brakes to the car Vivienne was driving."

"Will always drove that car," I said. "So you would think maybe someone had it in for him. Unless he cut them himself because he knew Vivienne would be driving."

Bobby let out a sound like an explosion and said, "I'd better get going."

"I'll drive over to Foxhall Manor to check on Faith," I said. "I'm only ten minutes away. I'll find out what's going on."

"Thanks," he said. "I'm texting Kit right now to let her know. . . . Hang on a sec. . . . She wants to know if you'll call when you get there. She can't raise anybody at the front desk, so she's starting to panic."

"Tell her not to worry," I said. "I'll call her in about fifteen minutes."

I found Will Baron before Bobby did.

He was leaving Faith's apartment as I stepped out of the elevator ten minutes later. The door closed behind me and he looked up, pausing in mid-step. Our eyes met, and in that heart-stopping moment I knew I had guessed right, that Will had planned his wife's death so he and the woman pretending to be Uma Lawrence could disappear with the money she'd inherited from Roxy.

I knew why he was here, too. Faith thought someone had poisoned Roxy and that she was next in line because of something she had overheard. Neither Kit nor I had believed her.

I believed her now. Roxy was dead. Was Faith . . .

"What were you doing in Faith Eastman's apartment? Is she all right?" My voice cracked with fear.

"You again." Will's face contorted, and now he

400

looked mean and dangerous. He ran toward me.

I spun around and smashed the elevator call button with the palm of my hand. The car hadn't left the floor, thank God. With a quiet whoosh, the door slid open and I got in, pulling my phone out of my pocket. He was right behind me, slipping in as it closed, trapping me with him. I reached for the button to open the door, but he shoved me against the wall so hard, my head rattled, then grabbed my phone and put it in his jacket. He wrenched my purse off my shoulder and kicked my cane, which clattered to the ground. Finally, he twisted my arms behind my back in a way that was painfully familiar.

He'd been my intruder the other night, smart enough to fake a Hispanic accent and send everyone in the wrong direction, looking for a disgruntled former employee or even someone sent by Gino Tomassi. That night, I had pleaded with my attacker to take what he wanted as long as he didn't hurt Hope. This time, I gritted my teeth, refusing to give him the satisfaction of knowing it hurt. He held my wrists with one hand while he punched the button for the fourth floor, the top floor, with the other.

"If you make any noise," he said in my ear, "scream or do anything stupid, I'll kill you. I've got a knife."

I felt something hard and long—like a knife blade—against my back. "Behave," he said.

401

"What have you done to Faith?" I said. "If you've hurt her—"

"You'll do what? A cripple like you going to take me on? Just try it."

"The police know about you," I said, and now I didn't care what he did to me as long as he got what was coming to him. "I talked to Faith's son-in-law before I drove over here. He's a detective with the Loudoun County Sheriff's Department and he's looking for you and your girlfriend. Whoever Uma Lawrence really is. You just made it personal for him."

"I don't know what you're talking about."

"Next time, don't pick such a dumb partner. She made too many mistakes. My three-and-a-half-year-old niece could have figured out she was an imposter."

"Shut up."

The elevator reached the fourth floor and the door slid open. Where was anybody in this place when you needed them—a maid, a nurse, even one of the residents? Instead, the floor was quiet and deserted.

Will Baron marched me down the hall to the emergency exit. He opened the door and said, "Let's go. Up the stairs."

"I can't climb stairs without my cane unless I hold on to a railing. Either let go of my hands or carry me," I said, and hoped he didn't know that wasn't entirely true.

He took a moment to consider his options and then released his grip on me.

"Get moving," he said. "And don't try anything. We're going to the roof."

"Where's the real Uma Lawrence?" I asked as I started up the steps. "And what happened to Roxy? Was her death timed conveniently for you, or did you do something to her?"

"Shut up," he said again. "I should have made sure you were dead the first time I had the chance."

"The night you broke into my house."

"You left the damn door unlocked. I didn't need to break in."

We reached the landing at the top of the stairs. The sign on the battleship gray security door said ROOFTOP TERRACE. Another sign on the wall said CLOSED UNTIL APRIL 1.

"Open the door," he said.

I pretended to push on the handle. "It's locked. Or it's stuck."

"Oh, for God's sake." He leaned around me and reached for it.

I drove my elbow into his stomach and then brought it up hard, so it caught him on the chin. He doubled over with a painful *ouf* and staggered, losing his balance on the concrete staircase. I didn't turn around to see what happened, but I think he fell back against the railing, because I heard a dull thud, followed by the sound of something clattering down the stairs. His knife. Once he found his footing, he would have to retrieve it.

I pushed the door open and fled outside. The long, narrow rooftop garden was surrounded by a wall that had been part of the facade of the original manor house. On either side of the security door, patio tables and chairs that were normally set out for the residents in warmer weather were stacked and covered with protective tarps next to a row of heavy umbrella bases lined up like soldiers. I yanked an umbrella pole from one of the bases and shoved it under the door handle, hoping it might slow Will Baron down temporarily. Then I took another pole as a makeshift cane.

I'd been there before to have tea with Faith. This part of the roof was at the back of the main building and was connected to what had been a large open-air pavilion that was now covered by an enormous glass-and-steel-framed skylight.

I can't run anymore. It still terrifies me to realize this, but I can't. So I walked as fast as I could toward the pavilion while the security door handle rattled ominously. The melting snow had turned the roof into an ice rink, and I slipped once, catching myself in time with the umbrella pole.

The drop from the roof garden to the skylight looked like it was about six or seven feet. I had no idea how much weight tempered glass could handle before it cracked, but I was about to find out, unless I slipped and rolled off when I landed. Or else fell through to the courtyard below. Then I'd know for sure. But Will Baron probably weighed at least twice what I did, and I was betting he wouldn't dare follow me. I hiked myself up on the wall and swung my good leg over. My foot caught on a small ledge on the other side that was about as wide as a windowsill. I'd barely had time to hoist myself completely over the wall when he started yelling that he would find me wherever I was hiding and make me sorry. I clung to the ledge like a limpet and dug my fingernails into the old mortar.

On the ground below, vehicles sped up the drive to Foxhall Manor, stopping in front of the building. Officers from the Loudoun County Sheriff's Department wouldn't have used their lights and sirens, since it would terrify the elderly residents, but I knew the cavalry had arrived and help was on the way by the sound of doors slamming and urgent voices shouting. I closed my eyes and prayed. How long until they figured out we were on the roof?

"You. Get up here." I looked up and saw the hatred and fury on Will Baron's face.

"No."

He put his foot on the ledge and brought his heavy boot down on my fingers. It hurt like hell, but I clung to my perch. "Two choices. Either

I'll throw you off and you won't survive that drop to the ground or you can come up here as my hostage. You'll be my ticket out of here."

"All right," I said, through gritted teeth. "You win. Help me up."

He removed his foot. As soon as my hand was free, I pushed myself off the ledge and fell, landing with a teeth-jarring thud on the skylight. The glass cracked under me and I was sure I'd gambled wrong and it was over.

But it didn't shatter, so I grabbed the nearest steel support and hung on to keep myself from sliding off. Then I looked up at Will.

"If it won't take my weight without cracking," I said to him, "it sure as hell won't take yours without breaking."

Then I yelled down to the officers mobilized on the ground below, and told them that I was on the roof with Will Baron and he had a knife.

The ambulance for Faith had come and gone by the time they got me back on the ground and took me into Foxhall Manor's small library, just off the main lobby. One of the officers who had rescued me told me Faith was unconscious but still breathing.

"She's Detective Noland's mother-in-law," I said.

"We know," he said, "and so does Detective Noland. His wife is going to meet the ambulance at the hospital. In the meantime, he wants you to wait here until he arrives. He's got some questions he wants to ask you."

I didn't see Will Baron being escorted out of the building in handcuffs and put into a police cruiser, but Bobby had just arrived and was sitting down with me when another officer showed up and said, "Detective, we found Uma Lawrence. She was in her grandmother's apartment and she says she's done nothing wrong. She wants to leave."

"Stop her." Bobby got up and walked into the lobby. I followed him.

Uma Lawrence's sulky mood from a few hours ago when she'd been at the winery was gone, replaced by the desperation of a cornered animal. When she saw me, her eyes blazed.

"You." She erupted with anger. "You're responsible for this. I haven't done anything wrong. You're trying to sabotage me because my grandmother left me money that you wanted to go to your friends."

"All I did was figure out why you didn't want the DNA test," I said, "because you're not related to either Johnny or Zara Tomassi. And Mac never asked Will Baron to deliver furniture to the house like you said he had. You two already knew each other and you'd planned this scam together."

"You're lying. None of that's true."

"We've been in touch with Scotland Yard,"

Bobby said. "Apparently, the real Uma Lawrence has been missing for two weeks. When she didn't turn up at work, her boss notified the authorities. And for the record, she's a brunette, about five two. It's only a matter of time before we find out who you really are."

"I want a lawyer," she said. "I'm done talking."

"It would go easier on you if you cooperated."

"Lawyer. Lawyer, lawyer, lawyer."

Bobby shrugged. "Read her her rights and book her," he said to the officer. "The charges are grand larceny, impersonation, and possibly the attempted murder of Faith Eastman. Once the British police find Uma Lawrence, they'll probably have her on kidnapping." He paused and looked hard at Uma. "Or another charge of murder."

"You're making a mistake," she said. "I didn't do anything. It was all Will's idea."

Bobby looked at her in disgust. "Get her out of my sight," he said.

THIRTY-ONE

Jay Gatsby would have loved our "Anything Goes" Valentine's Day party, which turned out to be more aptly named than I could have imagined. By Saturday evening, the news of Will Baron's arrest on suspicion of murder in the death of Vivienne Baron and the attempted murder of

Faith Eastman had gone around town like wild-fire. As a result, everyone headed straight for the bar, still trying to process the news that a cold-blooded killer had lived among us, becoming a liked and trusted member of the community.

I didn't wear Lucky's dress. I couldn't, not after what I knew about the conspiracy of silence to cover up Zara's murder and that a woman who was my namesake was complicit in it, along with Mac's grandmother and Quinn's great-grandfather. It would have seemed like I was somehow condoning it. Dominique, it turned out, had bought two dresses at a vintage clothing store because she couldn't decide what to wear. The beaded V-neck gold lamé sheath she didn't choose fit me perfectly and I got compliments all evening on how sensational I looked.

I would read Lucky's letters to Izzy someday, and as for Lucky's dress, I could always put it back in the attic in some dusty corner where it might remain for another century. Or maybe I could adopt the Santori-Tomassi solution to getting rid of toxic memories: a bonfire.

We had two surprise guests that evening. Gino Tomassi dropped by first with a large donation for Veronica House.

"I owe both of you," he said to Quinn and me. "And I pay my debts. After spending time at your vineyard, Lucie, I told Dante that we needed to think about buying land, maybe along the central coast, not the two vineyards in Angwin on Howell Mountain I was looking at. I have a lot of respect for what you two do here." He leaned over and kissed me on the cheek and gave Quinn's shoulder a light punch. "Come see me sometime at Bel Paradiso."

Then he was gone.

The other unexpected guest was Mac, who showed up as the party was winding down. He navigated his way over to Quinn and me through the crowd of friends and neighbors bombarding him with questions and said, "I need to talk to you in private."

We adjourned to Frankie's office and locked the door.

"I spent the afternoon with Bobby, answering questions about Will and that woman," he said. "I still can't believe I trusted him. And I let his . . . partner in crime stay in Roxy's house. I feel responsible for everything that happened. If it hadn't been for me—"

"You couldn't have known who he was," I said. "Nobody knew. He was a first-rate con artist, Mac. He fooled everybody and nearly got away with it, except for that slip the fake Uma made about DNA testing."

"Her name, by the way, is Wendy Underhill," Mac said. "The two of them met a few years back when he was on a study abroad program in London. She's an actress. Vivienne wasn't in the

410

picture then, so she wouldn't have recognized Wendy."

"I still don't understand how Will knew know about Roxy's new will in the first place," Quinn said.

"Easy," Mac said with a grim smile. "He found out from her lawyer. By accident, of course. Sam Constantine was on the phone with Roxy, discussing the changes in her will, the day Will delivered two paintings I sold Sam. Will obviously overheard Sam's end of the conversation and figured out what was going on. Plus, by then he had charmed one of the maids at Foxhall Manor, who let him use her master key from time to time. I'm sure he managed to slip into Roxy's apartment when she wasn't there and have a look around."

"I met the maid he charmed. Pilar," I said. "She cleaned Roxy's apartment and also Faith Eastman's."

Mac's face fell. "How is Faith? I heard she was in intensive care. Bobby said they found a box of Valentine's candy in her apartment that had been poisoned."

"She's still not out of the woods," I said, "but Kit says her mom is tough and she'll pull through. Will must have been hovering nearby the day you and Roxy were arguing. He was the second person Faith saw walk past her door. Skye Cohen told me he helped deliver furniture to

Veronica House that had been donated by residents or the families of someone who had passed away. I guess he knew his way around the place pretty well and no one questioned his presence. I wonder if Faith's right and he poisoned Roxy, too. Maybe Pilar knows something."

"If he did, I hope they lock him up somewhere and throw away the key," Mac said. "Roxy was a wonderful person. And I owe Faith an apology."

"Go visit her," I said. "Now, before anyone else knocks on that door and asks what we're doing in here, I think we should get back to the party. I nearly forgot that I need to talk to Dominique about something."

"I heard," Quinn said in my ear as we were leaving Frankie's office, "that she turned down the job of executive chef at the White House."

I looked at him in surprise. "How did you know about that?"

"Small town." He grinned. "Come on, there's something I want to show you. It's snowing again."

"Snowing?"

"Yup." He grabbed my hand. "Let's go."

We went outside onto the terrace, which we had to ourselves. White fairy lights outlined the balcony railing and gas lanterns flickered softly on either side of the four sets of double doors.

The soft, fat flakes weren't sticking and it wasn't serious snow, but it was lovely.

Quinn led me over to the railing and we stared out at the view of the dark, peaceful vineyard and the hump-backed outline of the Blue Ridge Mountains behind it. After a moment, he pulled something out of his jacket pocket. "This is for you. It's going on midnight and I wanted to do this while it was still Valentine's Day."

A velvet jewelry box.

"I don't understand."

"Open it."

The exquisite ring, a large, brilliant, round-cut diamond surrounded by a circle of diamonds and set in an old-fashioned filigreed white-gold setting, was obviously an antique. "It's beautiful," I said.

"It was my grandmother's," he said. "My mother's mother, not from the Santori side, or the Tomassi. My grandfather had it made for her in Spain. It fits, by the way. I had a little help from Eli."

"I don't know what to say."

The diamond flashed in the golden lantern light as he slipped it on my finger. "Say yes," he said. "Because I'm asking you to marry me."

"Yes," I said. "Yes, yes, yes."

"Happy Valentine's Day," he murmured, and kissed me.

ACKNOWLEDGMENTS

In October 2013, the Smithsonian Institution invited Michael Martini, grandson of pioneering winemaker Louis M. Martini, along with several other members of legendary California wine-making families, to the American History Museum in Washington, D.C. to participate in a discussion on the impact of Prohibition on the American wine industry. While Michael and his wife Jacque were in town we met for dinner, which is how and when the idea for *The Champagne Conspiracy* got its start.

I owe thanks to many people for research help with this book, especially Michael Martini for recounting his memories of growing up working for his father and grandfather. Rick Tagg, winemaker at Barrel Oak Winery in Delaplane, Virginia, answered questions about making champagne, as well as what happens at a vineyard in the dead of winter. (A lot more than I thought). Detective Jim Smith from the Crime Scene Unit of the Fairfax County (Virginia) Police Department answered law enforcement questions and my cousin Victor Thuronyi answered questions about estate law. As always, any mistakes are on me, not them.

Two books, *Last Call: The Rise and Fall of*

Prohibition by Daniel Okrent (Scribner, 2011) and *Florence Harding: The First Lady, the Jazz Age, and the Death of America's Most Scandalous President* by Carl Sferrazza Anthony (William Morrow, 1998) were especially helpful while researching this book. The love letters of Warren Harding and his longtime mistress Carrie Fulton Phillips, which were released to the public by the Library of Congress while I was writing this book, were a serendipitous resource.

Donna Andrews, John Gilstrap, Alan Orloff, and Art Taylor, affectionately known as the Rumpus Writers, read and commented on early drafts of the manuscript; André de Nesnera also read it and, as always, provided unstinting and loving support, in addition to making dinner. A lot.

At Minotaur Books, special thanks to Hannah Braaten, my sharp-eyed editor, whose suggestions and guidance helped make this book so much better, as well as to Keith Kahla, Shailyn Tavella, and Allison Ziegler.

Last but not least, thanks and love to Dominick Abel, my agent, who makes it all possible.

Center Point Large Print
600 Brooks Road / PO Box 1
Thorndike, ME 04986-0001 USA

(207) 568-3717

US & Canada:
1 800 929-9108
www.centerpointlargeprint.com